The

NIGHT

TRAVELLERS

Also by Armando Lucas Correa
The German Girl
The Daughter's Tale

The
NIGHT
TRAVELLERS

ARMANDO
LUCAS CORREA

Translated by Nick Caistor and Faye Williams
Additional translation by Cecilia Molinari

SIMON & SCHUSTER

London · New York · Sydney · Toronto · New Delhi

First published in the United States by Atria Books,
an imprint of Simon & Schuster, Inc., 2023

First published in Great Britain by Simon & Schuster UK Ltd, 2023

This paperback edition published in 2024

1 3 5 7 9 10 8 6 4 2

Simon & Schuster UK Ltd
1st Floor
222 Gray's Inn Road
London WC1X 8HB

Simon & Schuster: Celebrating 100 Years of Publishing in 2024

Simon & Schuster Australia, Sydney
Simon & Schuster India, New Delhi

www.simonandschuster.co.uk
www.simonandschuster.com.au
www.simonandschuster.co.in

A CIP catalogue record for this book
is available from the British Library

Paperback ISBN: 978-1-3985-2399-9
eBook ISBN: 978-1-3985-2398-2
Audio ISBN: 978-1-3985-2400-2

Printed and Bound in the UK using 100% Renewable
Electricity at CPI Group (UK) Ltd

MIX
Paper | Supporting
responsible forestry
FSC® C171272

To Emma, Anna, and Lucas

Contents

ACT ONE

One: Berlin, March 1931   3

Two: Berlin, March 1938   8

Three: Düsseldorf, June 1929   18

Four: Düsseldorf, March 1934   28

Five: Berlin, August 1936   40

Six: Berlin, October 1938   46

Seven: Brandenburg-Görden, January 1939   54

Eight: Berlin, February 1939   69

Nine: Berlin, March 1939   78

Ten: Hamburg, May 1939   87

ACT TWO

Eleven: Havana, November 1942   95

Twelve: Havana, April 1944   102

Thirteen: Varadero, December 1948   118

Fourteen: Havana, June 1951   131

Fifteen: Havana, March 1952   143

Sixteen: Arroyo Naranjo, December 1956   155

Seventeen: Havana, June 1958   166

Eighteeen: Havana, January 1959   175

Nineteen: Santiago de Cuba, March 1959   187

Twenty: Havana, March 1962   198

CONTENTS

ACT THREE

Twenty-one: New York, May 1975   211

Twenty-two: Düsseldorf, November 1975   220

Twenty-three: Düsseldorf, August 1981   232

Twenty-four: Berlin, August 1988   238

Twenty-five: Bochum-Linden, April 1996   246

Twnety-six: Berlin, January 2000   257

Twenty-seven: Berlin, March 2014   266

Twenty-eight: Berlin, June 1939   273

Twenty-nine: Oranienburg, January 1940   281

Thirty: Berlin, April 2014   290

Thirty-one: Pankow, May 2014   303

Thirty-two: Havana, May 2015   312

Thirty-three: Havana, January 1988   322

Thirty-four: Havana, May 2015   329

Thirty-five: Berlin, November 2015   333

Author's Note   339

Acknowledgments   343

Bibliography   349

Night travelers are full of light.
—RUMI

ACT ONE

1

The night Lilith was born, winter storms raged in the midst of spring.

Windows closed. Curtains drawn. Ally Keller writhed in pain on the damp sheets. The midwife clutched Ally's ankles.

"This time it's coming."

After the contraction, the very last one, her life would change. *Marcus*, Ally thought. She wanted to cry out his name.

Marcus couldn't answer her. He was far away. The only contact they had now was the occasional letter. Ally had started to forget his scent. Even his face had faded into darkness for a moment. She looked down at herself on the bed as though she were some other woman, as though the body in labor wasn't her own.

"Marcus," she said aloud, her mind increasingly restless.

After everything they'd been through together, after all they'd said and shared, Marcus had become a shadow to her. Their child would grow up without a father. Perhaps her father had never really wanted her after all. Perhaps this was always meant to be her daughter's destiny. What right did she have to interfere?

The night Lilith was born, Ally thought of her own mother. She

3

couldn't recall a single lullaby, an embrace, a kiss. She had spent her childhood surrounded by tutors, perfecting her handwriting and use of language, learning new vocabulary words and proper grammatical constructions. Numbers were a nightmare, science was dull, and geography left her disoriented. All she cared about was escaping into the make-believe stories that led her on journeys back in time.

"Join us in the real world, would you?" her mother would say. "Life isn't a fairy tale."

Her mother let her go her own way. She had sensed what Ally's life would be, and how powerless she was to stop it. Given the direction Germany was heading, she knew that her rebellious, headstrong daughter was a lost cause. With hindsight, Ally could see her mother had been right all along.

"You're falling asleep." The midwife's agitated voice interrupted her thoughts, her hands stained with a yellowish liquid. "You need to concentrate if you want to get this over with."

The midwife was seasoned: she could boast of the requisite nine hundred hours of training, had helped deliver more than one hundred babies.

"Not a single dead baby, not one. Nor a mother either, not one," she had told Ally when she took her on.

"She's one of the best," the agency had assured her.

"One day we'll enact a law to make sure that all babies born in our country are delivered by a German midwife," the woman at the agency had added, raising her voice. "Purity upon purity."

Perhaps I should have found one with no experience, no idea how to bring a baby into the world, Ally thought.

"Look at me!" the midwife snapped. "Unless you do your bit, I can't do my job properly. You're going to make me look bad."

Ally began to tremble. The midwife seemed to be in a hurry. Ally thought she might have another pregnant woman waiting for her. She couldn't stop thinking that this woman's fingers, her hands were inside her, delving around. Saving one life while destroying another.

The night Lilith was born, Ally tried to imagine herself back in the apartment on the riverbank with Marcus: the two of them, hidden in the moonlight, making plans for life as a family, as if such a thing were possible. The morning light always took them by surprise. Caught unawares, they began closing windows and drawing curtains to stay in the dark they'd made their haven.

"We should run away," she once said to Marcus, while they were lying curled up in bed.

She waited for his response in silence, knowing that for Marcus there could only be one answer. Nobody could convince him otherwise.

"If things are bad for us here, in America it would only be worse," he would say. "Every day that goes by, more people see us as the enemy."

To Ally, Marcus's fear was abstract. It lay in hidden forces, like a gathering wave they couldn't see, but that would one day, apparently, drown them all. So she chose to ignore Marcus's forebodings and those of his artist friends; she was hopeful that the storm would pass. Marcus had dreams of working in movies. He had already appeared in one film, in a minor role as a musician, and he had said she should go with him to Paris where he hoped to be cast in another. But then she became pregnant and everything changed.

Her parents were beside themselves. They sent her to live in their empty apartment in Mitte, in the center of Berlin, to hide their shame. They told her that it was the last thing they'd do for her. How she chose to live beyond that point was her problem, not theirs. In the letter her mother had written, she could hear her firm, deliberate voice, with its Bavarian lilt. Ally hadn't heard from her since.

Ally learned of her father's death from a notice in the newspaper. The same day, she also received a letter about a small inheritance her father had left her. She imagined that back in Munich there would have been prayers, Ave Marias, veiled windows, and stilted conversations that trailed off into murmurs. She thought of her mother shrouded in mourning, a mourning that for her began the day Ally left. Ally was convinced that when her mother died, she would leave instructions for the news of her death not to be made public, to ensure that her death would go unnoticed, so her daughter wouldn't get the chance to weep for her. Ally didn't deserve even that much. Her mother's vengeance would be silence.

She recalled the feeling of being alone in the vast Mitte apartment, losing herself in its corridors, its rooms full of shadows and painted a muddy green, which she felt would consume her. It was then that the letters from Marcus began to arrive. *This isn't the country I want for my child, don't come back to Düsseldorf, life here grows more difficult by the day. They don't want us in America either. Nobody wants us.* Sometimes they were not so much answers to her own letters but diatribes.

A cry filled the room. It had come from her chest, her choking throat, her stiffened arms. She felt torn in two. The stabbing pains in her belly spread to her whole body and she clung desperately to the bars of the bed.

"Marcus!" Her shout, guttural, startled the midwife.

"Who's Marcus? The father? There's nobody here. Come on now, don't stop, you're nearly there. One more push and you've done it!"

Her body stiffened and a shiver ran through her. Her lips, trembling, dry. Her belly tensed to a point and then shrank, as though the living being within her had dissolved. She had brought on a storm. She felt the gusts of wind and rain lashing down. Thunderclaps and hailstones pounded her. She was tearing apart. Her abdomen contracted. Opening her increasingly heavy legs, she let something out, a sort of mollusk. A smell of rust invaded the room's fetid air. The tiny body had taken all the warmth of her belly with it. Her skin quivered.

A lengthy silence. Ally stretched out her legs and closed her eyes. Tears mingled with sweat. The midwife picked up the inert baby by its feet and snipped through the umbilical cord. With the other hand she tossed the placenta into a dish of bloody water, and on one corner of the bed, began to wash the newborn with tepid water.

"It's a girl." The midwife's voice resonated in the room, which was otherwise glaringly silent.

What's happened? Why isn't she crying? She's stillborn, she thought.

Her throat was still burning; her belly throbbed. She could no longer feel her legs.

At that instant, the baby let out a soft whimper like a wounded animal. Little by little, the whimper grew to a howl. Eventually, it became a wail. Ally didn't react.

Meanwhile, the midwife began rubbing the baby, more relaxed now that she'd done her job. When she saw the bluish tinge of her clean face, her anxiety returned. A lack of oxygen, she deduced. Tentatively, she opened the baby's mouth and inspected the purple gums. Thinking there might be a blockage in the windpipe, she poked her index finger into the newborn's tiny throat. She looked at the baby, and at Ally, who still had her eyes closed.

The little baby wouldn't stop crying as the midwife roughly wrapped her in a clean sheet. Only her face peeped out. The midwife pursed her lips, handing the baby over to Ally the way one transfers a foreign object.

"It's a Rhineland bastard. You've brought a *mischling* into the world. This girl isn't German, she's Black."

Ally sat up and took the baby on her lap. The newborn instantly settled.

"Lilith," Ally murmured. "Her name means light."

2

Seven Years Later
Berlin, March 1938

D<small>usk</small>.

"Lilith, run! Run, and don't look back!" Ally cried, her eyes shut tight. "Keep going, don't slow down."

The streetlamps flashed silvery threads on the wooden and bronze benches in the Tiergarten. Ally twirled around with her arms outstretched, creating a whirlwind of leaves. For a moment she had made the world stand still, forming a protective cloud all around her. When she opened her eyes, it was the park that was spinning; the trees were falling in on her, and she couldn't steady herself. She felt she might pass out.

By night, the Tiergarten, in the middle of Berlin, was like a labyrinth.

"Lilith?" Ally whispered.

Her daughter had played the game perfectly: she couldn't be seen.

With the avenue in front and the trees behind her, Ally sighed. She thought she was alone, outside the halo of light from the streetlamp, but when she turned around, a group of young men was standing before her, wearing gray uniforms. She felt the prickle of fear. You might be able to hold back the tears, raise the corners of your lips, hide the shaking legs and sweating palms, but the dread would always be there, finding its way to the surface somehow and weakening you. The hunter can smell fear. But the uniformed youths smiled at her, raised their right arms in salute. She was the image of a vigorous, perfect German woman.

"*Sieg heil!*"

If they only knew, she thought.

A gust of wind cleared away the clouds. The moon shone down on her, on her blond hair and porcelain skin. Ally was radiant. One of the youths turned around to look at her, as though she were some kind of magical apparition in the Tiergarten, a Valkyrie on the way to meet her fate. The young men marched off. She was alone again, in the darkness.

"Mommy?" Lilith's voice raised her from her stupor. "Did I do well this time?"

Without looking down, Ally ran her hands over her daughter's curly, crinkly hair, as she trotted alongside her. Ally alone was bathed in light. Lilith was shadow.

"Let's go home."

"But did I do well, Mommy?"

"Of course you did, Lilith, as you do every night. You get better each time."

In the darkness they went unnoticed. The passersby ignored them, nobody looked at them in astonishment, pursed their lips in disgust, or lowered their gaze pityingly. Nobody hurled stones or insults, and the children didn't run after them, protected by their purity, yelling songs about the jungle or chimpanzees.

By night they felt free.

"By night, we're all the same color," Ally would murmur to her daughter when they walked, as though reciting one of her poems.

Ally was always writing, no matter where she was. She didn't need pencil or paper; her mind worked more quickly than her hands, she used to tell Lilith. She recited poems to her, poems with a musical cadence that filled Lilith with joy.

"What do you mean, Mommy?"

"What I mean is: the night belongs to us, to me and you. The night is ours."

• ✦ •

It was around Lilith's seventh birthday that Ally's nightmares began. *What sort of mother dreams about her child dying?* she thought. She only had herself to blame, for having brought her into the world. For having to live in endless flight.

In their apartment building, hidden in a shady, dead-end street in Mitte, they never used the elevator, but always walked up and down the dark staircase so that they didn't bump into any neighbors. She had heard the Strassers, who lived in the same apartment block, complaining, harping back to a triumphant past. The day she moved into the apartment, before Lilith was born, they had invited her in for coffee. The rooms were filled with trophies they had brought back from far-off lands: sphinxes, fragments of stone faces, clay and marble arms. They loved ruins. Frau Strasser went through life suffocated by a corset that left her permanently cantankerous, snubbing anyone who didn't dress like her and her magnificent offspring. The mere act of walking left her struggling for breath, and even in winter she was plagued by beads of sweat that threatened to spoil her makeup. They had two daughters, each one as perfect as the sun. The feminine ideal, the likes of which often graced the cover of *Das Deutsche Mädel*, the magazine of the League of German Girls that everyone adored.

Ever since Lilith was born, they had avoided Ally. One day Herr Strasser had even dared to spit at her as they passed each other in the street outside the apartment. Ally's bag of fruit had fallen to the ground, and the apples rolled across the pavement, gathering dark, wet dust as they went.

"Those apples are cleaner than you," Herr Strasser had said after launching the ball of phlegm that landed by her feet.

Insults were no longer veiled. Ally had gone through the bronze and wooden doorway into the building that was no longer her refuge. She saw her neighbors, the Herzogs, looking frightened, walking through the threshold of apartment 1B. They had witnessed her humiliation, and probably felt sorry for her. They too had been insulted, on more than one occasion.

The Herzogs owned a small lighting store outside the S-Bahn station in the Hackescher Markt. Ally had once thought about going into the store to shelter from an icy downpour, but in the end she hadn't: she saw the six-pointed star on the shop window, and inside it the most offensive word to describe someone at the time, *Jude*. She bowed her head and carried on walking, wet and trembling. The last time she got off the S-Bahn, she saw from a distance what remained of the shop. The windows had been smashed, and all the lamps destroyed. There was glass everywhere. It was impossible to avoid treading on it. She shuddered as it splintered underfoot; it was part of the symphony of the city. Each footstep reduced the fragments to dust, until they were gone. *Nobody in Berlin needs light anymore*, she thought, and turned in the opposite direction. *I suppose we'll all live in the shadows from now on.*

Ally had lost her capacity to feel shocked; nothing offended her anymore. Words didn't frighten her; nor did Herr Strasser's spit, which was merely a tiresome, petty nuisance.

Fortunately, she was alone that day, as she was almost every afternoon. Lilith had stayed home with Herr Professor, her neighbor and mentor. His name was Bruno Bormann, but they both called him Opa. He hadn't liked it at first. "Am I so old that you can call me Gramps?" he would say. But now he always announced his arrival in the apartment with "Opa's feeling tired," "Opa's hungry," "Opa needs someone to sing to him," or "Don't you have a kiss and a cuddle for Opa?"

"You know, Lilith," Herr Professor told her when they read together and she asked questions about destiny, "you're older than Opa. You have an old soul."

The three of them ate dinner together almost every night, unless Herr Professor was meeting his old colleagues from the university where

ARMANDO LUCAS CORREA

he had taught literature for over two decades. There weren't many of
them left. Some had died, and others had fled to America to escape the
horror and shame of what was happening in their country. Herr Professor had once been revered; devoted students often quoted his literary
musings. When he first became a lecturer, he imagined himself gray-
haired and with a walking stick still teaching students and was determined to continue teaching until he drew his final breath. But times had
changed. Fear and denunciations had set in, and he no longer trusted
the professors who had chosen to stay, or the new students. These angry
young people were the ones who now decided what should be taught in
the sacred German academy, and what should disappear forever from
the curriculum. The professors, deans, and even the university rector
were as afraid of being denounced by a student as they were of being
hit by a stray bullet. One morning he arrived at the university to find
several empty shelves in the library; first editions scattered on the floor
and trampled on.

"Books are no longer seen as useful in this country," he told Ally.
"Who cares about reading the classics these days? How long will it go
on, my dear Ally? You and I are survivors; we belong to another era.
The new generation only wants to listen to the Führer's speeches, the
Führer's tirades."

Herr Professor, with his mild manners and perfect enunciation, had
a voice that resonated without being raised, so that it could be heard in
every corner of the house. He was Lilith's tutor. Thanks to him, the little
girl had been able to read and write with startling fluency from the age
of five. She devoured books she couldn't fully understand, underlining
words on the pages of books that she took, without asking permission,
from Herr Professor's vast library.

Ally's and Herr Professor's front doors, side by side, were rarely
locked.

"We ought to knock down the wall between our apartments. Then
Opa wouldn't have to visit you both," Herr Professor had once suggested, teasingly.

Lilith had smiled at the idea, thinking she would be able to peruse his library anytime she liked, not just at night, the only time she was permitted to step outside the apartment, taking care not to let the ghosts—their name for the neighbors—see her.

Ally knew little about Herr Professor's life before they had met, but she considered him a key part of hers. She knew he had once, in his words, "made a blunder," that is, fallen in love. She had never pressed him for details.

"Mistakes like that can change the course of your life, but fortunately we don't normally fall in love twice. Once is enough," the old man had said.

At present, Lilith was engrossed in a leather-bound book, written in an unfathomable language, entitled *Eugenics*, a word she didn't dare say aloud. She pored over the illustrations of human bodies, diseases, dystrophies, perfection, and imperfection, and came to a halt on a little girl's flawless face.

"Opa, I want you to start teaching me English today, right now."

"If I teach you English, it won't be for you to read that book, but to understand the Great Poet."

Starting that night, they began reading aloud Shakespeare's sonnets, written in old-fashioned English, without bothering to try to work out what they meant.

"To learn a language, the first thing to do is capture its musicality, untangle your tongue, relax your facial muscles," Herr Professor explained. "The rest will follow in due course."

Lilith lit up, thrilled by this exciting new world that had just opened up to her. "Let's find Mommy so she can listen to us!"

"We should leave your mother in peace. She needs to write, and write a lot. It does her good, especially when she's weary."

"It's my fault that Mommy doesn't sleep."

"No, Lilith. It's the Führer's fault, the fact that he believes he's Odin. You've got nothing to do with it."

"Mommy doesn't like us to mention his name . . ."

13

From the moment she woke up, Lilith spent nearly all her time with Herr Professor. At lunchtime the three would eat together, and the little girl would be captivated by his stories, which ranged from the glories of ancient Babylon to Greek mythology; endless speeches about gods and demigods, or the Doric temples of the Acropolis, that might suddenly end up in the Greco-Persian Wars. Herr Professor was as happy talking about Aphrodite, Hephaestus, and Ares and their place in the Temple of the Twelve Olympian Gods, as the battles of the Nubians and the Assyrians.

One afternoon, Herr Professor found Lilith in front of the bathroom mirror, the only spot in his apartment without books. The little girl drew closer to the glass, as though trying to find an answer to her doubts, slowly stroking her hair and eyebrows. When she realized Herr Professor was watching her, she jumped, startled.

"Mommy is so pretty."

"And so are you."

"But I don't look like her. I want to look like her."

"You have the same profile, the same lips, your eyes are the same shape."

"But my skin . . ."

"Your skin is beautiful. Just look how it glows next to mine."

They stood together in front of the mirror. Lilith untied her curls. Herr Professor swept the gray hairs from his forehead and ran his hand down over his stomach.

"I'm going to have to do something with this belly, it's getting bigger every day. I may be old, but at least I still have all my hair!"

They laughed. To Lilith, Herr Professor was like a friendly giant who watched over them.

Some days he climbed up the wooden stepladder next to the wardrobe in the little room beside the kitchen. Perched on the top rung, he handed down boxes lined in red velvet. That was where he kept the family photographs that his mother, a tall, robust woman, had sorted in her final years. Lilith loved going through the pictures of strangers, people from so long ago that even Herr Professor couldn't remember their names.

"Little Bruno was afraid of the dark," he once said, pointing to a photo of himself as a toddler. "We're not though, are we, Lilith?"

The little girl burst into laughter at the sight of a bald, chubby baby perched on a lace cushion in one of the photographs.

"You've had a grumpy face since you were born! That couldn't be anyone but you."

"We were all babies once, and before we die, we go back to that time when we depend on someone doing everything for us."

"Don't worry, Opa, I'll look after you."

Late at night, after Lilith had gone to bed, Ally and Herr Professor would make a pot of tea to ward off sleep. They remained silent; they had no need of words to communicate. After a few minutes, Ally would lean her head on his lap, and he would stroke her hair, a smoky gray in the darkness.

"We'll find a way, we will," he repeated. "Lilith's a clever girl. She's a prodigy, very special."

"Opa, time's against us. Lilith is nearly seven years old," Ally said, her breathing ragged.

"We can trust Franz." Herr Professor's hands were trembling.

Franz Bouhler was one of Herr Professor's former students. His mother had insisted he study science so that he could go on to work in his cousin Philipp's laboratory. Philipp had begun research that, according to Franz, was going to change the way they saw the world. His true passion though, was for literature. He wrote poetry and had enrolled in Herr Professor's literature classes. After Herr Professor retired, Franz continued to visit him and share his writing.

"Franz is a dreamer," Ally said.

"We all are," Herr Professor said. "*When I waked, I cried to dream again.*"

Since Franz began to visit them, he had become their only contact with the outside world. Lilith was growing up quickly, and every day it was more noticeable that she was a *mischling* child, a Rhineland bastard, who by law would have to be sterilized to survive in the new Germany. They avoided the radio news, and there were no newspapers in their homes. When they went out at night, they lowered their gaze so as not to see the avalanche of triumphalist white, red, and black posters inundating the city.

Herr Professor would sometimes edit Franz's grandiloquent poems, which were filled with hope, in contrast to the dark, pessimistic lyricism of Ally's own verses. It was Franz's fresh, youthful spirit—he was four years younger than Ally—that drove her to seek shelter in him. Wednesday afternoons were their time. Ally felt safe walking around the small streets of Mitte alongside the tall man, with his strapping arms, clumsy movements, but with a sweetness that gave him an almost childlike air. He always wore gray flannel, and she a woolen trench coat in reddish tones that shifted color according to the day's changing light.

Franz read Ally's poems devotedly. He admired the simplicity of her verses. In his work, he was constantly looking for increasingly complex constructions to get across an idea that always ended up seeming trite within twenty-four hours. Ally tried to understand Franz's texts, his rhetoric, but was overwhelmed by his storm of words. She put it down to his innocence.

To Lilith, Franz was something between a Greek god and a big brother. When he arrived, she ran into his arms and buried her face in his neck, as he scooped her up and held her in the air.

"What do you have for me today, Little Light?" Franz would say to her. "Ask me anything."

They could while away hours telling each other how they had spent the day: for her, getting up, washing her face, having a drink of water, reading with Herr Professor, going to bed and smiling; for him, studying huge books about the parts of the body and writing the most beautiful poem a German had ever created, and which she would soon be able to read for herself. For Franz, this was the closest thing he had to a home. He avoided dinnertime at his house, with his mother, a widow who

16

only gave orders. She considered it a weakness to be writing poems that wouldn't get him anywhere and reading books that would one day end up in a bonfire.

"Germany doesn't need any more writers," his mother had said to him. "What Germany needs are soldiers prepared to serve their country."

Ally's home was the only one the young man visited that didn't have a portrait of the Führer hanging over the mantle. And the little girl could see that when Franz was there, her mother was happy. With him, they were not afraid of ghosts, or of the Führer. Nobody could hurt them. Franz was a barricade.

Then, they began preparations for Lilith's seventh birthday. The number kept them awake at night. There were no more smiles, they no longer recited poems in the dark. Dinnertime was a silent affair once more.

"Seven," Lilith repeated, as though the number had become her prison sentence.

3

Eight Years Earlier
Düsseldorf, June 1929

If you don't hurry up, we'll be late," Ally shouted, already standing at the front door.

When she saw Stella come out of the bathroom, she chuckled.

"Red? And with all that cleavage on display? Where do you think we're going?"

"To have fun!" Stella said.

"Wearing red will only get you noticed by the Vampire."

The two smiled and hurried down the stairs.

It was only eight at night and the city was quiet. The days were getting longer, and the streetlamps on each corner were still unlit. They crossed empty boulevards, avoiding the puddles a tentative summer shower had left behind.

When they got to U-Bahn station, on the Altstadt line, the platform was deserted. It felt as though the plague that had ravaged the world a decade earlier had returned.

"Everyone pays too much attention to the newspaper headlines," Ally said.

"How scary, the Vampire of Düsseldorf is lying in wait for us," Stella mocked. "Somehow I don't think we'd be the ideal bait for him."

"Ideal? I don't think this vampire is so discerning. His victim is just the first girl he comes across."

"Well, anyway, we came out to have fun."

They were the only passengers in their carriage. On one of the doors was a poster offering a reward for the capture of the Vampire: ten thousand reichsmark. The two looked at each other in surprise and traveled the rest of the journey in silence. They had never been afraid before, but now they were alarmed, although they didn't dare admit it. In a few minutes they would reach their stop, and there were bound to be plenty of people milling around the Brauerei Schumacher. Marcus and Tom were meeting them a few blocks from there. Why would anyone want to stay in on a Saturday night in summer? They had decided that no vampire—real or imaginary—was going to stop them doing as they pleased. The attacker—who had sexually assaulted little girls, women, old ladies, and even men in the area close to the River Rhine, and then stabbed them until they bled to death—had made the front page of every German newspaper. The police, business owners, and general populace were on high alert. And so were they.

The latest victim had been found near Central Station, lying naked on a mattress in a hotel room. She had been strangled, but her body showed no other signs of violence, and there were no traces of blood. Some doubted whether it was the work of the same killer.

Since they had moved from Munich to Düsseldorf together, Ally and Stella had promised themselves they would be independent. Although their families helped them out, they both spent the afternoons working in a department store in the center of town, selling perfumes. "Everyone hides beneath scents," Ally used to say. Berlin was meant to be their final destination, but they decided to stay a while in the city on the banks of the Rhine, because of the music. Stella wanted to be a dancer; Ally a writer.

Every Saturday morning, Ally wrote long poems while Stella slept. They would have liked to live closer to the center, in a two-bedroom apartment, but over time they had grown accustomed to living in such close quarters.

During the week at midday, they would try to memorize the ingredients of the perfumes, which came in little bottles made by craftsmen seemingly obsessed with eternal passion. Standing behind the counter of a perfumery that looked more like an apothecary, they spoke like experts about aniseed, Oriental teas, calamus, pomegranate, myrtle, cypress, and dried Bulgarian rose petals.

On Saturday nights, they crossed the city, all the way to the cabaret club where they met Marcus and Tom, relishing rhythms their parents would have despised.

"If our parents knew we were going out with Black musicians they'd disown us," Stella said, giggling.

"Marcus is German," Ally corrected her.

"And Tom's American," Stella added. "But they're both Black."

They pushed their way through the crowd, who, like them, had chosen to ignore the Vampire. The wall of the popular brewery was covered in reward posters. *Ten thousand*, they heard between laughter and snippets of conversation, like a litany. Everyone wanted to catch the Vampire, and kept their eyes peeled, trying to spot a culprit. Some tried to use themselves as bait. If you worked in a pair, it was said, you could catch the most feared and wanted man in Germany.

Conversations blended into noise. People shouted to one another, while Stella hurried Ally, who was bumping into passersby, thrown off balance by phrases that came at her like blows.

"I bet it's a stinking Jew. We need to do away with them once and for all."

"It seems to me that it's one of the Blacks who've flooded the city thanks to the Jews."

"More like thanks to the French. They are the ones who filled their army with Negroes."

"What would you do with ten thousand reichsmark?" Ally overheard a girl ask her boyfriend.

"We'd go to Berlin," he replied.

Berlin, Ally thought. *Marcus and I could go to Berlin.*

In the passageway under the soft light from the side door of Schall und Rauch, Ally spotted Marcus and her heart began to race. He smiled when he saw her, waving his hand to signal for her to hurry up. Ally left Stella's side and ran over to him.

"You kept me waiting for hours," he whispered in her ear.

"Don't exaggerate," she said, kissing him.

Marcus opened the door to let Stella through. He remained in the light of the doorway, Ally in his arms. Totally still and at peace.

"We should go in," she said.

"You're here now. I don't care if we're late going on."

He took a step back and drank her in with his eyes.

"You look at me as though I might evaporate any second."

He smiled at this, then he took her hand, and they went into the dark corridor. Climbing the stairs up to the stage, they sensed the hustle and bustle in the wings. Cigarette smoke mingled with the smell of beer. As she passed by, Ally brushed against the heavy curtains, sending up a cloud of dust particles that seemed to give off their own light.

They could hear discordant snatches of music from out on the stage. The comedian's voice rang out like howls of protest over the audience's laughter.

"Now you'll go out and calm them down," Ally said to Marcus, finally up in the dressing room.

It was small, a kind of attic, with clothes and musical instruments strewn about on the knotty wooden floorboards. There were empty beer bottles around the room, a bottle of whisky, glasses everywhere, piles of newspapers. Several photographs hung on the walls. She recognized Marcus in one of the images, and behind him the Eiffel Tower. He had his arms stretched out to either side and his saxophone at his feet.

Marcus picked up his horn, kissed Ally, and left her in the dressing room. She went over to a photograph of Marcus stuck to the mirror, and as she was reaching out to touch it, Stella interrupted her.

"Are you going to stay here all night, or do you want to listen to them? Come on, let's go."

They found a table near the stage but off to one side from which they could see the musicians and the audience. From where they were, the sound came to them distorted. Still, Ally, who had only recently been introduced to jazz by Marcus, reveled in those cadences. Few people in the audience paid attention. It was background music, meant to fill the interval until the next comedian came on, followed by the dancers with their bare midriffs. In the audience, women were sitting on tables. A couple of them were dancing in one corner. A boisterous group seemed to be making up a song about German excellence. At one of the central tables sat three young men with made-up faces, reddish-purple lips, and slicked back hair. Ally's puzzled gaze rested on a table at the back, where six men in suits and black ties were sitting. They still had their hats on. Their eyes were fixed on the stage, faces tense.

"Who are they?" Ally asked Stella, surreptitiously gesturing toward them.

"Them?" Stella asked, pointing. "No idea, but I bet they're not much fun."

When the music finished, the spotlights roamed over the club, from the musicians to the applauding audience. The light came to rest on Ally. One of the men removed his hat and fixed his gaze on her.

With the stage in darkness, a voice came over the loudspeakers.

"Ladies and gentlemen, the moment you've all been waiting for. Our illustrious Master of Ceremonies . . ."

A drumroll, a lengthy pause, and the lights came up on a man in full makeup, wearing an unbuttoned white shirt, no trousers, a suspender belt, garters, and high-heeled shoes. He took off his top hat, gave a curtsy, and as the cymbals crashed, he tumbled forward onto the floor. The audience roared. From the shadows, a white dog wearing a huge pink chiffon bow ran across to him, snuggling against his legs.

"Couldn't you be a little more discreet?" the MC stage-whispered to the dog, prompting another smattering of laughter.

The MC stroked the dog, a macabre expression on his face. The two of them waited in silence for some signal from the orchestra, a discordant note. Then the man stood up reluctantly, and the stage was plunged into darkness. Moments later, a pin spot illuminated a tiny piece of the stage, then opened slowly in time to a jaunty tune, to reveal the MC's bare backside, and that of the dog as well. A trumpet blared, and the audience clapped and cheered.

The show continued, but Ally didn't pay much attention to it, lost in her own thoughts. When a loud clang from the stage roused her, she found herself alone at the table. Ally glanced around the theater, wondering where Stella had gone. The men sitting at the back table had also disappeared. Ally got to her feet and went backstage, barging past the dancers to get to the dressing room. She was taken aback by the silence when she entered. She saw Stella in Tom's arms, looking distraught. Marcus was packing away his saxophone.

"They've taken Lonnie to Mühlenstrasse police station," Stella told her, stifling a sob. "Those men at the back, the dreary-looking ones? They were policemen."

"But why take Lonnie?" Ally asked.

Nobody answered.

"Come on, we should get going," Marcus said, taking her by the hand. They left the cabaret without saying goodbye to anyone.

They walked, heads bowed, for quite some time. Ally hoped Marcus would start the conversation, but in the end gave up waiting.

"What are they accusing Lonnie of? Can you at least explain? Are we just going to leave, without doing anything?"

"There's nothing we can do, Ally. They're the ones with the power."

"I don't understand," Ally said.

"You don't have to be guilty of anything, they can cart you off to prison anyway. Lonnie is Black. That in itself makes him guilty. Tomorrow it might be me. The week after, Tom."

"They must have had a reason to take him," Ally insisted.

"Don't be naïve. Because he missed a week at the club. That's why they took him."

"What does that matter to the police?"

"The week he was off work, a dead woman was found on the riverbank. You already know, if the Vampire really exists, he must be Black. We're always the first ones they point the finger at. We're the guilty ones. The savages, the murderers. One of the white musicians was off those same days. He hasn't even been questioned."

Ally didn't know what to say, leaning into him in a show of comfort. His friend had been taken away, and he knew it could just as easily have been him. Marcus had been lucky.

"Unless another body appears, they won't release him. As far as they're concerned, he's guilty."

He wasn't the first to have been detained. Their neighborhood butcher had made headlines a few months ago. Being Jewish and a butcher was the perfect combination for him to be suspected of the murders. Caricatures of the man filled the magazines and newspapers. The butcher ended up taking his own life in jail. He hanged himself using his bedsheets. A clear demonstration of his guilt, the judge had said. Girls, women, and old ladies could once more sleep easy in their beds; everyone could return to the park, to walking in the moonlight along the River Düssel. Peace returned to a city that had been plunged into terror. In one newspaper editorial, a city councilor went so far as to say that this was a sign that they needed to get rid of all the Jews, not just in the city plagued by so many murders, but in the whole country. Germany needed to recover its greatness. No more vampires. Then the *Volksstimme* published an anonymous letter that had been sent to the police. The real Vampire didn't want to be denied the limelight: *Today, just before midnight, you'll find the next victim.*

That night, a woman's naked body was discovered in one of the squares. The Vampire had raped her on the riverbank. Her body was found by a drunkard, who instantly became a suspect.

The summer had unleashed the Vampire's fury. A few hours after the first incident, a man was knifed as he sat reading the newspaper on a park bench, and a woman was repeatedly stabbed in the ribs while out walking in broad daylight.

It was only at night that Ally and Marcus dared to walk hand in hand, protected by the shadows. By day, one went in front of the other, Marcus in front, Ally behind. They knew that if they did the opposite, he could be arrested on suspicion of pursuing a defenseless woman. They were used to it now—it was the only way they could be together. Ally didn't care whether she was seen by his side in the light of day. She would have dared to kiss him in public, embrace him, if he had let her, but Marcus walked with her as if they were conspirators. He knew that everyone would always see the Black man as the guilty one, the threat. She would always be the victim.

Stella, on the other hand, would only see Tom in the little room where the girls lived, where she often used to say two people were a crowd. She didn't dare go out into the streets with him, and felt Ally was reckless, letting herself be seen with Marcus. It was one thing to have fun, enjoying themselves in the cabaret, and another to fall in love and dream of making a life together. Stella was forever telling her that such a thing would never be accepted in Düsseldorf, or anywhere in Germany.

But over time, Ally made it clear to her she was prepared to start a family with Marcus. His irreverence, his rebellious spirit, his sheer talent captivated her. With him she felt safe. Together they could take on the world, she thought. Since they only ever went out at night and met around the club, the festive atmosphere, music, and smoke were like a protective blanket to them. Some people saw her as a "loose woman," as their landlady had once described her, spotting her going out on her own at night despite the police warnings. When women saw her with Marcus, it frightened them. They studied her face, trying to work out if she had been forced, or if she was with this strange specimen of her own volition. Men undressed her with their eyes, she could feel it. But the ones she feared were the Brownshirts. They sent a chill down her spine, and there were more of them every day, as though the godforsaken plague had returned and was blighting the country once more.

When they reached his Ellerstrasse apartment that night, Marcus took off his shoes, then his jacket, throwing it on the armchair by the window. Tonight, he didn't bother hanging it carefully in the wardrobe to stop it getting creased. He climbed into bed. When Ally tried to get close, he rolled away from her.

"Do you want me to go?" Ally asked warily.

"Of course not. We need to sleep. We'll know more tomorrow."

Ally didn't ask any more questions. She looked around the room, which she was trying to make more homey every day: the bronze-framed photograph of his German grandparents, whom Marcus had never known; an oil painting of the family home on the border with Alsace, which he had never visited either; a *Chocolate Kiddies* poster, from when Sam Wooding's orchestra came to play in Berlin, and the only photograph of his mother, with her fair hair and languid eyes, on the bedside table that had a leg missing.

There were various copies of *Der Artist* piled up in one corner of the room, one with a headline in red: *Schesbend*. There was also Dvorak piano sheet music, and a program, signed by Sam Wooding, from the show at the Admiralspalast in Berlin three years earlier, the first time Marcus had heard the music of Duke Ellington. There were no pictures of his father. Marcus's mother had met him in France and gave birth to their son alone, in Düsseldorf, far from her family. Soon after the baby was born, she had gotten work as a live-in domestic servant, and the family who took her on soon recognized her little boy's musical talents, sponsoring piano lessons for Marcus when he was only four.

As a teenager, Marcus went to Paris, perhaps hoping to find the man who was no more than an image, a faceless shadow. His father. That was where he began to play the piano and saxophone, in cafés where people went to talk, not to listen to music, and he met other artists like himself. He could master any instrument from the moment he picked it up. One winter he received a letter from the family he had grown up with, the family that had accepted him: his mother had died, they told him, felled by the influenza ravaging the country. Devastated, he returned to Düsseldorf with a saxophone he had inherited from a musician friend who had grown tired of the bad nights and even worse pay, and Marcus began his nocturnal life as a musician in the city where he was born. In Schall und Rauch he met Tom and Lonnie, and they soon became an inseparable trio.

Ally was startled when Marcus suddenly roused himself, got up, and sat on the edge of the bed.

"I know where Lonnie was all week," he said gravely.

"Well, let's go to the police and save him then."

Marcus shook his head and somberly fixed his eyes on her.

"I can't."

"Why not? It's the only way to help Lonnie!"

Marcus looked at Ally. "There's nothing to be done. If they knew the truth, it would only make things worse."

4

Four Years Later
Düsseldorf, March 1934

The night Lilith was born, Ally thought her poetry writing days were over. What was the point in filling sheets of white paper with insipid poems if she couldn't be by Marcus's side, bringing their daughter up together? Lilith was going to need all her mother's attention. Ally's notebook disappeared into one of the nightstand drawers, and she no longer lay in bed inventing verses, playing with words, as she had once done. Then when little Lilith started to talk, Ally found her own words slowly started coming back to her.

She reread Marcus's letters time and again, hoping one day he would come and surprise them.

After the elections in 1933, Marcus stopped writing. That dismal autumn brought a victory for the Nazis: Marcus had officially become the enemy of the state. After not hearing from him for a month and a half, Ally decided to turn to her old friend Stella, writing to her in Düsseldorf. Then a fire at the Reichstag in the center of Berlin filled the city with terror. Everybody was a suspect. More elections followed, novena prayers for a republic that was already dying, yet Ally was hopeful. "The country will regain its sanity," she would say. "We'll be ourselves again."

Ally had never intended to stay in Berlin. Ever since she had arrived there pregnant, her suitcase was always packed and ready; the house tidy; the books, still in boxes; the typewriter in a corner beside an empty cupboard. The girl slept in a little crib trimmed with lace and ribbons, next to Ally, who seemed in denial when it came to preparing the baby's room, as though sending Lilith to her own room would mean admitting they would never return to Düsseldorf and form a real family with Marcus.

The day Lilith turned two, Ally told her they were going on a train journey to celebrate. The little girl stared at her in astonishment. All she wanted was a cream cake with two candles to blow out in the dark.

"Be careful what you wish for," Herr Professor had said, adding a playful wink to soften the warning. "Wishes can be very dangerous . . ."

The packed suitcases sat in the hallway for months. Ally couldn't make up her mind. Every night she would tell Herr Professor they were going to go, only to postpone the trip the following day. All the letters she sent to Marcus were returned unopened. She kept them in the drawer where she hid her poems.

One evening not long before her daughter's third birthday, as the three of them were sitting by the fire's dying embers, Ally announced that she had made up her mind. They would take the train the next morning.

In the morning when he saw she was indeed ready to leave, Herr Professor looked at Ally in bewilderment.

"I already told Stella we're coming. She'll be waiting for us at the station," Ally told Herr Professor.

"Are you sure about this?" he asked her quietly. "If it's what you really want, I'll come with you to the train."

Standing by the carriage, Lilith was fascinated by the steam from the locomotives and the constant whistles of the trains.

"Look after your mommy," Herr Professor told her, as he lifted her up to say goodbye on the platform. "She needs you."

"We're going to miss the train," Ally said. "We need to get onboard."

"Don't worry, my child, you'll only be gone a few days," he said to Lilith.

Ally fixed her eyes on Herr Professor. There was a pleading look in them.

"I'll look after the plants; I'll check the mail. If I hear any news . . ."

"About Daddy?" asked Lilith.

"If there's any news about Daddy, you'll find it in Düsseldorf, not here. Up you go, or you'll miss the train."

Find out about him, not find him, Ally thought. They clambered up into the carriage, Lilith first, trying to help her mother with the suitcase.

"It's too heavy for you," Herr Professor heard Ally say.

Lilith was determined to help her mother. She pursed her lips and tensed her whole body each time she tried to lift the case. Before they disappeared into the carriage, she tilted her head and looked for her Opa. She said goodbye with her right arm outstretched, and a broad smile on her face.

Opa held his hand out to wave goodbye.

Ally slept the entire train journey. When she opened her eyes, she saw Lilith at the half-open window, frozen, her eyes red from the wind. Ally had been dreaming and tried to remember whether or not it had been a nightmare. Marcus would be waiting on the platform for them. He would pick Lilith up, say to her, "My little sunshine." He would whisper in Ally's ear, "What has the most beautiful woman in the world got to tell me?" the way he used to wake her in the morning after they had spent the night together. He would pick up the suitcase and take them to a light-filled apartment with views of the River Düssel. They would have dinner together, talk about music, her poetry, friends. They would go to bed early, and she would sleep in his arms, protected from the storms shaking the city, the country.

The hours separating Berlin from Düsseldorf seemed to Ally like a few minutes.

An elderly couple were staring at Lilith in astonishment. Seeing her mother had woken up, the little girl ran over to her. The old people couldn't take their eyes off her, and Lilith clumsily tucked her curls away under her hat. Ally kissed her and looked out the window. The train had slowed. They were pulling into the station. Her eyes swept along the platform, at the people anxiously awaiting their families. She wanted to find Stella in the crowd and shuddered when she saw soldiers.

They went into the station that was so familiar to Ally, but she suddenly felt as if she were back in Berlin, as though the distance had been erased. As in the capital, there were flags emblazoned with swastikas hanging everywhere, in every corner of the station, as though the election wasn't over, as though they were living in a never-ending political campaign to ensure the continuous victory of the great seducer. A brass band was playing a march. The music sounded dissonant, vulgar. The instruments attacked her. *We don't want you here*, they seemed to scream.

She spotted Stella, standing still in the bustling crowd. Ally and Lilith hurried over. Stella was wearing a long Prussian-blue overcoat, her wavy hair tied back leaving her forehead clear; her lips painted a bright red.

"Stella," Ally whispered with relief.

Stella bent and greeted Lilith first.

"You must be the famous and brilliant Lilith."

Lilith held out her hand, serious, her eyes open wide.

"You can give Auntie Stella a kiss, she's a great friend of Mommy's." Stella flushed.

"We'll take a cab," Stella said. "It looks like it might rain. Come on, let me take your case."

"There's no need, we can manage. Isn't that right, Lilith?"

Lilith nodded and smiled. They were near the band, who were in the last bars of a rousing march. Behind them was a blown-up full-color image of the Führer. A group of youths were singing a song that Ally recognized. The singing grew louder, and Ally began to tremble when she heard one of the verses: *Denn heute gehört uns Deutschland, und morgen die ganze Welt. For today, Germany is ours, and tomorrow the whole world.*

The cab pulled away from the celebratory chaos, the posters, the intimidating chorus of voices.

"Look, Lilith. This is where Auntie Stella and I used to go for walks, before you were born," she said, looking over at the little tributary off the Rhine. "Sometimes, during the week, we would go down to the Neander Valley. Not on the weekends though—they were for watching your father onstage at Schall und Rauch. Everything looks so different now."

"We've all changed," Stella explained. "We live in a new Germany, Ally. It's about time you woke up. You can't sleep through it all."

Ally stayed silent until they got out of the taxi. She barely recognized her friend. When they were children, Ally and Stella had made a pact to go to study in Berlin together, where they would live in the same apartment until the day they married, and that they would have a double wedding. They would go to the altar together. They would build their houses next door to one another, their babies would be born at the same time, and just like them they would be best friends their whole lives.

"Did I tell you I managed to get in touch with Tom?" Ally said, following her up the stairs.

"I'm surprised he hasn't left yet."

"He's going back to New York as soon as he can. He's scared."

"That's the best thing he can do. There's no point looking back, Ally. It won't do any of us any good."

"He's going to meet me tonight, before he goes."

Stella sighed, shaking her head. "You must know what you're getting yourself into."

Stella's elegant apartment was on the fourth floor. There were dark silk curtains in the living room. When they drew one back, a faint light entered the room. Lilith ran to the window.

"Look, Mommy, the river."

"You two can use my bedroom. I'll sleep in the study."

"It's a beautiful apartment. Do you live with someone?"

"Yes, but he's away traveling for a few weeks."

"Don't worry. We'll be gone in a couple of days."

"As long as you need, Ally. But at this point I don't think you're going to find many answers."

"I only want to know where he is."

Stella's eyes fixed on the girl.

"She's listening to us."

"She knows we came to find her father."

"Ally, Marcus left more than a year ago. You told me that yourself."

"He didn't leave, Stella. They took him. Just like they took Lonnie. Or don't you remember that? How you cried?"

"I'll make us a cup of tea. You need one."

They sat at the dining room table, beside a bookcase where a portrait of the Führer stood in a bronze picture frame, with a red ribbon tied in one corner.

Stella saw that the picture made Ally feel uncomfortable and closed her eyes.

"I don't know what world you're living in," she said as she poured the tea and offered Lilith an iced biscuit. "They're delicious, Lilith. Your mommy and I loved them when we were your age."

Lilith took the biscuit and went back to the window.

Ally slowly sipped her tea. She was in the home of a total stranger. The light in the room was dim, and it was as if there were a thin layer of glass between them. Even Stella's smell was different. She felt the words they spoke condensing with the steam from her tea.

"I don't know what it's like there, but here everything's changed." Stella continued.

"We're not the same in Berlin either."

"For your daughter's sake, go back to Berlin." Stella's voice tightened. "You won't find anything here. Think of Lilith."

"Should I be afraid?" Ally said with a hint of irony.

"Yes, why wouldn't you?" Stella raised her voice. "I'd be scared if I was in your position. With a . . ."

"A Rhineland bastard?"

"You know what I mean. Your daughter . . ."

"She's my daughter, and she's just as German as you are."

"She's different. We should never have gotten together with the musicians. It was just a bit of fun. But you—"

"Stella, I loved Marcus," Ally interrupted her again. Realizing she'd spoken in the past tense, she stuttered, "He's . . . he's the father of my child." Her voice now weak.

"At least she didn't turn out as dark as her father, and she has your features. The hair though, the problem is the hair."

"Stella, Lilith is my daughter."

Ally finished her tea and fetched her coat and purse from the bedroom. She went to Lilith and knelt to embrace her.

"Make sure you behave yourself. You're going to stay with auntie for a few hours. Give mommy a kiss."

Lilith flung her arms around her neck, hugged her tightly, and Ally scooped her up.

"You're getting so heavy. In a few months I won't be able to pick you up."

"Be careful, Ally. I'll look after Lilith, don't worry," Stella said.

Ally walked carefully down the stairs. She counted every step, as though reluctant to reach her destination. She paused at the front doorway and looked around at the red-and-yellow-bricked buildings. Floral curtains in the windows, spotless doors, the polished brass of the numbers. A world away from the decrepit building where she and Stella had once shared a damp and moldy room.

She took the U-Bahn toward the center. At this time of the evening, the carriages were full. There were no more vampires on the hunt for women like her; now there were soldiers everywhere. She looked at the young men's faces, all of them glowing with the joy of purpose. She eyed the insignias on one youth's jacket, and he beamed at her with pride. His euphoria sent shivers down her spine.

She went up to street level, leaving the station behind, and walked toward the beer cellar. There weren't any long queues now, or couples hanging around outside smoking. There were lights missing from the sign above the club. The last "L" and the "R" weren't lit. The words no longer made sense.

She went inside and saw that all the lights were on. She missed the darkness. A white-haired man in a crumpled suit sat alone at one of the tables, drinking beer. Two women were sitting near the stage. The rest of the tables were empty. As she crossed the room, a bartender with small teeth waved hello in a way that felt familiar. She didn't recognize him. She heard footsteps on the boards of the stage, the heels ringing out like gunshots. There were no spotlights. A man wandered off toward the props cupboard. She heard the familiar *Ladies and Gentlemen . . .* and prayed for a miracle.

But Marcus didn't step onto the stage.

She went to the canopy on the left-hand side of the stage and opened one of the secret doors leading to the dressing rooms. The bright bulbs on each corner of the stage pierced the curtains with shafts of light. There were no dancers hurrying to get onstage. She walked to the dressing room where Marcus used to gather with the other musicians. Tom was waiting at the door for her. He gestured for her to come in and gave her a quick hug. She didn't recognize any of the other musicians, and noticed Tom was the only Black man in the room. Nobody bothered to say hello.

She saw Marcus's saxophone standing in a corner covered in dust, exactly as he must have left it. Ally was looking for clues, signs, anything that might lead her to him.

She went over to the instrument and picked it up. She gave Tom a beseeching look, and he approached her with the case. The instrument was the only thing of Marcus's she could see. Tom tucked it inside the case, covered with images of the Eiffel Tower, the Statue of Liberty, the Brandenburg Gate.

There was nothing for her to ask. What was she doing there? She felt herself collapsing, and she leaned against Tom, sobbing. She knew she would never find Marcus. It suddenly occurred to her that if they saw the saxophone, they would realize he was just a musician, one who had even played for a German film. Marcus was German, as German as she was.

"Marcus needs his saxophone," Ally said through gritted teeth, fighting back her tears, almost whimpering.

Tom held a bundle of letters tied neatly with red string. "These are yours. You should have them."

Ally looked at the letters she'd written to Marcus. All of them had been opened and read. Holding them was disorienting. She felt as if they had been written by some other person. She realized Tom had already grown accustomed to the loss of Marcus, Lonnie, and who knew how many others. Now it was her turn to do the same.

Tom explained how the police had found some copies of a clandestine political magazine in Marcus's possession. A magazine their friend Lonnie was supposedly associated with. Despite having no proof, they determined that Marcus was the author of some of the anonymous articles.

Ally knew Lonnie and Marcus weren't the first to be taken away, and they wouldn't be the last. Tom would surely be next if he didn't leave now.

Ally and Tom left the cabaret, Tom carrying Marcus's saxophone case. They stood under the canopy in the dark.

"Marcus always told me our relationship wouldn't last. He knew they would never accept us, but I always had hope. I didn't care if people saw us together."

"He was protecting you. He was so worried about you and the baby, he knew you had to leave here, but he was excited about becoming a father too."

Ally's eyes went wide.

"You're saying he agreed with my parents' idea to send me to Berlin."

"You couldn't stay here with him; it was too dangerous."

"And Berlin wasn't?"

"In Berlin you had an apartment. Where would you have lived here?"

"With Marcus."

"Nobody would have rented an apartment to a couple like you."

Ally lowered her head, feeling drained.

"You're tired. You should go home. I don't think it would be a good idea for me to walk you. You'll be safer on your own."

"Before, when Stella and I went out alone at night, we were scared of the Vampire. Now I'm afraid every minute of the day, even if I have someone with me."

Ally's gaze was fixed on the saxophone case. She felt all turned around, caught up in her own fear. She knew she'd never see Tom again, just like Lonnie and Marcus. At least Tom was going to save himself.

They walked a little way, heads down, in silence, counting their steps. A policeman approached her, stopped her, and clasped her arm.

"Are you all right?" The man looked across at Tom. "What's this Negro piece of trash doing? Has he hurt you?"

"You're the one hurting me!" she replied angrily. "Leave me alone."

She shook his hand from her arm, and they ran to the U-Bahn station without looking back. Crying, she hugged Tom and then got on the train alone. This was goodbye.

When she reached Stella's apartment, she went straight to the bedroom and lay down beside a sleeping Lilith. A little before dawn she got up and dressed. She looked out at the city, its calm murmur, the cold mist. In a few hours the bustle would begin, the hordes of youth prepared to build the new Germany, in which she and her daughter had no place.

She went over to the table with the bundle of letters and spread them out. She recognized her handwriting, but not what she had written. She went through them, one by one, rereading odd phrases that appeared time and again.

Wait for me, I'll come back.

She has your eyes and my smile. Lilith will guide us.

I hear you before I close my eyes, but every day your voice grows weaker. Don't abandon me.

What have we become, Marcus?

Come to see us. Lilith needs you.

She learned to say Daddy before Mommy.

Night . . . I always wait for night to come.

"Mommy . . ." Lilith went over to her, her hair a mess.

"Look at the state of your hair. I need to untangle it for you, but we must be quiet, Auntie Stella's asleep."

Ally went to the bedroom. Looking for a comb, she opened the wardrobe and found one in the top drawer. Next to it lay military insignias, metal stamps emblazoned with swastikas, and a revolver in a leather case. She saw various uniforms hanging up. She closed the wardrobe and went back to Lilith.

"It's time to gather our things, we're leaving here." Agitated, she started to untangle Lilith's hair.

"Are we going to a hotel?"

"No, we're going back to Berlin."

Lilith asked no more questions. She didn't know where she had woken up, or what her mother was talking about. Whether she had found her father or not. She wanted to cry, but she held back her tears with all her might. This wasn't the time to be a helpless little girl.

At only three years old, Lilith had already accepted that she had been born to a father she could never know. When she blew out the candles on her birthday cake this year, and every one that followed, her wish was not for herself, but for her mother. Her mother was the one who needed to find him. Lilith was happy to hide away. What more could she ask for than to get lost in Herr Professor's books, or the nighttime walks through the beautiful park that, during those hours, was theirs alone?

Holding Lilith's hand, as well as the suitcase, Ally left Düsseldorf for Berlin, without saying goodbye to Stella, or the city, as though they had never been part of her life, as though Marcus had never existed. The only thing that mattered to her was the here and now. Memory was no longer a shield. She had lost her refuge; Lilith was her present. This trip had not been what she wanted, but it was what she needed. At last, she understood that Marcus had disappeared from their lives forever.

5

Mommy! It's Jesse!" the little girl cried, and Ally and Herr Professor hurried over to the radio.

Lilith sat cross-legged on the wooden floor, avoiding the rug that made her itch. Her mother and Herr Professor joined her to enjoy the only contact they had with the outside world: a magical little wooden box with golden trim.

For five-year-old Lilith, the radio was a kind of holy temple with a woman's face. She could see her eyes, nose, and smiling mouth, and on the top the oval shape of a crown. On more than one occasion her mother had found her talking to it, as though it were a loyal friend. Lilith often fell asleep to the sound of it when the stations had finished broadcasting. The crackle, which to her was more like a whistle, had become her favorite lullaby.

Two thousand five hundred doves in the sky above Berlin. Now the cannons are being prepared to welcome the symbol of German Olympic glory. The voice of Paul Laven, whom the little girl adored, resounded throughout the building. All of Germany was on tenterhooks.

From the Reichs-Rundfunk-Gesellschaft, broadcasting all over the world, the radio presenter announced enthusiastically. *Millions are listening today, here, in new Germany. And now the moment we've all been waiting for, the hundred-meter dash.*

Ally and Herr Professor clasped hands, their eyes on Lilith, who was staring fixedly at the magic box. All three held their breath and closed their eyes. They all had hope. Jesse Owens, the Black American runner who had won three gold medals in the biggest and most famous sporting event in the world, had the chance to break a record and win a fourth.

A year had passed since the *Nürnberger Gesetze*. The new racial laws agreed upon during a meeting in Nuremberg had been published in *Der Stürmer*. The message was clear: Racial purity must reign in Germany. The survival of a half-caste, a mulatto, a *mischling*, a Jew, would depend on how impure their blood was. A chart published in the newspaper allowed people to work out whether the mix, the error, was of the first or second degree. It took into account skin color, head size, proportion of the forehead, nose and eyes, and physical and mental abilities. The day the *Law for the Protection of German Blood and German Honor* was signed, the race of each citizen began to be defined, and the results kept in a register. The impure were not allowed to marry and reproduce. Nor could they work in business or in a university. Breaking the law was punishable by a prison sentence, a fine, or forced labor. Leaving Germany was impossible. An exit pass was required, a visa, a sponsor. That was the day Ally began her vigil.

"Jesse's going to win, you'll see," Lilith said, eyes tight shut. "Have faith in him."

"Lilith, he's already won three medals, "Ally reminded her. "He doesn't have anything left to prove. He's a great athlete."

"The fourth! We need the fourth!"

Lilith had recently told her mother she wanted to be an athlete, a long-distance runner. She was of the same blood as Jesse, she said, and in a few years, she'd be as tall as him too. When they went to the Tiergarten at night, Lilith would sprint back and forth until she was out of breath. When she twisted her ankle and had to treat it with an ice pack, she lay awake for several days, running with her eyes closed, dreaming up tactics and tricks that would allow her to hold her breath, conserving just enough oxygen in her veins to get her to the finish line: first her nose, then forehead, head, shoulders, and torso. She knew she had to start with deep inhalations, hold her breath, keep that rhythm. Three strides, inhale. Three strides, exhale.

She spent hours listening to her mother read to her, and sometimes her mind traveled to far-off places where she would find herself on the running track in a deserted Olympic stadium. At the time, her mother was reading her a biography of Abraham Lincoln by Emil Ludwig. Their constant wakefulness meant they got to know Napoleon, Cleopatra, Goethe, all brought to life by Ludwig's words. For the little girl, these historical figures' stories were great adventures. Ally didn't dare read Lilith her own poems, which had started to be published in a university literary journal. The day Herr Professor brought her several copies of an issue containing her poems in print, Ally turned pale.

"This is going to get us in trouble. My poems aren't an ode to the new Germany."

"You'll be fine. I don't think they'll reach many people through this little magazine," Herr Professor said.

"But it seems like I published the poems in response to the race laws," Ally said.

"Those at the university know that these poems were written a long time ago. Nothing is published overnight. However, I think it's best if we keep these magazines away from Lilith, and even from Franz."

"I shouldn't have published them. I can't afford to attract any attention right now."

"Nothing's going to happen. To you or to Lilith. We don't have to worry, at least not for today."

A few days later, Ally and Herr Professor decided to take the precaution of removing any possibly damning books from their shelves. Lilith unwillingly helped them.

"We're keeping Emil's books," Herr Professor declared.

"One day Emil will write about Jesse, you'll see," Lilith said.

Emil and Jesse became her new imaginary friends. She had conversations with them, as though they were sitting in the living room
armchair, or at the bureau, writing, weary with concentration.

"I want a photograph of Jesse in my bedroom," she said to her
mother, clutching the biography of Napoleon.

"Be careful with that book," Ally replied. "Go and put it back on
the shelf."

"Somebody could get us a newspaper with Jesse in it. Maybe Franz . . ."

"I don't think that's a good idea," Ally interrupted her, turning to
Herr Professor for support.

"Jesse may be a hero to us, but in his own country, I doubt they think
so highly of him. As a runner, perhaps; as a medal-winner, yes. But from
that to him being a hero . . ."

Herr Professor smiled at Lilith. When he saw how excited she was
by the races, he confessed to her that in his youth he had been an aspir-
ing athlete. Herr Professor became interested in track and field ath-
letics, eventually becoming a long-distance runner. Nowhere near Jesse
Owens's standard, of course, but good enough to compete in races with
schools from other cities.

"And did you ever compete in the Olympics?" Lilith asked eagerly.

"My love of books soon won out over my love of sport. And anyway,
Lilith, seeing Owens now, I realize for me it was just a childhood thing.
In fact, I think I only took part in sports to please my father. Do you
know what I used to love? Holidays along the North Sea coast. One day
we'll go and get lost in the dunes . . ."

The announcer's deep voice on the radio rang out, expounding on
glories he was witnessing.

*The Olympic Stadium, the biggest building ever imagined by man, is
filled to capacity. Over one hundred thousand spectators are here to cheer on
our German sportsmen. Thanks to the Führer, our nation now boasts the best
sporting stadium in the world.*

"Could we visit the Olympic Stadium one night?"

"They close it at night, but yes, we could look at it from outside," Ally told her.

The crowd was tense. The presenter's shallow breathing could be heard. Suddenly, cries of *Sieg heil! Sieg heil!* startled Lilith.

"There he is," Herr Professor said. "They don't even need to announce his arrival."

There is only one superior race, and that is about to be demonstrated now, the presenter continued. *The Olympic spirit is, in essence, German.*

"I think they might get a bit of a surprise today," Herr Professor said through gritted teeth.

Lilith gestured for silence. She wanted to concentrate. She knew the race was short, almost like a sigh. A distraction, a blink, or a sneeze, and they might miss it.

"Three strides, inhale," Lilith said to the others' surprise. "Three strides, exhale."

And here they come. We can see the athletes stepping onto the track, one by one. They're on their marks. These will be the longest seconds in the history of German Olympic sport. We can feel the breeze. We hope the wind will be behind us.

Pause. Another too-lengthy silence on the radio.

They're set. There's the starting pistol! The Black is first away!

The ovation drowns out the presenter, who is so utterly engrossed he forgets to describe the race. Perhaps it isn't what he was expecting. And it all happens in front of the Führer, in front of the people. The superior race must never lose. Stay calm. One more second.

It's O-vens, Metcalfe, and Osendarp.

Paul Laven is left breathless, and hands the microphone to another presenter.

That's all we have for today.

Lilith, Ally, and Herr Professor don't react. Lilith's gaze travels over Ally, then onto Herr Professor, before returning to the radio. She wants to hear Jesse's name: O-vens. She wants Paul Laven to say his name. Nobody has mentioned him being the winner. A fourth medal. He only needed a fourth medal to be immortal. The three stand up, hold hands in a circle, and jump for joy.

They hear cheering from the little magic box: "O-vens! O-vens!"

6

Two Years Later
Berlin, October 1938

By the age of five, Lilith had been able to use the Pythagorean theorem with complete accuracy. She spoke about right triangles with wonderment, as though she were discovering the formula for the very first time.

"We have a genius in the family," Herr Professor had said.

Ally ignored the little girl's frequent lectures, which had initially amused her, but over time she found alarming. She wasn't sure whether her talents would work in her favor or against her. To Herr Professor, the girl's knowledge was the perfect riposte for those who wanted to see her as an inferior being.

Lilith was six when one day she woke up and, over breakfast, defined photosynthesis with the cadence of someone reciting the verses of Heine, Ally's favorite poet. The metabolic process of cells and autotrophic organisms when exposed to sunlight could be applied in reverse to the life they lived, she said. According to Lilith, she was living proof that moonlight was a source of energy and nourishment as valid as that of the sun.

"Do we need to control which books this girl has access to?" Herr Professor asked, taken aback.

"It's your fault, or rather your library's fault," Ally replied with a smile.

"Nobody should be denied a book," Lilith interrupted. "There's no such thing as inappropriate books. Every book can teach us something."

Faced with these quips, Ally and Herr Professor looked at each other, biting their lips so as not to laugh. Lilith, who had never set foot inside a school, was evidence there was no such thing as superior or inferior races, Ally told herself whenever she read the alarming news stories.

Ally often felt guilty. She had robbed her daughter of her childhood, forced her to grow up, to mature, as the days of the calendar flew by in seconds. There was no time to waste. There had been moments when she wished she could go back in time and return Lilith's lost childhood. But she knew that for now she had to capitalize on the little girl's brilliance. That would be her trump card.

With Franz's help, they had secured an appointment at number four Tiergartenstrasse, where he worked with his cousin, an expert in the new racial laws. If Lilith was approved by the commission, if she was found not to be inferior, she wouldn't have to be sterilized using X-rays. The time had come to demonstrate that Lilith was special, that the color of her skin, the texture of her hair, the proportions of her head and face were not an impediment to her thriving. Ally took Herr Professor's arm and he knocked on the front door of the villa. She had walked past it so many times, never stopping.

"Some friends of my parents lived here, and they used to bring me as a child," Herr Professor said. "I remember it was like stepping inside a museum. I wasn't allowed to run or touch anything. Carelessness could end in catastrophe. I think it eventually became home to some antique dealers before the government took possession of it."

He hoped that his chatter would relieve the tension in Ally's face, but she seemed oblivious. A woman opened the door and, without even asking their names or whom they had come to see, directed them to follow her. It seemed as if they didn't receive many guests.

The rooms were empty, as though nobody else was in the villa. The offices must have been located on the upper floors. To one side they saw the dining room, with its huge teardrop chandelier hanging in the center. They followed the maid as far as the library. She gestured for them to go inside and then left. Countless leather-bound books, all the same size, filled the shelves, stacked against bronze bookends. Egyptian figures: busts, jars, sphinxes, sat on a rectangular, dark green marble table. Herr Professor ran his eyes over each one, as though trying to commit them to memory. Ally fixed her gaze on the doorway, waiting for Franz. They sat down, still in their coats, as if they knew the visit would be brief.

It was within these four walls that her daughter's future would be decided.

"We're lucky we can count on Franz," Herr Professor said.

Ally turned her head toward the tapestries with their pastoral landscapes, scenes of Arcadia inhabited by adorable cherubs. She heard footsteps, and her cheeks flushed with color. She smiled. She was hopeful. When Franz came in, Ally felt the library had been lit up. She stood and embraced him. He patted her on the back distantly.

"Ally, don't forget that Franz is at work."

"My cousin," Franz corrected, firmly. "It's my cousin Philipp who works here. Let's go."

Philipp Bouhler had studied philosophy and had written for the newspaper *Völkischer Beobachter*. "A humanist in search of perfection," Herr Professor said with irony whenever Franz praised his cousin. Since he had become a *Reichsleiter*, he had been instructed to implement the racial hygiene laws, which were not being strictly followed by all doctors. Now, the Aktion T4 program, which took its name from the address where the villa was located, was being put into practice in every hospital in the land. Originally meant to prevent the passing on of hereditary defects, including physical and mental imperfections, the law eventually came to include racial impurity.

"I'm sorry to have asked you to come, unfortunately my cousin cannot receive us now," Franz said without looking at them. "There's nothing we can do to avoid it. Lilith has to pass the commission exam."

Franz walked them through the grand rooms with the self-assuredness of a resident. Clearly familiar with how to operate the ancient latch on the garden door, he opened it, and they left the building. The Tiergarten stretched away from them, the trees' canopies disappearing into tin-colored clouds. Rain was coming and the air in the gardens revived Ally. She just needed Franz to tell her what to do. She would follow his instructions to the letter. There was no other way of escape.

Women were pushing immaculate babies in their carriages along the well-tended paths. Flags waved triumphantly in the breeze. In the distance, trams trundled around the city like any other peaceful December day. For her, the impending storm had already begun.

"A commission can convict her," Franz said quietly.

"Lilith is passing the commission," Herr Professor clarified.

Franz was silent. Ally had been hopeful that his close relationship with Philipp, and the admiration he felt for his cousin, would free her from her torment. Still, Lilith had all the qualities she needed to save herself. She had been born in Germany, to a German mother, surrounded by German culture and traditions. She had never had any contact with her father, or his family. She didn't really know who he was, or what he was like. Lilith was the child of a ghost, an illusion.

"You won't find another girl as clever as our Lilith," Herr Professor crowed enthusiastically.

"Lilith is brilliant," Ally agreed with a smile. "You know, even before she could read or write she used to draw numbers. It was as if she were working out some complex formula. Lilith learns whatever she sets her mind to."

"They have to check that Lilith has no deformities," Franz went on.

"Deformities?" Ally asked, breathless.

"I mean the shape of her head. That her nose isn't out of proportion, or her lips. Her skin, fortunately, isn't cracked or shiny. It isn't too dark, but still dark enough to be rejected. And her hair . . . That's what gives her away too."

Herr Professor and Ally kept their calm. Ally gulped, her throat dry. She didn't want to understand what she was hearing. She felt as if they were discussing an injured horse who needed to be shot to put it out of its misery. Her daughter was a missing link in a zoo, a sample, a specimen to be studied.

"There are three panels to convince," Franz explained. "They certify whether you're a Rhineland bastard. They analyze what percentage can be passed on to your descendants. Depending on what they find, they determine whether or not you have to be sterilized."

"Franz, we know that. My daughter isn't going to be sterilized."

"I'm not saying . . ."

"We came here in the hopes that your cousin could save my daughter, not to subject her to some commission that might condemn her," Ally interrupted him, with a coldness that Herr Professor and Franz had never seen in her before. "What makes her blood any different from mine or yours?"

"*Some rise by sin, and some by virtue fall,*" Herr Professor recited, downcast.

Disheartened, Ally felt the weight of the clouds upon her. She wanted to explain yet again to Franz that a commission was not going to approve her daughter. However brilliant, the little girl would be deemed by the commissioners to be a stain on the German race, and on the country's future. To prevent the damage Lilith could cause, they wanted to sterilize her so that her impure womb could never bear fruit.

They walked toward the Brandenburg Gate. Ally understood now that villa number four on Tiergartenstrasse would not provide them with the help they needed. Salvation didn't lie in the hands of Philipp Bouhler. Aktion T4 could only condemn her daughter.

It began to rain. The cold raindrops shook Ally out of her mental labyrinth. She had to stop thinking like this. She wanted to be with her daughter, never to be separated by anything or anyone.

They were crossing Unter den Linden toward the River Spree when Herr Professor suddenly stopped them.

"The Herzogs!" he said triumphantly.

"I don't think they can help us," Ally said. "They've just lost everything. They're ruined."

"Who are they?" asked Franz.

"My Jewish neighbors," Ally replied. "On the first floor, as you come in, on the left."

"I've never seen them."

"Since their lighting store was destroyed, they've locked themselves away," Herr Professor explained. "Their only son was taken away to the Sachsenhausen, and they haven't seen him since."

"I don't know them well at all," Ally said shamefacedly. "How awful. I had no idea about their son."

"They've lost everything, and now they don't know how to escape," Herr Professor went on. "They've waited too long. They didn't want to go and leave their son behind. They're looking for a country to move to, well away from here."

"Lilith," Franz said.

"What's Lilith got to do with the Herzogs?" Ally was confused.

"We could help the Herzogs escape, and Lilith could go with them," Franz explained. "She could pass for a Jew, don't you think? She has dark skin, but not too dark. If we cover her hair . . . I could help them get tickets on a boat that's leaving Hamburg."

"Where to?" Herr Professor asked, suddenly hopeful. "I heard that some are going to Palestine. Even England has accepted a lot of them."

"What are you two saying? I'm not going to abandon my daughter!"

"What would you rather?" Herr Professor said breathlessly. "For her to be subjected to rays that could kill her? If we knew for sure it would only leave her infertile, but those rays . . ."

Franz and Herr Professor stopped speaking when they saw that Ally's eyes were red, her breathing ragged. They couldn't tell if she was crying or if her face was wet with rain.

After a lengthy pause, Ally collected herself. "Come on, Lilith's waiting for us," she said, taking Franz by the arm. "Winter will soon be here."

They didn't quicken their pace but walked slowly in the drizzle. They had left Lilith alone, and by now she would be waiting for them to come home, watching the raindrops run down the glass pane. "Seven years," Ally repeated. "Seven years . . ." Turning the corner of Anklamer Strasse, she spotted the window of her apartment, which looked far away. Even from this distance she could make out her daughter's happy face.

Lilith and Ally always longed for rainy days in the way most people await the first warm day of sunshine after a long winter. While other people hurried off in search of shelter, they felt free beneath the cold drops. Only when it rained did the daytime belong to them. In her hooded raincoat, Lilith jumped over puddles in Mitte's cobbled streets, and Ally ran behind her, out of breath, but free. Soaked to the skin, they leaped on the benches in the Tiergarten, their laughter drowned out by the noise of the storm, the clacking feet of those running for shelter, and the cars, sluggish in the rain. The police had disappeared: there was nobody left for them to keep watch over. Who was going to scold them? Everybody was sheltering, except for them.

They opened the front door, and the three of them looked toward apartment 1B. On the right-hand side of the doorframe was a thin cylinder affixed at an angle. It was the first time Ally had noticed the mezuzah on the Herzogs' door.

"Should we speak to the Herzogs now?" Herr Professor asked determinedly. "We don't need to make a decision yet. We can tell them we want to help and leave the door open. It's an option we shouldn't rule out."

"Later. Let's not keep Lilith waiting, she saw us."

Franz closed the front door and they stood under the resin light by the elevator.

"I'll take the stairs," Ally said.

"I'll come with you." Franz took her by the arm.

"See you later then," said Herr Professor. "At my age, the less I use my legs the better."

Before going up, Ally ran a finger over the Herzogs' mezuzah, making sure Franz didn't see. Herr Professor smiled.

When they reached the third floor, Lilith was out in the corridor, waiting for them.

"Come on, it's time to have fun," Ally said brightly.

Lilith hugged Franz, and he took a little rag doll from the inside pocket of his overcoat.

"For me?" Lilith asked, surprised. "Do I deserve it?"

Franz hugged her.

"She's called Nadine," he whispered in her ear.

The little girl looked at the doll. She had yellow woolen braids and a blue dress. Her name was embroidered with red thread in tiny letters on her white pinafore.

Lilith clasped the doll tightly, then gave it back to Franz because she was about to go out in the rain. She set off down the stairs.

"I'll stay here with Herr Professor," said Franz, looking at Ally. "We'll see each other soon."

He kissed her on the cheek, and she put her arms around him. They stayed like that until the elevator doors opened.

"Lilith will already be on the sidewalk by now," Herr Professor interrupted them. "That girl can't wait to get out in the rain."

7

Three Months Later
Brandenburg-Görden, January 1939

Ally woke at first light with a feeling of weariness. She felt that tomorrow had already been and gone. A person can lose their sense of time, in the same way that one can lose their sight, sense of smell, taste. She got up, dressed slowly, applied her lipstick, and saw Lilith by her side. But she seemed to be at a great distance, so far away she couldn't make out her features. She filled her lungs with oxygen, and she couldn't detect even a single particle of her daughter. She had lost all her senses.

Lilith was ready; she was always ready. Sometimes Ally would have preferred a daughter she could scold, lecture, nag to do her chores. One who had to be reminded to read, to have good table manners, to greet people with "good morning" and "goodbye." Goodbye was essential.

They took the train, getting off in broad daylight at the garden city of Brandenburg-Görden, where tiny frozen drops of rain melted as they fell from the sky. The dense air and bright light overwhelmed them. *So near to Berlin, and yet so different*, Lilith thought. A gust of wind nearly knocked them down. Lilith ran to her mother and clung to her.

"Why didn't we travel at night?" Lilith said with a shiver.

"Well, you can see there aren't many people about," her mother said, trying to get her bearings.

They crossed the main avenue. It was early morning, and the only soul around was an old lady standing on a corner. A car sped past. The old lady raised a fist angrily.

"Where is everyone?" the little girl asked, suspicious.

"Ninety-C Neuendorfer Strasse," Ally said aloud, without looking down at Lilith. "We need to find the first building. Franz has arranged everything. They're only going to ask you some questions, and examine you, like when you go to see the doctor."

Ally didn't believe her own words. She was doing the thing she'd told Franz she'd never do—submit Lilith to a commission for judgment. She followed Franz's directions with a calmness that disturbed Lilith. The girl felt they should have stayed in Berlin, hunted but safe, among their books, with the curtains closed. Darkness was their ally. What were they doing out in broad daylight in a strange city?

"I hope these silly doctors don't have cold hands," Ally said with a smile, trying to cheer her up.

"I'm not afraid of the cold."

The little girl recovered, took her mother's hand again, and the two of them crossed the deserted street.

The city was still asleep. There were no soldiers, no flags. There were no smashed windows. No marches or triumphal songs. They hadn't seen a single salute, nor heard a *Sieg heil!* The harmony unnerved them. When they had gotten off the train, they had crossed open countryside and entered the so-called garden city as if they were entering an unknown dimension. Franz had told Ally he was certain that if the commission were to evaluate Lilith, the little girl would be exonerated, that she would be recognized as a benefit to racial hygiene. "Hygiene": the word kept Ally awake at night, and Lilith would often find her in the library, rearranging the books on the shelves, after having swept away the dust that seeped through the walls of her increasingly fragile kingdom.

The specialized commission that would evaluate Lilith's physique and intelligence was not based in the prison that had been converted into a hospital, but one of the doctors worked there, and he would help evaluate the purity and mental development of the little girl in her seventh year of life. Ally was further proof of her purity. There wasn't a drop of Jewish, Black, or the blood of any other race in the Keller family. Nor was there any alcoholism or addiction of any kind. Nobody smoked, they had long since given up eating meat, and there was no history of disorders like schizophrenia, epilepsy, or depression. True German blood, dating back over several generations. Added to this, they were Catholics who had never drifted toward the Lutheran Protestantism to which most people had succumbed. That absolved Lilith from any sin. She had inherited from Ally a purity that very few Germans at that time could boast of, when an error, a tiny indiscretion, or an uncertain past could overshadow or even close the doors to a respectable job in the new Germany.

"We should move here, Mommy."

"Don't believe everything you see. There isn't much difference between Brandenburg and Berlin. It's all the same, Lilith dear."

The seemingly uninhabited compound was made up of four similar buildings of a greenish-yellow hue, with small windows, all of them closed. A column of white smoke rose from the chimney of one of them. They climbed a small rise and saw a soldier in a helmet, armed with a rifle. He approached them. Ally stood mesmerized by the odorless white smoke surrounding them. Lilith didn't take her eyes off the man's weapon as she tugged on her mother's coat to get her attention.

Ally greeted the soldier, handing him a folded document. He studied the little girl's face and hair.

"Follow me," he ordered.

They left the main buildings behind. Lilith turned back to the block with the column of smoke rising until it became just another cloud, as if it were feeding the sky. The guard took them to a separate two-story building with a red door. He paused in the doorway, and in a few seconds a man wearing a white coat appeared. Under it, he had on a black tie, gray corduroy trousers, polished leather shoes.

"Welcome," he said, holding out his hand to Ally.

His soft hands sent a shiver down Ally's spine. The man had a deep, pleasant voice. He had slicked-back dark hair, pale skin. Ally noticed his weary eyes. Once inside, the man took a pair of black-framed spectacles from his pocket, put them on, and with the meticulousness of a detective studied the little girl intently, as though she were a unique specimen, a special sample to be handled with extreme care.

They went into the lobby, where a vase of white roses sat on a central table, each stem competing for perfection. They went through a second door, whose noisy hinges groaned in the darkened room, adding to the creaking of the wood floor. At the far end sat three doctors, wearing white coats and with stethoscopes hanging around their necks. They all looked up together, their arms resting on a polished black wooden desk. The glow of the table lamp, with its golden base and green shade, blurred their faces. In front of them, in the center of the floor on the other side of the desk, a beam of light marked the spot where Lilith should sit, as though everything had been choreographed. Ally and Lilith were bewildered by the vastness of the room.

"Doctor Heinze," said a voice from the back.

The doctor on the far right came forward and signaled toward the beam of light.

In this room, the ceiling seemed almost to touch the sky, the bronze lamps were lost up in the heights, so that the light was little more than shadows cast on the red velvet curtains like dried blood. *Where was I? Facing a tribunal that was going to execute my daughter,* she thought. And she was the only witness for the defense.

Ally walked slowly behind Doctor Heinze, as he guided Lilith across the room.

"That won't be necessary," she heard the same voice behind her say.

Ally understood this was directed at her but couldn't make out who was speaking. She felt the words coming down from the heavens, like an order from God.

"Wait here," the sacred voice continued.

A woman gestured for her to take a seat in the opposite corner. The gesture made clear it was not a request.

There was a chair in the darkness, and Ally went over to the only place where she was allowed to wait. Yes, it had definitely been an order. Her daughter had to pass the exams by herself. They knew it would be like this and were prepared.

Another woman, also in a white coat and carrying several sheets of paper, came into the room. Her footsteps punctured the wooden floorboards. Lilith smiled, trying to appear friendly. The woman made no eye contact with the girl.

"Doctor Hallervorden," said the woman, handing the documents to the doctor who looked the oldest, the most experienced.

The woman immediately left the room by the door closest to the desk.

With her eyes closed, Lilith could float away to distant lands. In a second, she would be transported to sunny gardens or woods, in the full light of day. If she chose to, she could leave her body and look down at herself from above, flying over the city, hidden among the clouds. Opa had taught her to do it when she first started to read. "If we close our eyes, we can build our own impenetrable wall. If we close our eyes, there isn't a force in the world that can destroy us." Lilith was certain that, if she put her mind to it, she could overcome hunger or cold. She wouldn't need to use the bathroom or drink water. With her eyes closed, in this room surrounded by giants in white coats, she braved the immensity.

She felt one of the men taking off her coat with the utmost care. He made her lift one foot, then the other. Now she was barefoot. Clumsy hands tried to unbutton her dress. She felt as, one by one, each mother of pearl button slipped out of its buttonhole. Her dress opened and fell to the floor, pooling at her feet, as if it had melted. Somebody lifted her by her arms. Her body was inert, powerless, weightless. They lowered her down slowly, and she felt the warmth of the wood on the soles of her feet.

With her eyes closed, there was no danger of shedding a tear, uttering a sigh. Lilith was naked in the middle of the room, in front of strangers. And her mother? Best not to think about her. She felt stronger than every one of the people around her. Time had stopped. She wasn't there.

Ally watched Lilith in the distance, a tiny dot in the beam of light. Seeing her naked, she began to shiver for her. That was all she could do to absorb the cold, the fear, the pain, and the horror. Lilith stayed strong, so rigid that for a second Ally thought her daughter was suspended in the air.

While they were undressing Lilith, one of the doctors began to read one of the documents. Ally heard dates, pounds, ounces, and a time accurate to the minute. The details of her daughter's birth. They should have just said she had been born on the darkest night of the season, in Berlin. That her child was a child of the night. *A Rhineland bastard*, she heard in the midwife's report.

One of the doctors approached the little girl with a pointed wooden instrument and began to calibrate her skull. He focused on her forehead, then moved on to her nose. The last doctor left the desk and approached Lilith with a shiny pair of silver scissors. Weapon in hand, he went toward her and, raising the shears, examined Lilith's head and cut a lock of hair from the nape of her neck. Lilith gave a start at the snip of the metal.

Doctor Heinze made a note, watchful of every moment. *It only takes a millimeter to set us apart from the others.* Ally saw Doctor Hallervorden push Lilith's head backward, as though snapping it off.

"Open your eyes," he ordered.

Lilith did not react. Her body was there, naked, but she had escaped to the middle of the night in the Tiergarten.

With her head tilted backward and the light shining on her face, the doctor forced the girl's right eyelid open. No longer concealed, the iris contracted. The doctor held up a card next to it, full of pictures of eyes of different sizes, shapes, and colors, comparing them with Lilith's.

The light made her eye brim with tears. When she straightened her head, one ran down her cheek. She could see another doctor coming toward her with a pointed instrument. She thought they were about to pierce her, to analyze whether her organs were human or animal, and she closed her eyes again. She didn't want to see the pain.

The instrument ran down her spine. It went from her neck to her waist, then from one shoulder blade to the other. It left the shape of a cross on her skin. Lilith sensed the doctor standing beside her. She opened her eyes. He was taking notes.

"You can get dressed now," the doctor said after a lengthy pause.

As her open eyes began to focus, Lilith felt increasingly uncomfortable. She picked up her dress and covered herself. She turned and saw Ally hunched over in the chair, her face buried in her hands. She wanted to tell her that she hadn't cried, that the tear was just an involuntary reaction to the light.

Hearing a door slam, Ally pulled herself together. The beam of light had disappeared, and with it her daughter and the four doctors. She was alone in the huge room. Should she shout? She didn't have the energy. Cry? For whom? Why? Wasn't this what she herself had wanted?

She let herself collapse to the floor, but her body was now weightless. She didn't make a sound, or make any desperate movements; it was no more than a dull thud. She let out a long howl, an irrepressible moan. She remained like that for several minutes, curled up in a ball, expecting a kick, a blow that would shake her from her inertia. One more second and she would fall asleep. That was what she wanted most of all. To sleep until the nightmare was over. Awake, she was condemned to endless delirium.

When she opened her eyes—how long had she been on the floor?—Ally saw the woman who had brought the midwife's report.

"You can wait outside," the woman said, turning her back.

When Ally didn't respond, she continued.

"The girl will have to complete some physical tests, resistance tests. Then she will answer some questions."

"How much longer will it take?" Ally asked, picking herself up.

"That depends on her. They let some children go after the first round. Some manage to get to the second stage. Very rarely do they get through the third and fourth. She's only seven years old, and she doesn't go to school. I don't suppose she can read or write very well."

Ally stood up and went out to the lobby, a smile on her face. The longer her daughter was kept there, the more stages she had passed. She was certain Lilith would astonish every one of the doctors with her intelligence. For now, that was her only guarantee. She knew that if they let her go after the first panel, as the woman had said, that would mean she had been condemned.

Feeling like an insect, Ally left the lobby. The roses were too perfect, she thought as she opened the front door. The light blinded her momentarily, and she felt glad as she took a deep breath. But the smell of burnt oil turned her stomach. She moved away from the greenish-yellow building and climbed the little hill. There were no trees, there was no shelter. To the right in the distance, alongside the complex of buildings, she saw a group of doctors in their white coats with a line of men and women who had no coats on. She studied the doctors. None of them had been in the room with her daughter. She started down the small hill, and as she approached, she surveyed the faces of the other people, many of them with vacant expressions. Some were limping, one woman was missing an arm, an old woman's head was shaking, a young man scratched his forehead compulsively, one man was sucking his thumb, another one was spitting. They were heading for the building with the column of white smoke coming from its chimney.

Ally flopped down on the grass. It was the best place to wait, and she began counting the coatless ones. One, two, three, four . . . How many millimeters were they from perfection? A mistake, a shadow, an imbalance, an asymmetry. One mistake was enough to become one of the others.

"You can't stay here," said the soldier who had let them in that morning.

Ally stretched out her right arm, and the soldier helped her up. She saw him smile for the first time.

"Are you spending the night in the town?"

It was the first time she had been acknowledged. She wasn't simply a ghost, a coatless one seeking shelter at the foot of a chimney pouring out white smoke.

"We'll take the last train, before nightfall."

"There are fewer people here every day. It's always nice to see a beautiful woman."

"Thank you," she said, blushing.

I'm alive, she thought.

The soldier recommended the restaurant next to the hotel. It was a long trek to the train station. Perhaps she should wait until tomorrow to go back. Who knew how long they would take in there? He obviously needed someone to talk to. He must have spent hours awake, making sure the demented didn't stray from their allotted path.

She listened to him in silence.

"The doctors always take their time." The soldier wanted to get her talking, to stay with him a while longer.

"Yes, and sometimes it's a good thing they take their time . . ."

"Where's the Black girl from? You wouldn't believe how many come here calling themselves Afro-Germans. Who do they think they're kidding?"

Ally's face tightened and she struggled to keep her smile. "I should go back to the lobby, in case they're looking for me."

She left the hill, the soldier, the building with the column of white smoke. She opened the red door as if it were her own home and took a seat beside the magnificent roses. She looked at them one by one.

What makes you better than any other flower? Before long you'll wither and be thrown out, she thought.

She examined her freckled hands, her ragged nails. She brought one of her cold palms up to her face. When she was alone, she always ended up going through every possible solution. The only option she refused to consider was abandonment, even though there was a slim hope of finding each other again.

She knew that since her daughter had turned seven, the only way for her to be accepted into German society was by sterilization. Then she would never be seen as a danger, a contaminating parasite. But how could she subject her daughter to such an aggressive procedure? Yes, they had already explained to her that the X-rays were reversible, that in America they were used for temporary sterilizations, that it all depended on the dose. She could find a compassionate doctor who might take pity on her and certify that Lilith had been bombarded with enough rays to sterilize her for life. It was easier for males. You just had to cut a tube. But radiation? Wouldn't the electromagnetic rays end up mutilating her daughter?

She worried they wouldn't stop at the X-rays. She had heard that they could be separated. That they could take her Lilith away to an asylum for lunatics and the soul-sick, "cretins," as the newspapers called them, pedaling their alternative reality, arguing that Germany had to be thoroughly cleansed.

The woman in the white coat, now wearing a navy-blue dress and a string of pearls, seemed more friendly. It was as if the harshness had come from the white. She was leading a smiling Lilith by the hand.

"Your daughter has behaved very well," she said.

She had passed the test, they had realized that Lilith was as German as they were, as intelligent and articulate as them. Lilith was more mature than any other child of her age. Ally wanted to hear the woman say it. She wanted a document that certified that Lilith was no danger to society, a "cancer" as the Nuremberg Laws put it.

Lilith and Ally left without saying goodbye, without looking back. Lilith wanted to forget the building, the red door, the city, the doctors, the questions they had asked her. In her mind she was still standing naked before them.

The soldier watched them leave. When they passed by him, Ally put her arm around her daughter and kissed her on the head. Her daughter had passed the first, second, third, and God knows how many more tests they had put her through. Her daughter was more intelligent than that perfect, virtuous soldier, whose classical profile and pale-blue eyes supposedly made him superior. That soldier who could find her beautiful, but not her daughter, in whom he saw an error.

They hurried across the streets that ran alongside the buildings.

"I'm tired, Mommy. We don't need to rush anymore."

When they reached the station, the train back to Berlin was almost ready to board. Ally couldn't see the time and had no idea when they would arrive. As soon as the train started moving, she fell asleep. Lilith delighted in studying her mother's wonderful face in repose. The brisk walk had restored her color. Lilith discovered the pink of her cheeks, the still intense red of her lips. At this time of day, the grays had been erased. Lilith imagined her mother before she'd had a child. She must have been even more beautiful.

Ally opened her eyes and said, "It's going to be a long journey. Sleep, Lilith, go to sleep."

The little girl woke up when the conductor announced they had reached their destination. She opened her eyes and let out a panicked shriek. It was still daylight.

"Mommy?"

Shaken, Ally pulled Lilith's knit cap tightly over her curls, took her hand, and they stepped down from the train together. Nobody would notice them. They were just a couple of transparent shadows. Who was going to care about a mother and her daughter? Leaving the main station, they let themselves get lost in the buzz of the city, as if it was where they belonged. They were safe, Ally repeated to herself. Nobody could threaten them. They wouldn't take the S-Bahn, that was reserved for the pure. They would walk home, avoiding Unter den Linden, the fancy hotels, the busy restaurants. Shouldn't it be night already? The winter days should have begun to get shorter by now.

In the distance, the Tiergarten was still busy and noisy. They crossed the Rosenthaler Platz and noticed a group of boisterous youths on the far side, who began to saunter over to size them up. They got closer and closer. "Drunk. They must have been drinking all day," Ally murmured, squeezing her daughter's hand tight. The little girl looked up at her. Ally started to quicken her pace, just as she felt the breath on her neck.

Should we try to get around them? Hide in a café? Nobody was going to start a fight with them in front of customers enjoying a peaceful evening. Would they let her in? Nobody would stand up for them. Blacks and Jews couldn't go to school, buy a newspaper, use the telephone, listen to the radio. They couldn't sit on a park bench. They could only use the S-Bahn carriage designated for them. On some lines, there weren't even any carriages for them. Ally knew the laws. She repeated them, trying to find a loophole, some way they could fit in without being considered guilty.

"Show us the noise a monkey makes!" said a voice that resounded through every nerve ending in her body.

Ally turned and saw the young Brownshirt. That very second, a boy with pink cheeks and an angelic face had become an entire army.

"I don't think that Negro girl even knows how to speak," the Brownshirt's singsong voice rang out.

The boy spread his arms wide as though about to make a speech to his friends.

Ally quickened her pace, dragging Lilith who looked distraught.

"Like I said, it's an inferior race. If they keep contaminating us, they'll bring the rest of us down with them!"

In her haste, Ally tripped and fell hard onto the sidewalk. As she tried to get up, one of the youths stood in her way and she rolled toward the street. Now she was lying on the cobblestones. A couple walked by without looking at her, without caring that a woman as white as they were was lying by the side of the road. Ally's eyes darted in search of Lilith. She couldn't find her.

"That's the first time I've seen a Negro girl," she heard in the distance.

Lilith stood undaunted next to a streetlamp, following every gesture, every word. Ally tried again to get up.

"Mommy!"

"So, you like Negroes?" the Brownshirt said in Ally's ear, so close she could feel his moist lips on her face, her neck, all over her body.

Ally sought a trace of alcohol on his breath. There was none.

"Did you enjoy it?"

She finally managed to stand but kept her eyes on the ground. One of the other youths stopped her with his leg, and, as if unintentionally, feigned a stumble that sent her flying back down onto the street. Ally shrank into a ball, shielding her head in her arms. The boy kicked her in the stomach. Her stomach muscles tensed with pain. She remembered the instructions she had given her daughter in case of attack: always protect your head.

"Oh, sorry," the boy said with a smile. "Are you going to cry? I want to see a Negro lover cry."

One more kick, to the back of the neck or forehead, and she'd be unconscious, she would sleep, she'd be spared this horror. Her eyes were pricking, her vision was blurred. She felt faint. Once again, she lifted her head to look for Lilith, but all she saw was another youth, blocking her view like a wall. Shaved head, thin lips; his nose, well-proportioned, in a perfect line. She had never seen anyone so symmetrical in her whole life. The boy smiled. His blue eyes could not have been more piercing. Ally realized she found German beauty absolutely sickening.

She finally spotted Lilith in the gloom, by the iron streetlamp. Down on the cobblestones, she felt the damp dust of the street on her lips. "Run, Lilith, run," she wanted to beg her, but the dirt was like a poison, paralyzing her. Perhaps the time had come to die. *How many times can one person die in this life?* she asked herself. This was one of those moments, she was certain. It would be better to never wake up, it would be so easy.

The boy ran at the little girl. He tore off her woolen hat, grabbing her by the hair.

Lilith screamed, and Ally gathered all her strength, got to her feet, and threw herself at the angelic-faced, smiling boy in the brown shirt.

"Don't worry," said the youth, almost losing his balance, "you can keep the Negro girl."

A whistle blew in the distance. The boys ran off in the opposite direction.

Ally folded Lilith in her arms. She wanted to go back to the time when she had her safe inside her. She didn't want to look her in the eye. She was waiting for another beating, expecting to be devoured. But this time they would be together. She wanted one final sharp blow, one of those that spreads out like a wave, destroying you from the inside. She burned with the shame of being unable to protect her daughter. If a mother cannot defend her child, she loses her very reason for being. It was time to disappear, Ally told herself, now sheltered by the twilight. The sun was setting.

"It's getting dark, we're safe," Lilith said quietly. Only Ally could hear her.

"You see night before everyone else," Ally told her, lifting her eyes skyward. There was still the slightest glimmer of light. "Not long now, Lilith. A few more minutes and nobody will see us."

"I'm sorry, Mommy." Lilith began to cry. "It's my fault. I'm sorry . . ."

"Oh, Lilith, what have I done to you, my darling girl . . ."

They waited until the last ray of light had faded. Little by little, they recovered. Ally felt something like a contraction in her stomach, like the ones that had briefly made her want to die during that darkest night in Berlin. But this time the spasm in her belly made her happy. She saw herself back in her bed, with the midwife beside her, the pain leaving her, as though she was giving birth to her daughter for a second time. If she wasn't going to protect her, who was? Yes, it was time.

"You're going to meet the Herzogs," she said, as though they were already at home, just the two of them. "They'll save you. You'll grow up far away from here, you'll be able to go to school, learn another language, and go on reading. And one day, maybe not too far off, we'll be together again, in a world with no Germans. Can you imagine that?"

Lilith listened to her, terrified, not wanting to contradict her. She closed her eyes. This dream made her mother feel secure. When Lilith opened them again, she saw an old woman standing in front of her, her face covered in wrinkles, with gray hair, and she was small, as small as Lilith. She hugged her. It was her turn now to protect her mother.

"Let's go," Lilith said.

She had no need of light.

8

Wednesdays had become her days, the only time she didn't feel hounded, when she could spend a few hours free of the obligation to provide protection, when she felt warm despite it being winter. On Wednesdays she found joy in Franz's arms, moments when she could simply forget herself. On so many of those Wednesdays, as her body became one with his, she dreamed of the perfect escape, the three of them on an island in the middle of the Pacific, far from the vampires and ghosts. They would become different people, forgetting everything else on their island, surrounded by water, without borders.

There were Wednesdays every week, until one day they ceased to exist. Ally came home that afternoon from Franz's arms and as she opened the door she found Lilith, trembling, beside Herr Professor. There was terror in their eyes.

"They were here," he said.

Since she'd given birth to Lilith, Ally had learned to live under constant threat. With every passing year, the danger became more imminent. It was her punishment, she knew, but she couldn't calculate the scale of it. How long must she go on paying for having brought a child into the world who was different?

She had almost grown accustomed to having the terrible decision hanging over her. What had previously been completely out of the question now felt like the only option. She had acclimatized to the horror. She surprised herself more every day. When she saw Lilith's eyes that Wednesday, she no longer had any doubts.

When Ally entered the apartment, Lilith didn't run to her. From the corner where she was standing, she began to describe what had happened. She didn't change her intonation or struggle to find the words. She spoke as though she were reciting a frequently told story. Lilith had grown tired of living in danger too.

First there had been a sharp rap on the door. Lilith had just returned from Herr Professor's apartment. She stood frozen, listening, trying to think who it could be. Another sharp rap on the door. This was a different kind of knock than she was used to hearing: Herr Professor usually tapped lightly three times. The mailman slid the letters under the door and went on his way, his footsteps louder than his knock. Franz kept his fist against the wood, as though he wanted to suppress the inevitable clamor.

The third knock was like an explosion. As soon as she heard it, Lilith ran to her mother's bedroom. She filled her lungs with air and avoided the cracks in the floorboards so as not to make a sound.

She felt safe in Ally's room. From there, they wouldn't be able to hear her out in the corridor. She let out all the air she had been holding in and breathed more calmly. She could feel her heartbeats, and as she brought her hand up to her chest to soothe them, she heard the creak of the front door hinge. The only person who would dare open the door on his own was Herr Professor. It was the others; she was sure of it. They had come to take her away.

Whenever she was afraid, Lilith would calm herself by whispering songs or reciting her mother's poems, the old ones, the ones Ally had written as she walked along the River Düssel behind Lilith's father, always behind. She had never told her mother. She would be annoyed if she knew Lilith had rummaged through the drawer of forgotten papers. Lilith could hear the footsteps in the living room now, and she guessed that they were by the fireplace. There was more than one of them. Two, perhaps three. They walked as though they were stalking. They knew the prey was nearby, within their reach. Fear cannot only be seen. It can also be felt and smelled.

There was no time to lose. Her mother had trained her. If they were in the park, all she had to do was run, as Jesse Owens had taught her. She had studied his start, his initial position over and over. It was all about the start. If you don't concentrate, you lose. If they were already stalking her, or were surrounding her, she should curl up into a ball and protect her head with her hands. If they managed to get into the house, she should slip away, without making the slightest sound, into the bedroom. Once there, she should open the wardrobe door in time with her breathing. Behind the clothes hanging up, she should open the little secret door. She had to remember not to move the dresses, so that they would conceal the hiding place, leaving only the brick wall visible. Once inside, she had to become a dot, always making sure to protect her head. She mustn't forget to take deep breaths, getting as much air as possible into her lungs, then exhaling to empty them. That way she would calm down, forget her fear, and not even the hunting dogs would be able to smell the fear on her.

One man entered the bedroom. He walked around it and went over to the window. Lilith heard him draw back the curtains. She counted one, two, three, several seconds, until he approached the wardrobe and paused there, as though he was looking at himself in the glass. It was a soldier, and Lilith wanted to believe he was simply looking for a mirror in order to see how perfect he looked in his impeccable uniform. But the mirror from her mother's wardrobe had been missing since long before Lilith was born. There were no mirrors in the apartment, except for a small one on the shelf above the bathroom basin. She felt sorry for the man, looking for his reflection. He opened the wardrobe door and light shone through the cracks in the cedar planks. Lilith felt she was being lit up through the dividing line of the secret door.

She heard voices. The man left the wardrobe open, and the drapes too. He didn't care if he was discovered. In these times, no one needed to have the law on their side. They themselves were the order. She was disorder. She couldn't make out what they were saying. Her heart was thumping so fast that the beats merged into a single reverberation. She would have liked to silence it, stop the echo, make her heart stop once and for all. She heard someone else come into the living room. Was it her mother? Footsteps on the floorboards joined the sound of her heartbeats.

It was not her mother; she heard the soldiers asking about her. Then to her relief she recognized Herr Professor's voice. Fräulein Keller lived alone, he assured them. There was no girl. *Mischling?* He had never seen a colored girl in the building. Ally Keller was a young woman. She had been his student, he explained. He was convincing them. It was a relief there were no framed photographs in her apartment. But why weren't they leaving? Lilith's body was shaking. If she went on shivering, they might find her.

Another, even longer silence. She imagined a battle of looks and gestures, trying to make clear who had power over whom. But then it went quiet. The negotiations were over, and they were coming for her. She knew she must follow her mother's instructions. If not, what good had all the practice been, all that running to nowhere in the Tiergarten? She had to protect her head. Her arms would form a perfect shield, knees pulled up to her stomach. She was an invincible, tiny ball, behind an invisible door that only her mother and Opa had the power to see.

"Lilith?"

Herr Professor's voice always calmed her. She opened the door slowly, still unsure. When she saw the burgundy dressing gown, she emerged from her cave and threw herself at him, holding him tightly.

Ally listened calmly to her daughter telling the story, then went to the bedroom. She was bewildered. The smell of the soldiers still hung in the air. A stranger had touched her curtains and opened her wardrobe. She looked at the bed and imagined him brushing his fingers across the sheets. She felt nauseous. She went back to the living room and took Lilith in her arms.

"You did so well," she said to the little girl, who was on the verge of tears. "It's all over now. Let's make dinner. The Herzogs are coming to dine with us."

Albert and Beatrice Herzog arrived half an hour before they sat down at the table. Ally opened the door to them with the absolute conviction they were Lilith's only hope of salvation. The couple paused in the doorway, looking intimidated. She knew Herr Professor had explained the plan they'd devised that could save them and Lilith, yet she didn't know if they'd agree. Standing in her doorway, they looked small to her, like two shadows. Behind the thick glass of Alfred's spectacles, Ally saw the eyes of a man who had lost all hope. It was the first time the Herzogs had ever been invited in by a neighbor. Once, they had lit up not only the neighborhood but, Ally was certain, the entire city as well. The residents' lamps, bulbs, chandeliers, and even their candles had been bought at the Herzogs' shop. One day she'd seen their son fitting the lightbulbs in the awning of the Friedrichstad-Palast.

Now the Herzogs were viewed as pestilent worms, a disgrace, and a danger. The day their son was taken away, people stopped greeting them, and the couple busied themselves with their fragile lamps. We all need light, they thought hopefully. After their shop was wrecked, the Herzogs shut themselves away. They left only occasionally to go to the market or the police station to inquire about their son's whereabouts. One day they received a letter from Sachsenhausen: he had died of pneumonia. When they saw the body, there was dried blood on his wrists, and a thin, purplish line around his neck. His lips were swollen, and his tongue reduced to a piece of dry meat. From that day on, the Herzogs sank into delirium.

"We're like animals that eat their own species," Albert now said, staring at the bowl of steaming soup Ally had placed before him.

"And the worst thing is we end up getting used to it." Ally's voice was barely audible.

They had lived under the same roof, passed each other countless times in the corridor, and now, at dinner, by the flickering candlelight, their faces shared the same expression of anguish. Ally realized that the Herzogs had never mentioned their son by his name all night and, dismayed, she promised herself that Lilith would always be known by her name, no matter where they sent her. She would always be Lilith, to herself and everyone else.

The girl stayed in her room, dressing and undressing Nadine. She loosened the braids and the woolen knots, as though trying to re-create her differently, more like herself. She was still traumatized from the soldiers' visit. She gave the doll instructions on how to protect herself from others, endlessly repeating them. The Herzogs had seen Lilith on a few occasions, and knew she was different, as different as they were in the eyes of others. When Herr Professor talked about Lilith with them, he emphasized her extreme intelligence, her aptitude for languages, her obsession with numbers, the richness of her vocabulary . . .

"A little genius, drifting aimlessly. She has outgrown Berlin," he told them.

The Herzogs looked at each other silently, as if they felt he was exaggerating, the way an affectionate father would. How could such a young girl be so brilliant?

They had already finished dinner when Franz entered the apartment. His voice preceded him: strong, full, his words with a kind echo to them.

"I hope you've had a nice evening," he said by way of greeting.

Only his face was illuminated, turning his blue eyes a pleasant gray. Despite the fact that he was wearing his uniform, Franz brought a sense of peace with him. Albert and Herr Professor rose to their feet. Beatrice nervously picked up the delicately embroidered white linen napkin and began to examine every stitch. With the confidence of the man of the house, Franz sat at the head of the table. At the opposite end, Ally smiled

with a glimmer of hope in her eyes. Having heard nothing from the specialized commission, she was convinced that sending Lilith to another
continent, abandoning her, was her only chance of salvation. Her daughter
hadn't passed the three levels of scrutiny, her intelligence wasn't an effec-
tive enough weapon. A drop of impure blood was enough to condemn her.

Ally's mind was in turmoil. Her stomach clenched and she feared
she was about to be sick. Excusing herself from the table, she ran to the
bathroom, stood at the basin, and lifted her eyes to the small mirror, the
only one in her home, the smoked glass and lack of a silver layer denying
her the power of honest reflection. She turned on the light and shadows
assaulted her face once more. She had aged. She had become a wretched
old woman. Desperation made her miserable. Fear had corrupted her.
She was just another one of the brainless ones.

Her eyes weary, she returned to the table. Franz was smiling. Franz
was the only hope. Franz was the savior. She would be indebted to him
her whole life, however short or long it might be.

"They were here," Ally said. "Franz, they came for her. They wanted
to take her away."

"There's one possibility," Franz said. "There's a country . . ."

"It's no longer safe even to go out at night," Ally went on. "They
could snatch her from me."

"Cuba," said Franz.

"Cuba? Go to Cuba? What are you talking about?" Ally said.

"I already have landing permits for them, from Cuba's Department
of Work. I applied for Lilith's passport using the permits. It will be
ready within a few weeks."

"Just like that? It's that simple? I'd thought perhaps England."

"To an island," Franz said, trying to placate her. "It's a safe place."

The ocean would be the frontier, the fortress walls. The ocean was
invincible.

"After what happened today, and what happened to you a month
ago . . ." Herr Professor stopped, feeling he was talking out of turn.

Everybody was silent. Then Franz continued addressing the Herzogs.

"You would set sail from Hamburg. The journey would take about two weeks. You'll be comfortable on the liner, first-class cabins . . ." Franz's voice trailed off.

"A Cuban ship?" was the only question Albert dared ask.

Franz took a few seconds to answer. Before he spoke, he looked around at the others.

"A ship with a German flag, but don't let that worry you."

"What makes you think they'll be safe on a German ship?" Herr Professor asked. "What interest do they have in saving them?"

No answers, only silence. Ally's face showed resignation.

The ship already had a departure date. They would set sail in three months, on the evening of Saturday, May 13.

"Two months after Lilith's eighth birthday," said Ally, standing up.

Her hands trembling, Ally picked up the soup tureen and carried it from the table. "It'll be cold once you get into open sea. Lilith will need her winter coat," she said.

Beatrice helped Ally clear the dishes. She stacked the porcelain plates in a pile with the utmost care. They didn't exchange a word. Beatrice followed Ally, mechanically tidying the plates, cutlery, and glasses in the kitchen. Ally paused to watch her, seeing herself in the other woman. Would she survive, like Beatrice, without her child? Would she wake every day and count the seconds until dinnertime, clear the table, and go back to bed, to sleep, until the next day? There was no yesterday, today, or tomorrow. Her kingdom had begun to slip away.

Seeing Beatrice's wariness, Ally took her hands. They were cold, clammy.

"Franz is helping us. You can trust him. He's a good man, Beatrice. There are still some decent Germans left."

Beatrice nodded but kept her eyes on the floor.

Ally went back into the dining room. Beatrice followed her, a frozen smile on her lips. They both said goodbye to Herr Professor. Ally hugged and kissed the old man as though for the last time. He left, head bowed, conscious that the end was fast approaching. What would his days be like without Lilith? Franz went to the living room and threw himself on the sofa.

When Ally returned to the living room, the Herzogs were standing at the door. Beatrice turned and hugged her.

"Paul. His name was Paul," Beatrice whispered in Ally's ear.

Her eyes lit up at having spoken of her son, and she took her husband's arm. The moment the Herzogs left, Ally hurried to Lilith's bedroom with the urgency of someone who fears she has lost something precious, searching desperately for it. Lilith was there, asleep, with the light on.

Ally returned to the living room, comforted by the knowledge that her daughter was safe in the next room. Now alone with Franz, Ally collapsed on the other end of the sofa, far away from him. She closed her eyes and, lost in the cushions and the Prussian-blue blanket that had once belonged to her mother, she tried to remember when the pain of losing Marcus had eased, trying to work out if it would take as long to get over abandoning her only daughter. The bold young woman who had wandered along the banks of the Düssel with a man she would have run away with, hugged, kissed in public, was now a phantom.

Franz turned off the living room lamp and began gently undressing Ally. Translucent in the dark, she felt she should be grateful. One kindness deserves another. The idea that he found her attractive, loved her in a way, gave her a certain pleasure. She let herself be swept along by his caresses, the warmth of his kisses. Every time he pressed himself against her, her mind raced to other places. She saw herself in the middle of the ocean, floating aimlessly in the darkness. In the murky waters, she could forget Marcus, Lilith. It was the only moment she ceased to exist, and in that fleeting moment she was happy.

9

One Month Later
Berlin, March 1939

There was a cake with eight white candles.

The Herzogs, Franz, Herr Professor, and Ally were standing together on one side of the oval table, all watching Lilith. She stood on the other side, holding her rag doll, eyes fixed on the candles, waiting for them to be lit. The rest of the room was in darkness.

There was a small pink envelope, with no inscription.

"When I blow out the candles, can I make one last wish?" asked Lilith, wrapped up in her thoughts.

Her prior wishes had never come true, but she needed to try one last time.

There was also an indigo-blue box, the size of her fist.

"Of course you can," Beatrice said. "Wish for another hundred and twenty years of happiness."

"This time try one that's within our reach," Herr Professor suggested. "Don't ask for the moon, because that's for everyone to share. How am I supposed to ask it to shine only for you?"

"How about a dog, then? That's easy, isn't it?" Lilith said.

"What type of dog would you like? A German Shepherd?" Herr Professor suggested.

"Why would she want a German dog?" Albert said. "A cat would be better, any old cat."

"Oh yes, that's a good idea," the professor played along with the game. "Cats make less noise, they're less demanding. You can leave them to it, they don't need people looking after them the whole time."

"I want to be a cat!" Lilith said.

"That's not a bad idea. Let's all turn into cats! Come on, Ally. From now on, we'll all be cats. Close your eyes and wish it so."

Ally hadn't spoken all night, as though she were already trying to accustom her daughter to a life without her.

The six of them remained in the dark for a long while, staring at the extinguished candles and their threads of smoke. Then, all of a sudden, the telephone started ringing. Nobody had called them for quite some time. Ally didn't react. Beatrice was alarmed. Everybody froze, and didn't move until the ringing died away, as though the sound had come from another apartment.

After she blew out the candles, Lilith took Franz by the hand and led him out of the room. Standing in the corridor, she looked up into his eyes.

"You don't have to worry," Franz said to her, brushing a few rebellious curls from her forehead.

"I want to see my passport."

"Your mother has it, she'll give it to Albert soon,"

"Show me," she said.

"Okay. Let's go back in, and we'll ask your mother."

"No. Go and get it and bring it here to show me, please."

Franz seemed surprised and went back into the living room. The lamplight had turned the room an ashen color. Lilith waited for him, as if she had started to live in a different dimension. She felt completely alone.

On her eighth birthday, Lilith wanted to feel as if she were being born again. The farewell had begun, the only way her mother could breathe peacefully once more. Lilith understood they couldn't stay hidden away forever. She had agreed to be subjected to the investigations, interrogations, and medical examinations because she didn't want to go against her mother and Opa, but ever since she turned seven, Lilith had known what her fate would be. Her first death had begun. Hadn't her mother written in a poem that one is born only to die many times over? A cat. She would have liked to go to sleep and wake up as a cat.

She had never understood why they weren't able to find a country that would accept them all. With her mother, Franz, and Opa, they could start a new life, far from Germanic ideals of perfection. They would learn a new language, or as many as they needed to, and could even forget their own if they wanted to. What would they need German for? She could already pronounce the surname of her hero, *Owens*, in perfect English, not *O-vens* like those who had cheered him in the Olympic stadium.

Now, instead of staying a Keller, she had joined a different tribe, she had told Herr Professor. Overnight, she had become a Herzog. She was no longer a Black German; she was a Jew. Which of the two sins brought the greater punishment?

She would live on an island, with a new identity and a new family. She would learn a new language, become part of a new culture, and completely erase the past. Tomorrow had ceased to exist for Lilith, and from this night on, she began to devise a secret plan. She didn't want to dream it so as not to destroy it; one careless slip could betray her.

"Here you are." Franz interrupted her thoughts, handing her the passport with the swastika on the sacred eagle.

She opened it carefully, as though it were a fake document, whose ink might disappear as she brushed her fingers across it. She didn't recognize herself in the photograph on the greenish pages. She read the day, the city, and the country where she had been born, and finally read her name: Lilith Herzog. Beneath this a huge red letter had been stamped: "J."

She returned the passport to Franz with a smile as broad as the one in the photograph and hugged him. Here was the confirmation: the three commissioners must have decided she belonged to an inferior race.

"My Little Light," he murmured.

"It's time to have cake," she said, turning on her heel and going back into the living room.

Lilith picked up a plate and took a small bite of the cream cake, but it seemed to have no taste to her.

Finally, the time had come to open presents. They expected it of her, though she would have preferred to do it alone so she wouldn't have to smile, make pleasant gestures, and thank everyone with hugs and kisses.

She took the indigo-blue box in her hands and spent several minutes opening it. All eyes were on her. She took out a gold chain with a crucifix. In the center of the cross was a ruby. On the back, an inscription: *Lilith Keller*. It was a gift from Opa.

"So that you never forget who you are."

"Sometimes it's better to forget," Ally interrupted.

"I don't think she should wear it the day we leave," Albert said. "Or when we're in Cuba . . ."

"She can keep it in her suitcase," Herr Professor agreed. "It'll be your amulet," he told Lilith.

The little girl put the chain back in the box and opened the pink envelope. In it was a poem. She read the title: *The Night Traveler*. She folded the sheet of paper once more and returned it to the envelope. She put both gifts in a pocket of her dress.

She went over to her mother, gave her a hug, and kissed her.

"I'll read the poem when I go to bed," she whispered in her ear.

Ally busied herself going back and forth to the kitchen. She avoided Beatrice's eyes; the older woman looked lost.

Yes, loss has been assigned its day and hour, Ally thought.

Ally and Beatrice cleared the table and tidied up in the kitchen. Lilith went to sit on the sofa with Herr Professor. Albert said his good-byes and left to return to his apartment.

"We should go for a walk," Ally said to Franz, putting on her coat.

"What about Lilith?"

"She's busy with her Opa. Lord knows what they'll be debating."

They walked downstairs with Beatrice, and Ally said goodbye to her.

"I'll forever be grateful to you," Ally said.

"It's Franz you should be thanking, he made all this possible," Beatrice said.

Beatrice crossed the threshold to her apartment with her eyes fixed on the mezuzah, but this time she did not brush it with her finger. Nothing and nobody could protect her. She was losing her home.

"I need some fresh air," Ally said, opening the front door.

A cloud of smoke still hung beneath the Berlin sky. The air was charged with gunpowder, ash, leather, and metal. The streets were still strewn with broken glass. She walked arm in arm with Franz. Next to him, she felt free. When it came down to it, she was her own enemy, she told herself. It had been her decision to send her daughter to an island with two strangers, hoping they would take care of her.

Their eyes fixed on the ground, Franz and Ally crossed Oranien-burgerstrasse, shrouded in thick fog. The smoke was eternal, as if the fire that had destroyed one of its majestic buildings had refused to go out. Ally suddenly felt that the city was in ruins, under siege, at war. She was planning her farewell, which had become a sort of surrender. Her daughter had been born beneath the Berlin sky; she had hidden her beneath the trees of the Tiergarten. The night had always belonged to them, but not anymore.

"Don't you think we should go back?" Franz asked, tenderly.

"How far back can we go?" Ally replied with a sad smile.

She suddenly felt the urge to go to Franz's mother's house in Weissensee and visit the stoic widow Frau Bouhler. She would tell her that her son was safe, that his girlfriend was going to get rid of her mistake, that her son would no longer need to worry about being expelled from the university, or rejected, or condemned to the other side, that Lilith was going to cease to exist. The evening they had gone to meet Mary Bouhler, Ally had seen the delight in the woman's face; she had accepted her the moment she walked into the living room with its dark Lutheran furniture. Her son was in love with an Aryan woman who could produce heroic soldiers to serve the Führer.

During the meal they shared that night, her eyes had shone at being in the presence of her son. She recalled the time they had gone to the Berlin Sportpalast together, and for the first time, seen in person the man destined to drag his country out of its misery, to save Germany. A second in front of Him was enough to be transformed forever, she had said. He had talked directly to her, looked her in the eye like a dear friend who has come to visit, as if her conscience was talking to her, as if somebody else was voicing her very thoughts. Frau Bouhler could remember what she was wearing that day. Yes, it was cold, but she had warmed up straightaway. They had waited for hours, amid the cheers and marches. It had been an emotional evening. His first speech as Chancellor, an unforgettable moment in history. True Germans, those who voted for Him, the people, had listened to the Führer that day. Frau Bouhler could even recite lines from the speech from memory: *There was a time when a German could only be proud of his past; when the present caused nothing but shame.*

"See Fräulein Keller? Wasn't He right? Today we can be proud of the new Germany, and my son is part of that."

Ally had raised a piece of bread to her mouth and focused her mind on deciphering the ingredients: the quantity of flour, fat, yeast. There was a little too much yeast. She had tried to remember where she had been that February 10, which dress she was wearing. She guessed she would have probably been reading to Lilith, likely a legend, a story of elves and enchanted woods. Of flying high in the air and far away. But she couldn't remember. Her mind was a haze.

Frau Bouhler, on the other hand, could remember each instant.

She saw herself back amid the euphoria, with the thousands of ecstatic people filling the Sportpalast, hanging on His every word, His every gesture. She said every pause was filled with shouts. That whenever He had stopped, everybody had raised their arm with a *Heil!* That the stage was hung with a black swastika on a white circle and a bloodred flag. That the people were protected by the soldiers, that the soldiers were the people, that He had promised there would be no more division, that there was no longer anything to fear. That nobody was going to take away their children, take over their businesses, steal their fortunes. That there would be an end to hunger, and everyone would be able to build a home. That women would be free to produce the very best fruit from their pure and healthy wombs.

Before that, Frau Bouhler had never been interested in politics. She had never been to a rally or demonstration. She had never listened to a leader's speech in its entirety. If only she were young, she had said, if she could start again, she repeated, leaving the phrase hanging in the air, her eyes glassy. But at least she had her son. It was a great opportunity for an entire generation.

"I dream my son will follow in his father's footsteps," Frau Bouhler said. "I dream that he will become a courageous soldier, an honorable member of the Party. It's the least we can do for the man who has saved Germany," the woman went on, as Franz took Ally's hand.

Franz realized that Ally was miles away. She appeared drowsy. Her movements had become slow, deliberate. In that instant, Ally imagined herself next to Marcus, side by side, when they didn't need to talk to communicate: just a touch, a smile was enough. *Marcus?* She called out to him silently. What would her life have been like with Marcus? If they had obtained a permit to leave the country, a visa. But there was no way out for them. They were doomed. Only Jews received refugee quotas. Only Jews could get permits to leave the country, but there were few places that would take them in.

"I love you, Ally." Franz's voice brought her back to the present moment.

Ally observed him affectionately. Was it the first time he said he loved her?

"I love you too," she responded. "How could I not love you?"

She admired the young man who risked dating a woman with a *mischling*. But she was convinced that Franz would never have a future with her, and she had no future without her daughter.

In two months, when the departure date arrived, Ally imagined she would take a bath in jasmine water; the scent would be a lasting memory. They would travel in separate cars. The Herzogs and Lilith in one, she and Herr Professor in another. They would watch her leave from the car. Lilith would turn back to look at her and smile. That was how she would see her for the final time, holding Beatrice's hand, with the little suitcase almost dragging on the ground, holding everything she needed to cross the ocean: the chain with the crucifix, her mother's poem, and Nadine, the rag doll.

When the moment came for them to climb the gangway, Ally would be overcome, and would run from the car to her daughter, knowing she could never abandon her. Lilith would be happy again, grateful. They would tear up the passport that called her a Herzog, throwing it into the sea. Yes, they would say goodbye to Beatrice with a hug and a kiss. Albert would already be on deck. Beatrice would hesitate for a second. Should she go, or stay here, with her son's remains?

Ally and Lilith would return to the car together. They would sit in the back, beside Herr Professor. They would be a family again, escape the horror. They would take a train, crossing rivers and mountains, far from the country they had once been a part of. If they could, they would cross the English Channel, let the sea set them free.

But the little girl in this story doesn't have Lilith's face. And the old man was not Herr Professor. There were no trains. Ally was just another in a crowd of strangers.

One dreams of freedom the way one dreams of God, she said to herself. *Dreaming of God tricks us into believing we can endure the unendurable.*

But dreams, and God, had become meaningless for her. Her daughter was going to leave. The ship would sail away from the port. She would return to Berlin in the car with Herr Professor. There would be no hugs nor kisses. Nobody would shed a tear.

10

Two Months Later
Hamburg, May 1939

Night. Spotlights on the three officials sitting behind a table, next to the gangway. Albert Herzog handed over the documents, one by one: passport, Cuban landing pass, baggage receipt, tickets, the three ten reichsmark bills. In the glare of the spotlights, Albert's eyebrows looked bushy, his eyes almost lost. It was impossible to tell whether they were moist with tears. Lilith had the chain and her rag doll. Nobody asked about the poem she had hidden in the right-hand pocket of her woolen overcoat. She wouldn't need the coat in Cuba, of that she was certain. To Lilith, the poem had life, a heartbeat. She felt it through the fabric.

Nobody paid attention to the color of her skin. *By night, we're all the same color*, she said to herself, trying to stay calm. She knew her fear could give her away. The here and now could dissolve because of a mistake. And then she would be condemned. With her hair tied back and covered with a black woolen hat, none of the officials suspected her. Lilith had always tried to stay in the shadows. She was a Herzog, the red stamp on the first page of her passport: the "J."

Lilith sang, or rather hummed a tune the others couldn't make out and took hold of Beatrice's cold hand. It felt broken, as though all the bones in her body were splintered. She looked up and saw how red patches were beginning to spread over Mrs. Herzog's neck. *She's going to crack*, she thought. *She's going to cry. She's going to faint.*

"Mommy." It was the first time she had called her this. "When will we be shown to our cabin?"

Lilith wanted to sound like a good little girl, with good manners. A sweet little girl who had just learned to read. She carried her rag doll— white, blond, dressed in blue—under her arm. The name Nadine was embroidered in red on the white pinafore. Mrs. Herzog didn't hear her. She was caught up in her own terror.

"It's the biggest ship I've ever seen in my life," the little girl went on.

The official with the transparent eyes handed the passports back to Albert, without a second glance at the woman or little girl. They were his shadow. Sometimes fear makes you invisible. It's a way of erasing yourself. But one careless slip and they could be stopped.

They had to press on, get away from the others' inquisitive eyes. Lilith counted the steps, one by one. They still hadn't noticed her. Lilith was following Beatrice. The official heard her voice, her German accent, her enlightened phrases. An error, she should make a grammatical error, speak like a silly little girl so as not to arouse suspicion. Yes, everybody's eyes were upon her.

"One step, two step, all the way up the gangway!" Lilith sang. *Which verse would Herr Professor recite at a moment like this?* she thought.

She was about to cross the dividing line, everlasting and shifting, and suddenly she had the feeling they were being followed. She couldn't make out who was behind her. But without a doubt, they could spot a Rhineland bastard, a filthy *mischling*, perhaps by the way she walked or her mannerisms. The officials recognized her; the imposter, the Black one. The light was still scarce. Lilith shielded herself in the darkness. Invisible, she reached the top.

Her heart beat at a deafening speed. Everyone around her could perceive her fear, finally see the true color of her skin, her cursed hair hidden beneath a wooly hat so dark it made her face shine paler than it really was. It had all been planned, down to the smallest detail, by her saviors, those who decided to send her out into the abyss. In the end, the masks weren't enough. Anyone who put their mind to it, stopped for a moment to look at her, would have known straightaway she wasn't a Herzog. Beatrice's pained eyes, Albert's reluctance, and the distance between Lilith and her fictitious parents would be all the proof the officials needed.

If the island lay beneath an endless sun, she would find her true shadow there. She would find a big tree and make it her home forever.

When she reached the top and set foot on deck, Lilith turned and bumped into the captain. This elegant man, wearing white and black, doffed his hat and bowed to her. He wasn't like the captain in the bedtime story her mother and Opa had told her. This captain didn't kidnap lost children or tie princesses to rocks in lagoons or throw them overboard at sea.

"Welcome to the *Saint Louis*," said Captain no-Hook.

Lilith sighed and identified the enemy. The officials were still at the control point, stamping the red "J" in the passports like an indelible scar. Other families were climbing aboard.

"Mommy?" she wanted to shout when she looked down at the port. The others were down there, lost in perpetual abandonment. She watched those saying goodbye on the quayside, waving their hands cautiously, convinced nobody could see them, convinced they had already been erased from the memory of those they were saving, escaping to the promised island in the transatlantic liner.

The night before, she had sat on the sofa between her mother and Opa, the three of them staring at the ashes of the fire.

"We'll see each other again," Opa said, his voice cracking. "Somewhere in the world."

Lilith had the feeling that no, she wouldn't see him again, that this was their last night together. She hugged him tightly to soothe him.

"Little one," Opa continued, as Ally began to cry.

"Mommy . . ."

Lilith fell silent. She didn't have the energy to comfort them any-more. Her lips began to tremble. She was cold; she was frightened.

She didn't sleep that last night. She wouldn't sleep again until the ship was out on the high seas.

She opened her eyes and saw she was at the ship's rail. Below, men and women were lost in a gesture. *They were saying goodbye to her*, she thought. Lilith gave one last wave with her right hand, but now she was the one who couldn't be seen. She was lost in the mass of people filling the deck. She waved her hand furiously, hoping in vain that her mother would see her.

She was alone. The Herzogs had turned their backs. It was time to carry out her plan. Nobody would notice a little girl. Everyone was busy saying goodbye to those they had lost. She headed to the starboard side, where there were fewer passengers. There, she would find a spot, away from the life rafts. Arms in the air, she would count to ten, in time with the beating of her heart, and would throw herself off into empti-ness. The force of the fall would send her underwater, down to where the waters were darkest. She would start to release all the air she had stored in her lungs, and to the rhythm of the bubbles would rise to the surface. She would swim to the quay, avoiding the control point where some passengers were still waiting to be registered. She would catch her breath and wait for the pistol shot signaling the start of the most important race of her life. Like Jesse, she would get on her mark, ready to go, first her forehead, then her shoulders and chest, and with the wind behind her she would run, not looking back in case she turned into a pillar of salt. The only problem was she couldn't swim. She would have to let herself sink down to infinity, down where not even the moonlight reaches, with her back to the surface.

Her mother by now would be a dot in the distance, as far away as her life in Berlin. To Ally, the black, white, and red transatlantic liner was a huge necropolis. There was a before and an after. Tombstones were carved with two dates, the boundaries that set the size of the grave: the day you were born and the day you died. Everything happened in this limited period of time. The need to shoulder another's pain in order to ward off your own was very real. *There's always someone worse off than yourself*, she told herself. *Distance makes the heart grow fonder*. Platitudes were all she had left.

Lilith couldn't remember the farewell, if there had even been one. For her, the last time she had seen her mother was in bed, reading bedtime stories together. Why would she want to remember her face at the port or her crying on the couch? Ally and Opa were already fading in her memory.

Rather than throwing herself overboard, Lilith headed toward another abyss: that of the cabins. She pushed past people whose eyes were still glued to the port. She saw the sky was completely empty: the clouds, stars, even the moon had abandoned her.

"Now it's just me and the night."

Her words began to drown in the river.

In their cabin, the Herzogs heard the long blast on the ship's siren that signaled their departure toward the biggest island in the Caribbean. They climbed into bed, holding hands. As Lilith went to peer out the porthole, she detected the scent of jasmine. She felt light-headed. The boat had begun slowly edging away from the dock. Soon the port dwindled in the distance. She knew they would first sail along a river, then they would go out to sea, and finally the ocean.

"From the River Elbe to the North Sea," she said aloud, imagining her Opa as a child, holidaying among the dunes on the edge of an endless ocean.

Out in the North Sea, the waves crashing against the metal hull sprayed the deck with salt water. She gazed up at the sky and could make out a solitary star. She clamped her eyes closed, like at the end of a play when the curtain drops with its own weight to the stage. She was saved.

She was night.

ACT TWO

11

Three Years Later
Havana, November 1942

They're here, they're all over," Lilith heard Beatrice say as she came down the stairs. "Where will we hide?"

"They've already shot him. Nothing's going to happen to us." Albert's voice was adamant.

When Lilith walked into the kitchen, they both smiled and switched off the radio.

"They shot the Nazi spy," Lilith said, to show she knew what they were talking about. "I heard it on the news. The president refused to pardon him."

"We're surrounded by German submarines . . ." Beatrice was trembling. "How many more spies are hidden out there?"

"They'll find them all," Albert insisted.

"Why did he bother with us?" said Beatrice. "Enrique . . ."

"His name is August," Lilith corrected her. "It seemed strange to me that every time we spoke in German he would turn around and stare at us. A Nazi spy . . ."

August Luning used to visit the Herzogs' business to buy rolls of fabric, and on occasion stayed to drink coffee and chat with them, in perfect English. The Herzogs' Spanish was very limited. Luning had told them he was from Honduras and had left Spain to open a family business in Cuba, which was growing more prosperous by the day. He had also said he used to live in Germany, and in England. Indeed, a few months after he arrived, he had opened a tailor's shop, La Estampa, on Calle Industria. Mild mannered and hesitant when he spoke, Luning was tall, with a round face, dark hair, and tanned skin. The Herzogs would never have believed that the disorganized and forever tardy businessman, who didn't appear to be fully in control of his sales and purchases and couldn't negotiate a good price, was actually a German.

It had been a year since Cuba had declared war, first on Japan and then on Germany, sending ships to assist the Allies. Two of these vessels were sunk by German U-boats off Cuba's east coast, according to the island's newspapers, which Albert tried to keep out of his wife's sight. Despite the war, their fabric business on Calle Muralla prospered, and the Herzogs supplied the city's department stores.

Some months before, there had been a mandatory blackout in Havana. That day, Beatrice and Lilith had shut themselves away in Albert's office, curled up in a corner, covered with pillows. That was how they slept that night, when even the lighthouse on Castillo del Morro, at the entrance to the bay, was switched off for the very first time. Via Radio Berlin, Germany had threatened to bomb the Cuban capital. The state of alert consumed the whole city, and the authorities ordered blackouts across the entire Havana coastline.

For Beatrice, the days of terror had returned.

"They'll show up even here," she said, trembling. "We'll never be free of them . . ."

Since then, Lilith had to lock herself away with Beatrice in the office, and couldn't even go out into the yard, until they were told the Nazi spy, who had dared to make contact with them, had been arrested.

Albert had once visited Luning in his home on the second floor of a guest house in Calle Teniente Rey. He lived surrounded by different colored birds in cages, strategically placed in each window of the two rooms he occupied. As soon as he entered, Albert got the impression of being in a little jungle, partly owing to the heat and humidity the unpainted walls gave off. There were cobwebs all over the high ceilings, and dust everywhere, making it feel like an uninhabited room that Luning had filled at the last minute, just before he received his guest. As they finalized several fabric orders and Luning handed over a deposit, Albert took pity on the man with no family, a refugee just like him, who was doing all he could to keep his business going. He even considered inviting him to dinner when they moved to the house in Vedado, but never did.

Thanks to one of Luning's employees, Beatrice had received a letter from Berlin. More accurately, a document, which took over three months to arrive in Havana. Before the war, the employee had done business with a German textile company and still had good friends there, so Beatrice asked for help after hearing on the radio that the Germans were advancing through the countries of Europe. Beatrice told him she wanted to know the fate of her siblings, as well as Lilith's mother and Professor Bormann, whom she considered family. Beatrice had lost contact with her brothers and sisters. She knew they had been deported but had no idea where they had been sent. As for Ally, Beatrice couldn't understand why she didn't reply to her letters, why she had stopped contacting them, abandoning her daughter, although sometimes she told herself forgetting was also a way to survive.

Since her arrival in Havana, Beatrice had written to Ally every month, telling her about the little girl's progress. That Spanish came easy to her; that she had become an expert in taffeta, flannel, tulle, brocade, gabardine, and, of course, all the different types of linen, so popular on the island; that she had made a friend, Martín, at the new American school, where she had moved up a grade, and he had introduced her to his best friend, Oscar; that they had moved into a new house, some distance from the business, in a neighborhood where Lilith could grow up safely. The little girl had adapted to the sun and heat, she told her, but for them it was more wearing. They felt older every day, the days felt like months, and the months like years. Lilith on the other hand had a future on the island, and one day, when the war was over, Ally could come and be with her again. Beatrice told her Lilith had inherited her mannerisms and expressions. She watched her growing up, becoming a woman, more like her mother every day. It was just as she was writing this letter in the back of the shop that Luning's employee appeared with the document, a gloomy look on his face.

"I'm sorry," he said, the first time he had spoken to her in German.

Beatrice took the document and opened it in front of Albert, who could read the news in her face. She handed the sheet of paper to her husband and returned to the back of the shop. She rummaged for the letter she had been writing for days and ripped it up as if by doing so she could destroy the news she had received, make it not so.

The document stated that Ally Keller and Bruno Bormann had been sent to Sachsenhausen on June 17, 1939. Herr Bormann had suffered a heart attack shortly after arriving and did not survive. Seven months later, Ally bled to death.

"I don't think we should say anything to Lilith," Albert said.

"What do we achieve by lying to her?"

"She's happy here, she's forgotten what happened in Berlin."

"One day she'll find out," Beatrice said, emphatically, lips trembling. "If we don't tell her now, she'll never forgive us."

"Let's wait for the right moment, at least."

Then the news of the spy spread across the island, and they knew it was only a matter of time before questions would be asked about Beatrice's dealings with the spy's associate. When Luning was captured, the Herzogs sat Lilith down, and after a lengthy silence, Beatrice decided to tell her, getting straight to the point. Albert stared at his wife, unable to understand how she was telling a little girl that she had lost the only family she ever had. He wanted to curse, bang his fists on the table, shout out in rage. He felt he was going to explode, and his eyes filled with tears.

"Not long after we left Germany, your mother and the Professor were sent to the same labor camp where they killed my son. They're both gone. I'm so sorry."

Lilith didn't ask any questions, she didn't even want to know how they had died, or how the Herzogs had come by the information. She simply wept, motionless. The Herzogs went over to her. For the first time, Beatrice hugged and kissed her. She didn't often show her physical affection. Albert left the room, head bowed.

"We will survive, my dear, but the pain will always be there," Beatrice told Lilith. "Your mother never forgot you. You were in her heart until the moment she took her last breath. That's how we mothers are."

Lilith sat silently in the dining room. She clenched her hands as if she wanted to feel pain. Her chest was tight, and she felt Beatrice watching her. She wanted to be alone, but she couldn't. She continued to cry and felt her body shaking, uncontrollably. She had already lost her mother years ago when she boarded the ship in Hamburg, and now she was heartbroken because she realized she had begun to forget her face.

During the spy's trial, in which he was said to have confessed his crimes, a police detective appeared in the shop and asked to see their sales and purchase ledger. The spy was listed there as Enrique Augusto Luní. The detective was perspiring heavily, and beads of sweat dripped onto the counter. As he took notes, Beatrice handed him the document she had received from Germany.

"One of señor Luning's employees brought it to us some time ago," she said. When she realized the detective didn't understand German, she added: "It's confirmation our relatives died in a concentration camp."

Beatrice wanted to make it clear they had no connection with Luning, they had no reason to want to help Germany. They were victims too.

Magazines and newspapers dedicated a hundred pages to the spy's work on the island. His execution by firing squad in the ditches of the Castillo del Príncipe appeared on the front page of one of Cuba's most popular publications. There were no photographers present, but an artist re-created the scene. In one image, the spy stood facing the firing squad; another one showed the Nazi's lifeless body.

Beatrice stopped working at their store. She became a recluse, spending her time listening to the radio, deciphering the Spanish that she was gradually understanding more and more, but would never learn well enough to hold a conversation. In the afternoons, she listened to radio soap operas, romances, and adventure stories, and at night, a classical music station.

A wave of fury against Germans had been unleashed in Cuba, and so to avoid his family being caught up in it, Albert removed his name from his businesses. He had heard on the radio that Palma City, a village in the north of Camagüey that didn't even figure on maps, had a prosperous German community, and that all of the German men had been taken to Havana and imprisoned in Castillo del Morro.

"The new shop is now called Mueblería Luz," Albert said with a smile. "We added Luz for you, Lilith, our dear Little Light."

The day Mueblería Luz opened on Calle Galiano, Lilith's two best friends, Martín and Oscar, and their parents accompanied her to the shop.

The three youngsters ran around the store, throwing themselves on furniture that still smelled of fresh varnish, and hiding in mahogany wardrobes, while their parents raised glasses of champagne to celebrate the opening of the furniture and upholstery store. The furniture was made of dark, heavy wood, some with gilt trim, beveled mirrors, pearl inlay, marquetry, motifs of branches and garlands, marble and leather tabletops with chiseled bronze details.

"Just looking at this furniture makes me feel suffocated," Lilith said. "Did you know that the Nazi spy once came to the store?"

"So you knew the spy?" Oscar interrupted her.

"He was a strange man; he didn't seem German."

"You don't seem German either, but that doesn't make you a spy."

"I always got the feeling he could understand us when I spoke to my parents in German," Lilith explained. "His expression was weird."

"We should start catching spies," Martín said. "The city must be infested with Nazis. You know German, so you can help unmask them."

"Let's go catch spies!" Oscar shouted and ran off.

Lilith and Martín linked arms behind him, bursting with laughter.

The ribbon was ready. Lilith went over to her parents and took the scissors in her left hand. When she turned around, she saw Martín with the others. The photographer's flash blinded her as she cut the ribbon.

It was a happy day.

12

A Year and a Half Later
Havana, April 1944

The day Lilith turned thirteen, Martín Bernal snuck into the house quietly and crept up behind her in the kitchen. Covering her eyes with his hands, he asked her to make a wish.

"Don't tell me, say it to yourself, so that it comes true."

Lilith spun around. Martín was so close. One move and they would be in each other's arms. He leaned forward nervously and pressed his lips against Lilith's cheek. He moved cautiously, until she lifted her face and kissed him.

Ever since they had become neighbors, Lilith and Martín had paid no attention to the boundary between their houses. They jumped over the metal fence separating their backyards until eventually they cut the chain and padlock between the two houses. A stone wall divided the alleyways running down the side of the buildings. From on top of this, Martín could communicate with Lilith through her bedroom window. Every time he wanted to see his friend, he would jump down from the highest part of the wall and land with the grace of a lynx. One day, unbeknown to Martín's father, they quietly knocked down the wooden gate, and their yards were joined forever. He didn't punish his son: he knew if

Martín hadn't done it, he would have ended up crashing into the fence one day as he threw himself from above.

"Those kids are going to get married one day," Helena, the lady who helped the Herzogs with the house chores, used to say as she watched them conspiring in the yard.

Lilith and Martín built themselves a universe in the mango and orange-red flame trees, the castor oil plants with their yellow leaves, the hedge of red and white poinsettias that blossomed out of season.

"We've confused them," Martín said one day. "It's Christmas all year around for us."

When they had disembarked in Havana five years earlier, Lilith and the Herzogs stayed for a while in the Hotel Nacional. Lilith remembered her room had a sea view, and when she opened the windows in the morning it made her feel queasy. She felt as if her stomach was about to explode, and the only way to ease it was to imagine that one day, her mother, Franz, and her Opa would arrive to surprise them, in one of the boats that docked in the port. The hotel room made her feel as she had in the cabin out at sea.

During the crossing on the *St. Louis*, intoxicated by the bitter seasickness pills, her stomach shrunken by constant vomiting, Lilith imagined herself arriving on an island of carnivorous plants, which she would study, and wild animals that she would have to avoid. She believed that, with great care, she would calm the plants' appetites, and that she would adopt some kind of mammal of the sort that devour everything around them as they grow, but which, thanks to her dedication and a tireless process of domestication, she would end up humanizing. She was keen to prove it, to wipe cruelty from the face of the earth. But when she arrived, she found a beautiful city built alongside a placid sea; a clean city, full of elegantly dressed people covered from head to toe to protect themselves from the sun's rays. Instead of the wild island of her imagination, they had sent her to a European city, as bland as any German one, but far sunnier, and inhabited by people of all colors and races.

Back then, Lilith used to call her new parents "Herr and Frau Herzog." They later became Albert and Beatrice. It was only when they bought the store on Calle Muralla, and the family decided to move into the apartment above until the business prospered, that they became Mom and Dad. When the store had taken off, the Herzogs bought a house in a quiet neighborhood close to the sea. They chose it for its proximity to the bilingual St. George's School, where the Herzogs hoped the girl would study in order to master English and fit into Havana society, as well as lose her German accent in Spanish.

For the first time, she lived in a house filled with mirrors, and gradually grew accustomed to her reflection. The very thing her mother had tried to avoid in her home in Berlin, Lilith finding out she looked different, was no longer a danger. She didn't look like her parents in the slightest, but outside of the fortress where they lived, protected from the sun and the heat, she was just like everyone else. Her skin didn't stand out on an island where everyone lived in the glare of the sun.

When she arrived in the tropics, Lilith no longer had to prove her intelligence to anybody, her ability for languages, her passion for numbers. There was no commission to analyze her capacity for association and memory. For a while she had even tried to distance herself from books, but in the end, she couldn't do without them, especially late at night, when the hours dragged. She spent endless nights trying to get to sleep after terrible nightmares.

Since they moved to the Vedado house, Helena began living with them from Monday to Friday. Lilith talked more with Helena than with her adoptive parents. Helena, with an "H," as she always felt the need to clarify when she was introduced to someone, "an extravagance on my mother's part, obsessed with romantic novels from the last century," was a woman toughened by neglect. Her mother had sent her to Havana to rescue her from misery in her village. She had left her neighborhood, in the beautiful and peaceful Cienfuegos, a city she never went back to, for a city that was in a constant bustle. She married a man from Galicia who one day, a few years later, boarded a boat in search of fortune in the States, and that was the last she heard of him. Fate had led her to care for other people's families, who she often came to feel as if they were her own. "It's terrible being an only child, my dear, because you're left alone once your parents have gone," she would tell Lilith. "Look at me, no husband and no children, in this city that never has and never will be mine."

Helena seemed perpetually suffocated, as if her nostrils were blocked and she couldn't get enough oxygen with each breath. She had a mournful face and seemed to be forever on the verge of tears. She hated crowds, complaining they made her feel she couldn't breathe, that the people stole all the oxygen from around her, leaving her in an atmosphere more arid than a desert.

With her characteristic cough, as if constantly clearing her throat, Helena wandered around the house restlessly, stopping every now and then to catch her breath. "In my family, everyone was born with useless lungs," she would explain.

"My mother and my grandfather too, both died from emphysema that had been devouring them for years. That'll be my fate too, and there's nothing I can do about it," she had told Beatrice. "It looks as if I'll inherit my mother's weak lungs and my father's arthritis. My fingers have been twisted for as long as I can remember."

To begin with, the coughing fits were so intense that a terrified Beatrice would run down the stairs thinking Helena was choking, only to find her in a trail of smoke, a cigarette in one hand and a cup of black coffee in the other. They walked around the house, learning about one another, sharing afflictions and muttering, since words were nothing more than sounds. Neither understood what the other was saying, but they reacted to each other as though they did. They were like sisters, living out their final years together.

Helena taught Lilith to protect herself from the sun with parasols and hats, together with dresses, which she wore reluctantly. On the weekends, Helena massaged her hair with olive and coconut oil, and made her comb it with metal combs heated on the hot plate. Afterward, they would condition her hair with a homemade ointment of avocado, egg yolk, and honey. "Those curls need to be looked after and taken in hand," she used to say. The worst thing was when there was a school gala. To straighten Lilith's hair, Helena would insist on using the metal iron she heated over hot coals in the yard. Lilith's hair would give off an acrid smoke that left her nauseous all week.

"You've turned me into a chimney!" Lilith used to say to Helena, laughing, as Beatrice looked on, bewildered.

Over time, Lilith forgot the warmth of Berlin's oak floorboards, and began to appreciate the chill of tiled floors. Faced with the island's tranquil afternoons, she immersed herself in a stack of books about the age of chivalry they had inherited with the house or accompanied her mother to the Guanabacoa cemetery to lay stones on the graves of long-lost souls, and to keep the area reserved for Beatrice and her husband spick and span. Lilith wouldn't end up there. They both knew her grave would be in Colón cemetery, alongside mortal remains that, instead of stones, were honored with crosses and flowers.

When they had registered Lilith in the school where she would study English and Spanish, she had been given a number of assessments to determine which class she would join. She had never attended an educational institution in Germany. When they returned the following week, the headmistress and the American woman with a long face and perpetual smile met them.

"She will go straight into intermediate class," the headmistress said, in English, directing her comment at Beatrice even though Lilith stood right there. "We can't place her any higher."

All that Beatrice wanted for Lilith was access to a quality education, so she simply nodded. English would be more useful to her than Spanish, she thought, and it was high time the girl started to interact and get to know other families, so that one day she could create one of her own.

"She's ready to go to university," the headmistress went on, still ignoring Lilith, as though they were talking about someone else. "But that isn't a decision for me. She's tall, so nobody will notice the difference in class. She looks a lot older."

Long before term started, Lilith had decided not to stand out in school, not to learn more than she was taught. Her mother and Opa's obsession with her being the most brilliant girl was left far behind. She felt she had already learned everything she would need in life.

One afternoon, Beatrice approached Lilith when she saw her looking all gloomy after finishing her homework. She sat next to her, took her hand, and told her that she would teach her to knit.

"The pain never goes away, it's always going to be there, but knitting has done me a lot of good," Beatrice told her.

Helena, following Beatrice's instructions, began to fill the house with rolls of yarn of different colors and thickness and long and short metal needles that she bought in the shops on Calle Muralla. After dinner, Beatrice and Lilith began to knit scarves that they refused to finish, mixing different colors and textures.

Beatrice told her stories of relatives who lived long ago, and of the breads that her mother baked for Shabbat. It was as if her life belonged to the past, as if for her neither the present nor the future mattered. And yet she never mentioned her son.

When Lilith would say goodnight and go to bed, Helena would run and bring her a glass of warm milk.

"Beatrice loves you, even if she doesn't show it like I do," Helena said as she covered her with hugs and kisses.

On the first day of school, Martín had walked right over to her.

"So you're the Polish girl," he said to her, in English.

"I'm not Polish, I'm German."

"You're rather dark for a German."

Martín crossed his arms, and with an approving look, let her know that he liked her. Because she was different. From that moment on, they became inseparable. After school, they would take the long way home, along the tree-lined avenues of Vedado, trying to delay the moment they arrived and would have to go their separate ways. They spoke in English, and she corrected him and taught him new words. Before long, Lilith could pronounce certain Spanish phrases with a Cuban accent.

"You talk like an American," he would say to her, chuckling.

She practiced her Spanish accent with him every day since his teasing remark, and after a few months, Lilith spoke with a Havana lilt.

"Now you actually seem more Cuban than me!"

The day Martín said this, Lilith bubbled over with pride.

"You're the one who seems like you're not from here," she replied, crossing her arms the way he always did.

"And where does it seem like I'm from?"

"You look German. Yes, I would definitely say you were from a long way north."

Martín shook his head, smiling. "No, little girl . . . What you don't know is that Cubans are all different colors. There are blondes, people with olive skin, Blacks, mulattos, Chinese, Chinese-mulattos, so . . . And our president has the same skin color as you."

Martín was taller than her, with a long neck, and when he talked to her, he looked her straight in the eye and every millimeter of his face seemed to participate in the conversation so that the effect was mesmerizing, and she couldn't help but pay attention. Lilith felt secure in his confident presence. She felt as though she had found an ally in Martín, someone who understood her, without judging her or asking her about her past. Martín was the only person on the island who made an effort to pronounce her name correctly. From the moment she set foot in Havana, everyone had called her Lili. Except him.

Like her, Martín was a dreamer. From the day they met, he told Lilith about his love of airplanes. He was an expert in bird flight and talked about the design of their wings as though pigeons and sparrows were species created in a laboratory.

"One day I'll show you the island from above. In a few hours we can go from top to bottom. You'll see how beautiful it is . . ."

Lilith never told him she was scared of heights. That when she was on the deck of the *St. Louis*, the people saying goodbye down on the quay looked like ants, and this threw the world off balance for her. The slightest movement, or even just seeing something from above, made her feel queasy.

. ✦ .

That spring Martín became her best friend. At school it was said Martín lived with only his father, a cabinet minister and friend to President Fulgencio Batista, because the boy's mother had eloped to Switzerland with a European aristocrat. Others said she had died during childbirth. In actual fact, Lilith knew, Martín had lost his mother when he was young.

"It was an illness that took her," he had said, without elaborating, and Lilith was satisfied by his explanation, which had left him subdued for the rest of the day.

Lilith knew that some grief never goes away.

She dared to tell him, by a way of consolation, that her father had also disappeared before she was born, but she wasn't ready to talk about her real mother and Opa. Loss brought them closer, as if they had both learned to navigate the same winding path of pain.

They explored the city together. He took her to see the River Almendares, the rocky beaches, and the flying academy he one day hoped to join. On the weekends, they would go to the cinema together to watch movies: science fiction, cowboys and Indians, gentlemen in tuxedos and women in flimsy silk dresses, battles with happy endings, and during the week they disassembled the family radios to understand how they worked, before putting them back together with the precision of clockmakers.

No one else joined in their conversations, their walks. They ate their midmorning snack together in the school playground, far from their noisy classmates, until the day Oscar Ponce de León, a spirited boy Martín had known since he was young, dared to sit between them, grab their hands like a big brother, and take them out of school to walk down Avenida Línea, which was plastered with political posters as it was election time.

Oscar attended a Catholic boys' school around the corner from Martín's, which he sometimes escaped from during the day to be with his friend. If he couldn't convince Martín to join him on his adventures, he would go back to class, sweating, with the recurring excuse that he had an upset stomach. The teachers regarded him as a lost cause. He had lived in Paris for a time with his parents, who had been diplomats for the previous government and were exiled to New York for a few months after the election, which had left the island with nobody at the helm until peace and order were restored. Martín told Lilith that when Oscar returned from exile, his accent was even stronger than hers. Oscar spoke French with British intonation, English like a born and bred Englishman, and Spanish like a madman.

"You two are like night and day," Oscar used to say to them, not for any difference in temperament, but because Lilith had dark hair and olive skin, and Martín was pale, with curls that turned golden in the sun.

To Lilith, it was Martín and Oscar who were opposites. Martín was always daydreaming, while Oscar gave speeches, had strong opinions. She would listen to them carefully at the beginning, only to give up halfway through, since according to Oscar the world was coming to end, and she lacked the patience or strength to start over.

"The islands are like a sewer," Oscar had once said to Lilith. "Only useless things end up here. We're full of poorly educated Spaniards, illiterate Africans, starving Chinese, and Jews without a homeland."

"Don't pay him any attention, Lilith," Martín interrupted him. "He's just bitter."

"And you can add idle communists, fugitives from justice, fraudsters, and murderers to the list," Oscar added. "Put them all together, stir them up in a big saucepan, and that's how you make a Cuban. Cubans rise up out of misery every day, like the phoenix, and almost by inertia they crash again, but they get up and rise again, in a vicious cycle there's no way out of. The best thing to do on the islands is escape."

Oscar talked about politics like a king without a throne. He was an anarchist and believed that democracies could not be reproduced. He used to say nobody could be something they are not.

"My grandmother used to say that a monkey dressed in silk is still a monkey."

Oscar quoted this and other such phrases with extreme pomposity.

He knew Martín and his father were great admirers of Fulgencio Batista, the current president whom everyone referred to as El Hombre. Oscar saw El Hombre as a self-taught peasant who had only joined the military to stave off hunger, and who had turned to politics because it was a route to even greater power. Politics was a way to brainwash the masses that even the Church could not prevent, ever since the French Revolution had declared everyone free and equal before the law.

As far as Oscar was concerned, the only good thing Fulgencio Batista had done was to give space to others: the communists, the trade unionists. Not because El Hombre, as he was commonly known, thought they had any right to govern, but rather to give the impression that Cuba was a democracy. Martín interrupted him at this point to list El Hombre's achievements. Thanks to the president, the minimum wage was the highest since the island's independence, and the Cuban currency would be enviably strong once his father, following the president's instructions, acquired several million dollars' worth of gold bars as a guarantee. Oscar shrugged.

"Don't count your chickens," he told Martín. "The good times are coming to an end. Just you watch, your man will pack his bags, and his money, and run. People aren't going to put up with this."

When Lilith first met Oscar, she thought he was much younger than Martín. Given his size, she guessed he was ten or twelve years old, but to hear him speak, and with his practiced gestures, she realized he must be a year or two older than Martín. Oscar was the most articulate boy she had ever met. One summer, when he was sent to school in Switzerland for three months, Oscar had a growth spurt and came home taller than her and Martín, though he remained as skinny and skeptical as ever.

Following that trip to Switzerland, Oscar decided he wanted to study at the Sorbonne after the war, to get away from the tropical heat and the self-serving politicians.

"You'll end up bailing out as well, you'll see," Oscar told them.

The three friends undertook reading competitions: Lilith in English, Martín in Spanish, and Oscar in French. They began with stories of knights-errant. Then they read biographies of military leaders, and even ended up reading classic romantic novels, which Oscar always ridiculed.

"Who in their right mind would drink vinegar to make themselves look emaciated? Only a bourgeois French girl, bored and unfaithful."

At Martín's house, Lilith tried all manner of Cuban dishes, among them desserts like rice pudding, vanilla custard, and *torrejas*, recipes that had crossed the Atlantic over one hundred years before. At her house, Helena had adapted to the Herzogs' eating habits, and avoided the traditional Cuban meals that Lilith longed to try. Helena did sometimes experiment though, much to Beatrice's dismay, smothering the boiled potatoes in garlic, onion, and cumin; frying the meat; and drowning the chicken in fiery sauces with annatto and bay.

Lilith didn't have a huge appetite, as Helena would often grumble. But what she did enjoy, like Martín, was the after-dinner coffee. She was enthralled by the tiny cup, its contents profoundly black, dense and aromatic, both sweet and bitter, the intense burnt flavor. She loved drinking it with Martín, in either of their yards. On the island, even tiny babies drank milky coffee before going to bed. That was why Cubans lived on constant high alert, she thought.

Martín idealized a Cuba that, according to Oscar, was nothing more than a hazy mirage. Oscar believed that democracy would never take hold in the islands, that it would be like asking the tropics for snow. Politics was an addiction for the two friends, but Oscar felt Martín lived with his head in the clouds, driven by his father's passion and yearning for Cuba to be a developed, democratic country.

Since Lilith had come into his life, Martín's world had shrunk. He stopped visiting the sons of his father's friends: the Mena family, the Menocals, and the Zayas-Bazán. This worried señor Bernal somewhat, although he knew his son wasn't lonely. He had two close friends, was dedicated to his studies, and dreamed of becoming a pilot.

Sometimes, Martín would accept invitations to the home of the Lobos, a family that controlled the sugar industry, the country's main economic engine. Occasionally, he would take Lilith, whom he once introduced as his girlfriend, completely out of the blue. But Martín would soon grow bored at these formal gatherings. Oscar, on the other hand, was able to breeze through such social events. Lilith never understood how such a restless, rebellious, and intelligent boy could endure conversations consisting entirely of whether to spend Christmas in New York, or which sugar processing plants it made sense to buy and develop.

"He has the blood of a diplomat in his veins," Martín once said. "He's only himself when he's with us."

Lilith avoided señor Lobo's daughters, who were forever competing for the love and approval of their father, commonly known as The Sugar King of Havana. But it always fascinated her to hear the magnate's stories each time he acquired a new piece for his collection of artifacts that had belonged to "the greatest military leader in history," Napoleon Bonaparte. It amazed Lilith that here, on an insignificant island in the middle of the Caribbean, someone could possess thousands of personal objects, furniture, weapons, and even the death mask of the French emperor.

"One day you'll help me get hold of the Great Corsican's telescope," señor Lobo said to señor Bernal on one occasion. "It shouldn't be in the hands of El Hombre."

Señor Bernal gave a slight smile, excused himself, and left his son, Lilith, and Oscar to continue chatting with señor Lobo. Martín's father had already explained to Lilith that Batista was rejected by many of the island's most important families, who simply couldn't accept that the most powerful man in the country was the son of farmers from the east of the island, had only held the rank of sergeant, and, even worse, was mulatto.

The first time Lilith saw the President was at the Bernal family home. Martín and Lilith were coming into the house from the garden when a bodyguard stopped them in the hallway.

"Don't worry," Martín whispered in Lilith's ear. "It means El Hombre must be here."

When the bodyguard recognized Martín, he let them pass.

Señor Bernal and El Hombre were in the library with Martha, who despite being Batista's wife, was still not considered First Lady because he'd married her almost immediately after divorcing his first wife. Lilith was unsure how she should act in front of a president. She had no idea of the protocol to follow, whether to bow or curtsy.

"So, this is your girlfriend," El Hombre said.

Martín ran over and hugged him.

"It's terrible what's happening to the Jews," Batista went on. "The doors are open for them here. Nobody quite like them in business. That's just what we need in Cuba."

Lilith wanted to tell the president she wasn't a Jew but didn't dare. She didn't know whether to thank him for accepting more refugees to Cuba or explain she had arrived on the MS *St. Louis*, a ship where more than nine hundred Jews had been sent back to Europe, turned away by his predecessor. She and the Herzogs had been among the few fortunate enough to disembark in Havana.

Lilith fixed her eyes on the book Batista was holding.

"Emil Ludwig. The best biographer in the world," he said. "And he's German like you. Maybe you can help me when he comes to Havana. We'll need a translator."

"I read that biography of Napoleon when I was a little girl," Lilith said, surprised by the familiarity with which the President, whom so many feared, addressed her.

"Your Spanish is very good."

"Her English is even better," Martín said.

The second time Lilith met the President was at his residence on the outskirts of Havana, a modernist house surrounded by palm trees. Martha, now recognized as the First Lady, welcomed them while holding a sleeping baby in her arms.

"You'll always be welcome in this family," Martha told Lilith.

Lilith saw many men in white shirts and black suspenders, and military men who didn't seem to be armed. In the distance, she could make out cows standing in a paddock with lush green grass. They seemed to be pets, almost decorative in their stillness.

A row of palm trees lined the path to the main residence but provided little shade. There was nowhere to hide from the sun out in the open air. Lilith had always been surprised how at ease Cubans were in the sun. She, on the other hand, always sought out shade, whatever the time of day. In the Caribbean, sunlight creeps through every crack, permeates the thickest curtains, infiltrates every space, heats up every room. The sun always wheedles its way inside. Lilith suddenly felt thirsty.

Martín and Lilith walked straight to the library. The President was there, alone except for one bodyguard. Lilith spotted a telescope in a corner. *That must be the one señor Lobo wants to get his hands on*, she thought. On the desk were building plans, a golden telephone, and in each corner sat bronze busts of men she didn't recognize. On a rectangular wall, a map of Cuba with the mountain ranges in relief.

The air was fresh, but the room remained full of shadows. *The sun isn't allowed in here.* The thought made Lilith feel safe. Someone opened the doors to an adjoining room and the sound of religious music drifted in. Was it an organ? She had been told there was a chapel on the estate. A man in uniform was sitting in one corner, motionless but clearly vigilant. Two women in white aprons came in with glasses of lemonade packed with ice, on a silver tray. They offered them to the youngsters, and left the room without raising their eyes, trying to remain invisible.

There were suitcases and empty boxes everywhere. Books were missing from the shelves, as if someone had been gradually emptying the library. Lilith wanted to get closer, to see the books that were still on the shelves, which might not have been read for years.

She was engrossed in the books when the President approached her. "If you're interested in any of the books, just tell me."

Lilith saw his eyes were weary. His term in office was coming to an end. Martín had told her the Batista family were going to move to Florida, in the United States.

Martín used to say that El Hombre had the gift of the gab, and she could see it was true. Between sips of lemonade, he talked about battles lost, strategies of ancient armies, the downfall of great leaders. He also spoke of a city that must rise from the ashes. He went from past to future as though the present didn't exist. Time was the enemy, he said. Batista showed Lilith the buildings that would remain half-finished all over the island and spoke of his fear that when another politician took power, his own legacy would go out the window. He wanted to make Havana the most civilized city in the hemisphere.

A utopia, Lilith thought, surprised by the erudition of this man who had not had a formal education. From that moment on, she felt an affinity with him. *The sun destroys everything on this island*, she wanted to tell the President.

The third time Lilith met the President, she acted as his translator. A few days before, she, Martín, and Oscar had been to a lecture by Emil Ludwig in the School of Philosophy and Arts at the University of Havana. Ludwig's remarks had been translated by Gonzalo de Quesada, a distinguished professor from the Seminario Martiano. The President had wanted her to attend the conference of her favorite German biographer so that she could then translate for him at a reception in the residence of the president of the Havana Athenaeum's Literature Department. In his lecture, Ludwig won over the Cubans by talking about their national heroes with devout admiration. He spoke of Martí, the Apostle, saying that though Germany was world renowned for its discipline, it lacked a heroic spirit, even predicting that within a few years that country would disappear.

That night, Lilith and the German author listened to soprano Esther Borja sing, accompanied on the piano. The Cuban diva was short, and as she sang, she closed her eyes, smiling softly and tilting her head, raising her arms to chest height, just like the white marble virgins in the Lobo family house. At first, her voice was gentle, pitched low, before rising to become piercing, penetrating, filling the room and captivating the audience.

At the end of the short recital, Emil Ludwig approached the singer. "Decades ago, I planted a bay tree in the garden of my house in Switzerland," he said in German, with Lilith translating. "I always carry a few of the leaves with me that I occasionally give as gifts to artists or statesmen. They are a kind of good luck charm for me. If you believe in charms, I'd like to offer you one. You are a marvelous artist."

Lilith was deeply moved, as was the singer. The President looked on from a distance, delighted.

Lilith closed her eyes and saw herself as a child in her mother's arms, close to Herr Professor, while they took turns reading to her from one of Ludwig's books. It was an instant of peace. She would like to have heard their voices, but she couldn't. After the concert that April evening, as they were being driven home by the presidential chauffeur, Martín saw Lilith's eyes filled with tears. He took Lilith's hands and kissed them, not knowing what else he could do to comfort her.

13

Lilith's hands were always cold. Martín used to say that she brought winter with her to Havana. Sometimes they put on scarves and let their teeth chatter, pretending the temperature was dropping by the second.

Lilith dreamed of running away with him one winter's night.

"You can't think in the tropics," Martín used to say. "The heat just makes you feel like lying on the sand, by the sea, under the sun. Nothing good comes from the heat. We'll never amount to anything here."

"And in the cold, we'd end up killing each other," Lilith countered.

"And not here?"

Since El Hombre had left the country, Martín had become as pessimistic as Oscar.

They didn't even go to the cinema anymore because Martín said it was too dangerous. Attacks on police officers were increasing, and shootings were common in Havana, where random acts of violence were becoming the order of the day.

Martín and Oscar had left university amid the chaotic scenes of students fighting to overthrow a democratically elected president. Martín took evening classes in calculus and geography and studied aviation mechanics at the Inter American Aviation School, near his home. He began to accumulate flying hours, with the hope of being accepted by an institution in the United States, and to escape the country that in his view had fallen apart without El Hombre's leadership. Oscar had given up studying law, choosing to concentrate instead on reading widely and traveling with his father, certain he would one day agree to send him to study at a European university. But the ravages of the war had hardly begun to heal on the old continent, and Oscar's mother was worried there were still Nazis on the loose. Lilith, on the other hand, tried to continue her literature and philosophy classes, but the political demonstrations often prevented her from climbing the steps to the university. Students would throw stones, and the police would fire their guns into the air, running the risk of killing someone, which did indeed happen on one occasion. After that, Lilith chose to stay at home to read while Martín learned to fly in dilapidated biplanes.

"One day that boy's going to disappear, like Matías Pérez in his hot air balloon," Helena would say.

On clear mornings, Martín would drive to Chico airport on the outskirts of Havana to build up his flying hours. When he returned, he would talk to Lilith and Oscar about how he had defied gravity in the two-seater Piper that he could barely fit inside of, but which was capable of crossing the Gulf at eighty miles per hour and landing in the Florida Keys.

Martín's father insisted that the only way to restore stability to the country was for Batista to leave the comfort of his home in Daytona Beach, Florida, and set his sights on a seat in the Cuban Senate. People said that Batista kept up to date with his country's travails, the new political parties, and the latest elections, although he hadn't the slightest desire to interfere.

Those were terrible times, not only because of the gangster-like murders, but also a hurricane that smashed across Havana from south to north, leaving dozens dead in its wake.

In the elections of 1948, in an outcome that came as a surprise to many, El Hombre was elected senator in absentia for the region of Las Villas, representing a party that Lilith had never heard of. Batista returned to Cuba without any fuss, and Lilith was hoping she would once again have access to the beautiful library in the newly elected senator's estate, which had been locked up since his departure years before. Martín's father, señor Bernal, looked exhausted, having gone for days without sleep while traveling to and from Florida. He was the same age as El Hombre, but Batista could have passed for his son. Martín hoped that El Hombre's return to Cuba might bring his father some respite.

Martín and Lilith found that they were spending less time together, so they made a pact to get the most of every chance they had to see one another. Sometimes, when she was with Martín, Lilith felt so happy that she was inevitably overcome with sadness. She didn't want to lose the one person in the world she could trust, but life had taught her not to believe in permanence. She loved Oscar too, but she knew he belonged to a different dimension. Oscar would leave on his own. He needed independence. Martín on the other hand needed her. They needed each other.

More than anything, Martín loved Lilith's audacity. He could discuss politics and great historical figures with her or perform flight calculations: they talked about numbers and mechanics, the impact of the war, nationalism, Communism. Girls at school, the daughters of his father's friends, only ever thought about getting married and having children, dressing in the latest fashions, being invited to the best parties. When they were with him, they laughed and looked at him with doe eyes. But with Lilith, what had started out as a friendship had changed gradually over the years. She meant everything to him. He realized this one afternoon when he saw her on the arm of Oscar, whom he regarded as a brother. From that day forward, he couldn't shake the idea of Oscar and Lilith together. He decided that Lilith had to be his and his alone. Then one morning his stomach erupted, he got chills, his legs turned to jelly, and he had to go back to bed. Surprised, his father came into his room, sat by his side, and felt his forehead.

"You're running a fever," he said. "Forget flying today."

He wanted to ask Lilith to be his girlfriend, but he was worried she would misunderstand him and make fun of his childish proposal, or reply with something like: "Why would you want me to be your girlfriend when you're with me all day anyway? You're like a brother to me." Rather than face rejection, he decided not to say anything.

But Lilith had realized Martín was falling in love with her.

According to Helena, that winter was one of the coldest of the decade. She came down with the influenza that was filling the capital's hospital wards and threatening her weak lungs. Helena used to say that since suffering scarlet fever that left her bedridden for months as a child, typhus that left her nearly bald, and measles that had scarred her skin, she had become vulnerable to every illness that arrived on the island. But she also said that by battling against them, her body had learned to resist them.

"I'm a tough nut to crack," Helena told Lilith when she called Doctor Silva to come to see her. "If it weren't for my lungs, and this cigarette that's glued to my lips, I promise you Helena would be around for a long time."

Lilith didn't understand why the whole island shut themselves away at the first sign of a breeze, starting with Helena. People seemed to fear cold before it even arrived. She never ceased to be amazed by the apprehension people in the tropics felt toward the wind, mist, drizzle, and even dew. Standing on dewy grass might cause a cold. The chest had to be covered in even a slight breeze, you shouldn't go outside with damp hair, windows had to be closed after a warm shower. Cubans seemed to adore the sun, with the same intensity that they feared the moon and blizzards. Lilith on the other hand still lived in harmony with the night.

When Oscar saw that his friend was better, and that his fever had passed, he asked Martín to go with him to Varadero for a few days. He had promised his father he would prepare Villa Ponce, their summer house, for the winter.

"I'll come with you too," Lilith said.

When Lilith announced her plan at home, Helena shrieked and went to find Beatrice to back her up.

"Lilita, who in their right mind would go to Varadero in December?" she said. "And with two boys and no chaperone? You're crazy. Señora Beatrice, are you really going to let her go?"

Beatrice didn't answer. She didn't even lift her eyes from the book she was reading. She knew Lilith was mature and trusted her.

Helena looked on in horror whenever Lilith shut herself in her room with Martín and Oscar, saying things to each other in languages Helena couldn't understand and that gave her a headache when she tried to work them out. On these occasions, Helena would throw open the window to avoid any misunderstanding, and the room would be flooded with the smell of night jasmine, a scent Martín would forever associate with his friend. Every half hour, Helena would interrupt them to offer glasses of lemonade, fruit, buttered toast, or on any other pretext, just to make them aware that she might come in at the least expected moment, so they would feel obliged to behave. When Lilith went to the house next door to visit Martín, Helena took to praying her rosary.

"This might be normal and respectable in Germany," Helena had said, pursing her lips, "but here, in Cuba, it's not done by proper señoritas."

When she saw Lilith packing her blue overnight bag to go to Varadero, Helena put her head in her hands.

"It'll be fine. They're my friends."

"With men, if everything's easy for them they get used to it, and then they don't bother asking you to marry them. What's the point? You need to think what you're doing if you want Martín to give you a ring. That's the only way I'll be able to relax. You're alone, my dear girl. You need to get married and have children."

Lilith kissed her goodbye and Helena left for the weekend. She knew that going off with a boy in the middle of the night might terrify some girls, and that she could be rejected from certain social circles to which she had absolutely no desire to belong. She was adamant she didn't need any more friends. Martín and Oscar were enough. And if she ended up a spinster, so be it.

· ◆ ·

Before they left for Varadero, Oscar and Martín had planned to go to Havana's Chinatown, and Lilith was feeling annoyed about them having an adventure without her.

"Don't worry," Martín said to her. "We'll come and pick you up later."

"No way," Lilith said. "I'm coming."

"No respectable Cuban woman goes there, Lilith," Oscar told her.

"I can pretend to be an American tourist, can't I?"

"You look more Cuban than we do," Oscar replied.

"I can speak English to them, or German."

"Lilith, I don't think women usually go to that neighborhood," Martín insisted. "Only the ones who work there, and you can spot them a mile away."

"I'll wear one of your suits!"

Oscar and Martín looked at each other, open-mouthed. Oscar was the first to give in.

"All right, fine, let's do it. Come on, Martín. We'll have a great time."

It would be an adventure for the three of them. The only thing Lilith knew about Chinatown was that there were red lights, naked women, and drunken men. According to Helena, Chinatown, San Isidro, and Colón were tropical versions of Sodom and Gomorrah. If it were up to her, she would have wiped them off the map of the island. Lilith imagined a low-ceilinged room, with bodies strewn everywhere, people smoking cigarettes, opium, and anything else they could get their hands on. An ode to the easy life and carnal pleasure. Made-up faces, red eyes, louche behavior. She would wear one of Oscar's suits: he was slimmer than Martín, it would fit her better.

At 9 p.m., Oscar and Martín waited for her around the corner in the Buick, a few paces from the corner store run by Ramón from Galicia, who according to Lilith always looked at her with hungry eyes. The car engine was running, with the lights off, and the windows rolled down. At that time of night, the streets in the neighborhood were deserted. The only light came from old Ramón's place. He must have been counting his money and writing a list of those who had to pay him tomorrow for goods supplied on credit.

"You can have whatever you want for free," he had once told Lilith.

Oscar and Martín were anxious. Lilith was never late. They knew she would have to sneak out, as usual. It was easy for her; her parents went to bed early and Helena always left at dusk on Friday to avoid the evening damp. But this time she would be in disguise.

"You're not allowed to park here."

Behind the wheel, Martín gave a start when he heard the gruff voice. Oscar's snicker gave the game away. It was Lilith, leaning on the window, wearing a man's suit, her hair tucked up under a wide-brimmed hat.

"Aren't you going to let me in?" she said, this time in her own voice.

"Well, well, if it isn't the little German girl," Oscar said, getting out of the car.

Lilith stood in the headlamps, one hand in her jacket pocket. In the other, she was carrying her overnight bag. She spread out her arms for them to look her over, smiling.

"Even though you've drowned yourself in aftershave, I can still smell night jasmine on you," said Martín, blushing.

Lilith climbed into the car and kissed him on the cheek.

"Watch it, you two," Oscar interrupted them, getting into the front seat beside Lilith. "Remember she's dressed as a man."

All three of them were nervous. If they were found out, their parents would be informed. But why should anyone care if a girl was dressed up as a man? Perhaps it would be thought a moral outrage, but Lilith was sure that many of those who went to Chinatown weren't sailors, tourists, or curious youths. She knew married men also visited there, and that they took great pains not to be discovered.

They parked the car in Avenida Zanja and walked to Calle Manrique. Lilith took in the neon signs in Chinese outside the little pharmacies and the crowded restaurants. On the corner, a sign announced the Shanghai Theater, showing two movies and a burlesque show. Each of them paid for a ticket. Oscar went in first. Lilith strode after him, while Martín played bodyguard behind her. Oscar's legs were shaking. They went down the side aisle to the stalls, passing magazines hanging on a string with bare-breasted women on their covers. They sat in the back row. Oscar and Martín took off their hats. Lilith kept hers on.

The auditorium was in near darkness. Cigarette smoke snaked up to the ceiling. When the stage lit up, first they heard a drumroll, then violins, a piano. Four unsmiling, barefoot girls wearing scarlet capes strutted out dramatically. They had pencil-thin eyebrows, thick eyelashes, their lips painted almost black. They all had the same face and were the same height, but the color of their skin was different. One had porcelain skin, another was jet black, another, an intense rose pink. They looked like painted dolls. At the sound of a trumpet, they let their capes fall, the spotlights making them look almost liquid. The girls stood with exposed breasts, and instantly covered their pelvises with feather fans, which they wafted around in a clumsy routine. Lilith snuck a look at her friends, who appeared simultaneously embarrassed and fascinated. She wanted to make a comment, a joke, but the boys seemed hypnotized: there was no way to get their attention. The girls' hip movements were out of time with the drums, as if battling against a beat they didn't recognize. The audience sat blank-faced, spellbound. At the moment the girls threw the fans into the air, the spotlights went off. The theater was in darkness once more. After a few seconds, the crowd let out a roar.

The whistling started. A man sitting next to them shouted obscenities. They heard a group speaking English. A presenter announced the next show: *Amores de Varadero*.

"We should get going," Lilith whispered. She was in no mood to put on a man's voice.

"I'm sorry we brought you here," Martín said, without being able to look her in the eye.

Martín's heart was racing, and he was worried his friends would notice his excitement. After a few seconds, he took Lilith's hand; she gave in, and he moved closer and closer until he could almost kiss her. He looked into her eyes and smiled nervously.

Oscar interrupted them by standing up and motioning for them to follow him.

They walked back to the car without saying a word. Martín got behind the wheel and they sped off.

"There was a shooting last week on that exact corner," Oscar said.

"Gangsters," Martín agreed.

Lilith took off her hat, shook out her hair.

They left Havana, tinged with feelings of shame, something none of them was accustomed to. Even as they put more distance between themselves and the theater, they felt as if they were still in the audience. Lilith suspected Martín and Oscar were more embarrassed than she was.

They crossed on to the Carretera Central. The streets were so quiet, it was as if the city were under a curfew. They would get to Villa Ponce before dawn. They drove in silence with the windows rolled down, lulled by the bends in the road, the smell of the sea.

When they reached Varadero, the little town took Lilith by surprise. She saw the tidy houses with barely any space between them, as if they needed one another to keep standing, to prevent them from being blown away in a strong wind. It looked like a model village built on an empty beach. They drove slowly through the town, then left it behind. They skirted the coast on the left-hand side of the peninsula, until they could make out a rocky outcrop. In the distance, they could see a brightly lit mansion on the top of a hill.

"Are you sure it's this way?" Lilith asked as they continued down an unpaved road, littered with rocks. "I think we're lost."

"I remember this track," Oscar assured her, his voice weary. "I always get my bearings from the DuPont mansion. It's just before you reach it. What's the matter, surely our little German girl isn't scared?"

They drove closer and closer to the coast. Once they passed the mangroves, they could make out palm trees and a short road that went down to the sea. At the end stood a sturdy-looking, single-story house, hidden amid lush vegetation, built to withstand the Gulf's inclement weather. On the right, the tall, white Dupont mansion looked like a sleeping giant.

The car headlamps illuminated one side of the house. Lilith jumped out and ran to the shore. Oscar followed and hugged her from behind. Lilith felt Martín putting his arms around both of them, as if protecting them.

"Who dares go into the sea?" Lilith asked.

"You're crazy," said Oscar.

"Nobody goes in the sea at this time of year," Martín added.

"We're not nobody. Come on, into the water!"

"It's easy to see you're not Cuban," Martín said. "Even if we're all roasting in the heat, no one goes in the sea in winter."

"Winter? You think this is winter?"

They turned and went into the darkened house. Oscar switched on a table lamp shaped like a bouquet of flowers and opened the aluminum door at the far end of the living room, leading out onto the terrace. From there, the sea looked like a sheet of metal.

"Your rooms are on the right," Oscar said. "If you really want to, we can have a swim."

Lilith went first. She left her shoes in the living room. Out on the terrace, as though performing a ritual, she took off her jacket, trousers, and shirt, stripping off her disguise. She turned to look at them and continued undressing until she was naked. She was bathed in moonlight.

Oscar trailed after her and timidly began to undress. Martín followed behind, his eyes fixed on the suit Lilith had been wearing, now crumpled on the terrace floor. He didn't dare raise his eyes yet. For the first time, he was going to see her naked.

Martín and Lilith had been close before, under the tents they made out of brocade upholstery fabric from the Herzogs' wardrobes, much to Helena's displeasure. They would embrace out in the yard, dodging the rays of sunshine that filtered through the branches. Just after she had moved there, in those days when she wasn't reading and time seemed to stand still, Lilith had christened all the trees with German names: Ekhardt, Georg, Gunther . . .

"We should hibernate here, but in reverse," she once told Martín. "Sleep the whole lousy summer until we're woken up by the October storms."

What Lilith missed about Berlin back then were the nights and the winters, racing around in a park that had become her private garden.

She had grown accustomed to people who condemned her before they even looked at her, the imminent possibility of separation from the people she loved. When she arrived in Cuba and found she was taller than all the girls in her class and most of the boys, and smarter, too, she had begun to feel she had some control for the first time. Undressing in front of her friends was another step toward self-confidence.

In the darkness, Martín and Oscar stood looking at Lilith's silhouette, as though waiting for someone to tell them what to do. But Lilith didn't look back. She walked slowly toward the shore and stepped into the calm water, dense in the darkness. She was a silvery shadow, dissolving as she moved into the pewter sea.

"What are you waiting for?" she shouted over her shoulder.

Oscar stood there naked and, as if hypnotized, peering out to sea with no interest in getting in. He hoped Lilith wouldn't turn around. He wanted to cover himself up to his neck, but when he finally ventured into the water, it only came up to his knees. A few minutes later, Martín entered the sea, but then came to a halt. Timid waves were frothing around him; he felt as if the salty water was penetrating his pores. Nervousness made them forget the cold. Lilith saw them trembling.

"The farther you get from shore, the warmer the water feels."

"It's freezing!" Oscar exclaimed.

Martín watched Oscar draw nearer to Lilith, and the pain in his stomach came flooding back. The last thing he needed was to come down with another fever and spend their time in the beach house unwell, while Lilith and Oscar had fun. He joined Oscar, and he slowly approached Lilith, who was floating on her back. The silver rays shone on her breasts.

In the distance they could see scattered houses, their lights on.

Oscar brushed Martín with his arm, but his friend didn't react, his eyes fixed on Lilith's breasts. Nervously, Martín turned to Oscar and smiled, embarrassed. Oscar made a quick movement and his lips almost brushed against Martín's.

"I think we should get out, unless we want to spend all day tomorrow sick in bed," Oscar murmured before swimming back to shore.

Martín kept looking at Lilith, getting closer all the time. She lifted her head, trying to stay afloat.

"I can't touch bottom here."

"You can hold on to me," Martín said.

"Let's both swim to shore, that will warm us up."

Lilith saw that Martín could still touch the ocean floor, as the waves came and went around them. She leaned on his shoulders, pulled herself toward his neck, closed her eyes, and for the first time kissed him on the lips. It was no more than a second, but for Martín it seemed to last a lifetime. Lilith pulled away from him and swam back toward the shore. He stayed rooted to the spot, lost in thought.

On the terrace, Oscar, now dressed, was waiting for her with an enormous towel. When she came close, he closed his eyes. Then he waved to Martín to come back to the house.

Martín advanced slowly, head down. As if embarrassed, he stopped at the house's entrance. Oscar covered him with a towel.

"You're going to catch a cold," he said.

He began to gently dry Martín's back, but Martín grabbed the towel himself. Oscar blushed and they entered the house.

Dawn was breaking.

They said goodnight without looking one another in the eye and went to their rooms. Oscar fell asleep at once. Lilith wished Martín would come and find her, so that they could stay awake together, in silence, like when they were younger and would disappear under the tents. With that hope, she closed her eyes and dreamed they lived together, had a family, and explored the islands in a boat. Martín was wide awake and more than once he got out of bed with the intention of going to Lilith's bedroom. But each time he couldn't bring himself to knock on her door and quietly retreated to his own room.

In the morning, Lilith was the last to wake. She showered, dressed, and with her hair still wet, went to find her friends. They were drinking coffee in the kitchen, glued to the radio.

"It's about to start," Oscar said.

Lilith understood straightaway. The whole island was transfixed by a radio soap opera that had been airing for eight months. It was about a young woman who has given up her son, and her father's search for his grandchild after he discovers what she's done. The star of the show was a hugely popular Black woman named Mamá Dolores. In the episode being broadcast that day, she was going to meet her son at last.

They were about ten minutes into the episode, riveted by Mamá Dolores's histrionic weeping, when the sound of the ringing telephone intruded. Oscar rushed to the hall to answer it. A few seconds later, he reappeared in the kitchen doorway. In the background, the song *El derecho de nacer* was playing.

"Martín, we have to go home," Oscar announced. "Your father has had a heart attack."

14

Two and a Half Years Later
Havana, June 1951

Seven years had passed since El Hombre ended his term as Cuba's elected president. Now, having returned to the country as a senator, he had taken refuge on his estate, apparently uninterested in wielding executive power. Still, his return had altered the rhythms of the Bernal family. Martín's father, confined to a wheelchair since his heart attack, spent more time at home than in the presidential palace. He passed the time organizing what Oscar called trivial political campaigns, all while trying to convince Senator Batista to run for the presidency.

Although the world war had ended six years earlier, in Havana the explosions, attacks, and gun fights between rival gangs were endless. "One war leads to another. We don't know how to live in peace," Lilith would say to Oscar, shaking her head.

For her, the end of the war meant nothing, she had already lost those she loved the most. She still spoke to Beatrice and Albert in German, and avoided the stories of mass exterminations, concentration camps, piles of corpses and skulls that had filled all the magazines in Havana. There had been celebrations all around, but she'd had nothing to celebrate. The war had annihilated her family, and given her another name, another country, another language, another mother. She had nowhere to go home to, despite Beatrice's endless letters to European refugee help groups and the Red Cross. Beatrice wanted the world to know that she, her husband, and Lilith were still stranded on an island that to them would always be a place of exile. Her letters were smoke signals, lost in thin air, thought Lilith. How many letters had crossed, all of them wishing for an impossible reunion? For her to know that now she wouldn't be spit at in her native country, where previously she'd had to hide away, was cold comfort.

When the war ended, a girl at school asked Lilith if she would leave Cuba.

"Where do think I should go?" she replied.

"Lilith's not going anywhere," Martín said. "She's just as Cuban as you and me."

Now, five years after the war ended, the economy of the island was booming. Rickety trams gave way to shiny new buses and there was a sense of modernity in the air. People were proud that Cuba was one of the countries that repaid its foreign debt on time. The Banco Nacional was set up, bringing a wave of prosperity to the country. However, what most transformed the lives of the Bernal family was the arrival of air-conditioning. Martín and his father hermetically sealed the house and installed a metal box in every room except the bathrooms and kitchen. The motors made the whole house vibrate, and the noise gave the Bernal home the feeling of a constantly throbbing factory. From outside, it looked as if the house were crying. The air-conditioning units dripping at the windows formed a river of tears that ran down to the Herzogs' yard. Helena cursed these electric boxes, complaining that if all the rich families decided to install them, Vedado would turn into a swamp.

The Herzog household also changed after the war was over. Albert spent all his time in his office, reading old newspapers from overseas, which was how he referred to anything to do with Germany, brought to him by a customer at the furniture store. He also began winding down his businesses.

"The war's over. What's the point in carrying on, if the only place we're going, when we leave here, is to the cemetery? We have more than enough to see us through."

Albert still called Lilith "the little girl," which always brought back a memory she had from their time aboard the *St. Louis*. A few days into the voyage, he whispered in her ear, "You're a clever little girl. You'll find a way to go on. Not just for you, but for your mother." Then he kissed her forehead. Albert had always supported her, even taking her side against Helena, who thought Lilith was too independent and head-strong. "Leave her alone, she knows what she's doing," he used to say.

With her husband holed up in his office, Beatrice began to go to Old Havana in the afternoons, to have tea at the Hotel Raquel. Count-less refugees from Europe were arriving every day. Some showed signs of terrible malnutrition, and they usually refused to talk about what had happened. The families arriving at the hotel on Calle Amargura at the corner of San Ignacio, on the other hand, were people who had been able to hold on to some money and possessions. Beatrice still harbored the hope that she would find a neighbor, or someone from the village where her family had lived. Day after day, she would come home at dusk, empty-handed, and shut herself away in silence.

The heat at that time of year was suffocating, and they spent most of the day in the kitchen, where they could open all the windows onto the yard, protected by the shadows of the trees with German names. The living room was hellish in the afternoon, with the sun nosediving in, devouring the color of the rugs and the paintings on the walls. Lilith started complaining about the heat, in the hope of convincing first Hel-ena, then her mother, that air-conditioning would make their lives much more pleasant.

Oscar left on a trip to Europe with his parents and when he returned a few months later, he surprised Martín and Lilith by introducing them to a friend he had met on the ocean liner returning from Barcelona. Ofelia Loynaz was eighteen years old and belonged to one of the island's oldest and most distinguished families. Her ancestors included heroes of the War of Independence as well as presidents of the republic, a legacy that Oscar's father enjoyed boasting about. Ofelia gradually became a part of the three friends' adventures.

One day Martín took Oscar with him to practice flying and suggested the two young women spend the day together. Oscar wanted Lilith and Ofelia to get to know each other better, hoping that Lilith would warm to the girl. Lilith never went flying with Martín; she was scared of heights, and sudden movements could turn her stomach. For Lilith, the mere thought of getting into one of those noisy planes brought back the dizziness and vomiting that had plagued her during the endless ocean crossing from Hamburg to Havana. They didn't even ask Ofelia, since she was so small and fragile, they thought she might collapse the moment the plane took off.

At first, Lilith couldn't understand how Oscar had formed a tie with a woman as quiet and delicate as her. Ofelia's voice was so weak that Lilith often struggled to hear her. It was made worse by the slow lilt of her Spanish, and the way she separated the words as she spoke, adding silences and swallowing her *s*'s. He didn't even use her name, he referred to Ofelia simply as "she" whenever he mentioned her. The truth was, Lilith had long suspected that Oscar was in love with Martín. Oscar was always captivated by Martín's stories of his daredevil flights, and at times she had seen Oscar's eyes lingering on Martín's strong, veined hands. She thought of something Helena had once told her: Nobody knows where our heart will lead us.

While Oscar and Martín were flying, Lilith and Ofelia shared coffee, and after sipping her cup of coffee for over an hour, Ofelia told her that she planned never to marry, because she had no appetite for parties, nor the need for a husband. Her life's purpose was to worship Jesus, she said. Ofelia spoke of Jesus with such familiarity—He was the only one she trusted, she was completely devoted to Him—that Lilith was sure there was no way this helpless young girl would ever become romantically involved with Oscar, who always insisted his future would take him off the island.

After coffee, Lilith accompanied Ofelia to make a donation at the church. She and Ofelia walked along the pedestrian promenade down the middle of Avenida Paseo, under the shade of the trees, until they came to an enormous neo-Gothic building with two towers, which occupied an entire block. On one corner, the construction became more classical, as if the architect had grown bored while he was building the church. Ofelia said this was the convent of Santa Catalina de Siena. They climbed the modest stairs, and as they entered the building, Ofelia dipped her fingertips in a fountain and crossed herself with a slight curtsy.

Ofelia told Lilith she had wanted to be a nun since she was a little girl. Not just any nun, she said breathlessly as they walked along, every now and then dabbing the sweat from her brow with a pink lace handkerchief. Ever since she was born, she had been destined for contemplation and prayer, she said, and one night before bed she had silently made a vow of perpetual enclosure, as valid as one made before the Lord in the cloister. Her parents thought it merely a childish whim, until they realized she had become very close to Sister Irene, one of the nuns at the convent, who cared for lepers and found homes for abandoned children. Ofelia viewed the well-to-do families who visited her parents' home as selfish and frivolous if they didn't donate to the church causes. When her father watched her insistently pester his friends' wives, he understood that, despite her submissive appearance, Ofelia was something of a rebel. She had begun a battle on all fronts on behalf of an omnipresent being, he would say of his daughter to the rest of the family.

"One day you're going to come home with leprosy and infect your younger brothers and your mother," he yelled at her one day.

"Father, forgive him," Ofelia responded, raising her eyes skyward and muttering a prayer.

While they waited for Sister Irene, Lilith was hypnotized by the faces she could make out in the darkness behind the latticework of a window near the altar, beside the stained glass windows. *They must be the cloistered nuns*, she thought.

Sister Irene was a tall, stout woman. Lilith had imagined all devout nuns to be like her friend: small, fragile, and docile, but she was met with a strong woman, affable and affectionate, who clasped Ofelia's hands for several minutes while they chatted. Ofelia handed her an envelope containing a cash donation, and the nun made the sign of the cross in the air.

Looking at the heavy black and white robes the nun wore, Lilith couldn't understand how anyone could bear to wear that suit of armor in the tropical heat. She imagined her always in the shadows, lit only by stained glass windows, sleeping in a cell that was empty except for a hard, wooden bed and a cross. It was an image straight out of the novels she had read, where women shut themselves up to pay for their guilt after being jilted by a lover, casting off all their worldly goods.

Ofelia and Sister Irene discussed a newborn baby who had no home. The mother had died during childbirth, and Ofelia promised to do everything in her power to find a good family to take the baby in. Sister Irene had an almost maternal relationship with Ofelia, and Lilith began to get a glimpse of the world where her new friend had been tempted to lock herself away. To spend all day reading, praying, and meditating didn't seem strange to Lilith. She thought it must be challenging to memorize the Bible word for word, learn Latin, and navigate the twists and turns of a religion that felt entirely foreign to her, even though she knew in some way it was hers. At least on her mother's side.

Since the day they met the nun, Lilith decided to become closer to Ofelia. She let her talk, without trying to understand her every word. The main thing was to seize an idea, not to understand every sentence murmured by the girl who swallowed her consonants as if she thought that by letting them go, they might take all her energy with them.

On weekdays they went to Calle Obispo, spending hours leafing through the books in La Moderna Poesía, where they would eventually buy the latest editions of Cuban authors. They went for long walks to nowhere in particular, and every month went together to see Sister Irene to give her Ofelia's donation. Lilith also began donating, placing a sealed envelope in the nun's hands, never knowing if it was an adequate amount, or similar to Ofelia's offering. Lilith had never met a girl so young and so devout, a calling she herself had never experienced. She thought that if God did indeed exist, he had obviously forgotten about her and her family.

As the months went by, Ofelia became more and more a part of the group. Lilith began to feel close to her. Ofelia's parents allowed her a freedom that other society girls could only dream of. They didn't insist she was chaperoned on her dates with Oscar, and even let her go over-night to Varadero with him, Lilith, and Martín. They knew that for their daughter God was ever present, and therefore her virginity was not at risk: her devotion to the Lord acted as a permanent chastity belt. They also thought the trip to Varadero might help her forget the idea of cloistering herself, which for them would mean losing their only daughter. Sons, when they marry, leave home and never come back. If Ofelia became an enclosed nun, who would look after them when they grew old?

Oscar and Martín had been happy to see Lilith, who didn't make friends easily, form a bond with Ofelia. And Martín was pleased to see Oscar with a girlfriend. He no longer had to feel uncomfortable during the prolonged hugs his friend gave him. They were like brothers, he thought, and they would be inseparable all their lives. If Oscar had feel-ings for him that were not reciprocated, Martín knew his friend under-stood that he was devoted to Lilith, whom he was certain he was going to marry and have children with.

One afternoon, Lilith was in the kitchen with her three friends when Oscar announced that he was going to the United States with his parents for an extended trip. Ofelia paled; it was clear this was the first she was hearing of this. Lilith took her hand. Oscar, without even glanc-ing at Ofelia, said that they would first go to San Francisco, and then to

New York, where Cuba, as a founding member of the United Nations, had opened a consulate. Oscar had already accompanied his father on a couple of trips to Manhattan, which he called a "real" island, and had returned obsessed with a new dance, created by a Cuban, that had begun to take hold across the world. Helena was preparing lemonade when the radio news broadcast ended, giving way to music.

"Mambo!" Oscar shouted and began dancing wildly.

He took Helena's hands and taught her a few steps, which she copied almost perfectly. They took two steps, lifting their toes and stretching one arm forward and then back, together with a syncopated hip movement. Lilith tried to do it, which made Martín laugh. Everyone— even Ofelia—could follow the rhythm. Except Lilith. She could barely comprehend the movements.

"I can't breathe!" Helena said with a huge smile on her face and went back to preparing the lemonade.

Oscar took Ofelia as his next partner. He directed the choreography, with the four of them forming a chain, and Lilith let herself be swept along. She truly believed that for the people born on the island, dancing was a part of their birthright. Their gestures, the way they walked, sat down, shrugged their shoulders: there was a musicality to all of it. Martín took Lilith's hands so that he could define the rhythm for her. Just at that moment there was a knock at the front door.

Helena excused herself and went to see who was at the door. A moment later Helena called for Beatrice. An echo of a conversation drifted through to the kitchen. It was a man's voice, speaking German. Lilith went to the living room, where she saw Beatrice talking with an old man with a haunted face, dressed in what were surely someone else's suit and shoes. He was carrying a narrow black leather case, edged in bronze.

"You must be Lilith," he said, his voice hoarse. "I was one of Professor Bruno Bormann's students."

Lilith realized the man wasn't old. Helena returned from the kitchen with a glass of water and a cup of coffee, which the visitor hadn't asked for. He drank the water and the coffee without pausing for breath. Color gradually returned to his face, though his voice remained choked.

"This is for you," he said, and handed Lilith a sealed yellow envelope.

Lilith opened it, and inside found a dirty, tatty little notebook, its corners worn, in sharp contrast to the impeccable packaging it had been sent in.

"It's yours," the man went on, without taking his eyes off her.

Beatrice was silent, frightened the man would tell Lilith more about her mother's death than she had told her.

Martín, Oscar, and Ofelia came into the hall and the man introduced himself.

"Señor Abramson," he said. "An old friend of Lilith's family."

"Everything okay?" Martín asked Lilith.

She didn't answer. Her eyes were glued to the little notebook.

Her fingertips touched the line written in German on the front cover: *For Lilith, my night traveler.* She carefully opened the book and saw what appeared to be a riot of words and ideas, many of them crossed out or worn away, making them difficult to read.

Lilith looked up at the man, wanting to ask him so much: about her mother, Opa, Franz. Then she returned to the pages, written in faded ink, trying to decipher them. She lifted the book to her face, to smell it, and blushed when she noticed everyone watching her. Her mother's notebook must have crossed borders, rivers, and mountains before navigating the Atlantic to reach her. What trace could possibly be left of Ally?

"Mother had beautiful handwriting," Lilith said, unsettled by her own words.

It had been a long time since she had referred to her real mother as anything other than "Ally," especially not in front of Beatrice. She didn't dare look at her. From the corner of her eye, she saw her adoptive mother's frozen smile. She tried to follow what the man was saying, a halting story that had no beginning and no end.

". . . so, bringing you this notebook was for a debt I had to settle," he said in Spanish, with a Castillan accent. "Now I can die in peace."

She understood that Herr Professor had been his mentor. When he was expelled from the university, during the first round of racial cleansing, Herr Professor continued reading his poems and essays, and, when he learned his family had been stripped of their businesses, helped pay for him to flee Berlin, first going south, and then eventually to Spain. While his parents were being taken to a concentration camp, he took a train across the Pyrenees. He arrived in Spain during the final throes of the civil war, and as that ended, the next began, the war that drew in the rest of Europe, leaving him stranded in a village with no official borders. When he finally had a place to live, he began to write to Herr Professor. The letters between them, he said, always arrived late, and in the wrong order.

Before Herr Professor was sent to Sachsenhausen, he managed to send the notebook. "The only thing I could save from the bonfire," he wrote Abramson, begging him to guard it with his life. It was all that remained of a writer he greatly admired, he said. This notebook, and a poem that must still be in her daughter's hands in Cuba, he had added.

Hearing this, Lilith shuddered, overwhelmed by an unfamiliar sense of guilt. Since arriving in Cuba with the couple she now called her parents, she had refused to look back. The poem she had traveled with had ended up tucked away in a drawer in her nightstand, along with a chain and a crucifix she had never dared to wear, out of respect for her new family. She had never returned to her mother's words and didn't even know if the writing had faded away, like in the notebook. The only details Herr Professor had given Abramson were Ally and Lilith's names, and the name of the family she had traveled with to Havana.

Abramson had found the Herzog family thanks to all the letters Beatrice had sent around the world, searching for the whereabouts of any surviving members of her family.

"The paths destiny takes us along . . ." he said in wonderment.

Hearing people speaking German, Albert came down from his office and stood in the doorway at the foot of the stairs, out of sight of the others. He didn't want to be part of a story that, he knew, was bound to end in tragedy. What else could happen to his family? He had lost his son and his home and his business, and now a stranger came along to torment Lilith, who had managed to escape hell and rebuild her life.

Lilith waited anxiously for the man to mention Franz. Until Martín, nobody else had ever made her feel as secure and protected as Franz had. Being with him had been like having an entire army behind her. At first, she had imagined Franz alongside fiendish soldiers, dodging bullets, surviving the trenches, fighting for a cause which he never believed in. In one of her dreams, she had seen him asleep in a woods, which she took to mean he had died peacefully, his face intact, not disfigured by a grenade, as she had also once dreamed. The image of Franz handing her the rag doll was seared in her memory. For her, that had been his goodbye.

One of Abramson's uncles had ended up in Panama, he explained. He had set up a business trading with Cuba and had moved to Havana after the war, because according to him it was the most prosperous country in the Americas. His uncle had accepted the invitation of an old friend who had offered to help him set up a channel for live transmissions via a lightbulb in a wooden box, which displayed images. Cuba was to be the second country in the world to have television.

Homeless, with no family and no money, in the midst of a continent in ruins, señor Abramson decided to join his uncle in Havana, and thus fulfill the promise he had made to his mentor. Now he could die in peace, he repeated. Abramson went on his way, looking even gaunter than when he had arrived, as if telling his story had depleted him of some of his life force.

Lilith ran to her bedroom so that nobody would see the tears in her eyes. She sat on the bed, the notebook still in her hands, not daring to open the drawer to see if the poem she left Germany with over a decade ago had faded away.

She read through some of the passages in the notebook, trying to piece the random words together so they made sense. She changed the order, started at the end, went back to the beginning, and when she finally gave up, she opened the drawer. The first thing she saw was the little box. She picked it up. Underneath was the sheet of paper with the poem, folded in half inside its pink envelope. She opened the box, and the sight of the crucifix brought to mind fragmented phrases and the sound of broken glass underfoot. She read the inscription on the little cross: *Lilith Keller*. Beneath it, a number: 7. She carefully unfolded the piece of paper and read a verse: *The night you were born, Berlin was at its darkest . . .* When she finished reading the poem, she went back to the beginning, lingering on every line. She memorized every word, every gap, every space, the stroke of the letters, the color of the ink. She didn't want anything to be forgotten: the past had returned to her.

With the poem, the cross, the rag doll, and the notebook on her chest, she lay down and eventually fell asleep.

15

Dawn.

"Stay in the house, don't go out," Lilith heard Martín say. "I can't say any more."

The telephone had woken her. Startled, but still half-asleep, she had lifted the receiver without saying a word. She would have liked to ask him if they would see each other later, if he would come and pick her up, but he'd already hung up the phone. She sat on the edge of the bed, gripped by fear.

One of the things Lilith loved most about Martín was his steadiness. Why would he call her with that frantic tone in his voice? At difficult moments, he always used to look her in the eye, take her hands in his, and with the conviction of a wise old man, tell her: *We'll always find a way*. But on that tenth day of March 1952, Martín had left her feeling scared and confused.

The last time he'd surprised her had been a much happier moment. Two months earlier, he had proposed marriage. Christmas and New Year celebrations were coming to an end, and Lilith was on the patio that joined the two houses when Martín snuck up behind her. He covered her eyes with his hands. She could feel his breathing was agitated, like when they were children and chased each other among the trees with names.

"It's about time everyone knows that I love you." He sighed.

She turned and kissed him. They held each other for several minutes. Beatrice and Helena were watching them from the kitchen window. He took her hand and put a ring on it.

Within hours, the two families were all celebrating in the Herzogs' living room. Albert opened a bottle of champagne, and they toasted the happy couple. Oscar was strangely silent.

Lilith saw her wedding as something very far away. They hadn't set a date yet, and Martín had insisted it would have to take place after his graduation. They had talked about it the evening before when they had been out for dinner in Río Mar, just the two of them. They had chatted about Martín's upcoming trip to the United States, the time they would have to spend apart, and the days she would visit him. His training in Tulsa, Oklahoma, would take two or three months.

At dinner, Lilith had ordered two glasses of champagne. Martín was taciturn and silent for much of the evening, but she had thought nothing of it. It was understandable for him to feel nervous about winning a place at the Spartan School of Aeronautics.

She'd grown accustomed to Martín's regular trips to Daytona Beach in Florida. She knew he had to build up his hours as a pilot. Although his father would have preferred him to continue his legal training and get a job in finance like him, Martín had known what he wanted since he was a little boy. "My world is up among the clouds," he used to say, and his father would roll his eyes. In the end though, señor Bernal was proud of his son: he excelled at math, and spoke English fluently, while he himself despite having graduated from an American university, still found it almost impossible to pronounce the consonants at the end of words. When all was said and done, he knew there was no shame in his son becoming a pilot.

It had been three years since señor Bernal had suffered the heart attack which had left him confined to a wheelchair and frequently short of breath. He still attended dinners with senators and businessmen, always accompanied by his son. From his time at his father's side, Martín had learned that silence can be a powerful weapon, as he told Lilith on more than one occasion.

With her heart now racing, Lilith tried to call Martín back, dialing the number of his father's office, but there was no answer. She called Ofelia, and she didn't answer either. Ofelia would be at the convent, Lilith supposed. She showered, dressed, and hurried downstairs to the kitchen. It was Monday, and her parents were still asleep. She opened the living room curtains and saw that the streets were deserted, as if the city were on hurricane alert, one of those that every year blew roofs off houses with the precision of a machine gun.

Before making coffee, Lilith climbed the stairs to her parents' bedroom. Resting her hand on the marble bannister, she shivered. She felt she was living in another dimension, back in her recurring nightmare of being trapped on a sinking ship.

She counted the steps, studying the images hanging on the wall in their mahogany frames, some edged with gilt. She saw herself as a child in Port Hamburg, holding the hands of Albert and Beatrice, as they climbed the gangway the day they fled Germany on the transatlantic liner. The photograph hanging on the wall now was a clipping from a New York newspaper. A fabric salesman had appeared with it one day at the Herzogs' store on Calle Muralla, and before showing them the rolls of taffeta and silk, he had placed it on the counter.

"Isn't that you two?" he said, pointing to the face of the man wearing a hat and eyeglasses, and the woman. Then he turned to the teenager behind the till: "And you still have the same frightened eyes you had as a girl."

She didn't recognize herself in that little girl, nor could she recall much of anything about the two weeks they had spent at sea, only going up on deck at night.

Albert had the image framed, and after hanging in the office of the furniture store, it had eventually ended up on the staircase wall after Albert retired and sold off all his businesses in Havana.

As Lilith climbed the stairs, she hesitated at the photograph of Albert and Beatrice's wedding. It seemed to her that the two young people in the picture had died years ago, and the old couple she lived with were their distant relatives.

"We were young and happy," Beatrice had once said to Lilith, seeing her mesmerized by the photograph.

Another photograph showed the whole Herzog family, gathered around a table covered with lace: the grandparents, parents, brothers and sisters, children, all with fixed smiles for the camera. They were all strangers to Lilith. After all Beatrice's years writing to organizations that reunited families hoping to find some of them, she had finally accepted that none had survived the war, and she would have to endure her life sentence of memory and guilt alone.

One of Lilith's favorite images was the opening of the Mueblería Luz furniture shop. She was there, cutting the ribbon, with Martín by her side, watching her, enthralled.

"From that day forward, I knew he was in love with you," Beatrice had confided in Lilith the day she and Martín became engaged.

Although they had given up their traditions since arriving in Havana, Beatrice lit two candles every Friday, and, when the war was over, she occasionally met with friends, customers from the furniture shop, in a Hebrew community center in Vedado. She was always hoping she might meet a refugee from what had once been her home village, wiped off the face of the earth at the very end of the war. She went to bed every night for years with the belief that one day, in the not-too-distant future, she would know what had become of her brothers and sisters, nephews and nieces.

There had also been a photo of Paul, Beatrice's only child, but one day she took it down and Lilith never saw it again. Beatrice said she couldn't bear the pain of not knowing how his face would have aged. Beatrice had told her it used to hang on the wall of the Herzogs' lighting shop in Berlin. "We lit up the whole city," Albert would say, "but in the end they chose darkness." There was now a shadowy patch on the staircase wall where the photograph of Paul had once hung.

"We'll hang your wedding photo there," Beatrice had said, her hand on Lilith's waist after they announced their engagement.

Finally, there was a photograph of Lilith and Martín, both dressed in their white St. George's School uniform and black bow ties, in the school's interior courtyard, on the afternoon of their high school graduation.

At the top of the stairs, Lilith turned her eyes to the corridor that led to the bedroom, and her father's office, a cave-like space with walls lined with dark wooden bookcases, and drapes across the windows that did not let in a single ray of light.

She hesitated by the door to the office, struck by a terrible sense of foreboding. She went in and saw that the leather armchair where her father could spend hours by the greenish light of the bronze lamp, was empty. She hung her head, sighed heavily, and headed for her parents' bedroom. *They can't still be asleep*, she thought. *Perhaps they went out early. Perhaps . . .*

Lilith gave up speculating and knocked twice on the door. There was no answer, and she decided to go in. She felt a blast of cold air and a strong smell of naphthalene. Her mother was obsessed with preserving the woolen clothes they had brought with them on the ship. There was a hint of chamomile in the air too. Her father always drank tea made with the dried flowers, hoping it would help him sleep deeply, though he never did, as he complained every morning. Her parents' morning conversations always revolved around the fact that, though they followed the age-old custom of closing their eyes to sleep, they were convinced they had lost the ability to dream the night they fled Germany. What was the point in sleeping if you weren't able to dream?

If her parents had been in the bedroom they would have spoken when she knocked or reacted when she opened the door. But the room was so silent it made her blood run cold.

The light from the corridor lent a subtle glow to the mahogany headboard of the four-poster, the posts wrapped with gray silk and the canopy with transparent curtains drawn back. Albert and Beatrice lay on the bed in the half-light. Lilith took a step to her left, and the light fell on her parents. They were holding hands, side by side, face up. Lilith recognized the dark-blue dress and wide black leather belt that Beatrice had worn the day they boarded the *St. Louis*. Albert had on his gray flannel three-piece suit, and the tie knotted at his neck seemed to be strangling him. His shoulders were raised almost to his ears. Lilith couldn't make out their faces; she didn't know whether their eyes were open or closed. Perhaps they had fallen asleep, fully dressed, about to go out, she thought. Then she noticed they were both wearing their worn leather shoes. She had seen the image before, in the cabin of the *St. Louis*, that May night they boarded the ship, almost twelve years earlier. That day that time had stopped for them.

Lilith wanted to go over to them, stroke their foreheads, hug them one last time, but she didn't dare. She collapsed to her knees on the cold tiles.

When she was finally able to pull herself up, Lilith left the room, taking care not to make the slightest sound, as if trying to avoid waking her parents from the deep sleep they had yearned for all these years. She left the door open so that the air could circulate. She was unsure who to call first, Doctor Silva, the family doctor, or the police, to report their deaths. *How did they die?* It was only now she asked herself that question. It couldn't have been a natural death. Her parents had decided to take their own lives, this morning or the previous night, when she was not at home. Doctor Silva would determine how long they had been lying on the bed. *An autopsy, they'll give them both an autopsy*, she thought.

"I can't let that happen," she said aloud.

Beatrice had once told her they must never be given an autopsy, that it went against their beliefs. Lilith never asked why.

When she finally got through to Doctor Silva, he didn't seem the least bit surprised, as though he had been waiting for the call for several weeks.

"It's going to take me at least two hours to get there. The city's in gridlock," he said.

"I'll be waiting."

Doctor Silva had emigrated to Cuba from Portugal and had never got used to the evils of the Caribbean, he used to say. As well as his native language, the gangly doctor also spoke fluent Spanish, English, German, and French, which meant his consulting room was always packed with lost souls.

Lilith wandered out of the house in a daze, not really knowing where to go but knowing she needed to leave. She stood outside on the sidewalk, suffocated. The house seemed distant now, as though she had never lived there. It belonged to the Herzogs, not her, a stranger they had taken in.

Doctor Silva would arrive in two hours, and then what? They would take away the corpses and bury them in Guanabacoa cemetery, which they had planned since arriving in Cuba, and she would leave a stone on each grave, would visit them on every anniversary. At least she would have a place to remember them and lay stones for them. All she had of her mother, Franz, and her Opa were vague memories, a poem, a notebook, a rag doll and a little crucifix inside a blue box that had turned gray over time.

What should she keep of the Herzogs? Only the family photographs, she decided. She would empty the wardrobes, let Helena have the rolls of fabric Beatrice had kept when they sold the store.

Helena! Where is Helena?" she thought. *She always arrives early on Monday mornings to make breakfast . . .* She knew she should telephone her, but first she wanted to find Martín. Why hadn't he answered her calls?

Usually when she would go see Martín, she let herself in at the back door, but today she went to the front, as if she were a stranger. She knocked on the door. Nobody answered.

When Lilith returned to her house, she found Helena at the door, carrying two shopping bags.

"*¡Ay Dios mío!* I thought I was never going to get here," said Helena, wiping the sweat from her brow with a hand holding a cigarette. "Everything's closed today, it's crazy . . ."

"They're gone, Helena . . ." Lilith looked down at the floor when she said it.

Helena didn't understand. She took in Lilith's desperate look, her frozen expression.

"Who is gone? What are you talking about, Lilita?"

"Helena, my parents are dead."

Eyes wide, Helena dropped the bags, opened the door, and rushed in. She looked first in the living room, then turned to the staircase. She left her lit cigarette in an ashtray and ran upstairs. A few moments later, Lilith heard a scream. She didn't dare follow her. She would wait for her to come down, explain to her she had already spoken to Doctor Silva, and all they could do now was wait.

Her gaze on the still-deserted street, Lilith felt Helena come up behind her.

Helena, ghost-white and silent, went to embrace Lilith tightly. "Poor Beatrice . . ." she said finally, rocking them back and forth. "There's no pain greater than losing a child. Nobody ever gets over that. However hard you might try to rebuild your life; the pain is always there. At least they can both rest now."

Lilith let herself be cradled, staring blankly ahead through tear-blurred eyes. "Did they say anything to you? It's as though they planned it . . ."

"They waited for you to become a woman, for you to get engaged . . . What more did they have to live for? All these years here and they could barely even speak Spanish. They endured enough with a broken heart. But *mi Dios*, what a day they chose . . ."

"What do you mean? What's happened?" Lilith asked, suddenly remembering Martín's early morning call.

"Haven't you heard the news? They've . . . Oh, look—here comes the doctor."

Doctor Silva got out of his vehicle and took his bag from the back seat. His hair was a mess, and he was out of breath, as though he had been running rather than sitting behind the steering wheel in his green-and-white car.

"I'm sorry," the doctor said, taking off his spectacles to wipe them with a handkerchief. "Upstairs?"

He went inside without pausing for an answer, Helena following behind him. Lilith stood frozen on the sidewalk, waiting for word from Martín.

For the first time since arriving on the island, Lilith felt defenseless. How could she navigate this without Martín? Someone would have to help her go through the necessary formalities, ensure they weren't given autopsies, file the necessary police reports, make funeral arrangements. Her parents had resolved to die only once they had fulfilled Ally Keller's wishes, once they were certain their adopted daughter's life was guaranteed. Only then did they die, hoping to be reunited with the son the Nazis had snatched from them.

She heard footsteps descending the stairs and went back inside to hear what the doctor had to say.

"Cyanide," Doctor Silva said as he filled out some forms on top of his leather bag.

Lilith's eyes widened in surprise. She turned to the doctor and Helena, looking for an explanation, but the doctor seemed to be in a hurry.

"Where did they get hold of cyanide?" asked Helena in amazement.

"You can find everything on this island," the doctor said, holding his hand out to Lilith to say goodbye. He handed the signed documents to Helena. "I already informed the mortuary, but today is a difficult day to make arrangements. We'll have to wait and see what we can do." And he was off.

Helena took Lilith by the hand and led her to the kitchen.

"How about a cup of herbal tea? It will do us both good."

Lilith sat down where she was told, cupped a mug of steaming water with lime flowers floating on the surface, and tried to take a sip. Impossible. She began to cry. Her body shook uncontrollably. But when she saw Helena was also choked with tears, she calmed herself and tried to show strength to the woman who had suddenly become her only family.

An hour later, Lilith heard the doorbell, and hoped it would be Martín, but it was the men from the mortuary. Helena took them upstairs.

Shortly afterward, they came down with stretchers, the bodies covered with white sheets. They didn't make eye contact with Lilith, and she couldn't bring herself to ask where they were taking her parents.

Helena held her hand as they made their way out of the house. "It's as if they were still asleep," Helena said. "I saw their faces. There wasn't an ounce of pain, Lilith. They went peacefully."

As the vehicle drove off with her parents' bodies, Lilith saw Martín's black Buick pulling up outside the house.

She ran to him and buried her face in his chest. She couldn't hold back her tears.

"They've taken them," she said, composing herself. "I woke up when you called me this morning and I found my parents . . ."

She faltered. Helena went to Martín and whispered in his ear.

Back inside the house, Martín didn't have the energy to talk to Lilith, but he tried to comfort her by holding her in his arms. His eyes were red, his face weary. Lilith was still leaning on him.

"We all need to stay calm," he said. "Batista has taken control of the army. El Hombre is already at Camp Columbia. My father's with him. No shots were fired."

Lilith looked at Martín, taken aback. She didn't understand what he meant. He was talking of military actions, and she had just lost her parents. *Albert and Beatrice are gone,* she wanted to tell him again. *My parents are gone.*

"Not a single shot was fired," Martín repeated. "Nobody was killed, and there was no bloodshed."

"What will happen to us?" Lilith asked, anxious and overwhelmed.

"Everything will be fine, my love. We have a new president. El Hombre has returned to set things right."

The afternoon the Herzogs were buried, Helena packed her things and moved into the house in Vedado, occupying a ground-floor room opposite Lilith's.

"All my worldly possessions fit in this wooden case," she said. "One shouldn't accumulate material things in this life. They weigh you down and make you trip over them when you walk."

With the Herzogs gone, Helena brought God, the Virgin, and every saint under the sun into the kitchen.

"Before, out of respect for them, I kept all my saints locked away. Now they can breathe in peace and protect us, my dear girl, because I know you're not Jewish," Helena told Lilith. "Do you think I was born yesterday? A nonbeliever wouldn't keep a crucifix with her "real" name written on it."

Lilith wanted to reproach her for poking around in her drawers but realized that she no longer had anything to hide. She felt liberated.

Helena's mourning soon gave way to a volcanic energy and desire to cleanse the house of any hint of tragedy. Clenching her jaw, she went about her household chores obsessively. She emptied drawers, removed drapes, shook out rugs, and moved furniture to the other bedroom, trying to remove Albert's and Beatrice's presence from every bit of wood, ceramic tile, and plaster wall. After all her cleaning, she lit candles so that any trace of their soul or spirit would disappear from their lives forever. The dead had their place, but that place should not be this house, which was meant to be inhabited only by the living.

"*Ave María santísima,*" Helena said, appealing to the Virgin.

Lilith felt at peace watching Helena's determined paternosters; her prayers to Dimas, the saint of lost things; and to la Virgen de la Caridad, Cuba's patron saint, at whose feet three haggard fishermen begged for her to save them from the waves.

16

After the death of her parents, Lilith put all talk of a wedding on hold. She was overwhelmed with her losses. Since she was a child, everyone close to her had disappeared. In Berlin she lost her mother, Herr Professor, Franz. In Havana, Albert and Beatrice. But over time, as Martín patiently waited for her to heal, she came to see that he wasn't going to abandon her and that her future was with him. Still, for her wedding, she ruled out any kind of big celebration; instead they agreed on a low-key affair that would be held at El Hombre's weekend getaway home.

A few months before the wedding was to take place, Oscar suggested that Lilith, Martín, and Ofelia come to his family's house in Varadero for a carefree weekend, the kind they'd always enjoyed when they were inseparable teenagers. Lilith appreciated his gesture of friendship and hoped it would be an opportunity for Martín and Oscar to reconnect.

The night before going to Varadero, Martín and Lilith walked with Ofelia to the cathedral, but found themselves running away from the oracle women, as Oscar used to call the throng of old crones who lurked around the place. They dressed in white, with strings of colored necklaces, a bunch of basil tucked behind their ears, a lit cigar in their mouths. Whenever she encountered them, Lilith tried to be friendly and smile, but they unnerved her, and she often found herself desperate to get away from them. That night, one of the crones took her hand and immediately started to tremble. Ofelia was terrified and made the sign of the cross.

"Oh, little girl," the oracle woman said to Lilith. "What are you doing on this island? You should have never gotten off the boat."

"Don't listen to her," Martín said, trying to separate them.

"Just think about it. Why you, and not the others?" the woman said solemnly, her eyes filling with tears. "You know what I mean."

Lilith had tried to forget their arrival at Havana, the harsh midday sun beating down on those desperately calling out to their relatives onboard the ship. Only twenty-eight passengers had been allowed to disembark. They had been among the fortunate ones. The rest were returned to Europe, where war soon broke out.

Lilith turned pale. She had wanted to forget. Yes, it was true that at night she saw faceless bodies, the ship sinking in the middle of the ocean, nobody shouting or reacting. She had never told anyone about these recurring nightmares.

"Go, get away from here," Martín shouted.

The old woman took a sprig of basil from her pinafore and waved it over Lilith's head before walking away. Lilith hid her face in her hands.

Martín hugged her.

"Don't worry about it. You're not going to listen to a crazy old woman, are you?"

Ofelia looked at her with compassion. Now it was her turn to protect Lilith, and this brought them closer still.

The next day they drove to the house in Varadero. Since it had only three bedrooms, Oscar suggested the girls share the main bedroom, thinking that he and Martín would each take the other two, in separate wings of the house. But Lilith surprised everyone by saying Ofelia could have the room so that she would be more comfortable. She imagined Ofelia kneeling at the foot of the bed praying for hours before going to sleep. After hesitating a moment, she took Martín's arm. She had decided. Tonight, for the first time, they were going to sleep together.

In the privacy of their room, Lilith undressed, and stood confidently before Martín, ready and willing for her beloved friend to take her in his arms, and to finally experience something she had already rehearsed in her dreams.

The following morning, much to their surprise, they saw Ofelia leave Oscar's room.

· ◆ ·

Ofelia and Lilith never spoke of the night they had spent in Varadero. Ofelia seemed resigned to the fate her parents wanted for her and, spurred on by her new friends, she let herself be carried along. Her parents wanted to see her married, away from the convent. For them, Oscar was the ideal candidate for their daughter.

Ofelia grew paler every day, drawing attention whenever they went out together, not only for how white her complexion was but also for the floral parasol she carried, even at night, as if she needed protection from the moonlight as well. One evening, when they were leaving a theater on the Paseo del Prado, they saw scrawled in huge letters on the façade the words *Abajo Batista*. The red paint was still wet, and they were struck by a smell of burnt oil. Martín suggested they hurry back to the car, to get away before the police arrived. Everybody leaving the hall was rushing, scared when they saw the red slogan.

Not long before, a group of terrorists, as Helena called them, had attacked a military barracks in Santiago de Cuba, in the east of the country, an assault that had left several dead on both sides. The surviving attackers were imprisoned on the Isla de Pinos, south of Havana, but in the end El Hombre reduced their sentences. At the trial, their leader had given a speech that was to become the manifesto of the new political movement whose aim was to overthrow El Hombre. Although he might have seized power in a coup, señor Bernal explained to them, elections had been held after that, and Batista had been duly reelected president. Oscar, like many, insisted the polling had been fraudulent.

Oscar had given Lilith the transcript of the opposition leader's speech, "History Will Absolve Me." Reading the pages written in prison by a fanatical young man, the nightmares she had as a little girl in Berlin came flooding back. She heard her mother and Opa arguing about *Mein Kampf*, also written in jail by a man who would come to have an entire nation in his thrall.

Around that time, Ofelia dedicated herself to going to Mass at the convent and helping Sister Irene tend to the lepers in the Sanatorium of El Rincón on the outskirts of the city, driven there by the family chauffeur. Oscar spent a whole day with Lilith and Martín, and it was only in the evening that he announced that he was going to live in New York for an extended period, to finish his legal studies and oversee his father's investments. It was a farewell, and Martín didn't ask any questions. He knew Oscar was running away, not only from the storm raging over the country, but also from Ofelia, who was getting in the way of his plans. Oscar didn't want to be tied down for the rest of his life to a girl his parents had set him up with.

When Oscar left for New York, Lilith felt sorry for Ofelia and went to meet her at the convent where her friend was spending increasing amounts of her time. Sister Irene met Lilith at the gate and took her to her friend, whom she found sitting in a cloud of incense, engrossed in her prayers. It had only been a couple of weeks since they had last seen each other, but Ofelia appeared even thinner, her eyes sunken in dark sockets. Her skin was so transparent that the path her veins traced from her neck to her forehead was visible. When she saw Lilith, Ofelia ran to her and hugged her, but she soon lost all of her energy. They walked around the convent's internal courtyard, and Lilith felt as though Ofelia was walking with the rhythm of the cloistered nuns, eyes on the ground. As she said goodbye, Ofelia smiled and confessed the reason for her absence.

"I'm pregnant," she said, hanging her head.

In that instant, Lilith thought of her own mother, pregnant with her in Berlin all those years ago.

"Ofelia, listen to me. It's going to be okay. You can come and live with me; you don't have to shut yourself away or stay with your parents."

"I need to be here, at the convent. This is where I belong."

"I can write to Oscar. I'm sure, when he finds out . . ."

"It's not his fault, it's nobody's fault," Ofelia interrupted her, and Lilith saw immense peace in her friend's face.

They linked arms and walked to a bench under a flame tree. They sat down in silence until Ofelia, with a great heaving breath, leaned on the shoulder of her only friend. She quietly explained to Lilith that as she was getting closer to taking holy orders, she had wanted to experience sex before she put that side of her earthly life away forever. That way her sacrifice for God would be made with full knowledge of what she was giving up. "It will be a beautiful, healthy baby, you'll see. But I want you to promise me something: this has to be our secret. I don't want Martín, or Oscar, and definitely not my parents to know. You're the only one who really understands me."

The sound of a religious chant roused them from their thoughts. A group of nuns was processing down the corridor on the floor above them. A dog began to bark. The scrawny, mangy animal ran around in circles behind the fountain, as though tormented by the chant.

"We'll find a home for the baby." Ofelia gasped. "It won't be the first or the last child that we've helped."

Lilith realized Ofelia was talking about the baby as if it didn't belong to her, as if the child growing inside of her was one of the newborns that mothers left in baskets at the convent door, or in the hospitals where they were born, without even recording them in the Civil Register. When she got home, Lilith wrote to Oscar in New York, but before long it came back to her, as did all her subsequent letters, unopened and stamped "Return to Sender." Every Friday afternoon, she went to visit Ofelia in the convent.

Lilith felt drawn to those who, like her friend, had such faith because she did not. She was intrigued by people who had grown up with the fear of God, when she had grown up with the fear of a real man: the Führer. But the thing that most attracted her to religious life was the quietude of mysticism: to live your life, kneeling in prayer before an empty altar, far from any noise.

Ofelia stayed at the convent, and one day, three months later, Lilith bumped into Ofelia's parents as they were leaving, beside themselves with sorrow. When she went in and met Ofelia, she saw the pregnancy could no longer be hidden. Her parents had left the convent convinced it was their fault, that they had pushed their daughter toward sin. They knew there was no other way than for the baby to be put up for adoption and to accept that their daughter would don the habit, a destiny that seemed to have been Ofelia's since the day she was born.

But Ofelia could not resist the power of her namesake. One day she smiled at Sister Irene and left the convent for a stroll. After walking for hours, all the while immersed in an endless soliloquy with God, the only one she felt really listened to her, she threw herself into the River Almendares, wrapped in a long garland of flowers she'd assembled.

There's rosemary, that's for remembrance. Pray you, love, remember. And there is pansies, that's for thoughts, Lilith read, remembering her Opa, when she saw the obituary in the *Diario de la Marina*. It didn't say that Ofelia had drowned her child with her in the muddy waters of the river.

Lilith cried that night, more than she'd ever cried for any of her dead. Once again, it was Martín's steady nature and unfailing devotion that got her through the darkness.

A week before her wedding, Lilith went back to the convent to make a donation in Ofelia's name. Sister Irene didn't come to see her, instead she was met by an elderly woman dressed in a tightly buttoned gray suit rather than a habit. She took the envelope, opened it, and counted the money in front of Lilith. She assumed that Sister Irene had shut herself away, plunged into a deep depression by the death of Ofelia, and that she had taken to endless praying, day and night, to ease her pain. Lilith could take no comfort in prayers, but she would wear a garland of flowers in her hair at her wedding in remembrance of her friend.

* ◆ *

Helena was bursting with happiness knowing her little girl would be getting married in a chapel, as God commanded. Martha, El Hombre's wife, took over the planning as if one of her own daughters were getting married. Martín's father had always been a loyal friend to her husband, and Lilith was the victim of a war in which she lost her parents, her home, her very identity. Moreover, Lilith and El Hombre had a shared passion for Emil Ludwig's biographies. Yet the wedding itself would be simple, purely a formality. There were to be no priests and no religious service. But at least Helena could be content that it would take place in the small chapel that was at the rear of El Hombre's house.

Lilith had chosen her dress from an old catalog she found in Martín's house. It was pale blue, pinched at the waist, with a straight neckline, off the shoulder, and with three-quarter-length sleeves. The dressmaker copied the design perfectly. Lilith had told Helena she didn't want to wear a veil. She wore a white, moon-shaped fascinator with three pearls and a delicate crown of flowers. All Helena asked was that she let her straighten her hair.

Once she was dressed, Lilith felt she was in disguise. The paleness of the dress made her tanned skin luminous. The moment Martín saw her step out of the car, he ran over to kiss her.

"You're more beautiful than ever," he whispered in her ear, making her blush. "Today you are going to make me the happiest man in the world. What would I be without you?"

The whole event took no longer than thirty minutes. They stood at the front of the chapel and simply signed the marriage certificate in the presence of El Hombre's secretary, who acted as notary. Then they all knelt and prayed to the bare crucifix while Helena crossed herself.

"Now you're married in the eyes of God," she said aloud.

At the end of the ceremony, they exchanged gold and platinum rings, and when they left the chapel, Batista's children threw rice and released two white doves. Helena dabbed her eyes constantly, and when she saw the doves, she threw up her arms and begged the heavens to protect her little girl until her dying day.

The service was followed by a small reception, which took place in the Batista library, Lilith's favorite place. Lilith had been enjoying a daiquiri and speaking to Martha when she was summoned by Martín's father with a wave, and she hurried over to him.

"My dear, my daughter. You must surprise me with a grandchild as soon as possible. I don't think I'm long for this world."

When he heard him, El Hombre, who was standing next to Martha, interrupted them.

"Bernal, don't talk nonsense. You'll be around for a good while yet."

Lilith went looking for Helena and found her praying in the chapel. She knelt on the right-hand side, this time before the Virgen de la Caridad del Cobre, concentrating on her supplication.

"I need a cigarette, that'll set me right," Helena said to her, her breath ragged. "You know your mother would be so happy to see you like this."

Lilith pursed her lips. At that moment, she wasn't thinking of Beatrice, which was who Helena meant, but her real mother. Soon she too would become a mother. She felt in her bones that was the reason Ally had saved her.

Lilith saw Martín leaving the library, a frown on his face. She knew what was weighing on him: the absence of Oscar, his best friend, who was missing from the most important event in his life. They had been keeping in touch for years through letters back and forth. But after weeks of not mentioning his name, Martín told her on the eve of their wedding that a friendship beginning in childhood had been erased in the blink of an eye.

The night of their wedding, when they rode away from Kuquine in the Buick, leaving behind the small but festive party that El Hombre and Martha had organized, Martín and Lilith were both overcome by a sense of something shifting between them.

"Nothing can separate us," Martín said after a long silence. "I will always be by your side."

Lilith opened the car window and the breeze ushered in a sense of calm. They were going to live together for the rest of their lives. They would have children, and their adventures with Oscar and Ofelia would be left behind in a distant past, their lost youth. They had suddenly become adults.

They arrived at the Hotel Capri at dusk, and Lilith spotted the Hotel Nacional nearby, where she had spent her first months in Havana, after arriving on the *St. Louis*, when one of her many lives was just beginning.

At midnight they realized that they had spent an eternal hour exploring each other's bodies. They kissed as if starting a wordless dialogue. Martín felt as safe in Lilith's arms as when he flew hidden in the clouds. They wanted to stop time, and for a moment they did.

The next morning, when the sun's rays woke them up, Lilith turned to Martín in bed and whispered to him, "Our first child will be a girl, just wait and see."

She had dreamed this just before she awoke, seeing the gentle face of her German mother and her dear Opa saying goodbye to her.

"And she'll look like you," he said, pulling her closer.

Lying in bed in the hotel's honeymoon suite, with his body tethered to the ground, as Martín used to describe his time not flying, Lilith thought her husband seemed anxious.

"Do you ever think we grew up too quickly?" he asked her.

"No, Martín, it's a long time since we were kids."

"Oscar left because—"

"You knew Oscar's life was headed elsewhere. Now it's time for us to live ours. He'll show up again. One day we'll see him come home."

They slept naked in each other's arms.

· ◆ ·

At dusk on New Year's Eve, a car was to take them to the Tropicana cabaret club, where they would usher in the year 1957. It was part of the honeymoon that Martha and El Hombre had given them as a wedding present. Martín hoped the new year would restore calm to the island. They went down to the hotel lobby and, while waiting for the chauffeur, saw a brand-new, cream-colored Cadillac Eldorado convertible pull into the driveway. Inside it, Martín recognized señor and señora Fox, the owners of the Tropicana. As they walked up the steps into the hotel, Martín approached señora Fox, wishing her a happy new year.

"You're here, and we're going to the Tropicana," Martín said to her.

Martín and Lilith had met the cabaret owners when they had accompanied the president and his wife to a charity dinner held at the club.

"Well, Martín," señor Fox said, "we came to the Capri to see the new show that has just opened . . ."

"He might be here, but he never stops thinking about what's going on back there," señora Fox interrupted him.

"Nothing will ever outshine our cabaret under the stars," her husband went on in his gruff voice. "This is all the rage now, but you know, Martín, fashions come, they make a bit of noise, then they're gone and forgotten."

Lilith and Martín arrived at the Tropicana around 8 p.m. and found their seats at the table that had been reserved for them near the bar. They were to eat dinner before the show began. In one corner of the stage, someone was arranging the fireworks to go off at midnight. Martín was surprised to see that several tables around them were still empty. Lilith was captivated by the lush vegetation. A cabaret show under the shade of trees! A man at the bar was watching them impatiently.

Just as Martín was about to signal for a waiter to take their order, he was blinded by an explosion a few meters away, the table and the ground shaking. At first, he thought it was an accident, that one of the fireworks had gone off by mistake, but then somebody shouted, "Down with Batista!" He pulled Lilith under the table.

"Stay quiet," he said in her ear, his voice choking.

They could hear a girl whimpering. Curled up in Martín's arms, Lilith opened her eyes and saw a young girl passed out, in front of the bar, her arm torn to shreds. Two waiters picked her up.

"Let us through!" someone shouted.

Nearby, another couple had also thrown themselves down on the cold tile floor. Martín asked them if they were okay, and the man nodded. The woman was trembling.

Lilith coughed from all the dust and smoke. In the midst of the cries and sobs, a loud voice cried out: "Down with Batista! *Viva* the twenty-sixth of July!"

Among the crush of people at the exit, Martín saw their chauffeur, desperately trying to find them. He waved his arms, and the man ran toward them.

Lilith had remained calm on the ground until Martín helped her to her feet. Her pink taffeta dress was creased and stained, and Lilith began to nervously brush it off. She didn't want Martín to see her shaken, but she was.

"We'd better leave," the chauffeur said, out of breath. "The car's right out front. A waiter told me he thought the girl was going to drop the bomb in the bar, but it went off in her hands. People are going out of their minds."

As they made their way through the chaos, Martín looked Lilith in the eye and spoke to her with the conviction of a man defeated.

"This country is going down in flames."

17

A Year and a Half Later
Havana, June 1958

Señora Helena has died," said a voice on the telephone.

Lilith had nothing to say in response. She felt sadness and guilt in equal measure. She should make calls now, share the news, the grief. But Helena had no family. Lilith only knew of a former husband, who one day had boarded a boat in search of his fortune, and ended up in another country, perhaps even with a new wife too. There was nobody to tell. The news would end with her and Martín. Should she go to the sanatorium? She couldn't travel in her present condition, with the nausea, vomiting, and sweats that prevented her setting foot outside. A journey that would take all night could put her at risk.

"I'm very sorry, señora Bernal," said a sweet-tempered nurse named Rosa, who had been caring for Helena for the last four months. "There is no suffering in God's kingdom."

Rather than consoling her, the trite phrase left Lilith at a loss. Helena was never coming back. Helena had once told Lilith that from the time of her birth, her mother had taught her to care for others. Firstly, the old people at home; then, her sick father. She had never had to look after her mother because she had been struck down by a bolt of lightning as she was bringing in the laundry from a metal washing line during a storm. Later, Helena cared for her husband, and when he walked out, she began to care for strangers. But Helena was no more, that was a fact.

As Nurse Rosa continued talking, Lilith didn't shed a single tear. She imagined a smiling Helena finally at peace, after a lifetime of caring for others, free of the cough that had slowly devoured her, leaving her doubled over, stealing her voice.

Nurse Rosa collected herself. "Señora Helena left everything in order."

Lilith listened patiently. Helena had not wanted any funeral rites. She had already said goodbye to Lilith, and there was no one else. They were to wash her with Castile soap, wrap her in a white sheet, mist her with violet water, and lay her in what would be her final resting place, the little family vault in Cienfuegos cemetery. That had been her wish, and her savings would be dedicated to a modest burial. Helena hadn't wanted Lilith to be burdened by her death.

Lilith tried to remember all the signs of Helena's poor health that had made it necessary for the old woman to go to the sanatorium. One night, Helena had woken up with a start. She opened Lilith's bedroom door, not bothering to knock, and stood in the doorway like a ghost, slowly coming to her senses.

"Has something happened? Are you unwell?" Lilith asked, going over to the old woman.

"I haven't got long left."

"Don't be silly. What you need to do is stop smoking."

Helena had put up with the cough for so long now, she no longer feared it. "Let God do His will," she said over and over, accustomed to the pain.

When the cough became so prevalent it was almost her way of breathing, Helena began to neglect the house. She walked around in circles in the yard, avoided going upstairs, left pans of boiling water on the stove, forgot what she was cooking. The water boiled dry, and she would fill the pans again, the steam covering the walls like tears.

One morning, when Lilith went down for her cup of coffee, she found Helena in the kitchen with a plump woman with startled eyes and tangled red hair. Helena was shouting and gesticulating wildly.

When she saw Lilith looking puzzled in the doorway, Helena felt uncomfortable. She had wanted to train the new maid before Lilith came down for breakfast.

"Don't worry, she's not deaf or dumb. But she doesn't speak Spanish. Someone recommended her because she's Polish like you."

"Helena, you know I'm not Polish."

Lilith went over to the woman, reached out to shake her hand, and spoke to her in German. Helena assumed they were introducing themselves. The woman still had her handbag under her arm.

"Listen, while I'm here, you're only allowed to speak Spanish," Helena said to both of them. "I know how to make us understand each other. The day I die you can speak to her in any language you like."

After a pause, Helena whispered into Lilith's ear: "She says she doesn't speak Spanish, but in this life I don't trust anyone anymore. Trust has to be earned. Look how she's holding on to her bag; she won't let go of it, as if we might rob her."

The woman wasn't Polish, or German, but rather from a small border village with houses made from mud bricks of many different colors. The village had once been part of Hungary and later Germany, and then had completely disappeared from the map after the war. The woman preferred not to talk about what happened during the war, what little of it she hadn't forgotten or buried in her head like a terrible nightmare, she told Lilith in a rudimentary German mixed with Yiddish and Hungarian. Thanks to bombs that didn't kill her, and to the Swedish Red Cross, she had ended up on a boat heading nowhere in particular, she said. She had nobody left in the world, nowhere to go home to, and although her papers identified her as German, she in fact wasn't. The boat that took her out of Europe was a fishing vessel, and she went from port to port, cooking and cleaning the hold. After many months, she'd had quite enough of the constant seasickness and came ashore at the next port of call, not out of any particular interest in the country, but because she had been fascinated by the ancient, eaten-away cliffs protecting the port, making her feel she was entering Old Constantinople. As soon as she set foot in Havana, people had been kind to her, but she never imagined it would be her German, a language she detested, that would eventually open doors for her.

A woman from the new Hebrew Community on Calle Línea who had offered shelter to the refugee had approached Helena in old Ramón's store, asking her if it was true, she worked for a German. She told her she had a good cook, with strong arms, for whatever housework they might require, but that the woman had a slight problem: she only spoke German. She actually knew the odd word in Spanish, as well as Hungarian, Czech, and Yiddish, but that wouldn't get her anywhere.

The woman's name was Hilde.

"If her name begins with H, that's a good sign," Helena said, taking the stranger by the arm.

Helena led her home without asking a single question, and the woman from the Hebrew Community heaved a sigh of relief as she watched them leave.

From that morning, Hilde dedicated herself to the house with a fury that disconcerted Helena. A task that might take Helena a full day, Hilde would finish in under an hour. Where did this woman, who never took a break, find all her energy, Helena asked herself? She'd heard in Ramón's that Hilde had survived torture, forced labor, and hellish hunger in the concentration camps. The one thing Helena didn't like about Hilde was having to share a room with her, but she eventually got used to it; the woman collapsed exhausted in the evening and got up before Helena even opened her eyes. Lilith had offered Helena her old bedroom, but she had refused, saying it would be needed as a nursery before too long.

Helena couldn't bring herself to try even a mouthful of the meals Hilde prepared, but seeing that Martín and Lilith didn't complain, she let Hilde make theirs, assuming that the way she seasoned them was more in tune with a European palate. As far as Helena was concerned, Martín—although Cuban by birth—was from another country too, since he was always flying somewhere. Hilde always seasoned meat, cutting it into large chunks that were either boiled or roasted until they resembled lumps of coal. Helena couldn't understand how everyone around the table ate everything Hilde served them without batting an eye.

"We need to watch the new girl," she kept saying to Lilith in those early days. "Can you believe she doesn't even let go of her handbag when she sleeps? And do you know why she always wears long sleeves? It's to hide some numbers she has tattooed on her arm. I saw when she came out of the bathroom."

With the arrival of the new resident, the television was always switched on. They had bought it when *El derecho de nacer* became popular, and Helena would listen to the program, never looking at the images, maintaining that the light from the green bulb could make you blind. Helena didn't care that Hilde listened to soap operas while she worked, because it meant "the Polish girl," as she still called her, would learn Spanish.

Since Hilde took control of the house, Helena was like her ghost, watching her, until her strength gave way and she flopped down onto the wicker rocking chair on the terrace. And it was in that manner that Helena gradually wasted away, until she became nothing but skin and bone. Her face retained its peaceful expression, giving the sensation that the torso, arms, and legs were an external burden that didn't really belong to her. She still had a penetrating gaze, despite the fact that her eye sockets had taken on a yellowish hue. Her lips had turned dark purple.

On the day of Lilith and Martín's wedding, El Hombre himself had noticed Helena's persistent cough, and recommended the sanatorium to her. He instructed his secretary to make the necessary telephone calls to secure a bed with the best view, for "the good Helena" as he called her, perhaps because she was from peasant stock like him.

When she arrived at Topes de Collantes Sanatorium, Helena felt she had come home. The hospital was the pride of the area, and Helena felt eternally grateful for what El Hombre had done, not just for her, but every Cuban with withered lungs.

Helena had supported El Hombre since the Sergeants' Revolt, when Batista had triumphed in a battle against a group of army officers who had set up headquarters in the Hotel Nacional back in the 1930s. It was then that Batista, who would go on to become the most powerful man in the country, began to construct his legend, gaining as many supporters as he did adversaries. To Helena, he would always be the "pretty mulatto," no matter how old he was. Her devotion and loyalty intrigued Lilith; to her, Batista was an astute, well-read politician, as well as a second father to Martín.

"If the pretty mulatto tells us we're going in the right direction, we have to believe him," Helena told her one day. "The filthy rich all envy him, because he came from the people, rose from soldier to sergeant, and from there to colonel. They say it all happened quickly, but it took years of hard work and dedication. We country folk support and love him because he came from the village. He's like us. And he made it on his own, without connections and without family money."

"Don't mess with my presidente," she would insist whenever anyone dared to argue that he had acquired riches, abused his power, that he was a bloodthirsty dictator, that his police officers tortured members of the Student Revolutionary Directorate, that it was his fault the Jewish refugees hadn't been able to disembark from the *St. Louis*.

"Believe me, my girl, the fact that those people who came here on that cursed ship with you were sent back home had nothing to do with him," Helena had said vehemently. "No, I won't let that be said. The only one guilty of that disgrace, something we'll now have to live with for centuries, is, was, and always will be the shameless cretin Laredo Brú and the Americans. Do you think Roosevelt wanted more Jews in Cuba and the United States? No way, he washed his hands of them like Pontius Pilate, and we're left burdened with the blame. Look how many Jews were welcomed here. If you think about it, Batista was the one who took charge of things and went after that godforsaken Nazi spy who was going around Havana doing the dirty on his own people. And he sent him to his death, like he deserved."

On lazy Sundays, with Martín up in the sky, flying over the island from east to west on presidential assignments that made Lilith uneasy, she had more time to spend with Helena. The old housekeeper regaled her with stories from Cuba's past, and to Lilith, the attacks, counterattacks, martyrs, and saints that filled them seemed like the stuff of legend. At sunset they would collapse exhausted onto their beds. By dawn they were up again, coffee cup in hand, counting the hours until Martín returned safe and sound, Helena crossing herself in front of the virgins and saints in the kitchen.

It had been easy to convince Helena to go to the sanatorium. She had kept a picture postcard of it from when it was opened, as if she knew she would end her days there. It was the masterpiece, she said, of the man she most admired in the universe, and if in the end she had to die, there could be nothing better than to do so near the place where she was born and where her parents were buried.

As Helena finally packed her meager belongings into a leather suitcase, Lilith saw for the first time a photograph of Helena's parents and husband, to whom she had always remained faithful.

"Marriage is for life, it doesn't matter what happens along the way," Helena told Lilith as she was leaving the house, glancing back inside as a kind of farewell. "Look after the baby that's on its way."

A chill went down Lilith's spine and she brought her hands up to her belly. She knew she might be pregnant, but hadn't wanted to tell anyone, not even Martín, until Doctor Silva confirmed the news.

"It will be a big, beautiful girl," Helena said, walking with Lilith to the Buick, where the driver was waiting with the door open.

They embraced. Helena slumped down into the back seat of the car. As the car pulled away, Lilith watched the old woman disappear into the distance, never once looking back.

· ◆ ·

Without Helena, the house in Vedado seemed to grow bigger by the day, its corners filling with ghosts that Lilith did her best to ignore. It rained a lot, and Hilde kept the house shut up, as Helena had instructed her. Lilith suddenly felt disoriented. Listening to Hilde speaking in German in the semidark house, she wasn't sure whether she was still in Havana or back in Berlin. As the days went on, the nausea eased, as Doctor Silva had assured her it would when he confirmed the pregnancy. He also predicted that the baby would be born at the end of the year.

"This cheeky little scamp has chosen quite a date," the doctor said, smiling. "He's going to love parties."

It was around then that Lilith and Martín received a letter from Oscar, as if he had never disappeared. He sent it from New York, telling them he had become a lawyer. His parents had left Havana, tired of the explosions and attacks, and fearful of the bloodbath that was on the way, he wrote, as though his old friends had also run away and were safe.

Oscar predicted it was too late for the elections Batista had announced for November. You mustn't mess with democracy, he said, claiming the "military uprising" wouldn't last another year. The Americans no longer wanted anything to do with him. There was a new El Hombre now: Fidel Castro. In subsequent letters, Oscar explained to her, knowing Martín was too pigheaded to see it, that the future was now in the hands of the 26th of July Movement; Batista's days were numbered; and Oscar's parents, like many other Cuban families living in New York, were collaborating with Castro's Sierra Maestra rebels. And not only the Cubans, he added, many Americans had also opened their checkbooks for the rebels.

Lilith didn't dare tell these things to Martín. But she did suggest that they consider moving to New York, asking him if he wasn't tired of living in a perpetual summer.

"There is nothing quite like the change of seasons . . ."

Martín looked at her in exasperation. "How can I leave my family, and our president? They need us here. But I think you should have this, just in case."

He handed her a little revolver with a wooden butt and silver barrel. She reached for it but was unsure how to hold it. Martín explained how the safety worked and how to load the bullets, warning her it should be kept unloaded at all times. Then they went up to the bedroom and Martín put the revolver away in the top drawer of the nightstand, next to the gray box where the chain and crucifix were cocooned.

Lilith knew in that moment that Oscar was right. Life would never go back to how it once was. One day, perhaps not too far in the future, she would wake up on an island that would once again be unknown to her. Oscar's final letter, at the start of the summer, scared her. "I'm thinking about coming back to Havana. I want to be part of the revolution," he said.

This was something else Lilith kept from Martín, who since their wedding had spent more time up in the clouds than on the ground. He didn't need to know that he and his former best friend had chosen opposite sides in the looming battle for the future of Cuba. But she did finally tell him, without preamble, that she was pregnant.

"The baby will be born at the start of next year."

They clung to each other with their eyes tightly closed, as they each tried to imagine the future.

18

Seven Months Later
Havana, January 1959

As Doctor Silva had predicted, Nadine decided to arrive on the last day of the year. On December 31, 1958, Lilith woke up in wet sheets. Her water had broken, and she was shocked not to have felt any pain. She called the doctor, who instructed her to take a hot bath, then walk around, stay on her feet, and avoid eating any solids. He told her he would be there in the evening. Lilith had no idea how she was going to stay calm when Martín was a bundle of nerves, muttering phrases she couldn't understand and making mathematical calculations as if the birth were going to take place in the clouds. But Hilde asked Martín to leave them alone and took charge of walking Lilith up and down the stairs, slowly, taking care with each step.

"This will help you dilate," she said.

Lilith didn't dare ask the woman if she too was a mother. If she was, she must have lost her children, and she didn't want to reopen that wound. Either way, Hilde behaved like an expert, as if she had given birth not once but several times.

The doctor arrived at around seven in the evening, examined Lilith, and announced there were still several hours to wait.

"From what I can see, this child doesn't want to be born this year," he said, going to the kitchen to have supper with Martín.

Martín had his head down, as if guarding a secret.

"How's El Hombre?" the doctor asked but didn't get an answer.

A few minutes later, Martín stood up and asked: "What is your family planning to do?"

The doctor realized Martín had asked him the question because he hadn't decided for his own family.

"Look, Martín, we have to get out of here. This New Year's Eve there's nothing for us to celebrate. You, at least, are going to be a father. My wife and I have already decided we're going north."

As the hands of the clock on the wall neared midnight, Lilith experienced her final contractions, pushing with her last vestiges of strength, her eyes bloodshot and biting her lips to stop herself shouting. They suddenly felt the roof shudder. An airplane flew over so low that Martín feared it would crash into their neighborhood seconds before his daughter was born.

Martín was filled with foreboding. Everyone was concentrating on the birth, as Lilith was losing blood. Hilde changed the sheets around her so that when the baby was born, it wouldn't be intimidated by so much red. From the bedroom window, Martín looked up at the sky.

"A clear night," he said softly, and felt an overwhelming urge to cry.

Martín went up to the office when he heard the telephone ring. The calls that followed left him even more uneasy, fighting with his own doubts. He knew then that they should have taken a plane much earlier, traveled north, and had the baby in a hospital in Daytona Beach. Even being born in midflight would have been better than the baby opening its eyes on an island with no future. That way his child would have belonged to the clouds, like him. But he couldn't betray El Hombre, to whom he owed his whole career. He couldn't leave him, like a coward. El Hombre had instructed that two airplanes be readied at Camp Columbia, assuming Martín would pilot one of them. But Martín had to say no. There was a pause, and El Hombre sent him his blessings from the far end of the phone. Martín cried. He was afraid it was too late now. He was going to be alone on the island, surrounded by savages.

His father was with Batista in Ciudad Militar. He was ready to go, to leave the chaos behind. He said he would reunite with his son in Florida. But when he spoke to his father on the telephone, Martín thought he heard a note of uncertainty.

The baby's cries brought him back to earth, and he ran to the bedroom. He knew that when he opened the door, he would be in a different dimension, another atmosphere, like when a plane climbs through clouds and gains altitude, leveling off and stabilizing so that no wind can bring it down. Only then would he be able to breathe in peace. Trembling, he waited in the doorway, holding the handle, fixing his expression so he would be smiling the first time his child saw his face. He hesitated a moment before going in. He didn't want the newborn to see him afraid. At the door separating him from his child stood a terrified man.

"Happy New Year, Daddy," the doctor said, opening the door, bag in hand ready to leave.

The doctor patted Martín on the back.

"Don't waste any time, get out of here," he said softly.

The bed had been made up with clean sheets. The soft glow from the floor lamp in a corner of the room lit up Lilith's face. She was smiling, with her hair brushed and a slick of lipstick on her lips. The baby was wrapped in a soft yellow knitted blanket.

"Aren't you going to give Nadine a kiss?" Lilith said, her voice firm and slow.

As she and Helena had predicted, it was a little girl. Hilde seemed even more exhausted than Lilith. She was standing at the foot of the bed, watching for Martín's reaction. She quietly gathered up the bloodied sheets thrown in a corner and left the room.

Martín sat on one side of the bed and for a fleeting moment felt happy. Next to him was everything he loved the most. Enthralled, he stroked the baby's face, kissed Lilith, and lay down with them. Gazing up into the darkened ceiling, the room appeared enormous. It was as if he could see them from above, as if they were an altarpiece.

"The three of us are always going to be together," Martín said with his eyes now on the little girl. "Nobody and nothing can separate us."

There was no sound of the traditional New Year celebrations in the neighborhood. Instead an eerie calm reigned. A new year was dawning in a country that was sinking, in which they were likely condemned to drown.

Lilith clung to the baby as if higher forces were trying to snatch her away. She protected her, not only with her arms and her body, but also with her gaze. When she breastfed her, she felt as if pain had never before been so pleasurable. Her body was mutilated, she thought, but at the same time the sense of shelter gave her peace. She asked herself who was protecting whom, thinking that this tiny jumble of flesh, flushed pink, hairless, and with eyes as bright as lights, had come to save her. She had had a child. Wasn't it for this very reason that her real mother, Ally, had saved her?

She felt her eyelids growing heavy. She had Martín by her side, and between them slept the baby that united them. With the feeling that they were now inseparable, she let sleep overcome her, like falling into a dark abyss, free of either dreams or nightmares. Later, she heard Martín's voice. He was sitting in the armchair with Nadine. He was awestruck; she clasped one of her father's fingers, as if she didn't want to let him go.

"One day we'll fly together, just you and me, because your mommy's scared of heights. Not you though, because I'll show you the clouds from when you're young. High up there, everything is ours, everything's tiny. And we'll travel to far-off places, far from the noise and the dirt. Just you and me."

Martín saw Lilith was awake and smiled at her.

"She's beautiful," he said.

Lilith prayed for time to stand still, for the windows and doors to remain shut. She didn't want to know anything about the outside world, or about the new year that had just begun. She had the strange feeling of being, for a moment, happy.

After the birth, they lived through days that felt like weeks, as they watched over the baby's sleep. Nadine clung to Lilith's breast whenever she was near, and they had to wait until she was asleep to separate them. Martín counted the little one's fingers over and over again, pored over every inch of her body, committing it all to memory: her wrinkles, her folds, her every shade of pink, her shadows, her movements.

In their Vedado house, with the windows closed and the drapes drawn shut, they lived in darkness. Outside, the sun was aggressive, and even at night the air was dense and stifling. But inside the house all was calm, a haven from the chaos outside.

"Revolutions are like tornados, they bring nothing but devastation," Hilde would say in German, peering through the gaps in the curtains. "Only the weeds are left standing."

Martín and Lilith heard Hilde like a distant murmur. They wanted to enjoy every second with Nadine. Outside there was a sea of confusion. Hilde told them the streets were full of craters from the tanks the rebels had driven into Havana. They had destroyed traffic lights and parking meters, taken over the hotels; their neighbors had left the country on one of the few remaining flights leaving the airports. Some were escaping on their yachts, leaving behind their pets, but the most terrifying thing was that the houses they abandoned, to be looked after by their domestic staff, were being ransacked by criminals who smashed down doors and windows. If it went on like this, there would be nothing left when they returned, whether that was in days or weeks, when order had been reestablished.

"I think we should show some sign of life, so they don't think the house has been abandoned," said Hilde, her memory suddenly flooded with the smell of gunpowder and burnt rubber. Her blood ran cold when she saw the broken glass of the neighbor's windows.

When Hilde opened the front door to go to Ramón's store, Lilith could hear the cheering and chants of people celebrating. She imagined the city as a huge bonfire where they were burning books, and youths were marching with red-and-black flags, the number 26 in the center, like the swastika, shouting about a new world in which the people alone held all the power. Mob rule once more, keeping time with the soldiers who marched to a new anthem.

Focused on feeding her child, Lilith tried to ignore Hilde's premonitions, although hearing them filled her with dread. She didn't admit this to Martín, who had found refuge in the little one, and she let him stay in that place until the day they heard a knock on the front door. A loud bang.

Martín opened the door. A man was standing there with señor Bernal's wheelchair. Martín looked at the wheelchair, then at the man, and the black Buick parked opposite his house, then at the wheelchair again.

"I thought I should bring you back the wheelchair," he said in a low voice.

Lilith, the baby in her arms, came down to the hall. Martín's body was blocking her view of the man. The wheelchair was broken. One wheel was twisted, the brake was missing, and the backrest was ripped. She switched on the light and stood beside Martín, to protect him from the horror.

It's time. Lilith's thoughts raced around her head, with no answers. She looked up and recognized the messenger. She had seen him before at the Kuquine estate: he was one of Batista's bodyguards, she was sure of it. He hadn't come to take her husband away. Perhaps El Hombre, the real one, the powerful one, had sent him to save them. She smiled, to give Martín hope, but he had understood the message. His father was in trouble. He hadn't left on the airplane with Batista.

"He changed his mind at the last minute. Nobody had a chance to convince him to go."

Martín and Lilith stood in silence. Nadine started to wriggle, as if sensing her parents' tension.

"I couldn't leave either," the messenger went on. "How could I abandon my family? We are many, and they all depend on me. Señor Bernal had time to ask me to come and warn you, but I was scared they would come for me too. I waited for things to calm down a bit, and I've only just dared bring you the wheelchair. This is going to end very badly. They've started executing people."

The man turned and left, without saying goodbye. Martín didn't have time to ask anything, or even to thank him.

The following morning, they took Martín.

Lilith and Martín had been awake throughout the night. They left the wheelchair in the hall, under the window onto the street, as a reminder. Martín spent hours mulling over possible ways out; ones that he could have taken, ones he'd ignored, ones he should now be trying to find. He hadn't said goodbye to his father. They hadn't come up with any plan to survive the possible downfall of Batista's government. Collapse and flight were possibilities they had never even considered. Batista had been not only the country's strongman, but also his father's friend for as long as Martín could remember. How could someone with all the power in the world become defenseless overnight? They knew the rebel forces were advancing, but the army had most of the island under control. Batista had said during a trip to Daytona that the Americans supported the rebels, were sending them money and weapons as ransom in exchange for liberating U.S. citizens taken prisoner by the rebels. But run away? The option hadn't even entered Martín's head.

When the messenger had left, Martín was overcome by the feeling he would never see his father again, and that he had never given him a final embrace. With his daughter in his arms, he roamed the house. He went up and down the stairs, stood in the office, went to the kitchen, passing the time until she was due to be fed. Then he laid her on Lilith's breast, and stretched out beside her, his eyes open, trying to make sense of the loss. When the baby was asleep, he took her in his arms again and patrolled his fortress. The cycle was repeated time and again. Every time he put the little one down, he said goodbye with a kiss, until they knocked at the door again. This time, Martín had known it was coming.

Hilde opened the door to four bearded, long-haired men dressed in olive green, each wearing a red-and-black 26th of July Movement armband on their right arms. They began to talk, and Hilde smiled, as if she could understand them. The only thing she could make out was "Bernal." Her heart accelerated so fast it left her breathless, but she kept the frozen smile fixed on her face, hiding her fear. She had been trained.

Martín came downstairs, freshly shaven. He was wearing a blue checked shirt; loose-fitting, dark trousers; and black, polished shoes. He patted Hilde on the back, trying to calm her.

"We thought you'd run away like a coward, just like your boss," one of the soldiers said, apparently the one in charge.

Martín sensed Lilith and the baby behind him. He turned and hugged them.

"You have to leave. Go with Hilde, anywhere," he whispered to her.

Lilith eyed the four soldiers accusingly, waiting for an explanation.

"The trial will be held in Santiago de Cuba, señora," the soldier went on. "These pilots have to pay for the bombs they dropped on us in the Sierra."

When they left, taking her husband with them, Lilith closed the door. Nadine was asleep in her arms. Hilde began to weep.

Lilith was focused. She turned to Hilde. "I need you to look after the baby from now on. At some point, I'll have to go to Santiago, and I don't know how many days I'll be away."

After having been cut off from the revolutionary chaos for several days, Lilith began watching the news again. It showed the impassioned people singing and chanting slogans, and the new leader, bearded and wearing the same olive-green uniform he had been wearing when he arrived in the capital from the Sierra Maestra at the head of a column of tanks. He appeared to be forever haranguing the masses, sowing hostility between different groups. Suddenly, she had once again become the "other." Those who weren't with him, out in the plazas, those who didn't belong to the new class, the only class, were all enemies. During one of his endless speeches to a sweaty and servile crowd, a white dove had settled on the shoulder of the new El Hombre, the one who many were beginning to adore with an almost religious devotion. Churches were becoming suspect. Priests and nuns were being expelled, accused of being enemies of the fatherland. The synagogues were taken over as well. Religion was declared the opium of the people, as the leader endlessly repeated in his daily speeches. Only one God ruled on the island, and that God wore olive-green fatigues.

The day after Martín was taken, Lilith received notice of señor Bernal's death. She had to delay her journey to Santiago to organize the funeral. It was then that she received a phone call from Oscar. He promised he would go with her to Santiago de Cuba.

· ◆ ·

Oscar had arrived with his parents in Havana on January 2. His father had been given a diplomatic position in the United States, and was preparing to travel there with Fidel, he told her when he called a few days after Nadine's birth. He had no interest in speaking to Martín.

"I thought you had all gone to Santo Domingo with Batista," Oscar then said coldly.

"We couldn't leave, I was in labor," Lilith stammered.

"And the baby?"

"Here, with me. Her name is Nadine."

The conversation was stilted, as if they were strangers. The distance was real.

She didn't hear from Oscar again until the day after Martín was taken to jail.

"Martín has been taken to jail, and his father is dead," Lilith said, trying not to weep. Oscar could hear the baby crying. "They killed him."

Now, together, in Colón cemetery, they stopped at the Bernal vault. A devastated Lilith, with Nadine in her arms, leaned against Oscar's shoulder.

The sun was glinting off the marble of the vault, dazzling her. Lilith laid a bunch of withered yellow roses on the family mausoleum. They were the only flowers available to buy at the entrance, roses nobody else had wanted. When Castro's rebels arrived in Havana, even the street sellers had disappeared, and with them the flowers.

Executions by firing squad had become commonplace. Hundreds were thought to have been riddled with bullets in La Cabaña. The new government, which had taken power by force, with public support, chose to broadcast summary trials on television, and even executions.

Martín's father was shot after a summary trial. He had been detained on New Year's Eve, in Ciudad Militar. He could have left in the same airplane as Batista, trusting that his son and the grandchild about to be born would follow in another airplane. But señor Bernal changed his mind at the foot of the steps. Once the planes had taken off, he asked who would take him home. It was the first of January of a year that never really began for him.

"Where is your son?" he was asked by a colonel who had been in the Isla de Pinos prison serving a sentence for collaborating with the rebel soldiers.

Señor Bernal gave no answer. The man thought Martín, El Hombre's trusted pilot, was flying one of the planes the president and his closest allies had escaped in.

The old man heard him making telephone calls, talking with his superiors. He knew they had opened the prisons, and that prisoners had left their cells, filling the streets with convicts. Camp Columbia in Ciudad Militar was now controlled by the rebels in olive green, and some who still wore the uniform of the old power they had turned their back on.

"So your son abandoned you," said one of the new soldiers.

They lifted señor Bernal from his wheelchair and threw him in the back of an army jeep. He didn't complain, but grasped the gold crucifix hanging from his neck, and began to pray aloud.

"Who are you praying to? The God of the rich?" barked a rebel, the musty smell of life in the Sierra still on him.

Señor Bernal was transferred to a fortress on the outskirts of

Havana. There they put him in a windowless cell with a stone bed. *A dreary journey toward the bitter end*, he thought.

Oscar had made the arrangements for señor Bernal's body to be collected and organized the burial. He and Lilith were the only mourners. The casket was closed, so she couldn't say goodbye, or see him one last time. *Another person I never got to say goodbye to*, she thought, *another person she loved who died alone.*

Oscar gently shook Lilith to try and rouse her from her daze. "I can help you get out of the country."

"I'm not leaving without Martín. I'm all he has left."

"Let me see what I can do."

On the way home, Oscar couldn't bring himself to look at Nadine, whom Lilith was breastfeeding every half hour to keep her calm. Only six weeks old, she was a strong baby, chubby, hairless, and with big eyes that shone bright blue in the light.

"She looks more like her grandmother every day," Lilith told him. "With her I have recovered my mother's face."

Oscar only smiled. "Perhaps she'll grow up to be a poet, like her grandmother."

When she returned home from the burial, a letter from Martín was waiting for her.

Santiago de Cuba
February 15, 1959

My dear Lilith,

I haven't heard any news about Dad, but I'm not very hopeful, though I would like to be. Everyone who was on Batista's side in some way or another will be sentenced. To how many years? I don't know. I don't want to worry you, nor do I want my daughter to grow up surrounded by fear, ashamed of her father locked up for being a traitor. All I ever wanted to do was fly. Now I must pay for that.

Before I go to sleep, I see Nadine growing by the minute. Last night I saw her walk, say her first words. Perhaps today when I go to sleep, she'll be a teenager. Soon I'll see her at university, married, with children, happy. See? It's easy to be happy. We once were.

Ever since you arrived on the island, my life began to have meaning. What would I have been without you, my Lilith? Help me now to make sure Nadine grows up to be a happy little girl. I can't make that dream come true. You can.

Promise me our daughter will grow up far from this approaching inferno. Promise me she will soon be safe. It's the only way I can bear the years of my sentence.

All my love for you. Every night I sleep with you both in my arms.

Martín

The handwriting was shaky. The paper creased. There were dark stains. Lilith read Martín's letter so often she learned it by heart. She was going to write back to him with the news of his father's death but thought it better to close her eyes and wait for the judge to pass sentence. They might have the good fortune of a compassionate prosecutor, who understood they were simply aviators, that Martín was not a fighter pilot or soldier.

The day she flew to Santiago, Lilith didn't say goodbye to her daughter. She left her in her crib. When Nadine woke up, it would be Hilde's arms that picked her up. When the plane took off, she began to sweat. She closed her eyes and saw how the world was collapsing under her, yet again. She was traveling at dusk now, she, who had always been a night traveler. *By night, we're all the same color,* she said to herself.

19

As Lilith opened the shutters on the balcony of the Hotel Casa Granda, the shouts from the street spilled into the room: "Lackeys!" "Murderers!" "Shoot them all!" A group of youths had gathered in the park opposite the Santiago cathedral and were chanting revolutionary slogans Lilith could only half understand. She felt as if she had suddenly forgotten her Spanish. She hung her head, eyes closed, and the darkness made her retch. The air around her felt heavy and dense. When she opened her eyes, the sidewalk seemed far away, infinite, and the idea occurred to her to throw herself into the abyss. It was bottomless, she would fall into eternity.

From the moment they had taken Martín, the days had become shorter for Lilith. She sensed the hours ticking away as she fed her daughter, burped her, cleaned her. When she arrived at the hotel, she changed and immediately went back downstairs, heading for the court-house. In the lobby, she muted all her gestures so that her mannerisms were no longer like those of the people of the island. One of the hotel staff spoke to her in English.

"Can I help you, señorita?"

"I'm going to the courthouse," Lilith replied, in English.

Overnight, she had become a foreigner again. The man began to give her directions, but then she spotted a group of women dressed in black. *Mothers and wives of the pilots*, she thought. Lilith was wearing a pink gabardine coat. She turned away from the man and joined the group of women. Together they walked through a crowd of people carrying red-and-black flags. As the women approached, the square fell silent, and the protestors moved aside to let them through. A gust of wind revealed the sky-blue dress Lilith had on under her gabardine coat, sharply contrasting with the other women's all-black attire.

Solemnly, they climbed the steps of the gray building that bore the Cuban coat of arms over its entrance. Lilith let herself be swept along with the women's grief. Some wept, as if they already knew the sentence the pilots would be given. An old woman took Lilith's arm, causing her to slow her pace.

"At my age, I can't cope with all this upheaval," the woman said, looking straight ahead. "I've just turned seventy-five, and these revolutionaries believe now they can tell me how to think, how to live. And who have you got here? Your husband?"

"I'm señora Bernal."

"Ah, well your husband's definitely in for a hard time."

Lilith stiffened, offended, and the old woman noticed.

"I mean they all are, not just your husband. The problem is that Martín Bernal was El Hombre's friend too. You're not from here. Are you American? The best thing for you would be to go back to your country."

"I'm not going anywhere without Martín."

"I understand, it's the same for me. My three daughters left with their husbands, taking all my grandchildren with them. I'm here with my only son, waiting to hear his sentence. My husband and parents are buried in Colón cemetery, so I can't leave. If anyone should leave, it's him and his cronies."

She spat out the "him" with contempt and a trace of disgust. The old woman took great care over every footstep, as if frightened she might fall and tumble down the stairs.

Inside the courtroom, an improvised meeting room with all the windows closed, the judges were already sitting at a rectangular table with a single silver microphone in front. The first five rows of wooden benches were reserved for the accused. An official indicated to the women that they should sit to one side, opposite the press. The general public would sit behind the accused, the official explained, in an accent Lilith didn't recognize.

"Do you think they'll let us see them? *Ay, Dios mío.* Why did that boy have to become a pilot? Can you imagine if he'd been a doctor, like his father? We'd be in Miami now, far from these savages."

When they sat down, the old woman lowered the net of her little hat, which she wore at an angle and fastened with clips, partially covering her face, and spoke to Lilith once more.

"You were right to wear a bit of color. You're not a widow. Your husband will recognize you from a distance. The rest of us look like buzzards, all in black, but I am a widow, so I can't dress any other way. You can call me Carmen, nowadays being señor or señora could land you in jail. Overnight we've all become Comrades."

The old woman muttered and crossed herself.

"My name is Lilith," she said, trying to make the woman feel better, though her own hands were shaking.

The room slowly filled up. Only the benches at the front remained empty. Then everyone stood, trying to make out what was happening at the entrance.

"They're bringing them in!" someone yelled.

In the deafening roar, she heard another shout.

"Murderers!"

At four o'clock in the afternoon, the twenty pilots, fifteen gunners, and eight mechanics were brought into the courtroom. They sat down amid cries from the public calling for them to be shot. Strangely calm,

Lilith stopped listening to Carmen, who was grumbling incessantly. She muted her ears to the political outbursts and the women's weeping. When Martín came in and sat in the front row, still in the checked shirt he had been wearing the day they took him, Lilith stood and opened her gabardine. Martín recognized the sky blue.

Finally, the prosecutor opened Case 127 of 1959. After some introductory legal rhetoric, the court clerk read out the names of the accused, one by one. On his feet, Martín stared at the prosecutor, and Lilith sat down. When she heard the charge of genocide, in which the name Martín Bernal was repeatedly mentioned, Lilith felt her hands shaking. There was nothing she could do. They were already condemned, even before the hearing, just as Carmen had said. The old woman had taken a pair of long, golden needles from her bag and begun knitting, red yarn slowly emerging from her black patent leather bag.

Lilith was afraid. She smiled at Martín, and he smiled back. He lowered his eyes to Lilith's arms, as if asking after Nadine. They both closed their eyes. For a moment they felt they were alone, as if they had escaped. She let herself be taken to that place.

"Turn around, my love," she heard her husband say.

"Martín," she said, and smiled. She didn't have to turn her head to know he was beside her, like before. The noise of the engine and the propellers shook her whole body. Never had the thought of being in an airplane given her such pleasure. They were up in the middle of the clouds. How on earth had Martín persuaded her to climb into this little metal bird?

"See? That wasn't so bad, was it? Nothing's moving here. We're safe. You and I could live up here . . ." Martín left the sentence hanging, as the airplane descended.

Lilith could no longer hear Martín. The deafening roar once again came between them. The propellers stopped, and the plane headed down toward the calm waters of an ocean. Night descended outside the windows, and she felt Martín embrace her. With him beside her, she could let the dark waters swallow her up. There was no moon or stars.

Scattered clouds slowly drifted by. No horizon. The sky and the sea were one. She was struck by a sense of peace she had not experienced since Nadine was born.

Martín Bernal's name was shouted again by the public. Lilith didn't want to wake up, she wanted to stay by his side. If she opened her eyes, she'd be back in that hell.

She was roused by a sobbing witness. The young woman was showing the court the burns on her arms, telling her story as if it had been learned from memory. Lilith closed her eyes to find Martín. She wanted to dream again, but she couldn't shut out the witness's anguished voice.

Batista's pilots had been accused of indiscriminately bombing the mountains where the guerrillas operated, decimating entire villages in the eastern part of the island. The attorney called for the pilots to confess, but they never did. At two o'clock in the morning, the first session was concluded. The accused were first to leave. Then the journalists. When the women in black started to file out of the courtroom, the public jeered and heckled them.

Back in her hotel room, Lilith undressed and curled up in a ball in bed, as her German mother had taught her. She was awake all night, or perhaps she slept with her eyes open, still conscious of every minute that passed. The following day she took a cold shower and dressed in the same sky-blue dress and pink gabardine coat. Oscar was waiting for her downstairs.

"I only managed to get a flight today," he said, nervously.

His briefcase was open, stuffed with papers. They walked to the courthouse together. He explained he had managed to compile Martín's flight logs for the last few months, but she wasn't listening.

At the trial, Oscar joined the team of defense attorneys. When Martín saw him, he looked over at Lilith. It was going to be another long day. Lilith watched Martín and Oscar hug. She was far away, so far she couldn't feel his presence. She saw Martín smiling at his friend, just like when they were children.

The defense lawyers were the only ones wearing white shirts, suits, and ties. The presiding judge was a rebel commander, shielded by the olive-green uniform. At one point, the prosecutor paused and, to everyone's amazement, started to read the encyclicals of Pius XII where the Pope made reference to conscience, guilt, and punishment. Then, relying on the encyclicals, the prosecutor called for the pilots to be condemned to death by firing squad.

One of the women in black started to scream.

"To hell with them all," she yelled. "To hell with the prosecutors and the lawyers. To hell with every member of this court, and to hell with Fidel Castro!"

The woman's family grabbed her and dragged her out. A man shouted, "Yes to Cuba, no to Yankees!"

In the distance, the woman's desperate sobs could still be heard. "You can't kill my husband! You'll orphan my children! Sons of bitches!"

On Sunday the court was in recess. The same on Monday. Another trial, in Havana, against one of Batista's "henchmen," had the whole country on tenterhooks. Oscar spent those two days working with the defense attorneys on a strategy Lilith suspected would get them nowhere.

Lilith took shelter in the Santiago cathedral, praying to a God that wasn't hers. She listened to prayers and masses she couldn't understand and wandered through the city assailed by a sun she kept at bay with her pink gabardine. Within its folds, the air was icy.

She lost herself in Santiago's noisy streets, and, feeling tired, entered a six-story building. The barred gate was open, and she walked hesitantly inside. She came to an inner courtyard draped with red-and-black flags, the number 26 in the center. She lifted her face to the sun, closed her eyes, and took a deep breath. Suddenly, she recovered her calm. She had escaped the noise, the crowds. A group of soldiers marched past, avoiding her. She felt invisible. She stood there for several minutes, overwhelmed by the marching men. She was damp with sweat. She lost all sense of time. She had become the island. When she opened her eyes, she realized she was in a military barracks, occupied by the new army.

There was a breath of hope in the following day's hearing. The defense lawyers had persuaded one of the prosecution witnesses, a pilot who had defected to the winning side, to give a statement in favor of the accused.

"If anyone's guilty, it's the twenty-nine pilots who fled with Batista," the witness said, hanging his head. "That's why they ran away. They're the guilty ones."

Every morning, before going to court, Lilith telephoned Havana. Hilde waited by the telephone at nine o'clock. Before the first ring had sounded, Lilith heard Hilde's voice begin rattling off her account of the day, packed with endless facts and figures. How many feedings the little girl had taken throughout the day, how many diaper changes, how many times she'd sat her in the sun, how many lukewarm baths she had given her with chamomile leaves to reduce the heat, how many drops of star anis to alleviate her colic, how many naps she had taken. She didn't once ask about Martín or when she was coming back, and this worried Lilith.

Every night over the phone, Lilith sang German lullabies to Nadine, so that she herself could get to sleep. At times she thought she would drift off when she was able to feel her daughter's soft skin against hers, and the pressure in her breasts, still full of milk. When Lilith returned home, she knew she would no longer be able to breastfeed her. She would be empty, dried up. She feared Hilde might run away with the girl on a boat, back to her home in the middle of the ocean.

On the ninth day of the trial, the prosecuting attorney ranted for five hours. Each day they wheeled out more and more prosecution witnesses: a baker, a farmworker, a mother, a crippled young woman, a man who had lost his right arm, a miner, a shopkeeper, a soldier, a sergeant, a Capuchin monk, a civil engineer, the man who composed the hymn of the 26th of July Movement. They all concurred that Batista's planes had bombed civilian populations with no rebel presence. Indictments against the accused were mounting, they were all equally guilty, individual responsibility was superseded by collective blame.

At one point, Oscar took the stand and addressed the tribunal. There was peace in his voice. His speech seemed like a prayer. "Who could prove these pilots were the attackers, and not the twenty-nine who had fled with Batista?" he asked.

"If they had committed a crime, if they had guilty consciences, all those standing before us had the chance to run away. None of them did. There is no evidence against them. Every single one of the accused must be declared innocent."

There was applause, and shouts against him. When quiet was restored, somebody shouted "To the firing squad with them!"

"It's hard losing a husband, the father of your daughter," Carmen said to Lilith, tears in her eyes. "You become a widow, and your daughter, an orphan . . . but I will lose my son."

Still, Lilith did not cry.

It had only been a few months since Martín had become a father, and scarcely two years before that, a husband. But he had always been a friend, her best friend. Losing her friend was more painful than losing her husband, Lilith wanted to tell Carmen.

It was the closing session of the hearing, and Lilith didn't want to miss a single detail. She wanted to concentrate on every single movement the prosecutors made, as they prepared to pass sentence. But Carmen distracted her, and the legal phrases were filled with rhetoric that was hard for her to understand. She might have understood better if they had spoken in German or English. It proved to her once again that she was only a visitor on this island, even though it was a place that she had once considered her own.

· ◆ ·

After two weeks of judicial proceedings, the Revolutionary Tribunal returned the verdict: not guilty. The twenty pilots, fifteen gunners, and eight mechanics, all of them declared innocent.

The verdict was delivered with so much legal verbosity it took Lilith several minutes to take it in. Oscar approached her nervously. He seemed to doubt the new government would accept the verdict. He had packed his papers away into his leather case and put a hand on Lilith's shoulder. Oscar wanted her full attention.

"I'm taking the next plane back to Havana," he said to her.

"Will they release Martín to me now?"

"No, they're being taken away again."

Lilith felt like she was going to faint.

"Where to?"

"A high-security prison."

"I can't stay in Santiago. My daughter—"

As she was talking to Oscar, the now-absolved accused were pushed and shoved out of the courtroom.

"Wait for my call in Havana," Oscar interrupted her, and left the room with the group of defense attorneys.

Waves of protest swept through the streets of Santiago. Lilith, once more on Carmen's arm, could barely cross Céspedes Park to get back to the hotel. She walked at the pace of the old lady, who was cursing repeatedly. As they passed a group of youths calling for the death penalty for the pilots, Carmen spat on the ground.

A shirtless boy holding the red-and-black flag pushed between Lilith and Carmen.

"Fucking bourgeois bitch," he shouted at the old woman, almost in her ear, stressing every syllable. She began to tremble.

The next day, Lilith left her room in the afternoon. For the first time since arriving in Santiago, she wasn't wearing the sky-blue dress and had packed it away in her suitcase. She wouldn't be needing it again. Now was the time for black. Her mourning had begun.

The waiting dragged on for days. The newspapers rallied the people to oppose the aviators' release. Fidel Castro announced on national television that the pilots were criminals working for Batista and called the officials of the first trial traitors. The rebel commander who had presided over the trial had gone from being a hero to a pariah. He flew to Havana and was later found at Camp Columbia with a bullet in his head. The women in black were sure he had been killed.

"They'll devour each other, like animals," one of them said.

Only three days after the not guilty verdict, they received a sudden notice that the trial would resume on Thursday night. The headlines in the press that day had been chilling. Lilith listened to the cries of the women in the adjoining rooms. Their pain seeped through the walls of the Hotel Casa Granda, it crossed the cold, tiled corridors, whispered through the windows, and reached as far as Céspedes Park. There, the chant continued: "The pilots of Batista's tyranny will not be freed." The people held the power, not the court. The court was the people. The people were Fidel.

The pilots refused to participate in the new mock trial. Lilith chose to stay in the park. She might go to the cathedral and kneel once more to pray for him, for her daughter, for herself, for all of them. Her husband wasn't at the trial, her sky-blue dress was packed away in the suitcase, her presence wasn't necessary. It was a trial without defense. What else would she have to listen to? There was no need for her to attend a summary trial where, contrary to law, the judge and prosecutor were one and the same. They would all be convicted of genocide. They would be declared war criminals, and their punishment would be execution by firing squad, or life imprisonment and forced labor on a small island to the south of the mainland. They would go to a prison made up of circular buildings, and in each one a hierarchy of evil would reign, like the circles of hell, far from light and reason. They should condemn them both, her and Martín. She prayed that they would both fall into the last circle, that of the night. Eyes closed, she prayed to the Virgin's deaf ears within those impenetrable walls, far removed from the torments outside, where the families of sinners gathered, to plead in vain for their salvation.

During the tribunal, as they heard the sentence, several of the women in black fainted. Lilith raised her eyes to the miraculous Virgin with unbridled hatred. Her body trembled; her hands were clammy. The cathedral was hell's waiting room; the court was the cliff's edge. She had known hell as a child, and her mother, her real mother, had saved her by sending her on a journey through the night. She had descended the circles until she fell into the ninth and final one. And at that moment she felt guilty for having brought hell closer to Martín.

She wanted to disappear into her dreams and directed one last plea to each of the lifeless saints and virgins of the cathedral. Nobody else could control her dreams, and she prayed she and Martín could go back to being those eternal children who met within the walls of St. George's School. Together they had wandered the streets of Vedado, which had become her Neverland, since *"Neverland is always more or less an island. All children, except one, grow up. Why can't you remain like this forever!"* She heard her Opa's voice, and started to weep, as one weeps for the dead.

At dusk, Lilith returned to Havana by train, protected by her pink gabardine coat, certain of her sentence, ready to descend to the fourth and final round of the ninth circle of hell. She felt she had lost control. She would arrive after midnight the next day. Oscar would have already landed in Havana. Martín would be on his way to Castillo del Príncipe, piled into the back of a truck with the other prisoners. From there, he would be taken by ferry to the tiny island with the circular buildings, where people are forgotten.

20

On an island where the only green allowed was that of the uniforms, even the old flame tree in the convent's inner courtyard had withered. That afternoon, the silence was particularly profound. Before, at least, you would hear some prayer or other, or the murmur of the branches. The heat persisted, hanging over the city, salty and viscous. Lilith defied the stifling air wearing her gabardine coat. Nadine was sweating, her cheeks flushed.

A door slammed and Nadine ran over to her mother, who was standing in the shade of one of the side galleries. The little girl looked around, making sure they were still alone, then carried on jumping and doing cartwheels in the courtyard, which looked abandoned, as if everyone, even the enclosed nuns, had run away.

"Everyone's leaving." Hilde never seemed to grow tired of repeating this.

It was harder every day to obtain a visa. Flights had been suspended. According to Hilde, the only remaining escape route from the island was through the Catholic Church, but the new government was hanging over it, like the Sword of Damocles. Hilde had come to the conclusion that her own destiny was to be found elsewhere, and she reminded Lilith she was running out of time every day.

"*You have to save our daughter,*" Lilith heard Martín's voice say, as though she didn't already know.

If only she could count on Oscar, Lilith said to herself at night, wishing her friend—not the lawyer who had defended Martín in Santiago, but the boy with whom they had played at being grown-ups at the house in Varadero—would come back and extend her a helping hand. But Oscar had achieved what Martín never could, becoming lost among the clouds.

The little plane that took off from Santiago de Cuba heading to Havana, with the three lawyers who had defended Batista's pilots onboard, never reached its destination. It was said it had been shot down by the rebels who had seized power, thirsty for vengeance, as it crossed the island toward the north. For fear of being condemned themselves, they had given up case 127 of 1959, leaving the pilots in limbo, the mother of one of the accused had declared on national television. Others celebrated the lawyers' deaths, calling them traitors and counterrevolutionaries. The more circumspect called it an accident. The weather was bad, said one broadcaster, nervously. A few months later, another little airplane, this time carrying Camilo Cienfuegos, another leader in olive green to whom the people paid homage, had also been lost in the middle of the ocean. Hilde had whispered, fearing that even the walls might be listening, that in old Ramón's store everyone said that He, the new El Hombre, had ordered his assassination, fueled by jealousy. No remains of either airplane were ever found. The passengers of one were called traitors, the other, a hero. The government mandated the island's children to throw white flowers into the sea every October, as an act of remembrance. Perhaps they thought the flowers, over time, would obscure their guilt.

Lilith had Nadine in her arms when she received the news that Martín had been executed. It was six months after he had been transferred from Havana to Pinar del Río, and from there to Isla de Pinos, and from there to hell: the five circular blocks of cement of the Model Prison. Hilde read the news in Lilith's eyes. She didn't need to be told in German to know what had happened. From that moment on, Hilde began to pack her bags and to look for a boat to rescue her from further torment.

They had taken Martín, naked and barefoot, from his solitary cell, and led him to the firing squad: a flaking wall with dark, damp stains, thick enough to absorb bullets. He came to a halt in front of his executioners and scanned the faces of all those who were about to take his life. Then his eyes were covered with a filthy blindfold, still wet from the tears of the previous man to be put to death. He could feel the cold grass beneath his feet. A cloud blocked the distant sun. *If only it would rain*, he thought. He wanted to dedicate a smile to Lilith, to Nadine, to his father. He forgot the rifles trained on him, and the anxious soldiers, whose job was to dole out death, and who took aim without really knowing why each prisoner lined up before them deserved a bullet in the chest. The order was that everyone who had been close to El Hombre, who had helped him escape with suitcases bursting with the people's money and gold bars from the country's coffers, must pay with his life. There was no need for trials or courts to sentence them. The people had the final word. The people were the executioners now.

It began to rain, and Martín raised his face. With his eyes closed, he could drift up into the clouds one last time, where he saw himself alone, shielded from the roar of his airplane's engines. He had never felt so safe. As he gained altitude, the storm intensified. The challenge was to remain stable, until he reached the infinite. Higher, a little higher, and he would be beyond the atmosphere, in a place where even the wind didn't blow. He heard the shots. It only took one bullet to bring him down. He felt an intense burning sensation in his chest, and his legs gave way. He couldn't hold himself up. He lifted his arms, filled his lungs with cold air, and let himself fall.

· ✦ ·

After Martín's death, Lilith began emptying the house. Cuba had never been the present, but only a transitional island, one more death.

One morning Hilde knocked on Lilith's bedroom door. She was holding a bag with what little she had been able to buy from Ramón's store.

"It's time, Lilith. We both know there's only one way."

Hilde's German now sounded imperative: the new government would indoctrinate the children, the men in olive green would eliminate parental rights, all children born on the island would belong to the people's government.

"And any children who don't obey will be made into Russian meat and put into cans," Hilde said, pulling a can out of the bag, with Russian writing on the label and a picture of a black cow's head. Lilith didn't understand. She thought that Hilde, with her poor Spanish, had misunderstood something she had heard at Ramón's.

According to Hilde, all exits from the country had been closed. The only hope was through the Catholic Church. The few priests and nuns who remained on the island could prepare documents for desperate families and those who ran the risk of persecution.

"Your husband was shot; they will help you." Hilde sounded confident.

Lilith still didn't understand what she was suggesting. She left the little girl in bed and opened the bedroom window. It was cloudy. The shadows made her feel at peace. She suddenly felt as if she had been there before, her belly clenched, anxious, sick, desolate. The room became the cabin of an ocean liner, adrift on the high seas, and Lilith told herself she had never left the *St. Louis*, that she hadn't been one of the twenty-eight passengers allowed to disembark in Havana. What difference was there between those who were sent back and those the island accepted? Ever since they left Hamburg, the nine hundred and thirty-seven passengers had no future.

"Your friend the nun is the only one who can help us." Hilde raised her voice, trying to convince Lilith. "You have to prove to Sister Irene that Nadine is Catholic, like her father, like her grandparents . . . Like you."

Hilde began telling her about the hundreds of children escaping Havana in Dutch airplanes without their parents, met by priests in Miami and then hopefully taken in by charitable families. Lilith once again saw herself in Ally, her mother. It was time for her to do what her mother did: to choose the impossible. Her fate had been mapped out.

"We haven't got much time. Those monsters are only allowing the children to leave because it makes the mothers look heartless, but one of these days they'll shut it down, and throw every last priest and nun out of the country. History repeats itself. Can't you see that, Lilith?"

Lilith nodded. She would accept Hilde's proposal. Her daughter was just another pawn in the game being played by the olive-green army. Martín had fallen, now it was her turn.

The night Hilde said goodbye, leaving with the same battered suitcase she had come into their lives carrying, Lilith and Nadine stood in the doorway, with the faint hope that Hilde would change her mind and stay with them in the crumbling Vedado house.

When Lilith hugged her, Hilde whispered in her ear, trying to convince her to act soon and get her daughter out of the country.

"Look at me now, alone, with no family, trying to forget. I didn't dare to give up my children, to send them far away, on their own. And I could have done so, like lots of people in my neighborhood and my family did. I thought, if we're going to suffer, it's best we suffer together. Where did that get me? I lost them forever. Today, who knows if they would be with me here or somewhere else. But no. We traveled through countries on a train, and when we arrived, when we got off, they split us up and killed them. Do you want that for Nadine?"

The first letter from Hilde arrived three months after she had left, when Lilith had already met with the nun. Hilde was spending her days making greasy stews, she said in the letter of several pages that ended with a drawing of a little boat beneath a sun and passing clouds. She said she had been through the Panama Canal, where she had posted the letter, and that she would soon get to see the Pacific Ocean. Who would have ever thought it, a woman born so far from the sea? she wrote. Lilith began to write back to Hilde, and spent all night awake.

The gold crucifix with her name on it was the only proof she needed to convince Sister Irene that the little girl was Catholic. The problem now was to find a family that would take her in. Most of the children leaving were already teenagers, or at least old enough to be in school. They knew how to speak and stick up for themselves. Nadine could walk and fire out words, but she would be the youngest child to be taken out of Cuba via the Church program. One day Sister Irene telephoned Lilith and asked her to come to see her urgently: they had found a family in Queens, New York, thanks to the archdiocese. Irma Taylor, a German-born housewife and her husband, Jordan, an electrician from New York, were prepared to take the little girl. They were both Catholics, had been married for several years, but had been unable to have children. Since Nadine was the daughter and granddaughter of German Catholics, the Taylors had decided to pay for the child's journey from Miami to New York.

Lilith wrote to Hilde that she had started speaking to Nadine in German and singing her German lullabies. Every night before bed, she read her the poem her mother had written her on her seventh birth-day. Since Hilde left, Lilith had found solace in her deceased mother's poetry. After many years without opening the envelope with the poem and the box with the crucifix hanging from a chain, she now repeated each verse in German and heard her mother's voice in them.

"By night, we're all the same color," she said aloud as she wrote.

The little girl had started to play with words, combining German and Spanish to create a dialect that fascinated Lilith. When she finished writing Hilde's letter, she folded it and put it in a drawer in the kitchen cupboard, next to the linen napkins. She had no address to send it to.

● ◆ ●

The house in Vedado, first without the Herzogs and Helena, and then without Martín, and then without Hilde, had become far too big for Lilith. She felt she and her little girl were like ants, scurrying up and down, never finding a comfortable place to settle. Lilith started taking daily trips to Ramón's store, which was still called that even though the Galician man who had set it up with the savings he brought to Cuba at the beginning of the century had gone to Miami with his family. A stranger now handed out the bread, rice, beans, and the meat that was only available once a week. Eggs disappeared, and Lilith was gradually using everything Hilde had been able to stockpile in the kitchen cupboard. She didn't need more, she told herself out loud, because she knew her daughter would be leaving soon and would make her own destiny.

In the evenings, when the sun was setting, Nadine went out to the yard and Lilith followed behind. She could hear the sounds of the family who had moved into the house where Martín was born and had lived as a child. She didn't dare look through the fence. The wooden gate that divided the two yards was shut again, locked with a chain and padlock. The castor oil plants had grown to form an impenetrable barrier.

All the neighbors on the block were strangers to her now. The people she saw in the store had a different accent, different mannerisms, and even dressed differently. They called one another Comrade. She heard it said that the title señor or señora was now simply a bourgeois relic that had to be erased from the people's vocabulary. They all seemed to have been baptized in a miraculous river, going in a señor or señora and coming out a Comrade, thanks to the revolution, an old man leaning on a silver-handled cane told her. He had always had a beard, but now he chose to shave. Having a beard had become a symbol of shame to him, he concluded in a broken voice, gesturing airily.

As the days went by, Lilith reduced her home to the kitchen. She and Nadine stopped sleeping in the room Lilith had shared with Martín and ended up in the small downstairs room that had once belonged to Helena. She began covering the mirrors with silk handkerchiefs, and the living room furniture with white sheets. As nobody was sweeping, the corners of the ceiling and teardrop lamps became veiled with spiderwebs.

Every evening after sunset, Lilith and Nadine visited Sister Irene in the convent. Lilith saw there was a fresh crack in the building's formerly solid walls. With Martín's death and Hilde's departure, Lilith felt her life becoming more and more like that of the cloistered nuns. Her thoughts often turned to Ofelia. The convent's inner courtyard became Nadine's playground. Nadine collected shiny white, gray, and black stones, dusting them off on her dress. With each visit, Sister Irene looked more haggard, as if the habits she wore had grown heavier and heavier.

"Everybody has left, but I'm still here," she said to Lilith one day. "Now even if I wanted to go, it's impossible. There are no flights to take me out of here. Nobody wants us, and little by little they'll forget us."

The two women stood side by side, faces turned up to the sky, waiting for a sign, a trailing cloud, a storm.

On Wednesday evening, the day before Nadine was to leave, the nun asked Lilith to attend mass. The hall was almost empty. An old woman was praying to a virgin on her knees, her face wet with tears and her head bowed, as if she were avoiding her prayer being overheard. A one-legged man on crutches hobbled up to one side of the altar toward the statue of an aged saint in a purple tunic surrounded by dogs. When the priest began the service, Sister Irene came over to Lilith, who was standing with Nadine asleep in her arms.

"Come on, let's go to the front. It will do us good. May I hold her?"

Lilith handed Nadine over, as if she no longer belonged to her.

At the end of the mass, they approached the altar. The little one weighed heavy in the nun's arms, leaving her out of breath.

"Nadine is leaving tomorrow," Sister Irene told the priest.

"So young?" The priest seemed confused.

"She's three years old," Lilith said anxiously, as if the priest's question could invalidate her daughter's ability to depart.

The man drew the cross in ash on each of their foreheads.

"Sometimes crying does you good," said the nun, handing the little girl back. But Lilith's eyes were dry.

The following day, Lilith dressed Nadine in a white dress with embroidered borders, fastened the chain with the crucifix around her neck, and tucked two white envelopes into her case, with no addressee or return address. In one was a sheet with Martín Bernal's initials embossed at the top. On it, meticulously and in her neatest handwriting, she had written the names of her mother, the poet Ally Keller; her Opa, Bruno Bormann, emeritus university professor; and her angel, Franz Bouhler, whom she thought might have survived the war. She also included Nadine's date of birth and the address of the apartment in Berlin where she had lived.

"Only a true angel could fly unscathed out of hell," she said out loud.

She hugged the little girl and began to speak softly to her.

"Your grandmother was a great writer. She did everything she could to save me. Sometimes you have to abandon what you love the most. Can you imagine? My mother was a very brave woman. I'm alive thanks to her, my dear Nadine. And if you had met Herr Professor. What a wise man! He taught me everything I know. Franz . . . we called Franz our angel, and thanks to him I was able to leave Berlin. They were my real family, Nadine, your family."

In the other envelope, folded in four, she slipped the poem written by her mother on the yellowing sheet of paper that had traveled with her to Cuba. Now it was her daughter's turn to travel with it.

She took the little girl to the convent, and when they reached the central courtyard, at the foot of the withered flame tree, she lifted her up.

"One day you'll understand why you're going away," Lilith said to her, in German. "One day we'll meet again."

Lilith trembled. The little girl smiled. She wriggled to indicate to her mother that she wanted to get down and ran to Sister Irene when she saw her emerge from the corridor leading to the cloister's chapel. Sister Irene hugged the girl, and when she looked up, Lilith had gone.

Back in the old house in Vedado, Lilith closed her eyes and took a deep breath. She had done the thing she dreaded the most, what was there left for her to fear? She fell asleep in the bed where she had spent the last night with her daughter. Then her nightmare began. She saw tens of thousands of children fleeing desperately, in planes, onboard ships; entire families throwing themselves onto ramshackle rafts to escape hell. She knew she herself was already condemned, there was nothing she could do. She saw her mother's face, that of her real mother, the one who had sent her away to save her, and she called on her spirit— she, who didn't believe in gods or virgins or saints or prayers—to give her the strength never to wake up. She had abandoned her daughter to save her. We give up what we love. We forget as the only means of salvation. It was her daughter's turn to be the night traveler, just as she had once been.

At dawn, with shadows looming around her, Lilith went into what was once her and Martín's bedroom, walked to the head of the bed, and let herself surrender. She squeezed her eyelids shut and looked inside herself. Her eyelids were now the walls. The room had been reduced to a labyrinth of veins and arteries. She opened the nightstand drawer and took out Martín's revolver. When they were still a family it had been a means of defense. Her hands were icy. She held the little revolver by the grip. The smell of metal, grease, and gunpowder filled her nostrils. Following Martín's instructions, she loaded the cold bullets into the chamber.

"Goodbye, Lilith."

She said goodbye to herself with the calm of somebody already dead. She hid the loaded revolver, with the safety catch off, under her pillow.

She was ready to travel by night once more.

ACT THREE

21

As a little girl, Nadine used to play at being a mother, treating her dolls with a tenderness she herself had never known. Irma and Jordan Taylor's home ran on discipline, respect, and order. She had wanted for nothing. Her parents had registered her in the best school in their neighborhood in New York; at Christmas she was given the toys she had asked for, and even a pair of skates and a bicycle; they let her watch her favorite television show and took her to the cinema on Sundays. Yet she always felt like a guest, someone passing through, the beneficiary of her parents' act of charity. If she woke in the night crying after a nightmare, Irma would get up, switch on the light, and soothe her from a distance. If she was running a fever, Irma would fetch the thermometer and hold cold compresses against her forehead and armpits. She had nothing to complain about. She'd had a happy childhood. She had never been mistreated, she was a good student, she did her homework, and her only chores were keeping her bedroom tidy and taking out the trash. Irma never took the time to teach her to cook, embroider, or knit, as she was convinced Nadine would become a doctor rather than a wife or mother. Perhaps she wanted Nadine to have what she never had, for Irma too was a victim of the war. If it hadn't been for the Nazis, she said she would have gone to work in a hospital, helping those in need.

"Your mother has such a good heart," Jordan had once told her, after Irma had barked an instruction at Nadine, in German. "She just wants you to do your best."

She was fond of them both, although ever since she was little, she had always been afraid that if she made a mistake, they would send her back to the convent in Havana.

Nadine didn't want to know anything about the past. When she slept, she was frequently besieged by the recurring nightmare of being stranded among the clouds or in the middle of the ocean. Since she was little, she had heard snippets from Irma of the story of her German grandmother, a poet and rebel in a country where being different could cost you your life; of the Jewish family who had rescued her mother, taking her from Berlin to Havana; of her own sudden departure from Cuba, leaving the mother who had sent her away in order to save her. She didn't want to know more. If Nadine didn't acknowledge her past, then it had never happened.

She was an orphan, that much she knew. She had been born in Cuba by accident. Her Cuban parents were dead, and the only person she knew of who might still be alive from her childhood was the nun who had organized her departure from Cuba. If she delved farther back, into her birth mother's past, the thread soon got lost in an unfathomable war. Nazism had destroyed her family; then Communism had robbed her of the one thing she could call her own. In the end, the Taylors were the only people she could count on.

One day, alone, when her parents went to Manhattan, she found a shoebox in her mother's closet containing letters arranged in chronological order, tied together with a yellow ribbon, their envelopes dogeared with the years. Nadine would have liked to read them, sensing they belonged to her even though she was neither the sender nor the addressee, but it was a long time before she dared to look at them more closely.

In the kitchen, while Irma was preparing dinner, Nadine asked her what had happened to her mother. Irma tried to avoid the question. Jordan watched nervously from a distance.

Not giving up, Nadine said, "I'd like to see where I was born—"

"There's nowhere to go," replied Irma, interrupting her. "You can't travel to Cuba, they're still in the middle of a revolution. You need to put all that behind you. Your mother is dead. You're a good American girl now."

That evening, Nadine felt her parents were on edge. She thought it was because she'd brought up wanting to go to Cuba, but what had really shaken them was a phone call from a stranger. The caller then unexpectedly showed up at their house just before they were sitting down to dinner the next night. He said he was a journalist investigating war crimes.

"Are you Irma Brauns?" said the man, holding a heavy leather briefcase.

Without being invited, the journalist walked inside and sat down in the living room. Irma and Jordan looked at each other and remained on their feet, facing the man.

Nadine started to tremble, without understanding why. Her mother sighed with resignation and sat down on one of the armchairs. She looked like she had been expecting this moment all her life.

"You better go up to your room," Jordan told Nadine.

Beginning the day after the journalist's visit, Nadine's parents regularly started taking the subway into Manhattan, consulting with lawyers and sending documents that proved they were American citizens and had never committed any crimes. When the Taylors were away on one such trip, Nadine and her best friend, Miranda, took out the shoebox of letters that Irma had hidden in her closet.

They were letters between her adoptive mother and the nun from the convent who had managed to get Nadine, along with more than ten thousand other children, out of Havana to save them from Communist indoctrination, via a program that some bureaucrat later ironically dubbed "Operation Pedro Pan."

Nadine stopped Miranda from emptying the box onto the dining room table.

"We have to leave it all exactly the same," she said, memorizing the way the letters were tied and set out.

Miranda read out odd paragraphs in English that made no sense to either of them, while Nadine rummaged through envelopes and documents she couldn't comprehend. They referred to Nadine's German blood, of the closeness of her parents to the Cuban government that had been overthrown. Of fear and persecution.

At first Miranda assumed this referred to the Nazis. For her and her family, any mention of persecution always had to do with the Nazis. But Nadine explained that the nun, Sister Irene, was talking about recent events in Cuba, where she had been born.

In a copy of a letter Irma had sent to Sister Irene making the case for the Taylors' suitability as adoptive parents, she made reference to her Catholic faith, her own childhood in Vienna, her dreams of becoming a nurse, the changes brought about by the war. She mentioned the years she spent in Berlin, where she met her husband, an electrician from Cleveland, Ohio, who fought for the Allies. Irma had been working in a hospital in Berlin, she wrote, when she met the American. Shortly after, they got married and she accompanied him to New York. They had lived ever since, she wrote, in a comfortable home with a spare bedroom for the little girl. With the letter there was a document from the archdiocese of New York endorsing the Taylor family and remarking on their religious devotion and good nature.

Nadine was hoping to discover some secret, but the letter only contained details of a story she already knew in broad strokes. In another letter, the nun said that she had lost contact with Lilith Bernal, Nadine's birth mother, and that what became of her "only God could know." Lilith was worn down by so much loss, the nun said. However much you pray, pain still weighs you down.

As she went through them all, Nadine found one letter separate from the others and without an envelope, folded in half. The nun's handwriting had passed through to the other side of the paper, and Nadine opened it with utmost care. The paper had aged more than the rest. It was yellowish, tattered, and ink-faded, as if it had survived a shipwreck. Inside was a sepia photograph, printed on a little piece of cardstock with serrated edges. It was a woman with a baby in her arms. Nadine showed it to Miranda, whose eyes grew wide as she lifted a hand to her mouth. They sat and studied the image.

"You look just like your mother," Miranda said in amazement.

Nadine's name was written on the back of the photograph, in handwriting that differed from the others.

"That's my real mother's handwriting." Real mother. She had never said it that way before. For Nadine, the only parents who existed in her life were the Taylors. Irma was her only mother.

Nadine felt as if she had discovered a treasure that had been hidden for years. Her real mother, Lilith, had tied back her hair leaving her forehead exposed. The baby was wrapped in a knitted blanket trimmed with lace. Both of them were looking at the camera, as if seeking approval.

Burning with curiosity, Miranda snatched the letter from Nadine and began reading aloud in a soft, almost inaudible voice. Nadine followed the writing as she read, scrutinizing each word, each phrase the nun had written in her rudimentary English. It was a kind of summary that the nun had obtained from her mother once the Taylor family had agreed to adopt the little girl.

She read her real name: Nadine Bernal Keller. Her birth mother was called Lilith Keller de Bernal, although it had been written as Herzog in an old German passport. Señora Keller de Bernal had come to Cuba thanks to paperwork prepared by Franz Bouhler, whom she called her guardian angel, Professor Bruno Bormann, and a Jewish family who had adopted her as their own child. Lilith was the daughter of a German writer, Ally Keller, killed by the Nazis in Sachsenhausen concentration camp, on the outskirts of Berlin, around 1940. According to the nun, although the baby was fair-skinned, her mother, Lilith Keller, was mixed race, and therefore her mother (Nadine's grandmother) had needed to get her out of Berlin to spare her from suffering under the Nazi racial hygiene laws. Lilith was the daughter of a German Catholic woman and a Black German man, who in turn was the son of a German woman and an African man.

When they finished reading the letters, they fell silent.

"And what happened to your mother in the end?"

"My mother . . . Lilith, she is dead."

"It must be painful to have to give away your daughter. My grandmother says that there are people who die of pain."

Nadine's head lowered.

"So you're Black?" Miranda couldn't get over it.

As Miranda read the last sentence, Nadine stood up. She had heard a car pulling up outside the house and realized her parents were home.

"We need to put everything back just as it was," Nadine said, flustered.

For months, her father continued to hide the truth about what had happened when the reporter visited them. One day when Nadine got home from school, Irma was no longer there. Jordan sat her down in the dimly lit living room of their house in Queens, and after a long silence, his arms hanging limp and his face haggard, told her something she didn't want to hear.

"Your mother has been taken to a German jail. They say she was a Nazi during the war and did some very bad things. We're going to Germany to support her during the trial."

She could see even saying this much was painful for him.

"Your mother is innocent," he declared with absolute certainty.

The next day, Jordan collected Nadine from school to tell her it was best she didn't go to class or see her friend Miranda for a while, until things had returned to normal. Nadine wasn't about to give up her best friend.

In the end, nothing returned to normal. Her father stopped sleeping, spending all day locked up in his room, making telephone calls and selling the properties they owned, including his share of the small electrical business, bought by one of his partners for a pittance. Jordan Taylor's face became furrowed, his hair started to thin.

"I'm shedding my leaves," he said one evening, trying to lighten the mood during one of their slow, silent dinners.

Now that they were alone, it was Jordan who went into Nadine's room at bedtime and asked her how she was, if she wanted a glass of warm milk. He occasionally ran his hand over her head absentmindedly, his way of giving her a caress.

They were going to leave the country, she knew it, and the house with its lace curtains made by Irma, the only home she had any memory of, would belong to another family. Jordan explained that Nadine would accompany him to Düsseldorf to help her mother, who had found herself locked up in a cell because one day a stranger had knocked on the door and asked to speak with her.

Jordan knew that he would never be able to convince Nadine to fly. She had been sent off, alone, on a plane when she was barely three years old, first to Miami and then to New York, a city so far away it forced her to give up any hope of ever returning to the place she came from. Over the years, she had told her parents many times that she would never fly again. In her mind, all the anxiety and grief she experienced as a small child became associated with flying in an airplane, and her phobia of flying only intensified as the years went by.

One evening her father told her they were going to cross the Atlantic on a boat, from there they would take a train to where Irma was being held in Germany. With nostalgia in his voice, he said he could still remember the beer he drank in Berlin after the war. He had never tasted anything like it since, even though most bars in their Queens neighborhood supposedly sold the same brand.

"It'll be an adventure, Nadine. We'll finally find out what happened to your German grandmother, the writer," he said. "It might even help your mother. She needs us—both of us—now more than ever."

The thing Nadine most resented about having to leave New York was losing her best friend. She and Miranda had been inseparable since kindergarten. Jordan never said this was a one-way trip, but all the signs were there. They had put the house up for sale and offered all of her mother's jewelry to the pawn shop on Lee Street. One weekend, not long before they left, Nadine noticed her mother's closet was empty, except for bare coat hangers and a box tucked on a high shelf. When she saw the shoebox of letters from Cuba was still in the same place her mother had hidden it, Nadine decided to take the letters and tuck them in her suitcase.

Miranda was as stunned by the suddenness of her friend's departure as Nadine. Still, during Nadine's final weeks in New York they only saw each other in class. Miranda was busy discovering her body with the help of an Italian boy whom she described as a kind of octopus.

The two of them used to walk around the neighborhood after school and often ended up at Miranda's house. Nadine didn't like any of the boys at school. She told Miranda that she wouldn't have a boyfriend until she got to college.

"One day I'm going to be a doctor and I'm going to marry a doctor too," Nadine would tell her.

"That's too many years of studying for me," Miranda replied. "I'll end up a teacher, like my mother."

What she never told Miranda was that she had plans to go study in Germany.

"We will go to the same university together, you can be sure of that," Miranda said.

"And one day we'll live together in Manhattan."

Nadine recalled that at one of the last family dinners she was invited to at Miranda's house, Miranda had insisted that every German who wasn't Jewish and had survived the war must be a Nazi. This was something Miranda had heard her grandparents say for as long as she could remember. There were no innocent Germans, she had said. People who didn't look like them were thrown into the ovens, and people who opposed them got a bullet in the head. Nadine told her friend she believed her mother Irma was born in Vienna and had only taken German citizenship after the war to avoid starvation.

"Well, there's always an exception to the rule and, in the end, you are adopted," Miranda answered, shrugging her shoulders. "One thing's for sure, you and I wouldn't have survived in Germany. We would have been gassed, and from there to the ovens. You for having a Black grandfather, me for being Jewish."

The two friends played with makeup and would often compare themselves in front of the mirror, trying to pick out the physical characteristics that most defined them. They traced their profile, then their ears and forehead, finding hardly any differences that set them apart. They were the same height, both had long necks, pale skin, blue eyes that turned green in sunlight, and wavy chestnut brown hair. Spending so much time in front of the mirror had made them experts in applying eyeliner and lipstick and drawing beauty spots on their cheeks.

Although Miranda's mother didn't observe many Jewish traditions, the one thing she refused to give up was the Sabbath meal. From time to time, they invited Nadine, who would join in with the other women in the house, lighting candles as the sun started to set. Nadine was fascinated by this family with so many aunts and uncles, cousins, and grandparents, all talking over one another, shouting, and swearing, the older generation speaking to the youngsters as if they were scolding them, then smothering them in hugs and kisses.

If the telephone rang during dinner on a Friday and Miranda ran to answer it, knowing it was her boyfriend, her mother would take off her shoe and threaten to throw it at her and cut off her hand if she as much as touched the receiver. "You yourself told me to forget that I'm Jewish, yet you won't let me answer the phone on a Friday," Miranda would say to her mother, who sat there, the shoe still in her hand, poised to throw it.

When they finally had to say goodbye, with Jordan already waiting in the car that would take them to the ship, both girls wept.

"You'll be going to college in a few years, and so will I. Well, as long as I don't get married and start popping out little Italian octopus babies," Miranda said, giggling, determined to lighten the sadness that hung over them.

The two girls laughed at the idea and embraced. They separated, knowing but not wanting to acknowledge that they would never see each other again.

22

Six Months Later
Düsseldorf, November 1975

Nadine spent the whole crossing in their cabin, being sick, while her father whiled away his time at the bar, returning late at night. Each day he'd rise, shower, put on fresh clothes, and disappear. Almost two weeks passed like this, until they reached Hamburg, where they caught a train to Düsseldorf. At age sixteen, her home in New York was already a distant memory. Jordan told her they were both needed in Düsseldorf if they were going to save Irma. When they disembarked from the train, they were met by Frau Adam, a stocky German woman who took them to her guesthouse and led them to two adjacent rooms on the second floor, each with its own bathroom. In her little bedroom, Nadine could hear her father's every sigh and sob through the faded floral wallpaper.

Nadine wandered the streets around the River Düssel, feeling both frightened and ashamed. The buildings, the smell of the trees, the trams, and the restaurants all seemed somehow familiar. The streets were nothing like this in Maspeth, Queens, where she had grown up. The atmosphere there was always the same, whatever the weather: mixed spices, blended with the incessant noise of the city, and the voices and gestures of people rushing to get to wherever they were going.

It was calm in Düsseldorf, but a calm that had nothing to do with quietness. The space felt compressed, intensified. In a stupor, she crossed a small bridge and approached the block-columned building where Jordan had been all day, and indeed all week, leaving her shut away in Frau Adam's decrepit guesthouse.

She had read every book she found on a shelf in the closet under the staircase in the guest house and was growing tired of Caesarius's texts in *Dialogus Miraculorum/The Dialogue on Miracles*, and of the story of Germanic power versus the decadent Roman empire as told in the *Gesta Romanorum/Deeds of the Romans*. When she was a little girl in Queens, she spoke and read German with Irma, although she knew, despite never having been told so, that Spanish had been her first language, which she one day hoped to regain the use of. After all, she'd been born in Havana, and although she was very young when she came to New York, she was certain she must have learned a few words.

But Germany was the place her parents always talked about. Irma had told Nadine ever since she was a little girl that one day they would go to Austria together and see where Irma had been born. They had even talked of Nadine applying to go to university in Berlin once she had finished high school.

This wasn't the trip they had planned. This felt more like an accident. A terrible mistake.

It had been a year since her adoptive mother had been taken into custody, yet still no one had explained the actual reasons for Irma's arrest to Nadine. All she knew was that Jordan had uprooted her from everything she knew and brought her with him to find Irma in this city that felt so strangely peaceful. Jordan seemed to be aging dramatically, running out of words, beginning a conversation then stopping halfway through. She wished they had never left New York.

For months, Nadine had been plagued by nightmares. Her father, on the other hand, battled insomnia. They had turned into wandering ghosts, Jordan clinging to the hope he would one day get Irma back. Nadine came to understand that Irma was her father's only true love.

They'd been in Düsseldorf for a fortnight, and Nadine spent her free time roaming the city without a map, memorizing the street names to be certain she'd find her way back. One morning, after breakfast, her father asked her to come to the courthouse that afternoon. He said they might need her, which was the same thing he had said the week before. She had waited at the courtroom for hours without being called, and eventually they had sent her back to the guesthouse.

Her father had insisted she stay away from stalls selling newspapers and magazines, and that she not listen to the radio. From then on, every time they approached a newsstand or saw someone reading a newspaper, she lowered her gaze. Frau Adam must have been warned too, as she never mentioned Nadine's mother's trial in front of her. The conversations over breakfast or in the evening were restricted to discussing recipes or talking about how prohibitively expensive life in Germany had become. But over time, Frau Adam, whose age was hard to guess, started to feel more comfortable around the teenage girl.

"You must really miss your mother," she said to her one day, noticing Nadine sitting alone in the dark living room.

The truth was, she didn't miss Irma. The woman who had raised her had vanished one day, without saying goodbye. That was all.

Nadine's time in Düsseldorf had so far consisted mainly of going back and forth from their lodgings to the courthouse. She had grown tired of waiting in room 4C and never being called upon. Then, one day, that changed.

A policewoman and a court official approached her, indicating that she should follow them. Without saying a word, they walked her through an imposing set of double doors, and the sound of many voices murmuring suddenly assailed her ears. Seeing the courtroom in all its grandeur, Nadine's heart started to race so fast, she thought she might faint. She waited at the entrance to the courtroom, closed her eyes, filled her lungs with air, and stood tall.

When she opened her eyes, she saw her father sitting at a long table, behind a mountain of papers, files, and folders. Spotting her, he signaled for her to join him. Nadine quickened her pace, feeling as if she were the one on trial, and went to sit by his side. From there, she looked around at the faces of those sitting at the tables at the front, and the men in dark suits and white ties who sat opposite them. She could hear the din rising in the room, and most people stood up. At the entrance to the courtroom, she saw a vaguely familiar woman in a brown overcoat and white hat from which wisps of grayish-blond curls were escaping. She was flanked by two lawyers. It was Irma.

Irma, now being referred to as Frau Brauns, was followed by two other defendants, as the journalists' cameras flashed. Nadine noticed that, unlike her mother, the other two women hid their faces behind newspapers. Irma was the only one who showed her startled eyes and pursed lips, in a strangely dignified expression. When Irma's and Nadine's eyes met, neither gave even the slightest flicker of recognition. They both turned their attention to the prosecutor, who had begun an impassioned address. The man pronounced his words with too much intensity, and his phrases clashed like spears. As he continued his onslaught of words designed to move and arouse pity, his face grew red, and his forehead became covered with a thick film of sweat.

Without understanding all the legal terminology he was tossing around, Nadine pieced together what was going on. She heard the prosecuting attorney impugn her mother, without mentioning her name, petitioning the judge to impose the maximum sentence. She wanted to ask her father, the lawyer, or the court official who had escorted her into the room and was still standing behind her, what this sentence was, but none of them paid her any attention. Nadine asked herself what a sixteen-year-old girl, born in Cuba and adopted by a family in New York, was doing at the trial of an Austrian who had become a German citizen, and then an American one. She only caught the odd word or phrase: mentions of crime, abuse, neglect, escape, refugees, camps with names that were difficult to remember, and then, repeatedly, the word "kicking": children said to have been hurled off packed trains by her own mother. The kicking was mentioned over and over again, as if the crime had been committed only by the tip of a shoe. The attorney stopped and looked at Irma, at Jordan, and finally at Nadine, as if all three were guilty.

The defense lawyer finally rose to speak: Irma Taylor had adopted the daughter of a Jewish German woman who had escaped to Cuba, and who had been orphaned by Communism. When he said daughter, the defense lawyer pointed to Nadine. The entire audience turned to her. Nadine closed her eyes. He said that the woman sitting in the dock couldn't hurt a fly. He said that the woman brave enough to show her face unashamedly in court was innocent. Irma Taylor, he insisted, was in fact yet another victim of a war that had drained everyone. After the war, a small minority, thirsty for vengeance and looking to make their fortune, went after those who had only followed orders, as any decent German citizen would have. How many generations would have to bear the blame? How many times could a woman be dragged before the court for simply doing her job and following the orders of her superiors? The defense attorney seemed overwhelmed by his own words.

The defense emphasized, despite regular interruptions from the prosecutor who insisted they focus only on events that took place in two concentration camps, that Irma Taylor—he refused to use Brauns, her maiden name—could not be tried twice for the same crime. Apparently, after the war, Mrs. Taylor had been able to escape from Majdanek concentration camp before the Red Army arrived and return to Vienna, her city of birth. There, the Austrian police had arrested her and handed her over to the British Army, who kept her imprisoned for almost a year before bringing her to justice. She'd been found guilty of torture and mistreatment of prisoners, and crimes against humanity. Mrs. Taylor had served three years in prison, after which she had married an American soldier and rebuilt her life in the United States, where she had changed her name and formed a respectable family.

Nadine left the courthouse disoriented. Suddenly, she didn't know what city she was in, which year it was, or where she had come from.

Later that day, back at the guesthouse, in her room, which she sensed would become a cell over the coming months, Nadine stood in front of the gold-framed mirror that hung next to the window. The gray light erased every line from her face, and she stared at her reflection, as she had done in the past with Miranda. She wished they had been able to stay together, that her father had left her behind, that Miranda's mother had taken her into her home instead. Better still, she wished that her real mother had never given her up, had allowed her to grow up with her in Cuba. The image reflected in the mirror was not really her, she told herself. She smiled, imagining herself back in New York.

Nadine tried to understand why they wanted to sentence her mother for an offense, a murder, despite her father continually insisting that without a body there was no crime. She asked herself whether her mother might be looked on with compassion and forgiven, and she wrestled over which way led to the truth. *But who knows the truth?* she asked herself. She had heard it said history was written by the victors. So, what happened to those who were defeated?

Late that night, she heard noises coming from downstairs and left her room, hoping to find her father. She might not be able to comfort him, but at least she could offer him some company. Instead she found Frau Adam, emptying a shelf stacked with porcelain. She went and joined her, helping her wrap each item in scraps of fabric and old newspapers, before laying them carefully in a suitcase.

"It's my mother's dinner service, and I suppose it would have been my grandmother's before her, but what use is it to me now?" Frau Adam said quietly. "Now I just need to work out how to get it to my sister, with a pound of coffee hidden inside the coffee pot."

Her sister was an old woman who lived alone in East Berlin. Frau Adam explained the city had been separated by a wall that the Soviets had built overnight to divide Germany. It was the price the country had to pay for defending an idea, she told her.

"There's nothing left of us Germans now," she went on. "We're no longer a nation. Nobody respects us and we're still held accountable for the deeds of others. Can you believe my sister can no longer get hold of coffee? What's become of us? At least on this side . . ."

Frau Adam told her the house had belonged to her husband's family for several generations. During the liberation, the neighborhood had been destroyed by bombs, but the villa remained standing amid the ruins. She confessed to Nadine that with no money and her husband in jail, she had no choice but to open it up as a guesthouse. Given its proximity to the courthouse, she'd had defendants, witnesses, attorneys, the guilty and the innocent under her roof, always taking care they didn't coincide.

"We're all guilty, and do you know why? Because we survived. They would rather we had died."

Her husband was a surgeon, sentenced for his affiliation with the ruling party at the time, she told Nadine. It surprised her that Frau Adam never once uttered the word Nazi.

"A doctor, just a doctor, and now he's rotting in jail until someone remembers about him and decides it's been long enough, that we don't need to keep carrying the weight of the guilt. Look at your mother . . . Twenty years later. Does that seem fair to you? She never tried to hide. She's already been tried once and served her sentence. Why do they have to dig up the past?"

Seeing Nadine's startled face, Frau Adam apologized.

"You've nothing to be ashamed of," she said. Then she stood up and took her hand. "Come with me, I've got a surprise for you."

They walked through dark rooms to the other side of the house, where Frau Adam led Nadine down a corridor to a little library, which had once been her husband's study. She had kept the room just as it was, as if she harbored hope of an amnesty that would allow Herr Adam to come back home as if nothing had ever happened. But he would never go back to the clinic or use the white coat hanging up in a clear bag in one of the bedroom closets, of that she was certain.

Frau Adam seemed more like a housekeeper than the owner of the house. She refused to hire anyone to help her clean or serve, and she herself prepared breakfast and dinner every day for those guests who requested it. The only thing she wouldn't do was wash the dishes. She was helped by a young Polish girl who furiously scrubbed the saucepans and gently polished the silver cutlery, as if afraid the knives and forks might wear away with too much rubbing.

Frau Adam suffered with survivor's curse, as she called it, a lack of belonging. What gave them the right to go on living despite the deaths of so many others?

In the library, Frau Adam lifted a heavy photo album from one of the shelves. It had an orange-colored cover with gilt trim, and stamped on the spine was a dull swastika that showed signs of having been vigorously rubbed out. The two of them sat down on the sofa, letting themselves sink into the silk cushions, then Frau Adam opened the album. Her sunken eyes lit up, regaining something of their former blue.

Nadine saw a photograph of a tall, slim young woman with narrow hips. The older woman beside her had hefty arms, a large bosom, and thick legs, and her head looked like it was buried inside her body. Her neck had disappeared.

"It's hard to believe thirty years have gone by. I don't even recognize myself. This is a photograph of me with my mother."

Most of the photos were of Frau Adam with her husband, nearly always in his military uniform. There were none of him wearing his white medical coat. Herr Adam's face exuded control, and in every snapshot, he was staring defiantly at the lens. Other photographs showed Frau Adam with a baby in her arms, sitting beside her husband on the bank of a lake. Others with a boy dressed in the Hitler Youth uniform, and then later the same young man, older now, dressed as a soldier.

"I always wanted a daughter, but it wasn't God's will. Men are sent to the battlefield, and very few return from war."

Toward the end of the album there were many empty spaces where photos had obviously been removed. One of the remaining photographs was of a trip to Lake Wannsee: a beautiful villa, Herr Adam sitting at a small table in a courtyard, holding a cup of coffee.

"That breakfast was the reason they condemned him. They accused him of hundreds of thousands of deaths. For a mere breakfast. He had been invited to Wannsee as an expert, that's all. They took away all the photos of him with other people that day, and made me identify every one of them, as if I had been there. They treated me like dirt. Do you think we would have stayed in Germany if my poor husband had actually been guilty? We would have run away, as so many others did. But my husband had nothing to be ashamed of or feel guilty for. They said he had decided the fate of millions of people, there at that breakfast with only doctors, lawyers, and journalists. They weren't executioners. Nobody believes that."

Frau Adam stood up, incensed, and put the photo album back on the shelf. Her eyes began to mist over.

"You know, if you want a book, there's no need to ask. Come and read whatever you want, although I don't think there are many romance novels. My husband loved science and history."

Time seemed to have stood still in the room, its walls lined with dark wooden shelves, two cracked leather armchairs sitting on a thick, reddish-brown rug, and on the wall an oil painting of an abandoned garden. *When was the last time Herr Adam had sat in an armchair behind the beveled glass table?* Nadine wondered, holding her breath and casting her eyes around every corner of the room, looking for signs of his presence. An empty space where an object that had once taken pride of place had been taken away, banished to the attic out of shame ever since the defeat. An eagle? A swastika? The image of Hitler on the wall for all to admire? Frau Adam had no photographs of her husband or son hanging on the walls or on the table, or the shelves. The uniform gave the game away. It had to be hidden.

She recalled Miranda's voice, or rather the voice of Miranda's grandmother, who had run away from Europe, her young daughter in her arms: "In every German family that survived the war, there's at least one Nazi."

Nadine found herself in the library of a man imprisoned for crimes against humanity. Frau Adam herself had insisted her husband had never shot or tortured anyone. Nadine now wanted to know the exact nature of the crime her mother was thought to have committed. Perhaps, like Herr Adam, she had been on the wrong side, the losing side. Her father had once said that in a war, everybody loses. She felt sympathetic toward Frau Adam, and that worried her. One can become accustomed to horror.

Nadine chose a book at random. Standing before Frau Adam, she tried to see herself in every gesture, every wrinkle of the woman who lived in the shadow of her husband's guilt. *Just like Frau Adam, her face would become blank, her eyes sunken, she would get so fat that her neck would disappear*, thought Nadine. With the book tucked under her arm, she said goodnight to Frau Adam, who remained standing in the dimly lit room.

Nadine wandered along the upstairs corridor. She went to the bathroom, splashed her face with ice cold water, brushed her hair, and went to bed. She decided to read to stop the thoughts going around her mind, convinced she would end up like Frau Adam, spending years hoping for an amnesty that would free Irma. Nobody, however wicked they might have been, should have to pay the price for a war that only one person was responsible for. One man had led the German nation into ruin, her father had told the defense lawyers.

After six months in Germany, and with the trial dragging on and on, New York was a distant memory for Nadine, and her old friend Miranda a stranger. Even her own voice felt alien to her. She felt as if she had arrived a little girl and become a woman overnight. Even her name was no longer hers. She was a Taylor but could also be a Keller like her real mother, or a Bernal like her father, or worse still, a Brauns, like her adoptive mother. She had begun to build a life in Germany but still couldn't imagine a future for herself.

One morning she woke breathless, suffocating. She ran to open the windows and shivered in the blast of cold air. She was living in a murderer's house. *Not all killers have bloodstains on their hands*, she thought. She was complicit, as were her adoptive parents, and Frau Adam. She would soon be starting school in Germany, and she had no idea what to expect, how to behave.

The judge declared a week's recess, during which time her father stayed in his room. Frau Adam took him his breakfast on a tray, which he barely touched, the Polish maid taking it away again at midday.

The day the trial resumed, the prosecution said they intended to call several witnesses, all of them from different countries. This news was a terrible blow to Jordan: there was no end in sight. His rage was all-consuming, and Nadine felt he had forgotten about her altogether. At dinner he looked straight through her. The only thing that mattered to him was saving his wife. He grew thinner every day, and his hands became stained with age spots. Driven mad by the throbbing in his temples, he had a habit of squeezing his eyes as if he was trying to look inside his own head, bringing his finger up to his forehead and pressing so hard it left a red circle.

Nadine looked at him and felt nothing. With the plate of untouched food before him, Jordan looked like he was letting himself die. That night, for the first time in her life, Nadine felt alone in the world. She had spent her whole life living with two strangers. Who were her parents really? The only person she spoke with was Frau Adam, who in the end Nadine was convinced was a Nazi. And her parents? What crimes had they committed?

Leaving the courthouse the next day, Jordan and Nadine quickened their pace.

There were reporters with cameras outside, and a clamoring crowd, itching for a spectacle.

"Let's hurry," Nadine's father muttered. "Who knows when this circus will end. All I ask is that they let us visit your mother."

Turning the corner, they dashed across a busy street and made it to a traffic island, cars whizzing past on either side. Nadine realized a photographer was still following them. He had pushed through the crowd to take their picture. The flash startled Nadine and she almost lost her balance. The mob behind the photographer drew closer. Cars went speeding past all around her. Nadine suddenly found herself separated from her father. For a second, he disappeared from her sight, and she brought her hand to her chest, trying to feel her own heartbeats. Nadine imagined her father poised to launch himself in front of the speeding cars, as if killing himself were going to end his torture. In her mind, Nadine couldn't stop seeing her father's body on the asphalt, his face calm, peaceful. It seemed to her that her father had been dead ever since they left court. He had been rehearsing the constant pain of living without his wife since leaving New York. The pain would never end.

A woman's shout made Nadine turn for a moment. The woman pointed a finger at her, as if accusing her. She spat out a phrase in German, in an accent Nadine couldn't place, a disgusted expression on her face. Her words throbbed like an echo. Nadine felt her body burning. Another phrase, clearer now. Now back by her father's side, to stop herself from falling, she leaned against her father's shoulder. He was swaying too, and she wanted to throw her arms around him to keep him stable, but she couldn't. They were standing on the dividing line between the living and the dead. Around them, cars passed in both directions. Behind them, the mob. Nadine prayed she could open an imaginary door, as she had once dreamed back in Maspeth, when she wanted to get rid of the nightmares. A door, she needed to open a door. If she found one, would she go through by herself?

The shout came again, nearer all the time. Her father was shivering, his hands sweating. Nadine felt again that she couldn't breathe, that her heart had stopped beating. She was drowning.

"That's the monster's daughter!" she heard the woman shout.

Nadine felt the truth of it. She was the daughter of a monster, undeserving of love or pity.

23

Nadine had found school in Düsseldorf boring, the only classes she was interested in were biology, taught by an old man, and Spanish, taught by a German woman who had lived in Seville as a child. The Spanish teacher told her she had a natural ability for languages and accents, as did many Jews. Nadine interrupted her to clarify that she was Catholic and had been born in Cuba to Cuban and German parents. The teacher stared at her in wonder, and from then on, she became known as "the Cuban girl."

Her mother's trial had dragged on in an endless circus of appeals, new accusations, rebuttals, and legal maneuvering for nearly six years. Gradually, the television news and newspapers stopped covering the story, but one journalist reported that this trial had become the longest and most expensive in the country's history. Jordan had retreated into a profound silence, and Nadine only ever saw him over breakfast on weekends. Her life consisted of going from school to the guesthouse and from the guesthouse to the library. With the money Jordan pushed under her bedroom door in an envelope each week, she went to the cinema to watch badly dubbed Hollywood movies. Thanks to her biology teacher and her excellent academic grades, she was accepted into the Freie Universität in Berlin, which its students called the FU, finally allowing her to make a clean break from her parents. She felt free the moment she received her letter of acceptance. She filled out the registration documents using her real name: Nadine Bernal.

Shortly before classes began at the university, Nadine had to return to Düsseldorf. The trial against Irma was coming to its end and as a last gesture of hope, the defense attorney wanted Nadine to be present. A crucial witness was finally going to testify at the trial, and the lawyer thought that Nadine's presence might elicit a little compassion for Irma. She resented the fact that she had to be there, just when she felt she was starting a new chapter of her life.

The courtroom was ice cold, and once she was back there, Nadine felt like a vulnerable little girl again. She had the impulse to hide behind her father, shielding herself from the prosecutor's barking and the unkempt woman in the witness stand, who had instantly recognized Irma. Try as she might, Nadine couldn't help but feel compassion for Irma, who looked so fragile, with her restrained gestures and deeply furrowed face.

"It's her," the woman on the witness stand said, pointing at Irma.

They asked her to state the defendant's name.

"Everyone in the camp knew her as 'the Stomping Horse'," she declared.

An uncomfortable murmur ran through the courthouse.

"Did you see her kill anyone?" the defense attorney asked.

"No."

"Did you see her take anyone to the gas chamber?"

"No."

"To the crematorium?"

"No."

"Did you see her armed with a pistol at any time, or aiming a pistol at anyone?"

"No."

Another uncomfortable silence.

"She . . ." the woman continued. "She mistreated the children arriving at the camp, the ones getting off the train, that were separated from their families."

"Did you see her kill a child?"

Another pause.

"She was so cruel to the children, only the children." The woman's voice could barely be heard, as though every word pained her.

The witness was growing smaller by the second, in front of Nadine's eyes.

"The children . . ." the woman repeated.

"Come now, what happened with the children," the defense attorney prodded her.

"She . . ."

"Can you finish the sentence once and for all?" the lawyer urged her, raising his voice.

"Take all the time you need," the judge said calmly.

"She was in charge of . . ."

"Of what?" the attorney asked.

"Of the children . . . when they . . ."

"She split them up?" the attorney offered, losing patience.

"Yes."

"At least that's clear then."

"Who ordered the children to be taken away from their mothers?" asked the lawyer.

"The captain." The woman's voice was stronger now.

"So, she was following orders?" As the defense attorney asked this, he turned to the public, then looked at the judge, and finally at one of the other witnesses who was looking accusingly at the woman in the witness box, as if she felt she were protecting the defendant.

"But she split them up," the woman repeated.

"Forcefully, yes. That was her job, don't you agree?"

"She kicked them."

The defense lawyer started to say something, but the woman now spoke in a torrent of words.

"When the children ran to their mothers' arms, she launched herself at them, kicking them. It was as if she didn't want to get her hands dirty. Kicking them once, twice, three, four times. She kicked them to the floor, and the children struggled to their feet again, running, screaming. If they fell, they got another kicking. That's why we called her the Horse. I never knew her name, but I remember her face, her eyes, her profile."

"Why did you pay her so much attention?"

Another pause. The woman looked lost.

"Do you need a break?" the judge asked, preparing to call a halt to the proceedings.

"A break? Why?"

"In that case, go on," the judge said.

"Do you recognize the other two defendants?" the defense attorney went on.

"I don't remember them. I can't remember all the guards who were there. I only remember the captain's face, and the Horse's."

"How many female guards watched over the camp?"

"Lots."

"So it could be that you're confusing her with someone else? How do you know it was her?"

"It was her."

"How can you be so certain?"

The woman looked tired, exhausted by so many questions.

"She stomped on the children."

"There were other women who kicked people too, isn't that right?"

"Yes."

"Do you remember the other women's faces?"

"I already told you, I don't."

"So, you could have confused the defendant's face. It's been a long time. Thirty years!"

"No!" she shouted.

"You seem very sure about it. Could it be that you want revenge, and you're setting your sights on her?"

"Yes, I did dream of getting my revenge . . ."

"For everything you went through, we understand that, but . . ."

"I survived, for this day."

The murmur in the courtroom grew, but the woman's voice rose above it.

"The Stomping Horse . . ."

"This is not the time for insults."

"That's what all the prisoners called her."

"But you're asking us to trust your memory three decades on. I'll say it again, to make it clear, thirty years! It sounds like nothing. I bet you can't remember the color of the wallpaper in your hotel room, and yet you insist on pointing the finger at this woman whose real name you don't even know. Why?"

"Because she separated me from my daughter."

Silence fell. The lawyer lowered his head. Nadine heard a dry cough, a low whisper, the blades of the fan.

"She hit my daughter. I fell to the ground, on top of her, to protect her, but the Stomping Horse kicked us apart. She stomped on my fingers, with one boot, bearing down all her weight. With the other, she kicked my daughter in the face. Then another kick, and I saw she was bleeding from her mouth. My daughter couldn't walk, she was dizzy. I wanted to cry out, but I couldn't, I was choking. We'd gone days without water. I saw my little girl stagger. The Horse, she turned to look at me, she knew I was watching her. I was remembering her face, committing it to memory."

"And what happened to your daughter?" the defense attorney persisted.

The woman heaved a deep sigh and fixed her eyes on the accused.

"I never saw her again. That was the last time I had her near me."

The swelling murmur in the courtroom made Nadine cover her ears.

"But do you know what hurts most?" the woman went on, her voice deliberate. "The effort of not forgetting a single detail of the Horse's face, memorizing it and re-creating it every night, has made me forget my own daughter's face. All I remember is that she had long plaits and blue eyes, like her dress, and she was wearing a dirty white pinafore. But I can't remember her face."

The woman's voice cracked. She gulped and began to cry. "How can a mother forget her own child's face?" she asked herself, her eyes misting over.

The noise in the courtroom was deafening. It suddenly died down, or perhaps Nadine stopped listening. She wanted to go home, but she didn't know where home was. She felt darkness engulf her. When she came round, she realized she was crying. She looked all around her in utter confusion. The floor was vibrating. She wasn't in the courtroom anymore, she was in a train carriage on the way back to Berlin. On her way to finish her education. On her way to build a life far from the Taylors where no one would ever again ask her to remember all the losses of her youth, or feel compassion for a killer, or love those who abandoned her. The past was finished, she would only care about the future.

24

The first time Nadine saw Anton Paulus he was wearing a hat pulled down low over his forehead. She called him "the hat boy" from the moment they were introduced. When they met at university, he told her he was finishing a PhD on "the recovery of what is lost," without going into further detail; she was working as an intern at a laboratory committed to laying to rest what had once been alive. They entertained themselves with wordplay and silly stories, they would finish each other's sentences, and gradually grew to know each other. Although he wasn't looking for a girlfriend, let alone a wife, when Nadine came into his life Anton knew he had lost control of the wheel—his destiny was no longer in his hands. They were a couple now, and they let themselves be swept along, not concerned with where they were heading as long as they were going there together.

They'd always felt a kinship: both of them loners, both accustomed to abandonment. Although Anton did have parents, they didn't live with him in Berlin. They were in touch through the occasional letter or telephone call, and he would sometimes visit them at Christmas at their apartment in Lucerne, Switzerland, where they had taken refuge before the war broke out. Thanks to a cousin on his mother's side who had married a Swiss-Scot, Joachim and Ernestine Paulus were able to settle in the pristine medieval city where the past wasn't defined by the recent world wars but dated back centuries. Anton had been born in Berlin purely by chance, while his parents were there on a work trip.

He grew up in Lucerne, with his aunt, who only read classics in French, and his parents, who spent their lives trying to alleviate the guilt of being German by making their people return, pay for, or restore the things they had destroyed. The Pauluses had placed all their savings in a foundation dedicated to recovering assets the Germans had stolen during the war, in particular the works of Max Liebermann, a painter who had been a family friend and who, as an old man, had chosen to swallow a cyanide pill rather than board a train with no destination. They had fought for decades to recuperate Liebermann's home by Lake Wannsee, which had fallen into the government's hands, and each time one of his paintings came up for auction, they investigated its provenance to see if it had been stolen by the Nazis during the war. If that turned out to be the case, they launched a vigorous legal battle to ensure that the painting was returned to its original owner.

Anton now ran the Paulus Foundation, and one day Nadine accompanied him to the cold, dark warehouse where they kept the paintings, protected between wooden dividers that allowed them to be visible. Any with a dubious past, that had belonged to families the Nazis had stolen from, could not be auctioned or exhibited until descendants of the prewar owners had been located. Nadine thought it was a shame that such masterpieces were condemned never to be seen.

Soon after Nadine began her university placement in a laboratory in Berlin, Anton convinced her to change direction and abandon the career in medicine her mother had chosen for her. She enjoyed biology but didn't feel capable of dealing with an endless stream of patients each day. She didn't have the gift of giving comfort, she used to say. She had dreamed of studying neurosurgery one day, so she could probe the brain's labyrinths, finding physical reasons to explain human behavior.

She came to prefer research, analyzing each particle of the thing that controls us on a biological level. But working in the brain research center raised a host of ethical and moral issues for her.

"All the brains, samples, and slides stored in this laboratory, however small, belonged to victims of the Nazis," Nadine told her professor during a class crammed with students desperate for the debate to end so that they could go and watch a soccer match. "They bear testimony to an atrocity. We're all benefiting from a crime."

"Perhaps you'd rather we threw away decades of study, from which we've learned so much and with which we've been able to decipher the human mind, helping future generations?" the professor asked her.

"Not throw them away, no," Nadine said, raising her voice to fill the lecture hall. "Bury them. I think the best thing we can do is lay them to rest."

The debate was interrupted by the commotion of the students getting up to leave, some gesturing angrily at Nadine.

"How long does this have to go on?" a young man said to her, pushing to get past. "If it bothers you so much, change classes or go back to your own miserable country."

As well as biology, she enrolled in Spanish and English, as it was an academic requirement to study two languages. Her Spanish classes were taught by Gaspar Leiva, a Chilean man who had sought refuge in the GDR, the other Germany, after first passing through Cuba, then eventually escaped to West Berlin. When she told him she was Cuban by birth, Gaspar felt a flash of connection with her. He had been the victim of a right-wing coup in Chile, he said, and then of the worst of "isms": Communism, like her family.

In Gaspar's Spanish class, Nadine met his teaching assistant, Mares, a fellow Cuban. The girl's name had caught Nadine's attention. Mares means *seas* in Spanish. Eventually she learned it was a name she had taken when she arrived in Moscow. Her real name was María Ares, but in her Soviet documents it appeared as M. Ares, so she joined them together.

Mares wrote poetry in Spanish mixed with German, Russian, and even English. It all came down to her experiences, she said. In Cuba she had been obsessed with American culture and music, despite not knowing a scrap of English. Later, desperate to leave the country that had caged her in, she ended up accepting a place to study cinema in Moscow, where she fell in love with a Kurd with a German passport who, when she graduated, got her pregnant and gave her a black eye.

Mares had two options: leave the Kurd and go back home to have her baby in Cuba, where she would be locked away, or marry the Kurd, go to West Germany, and have a Cuban-Kurdish-German child. Neither option appealed to her, but she settled on the second as she knew it would afford her child the freedom she never had, and she figured she could always survive the occasional beating from the Kurd.

Mares had arrived in West Berlin only a few months before the baby was due, and she and her husband moved into an apartment with only one window in an area where almost no one spoke German. Without a single mark in her purse, Mares spent her days alone, the fridge and pantry empty. One day she awoke to find herself in a clinic, several stitches in her head, a fractured rib that had punctured a lung, and an empty belly. Despite having been unconscious for several days, the doctors assured her she would make a full recovery, with no lasting damage. Her son had not been so fortunate. He was stillborn.

After the beating, the Kurd had fled, and according to authorities had ended up in Iran. For the first few weeks, Mares suffered recurring nightmares. She dreamed her son had survived and her husband had taken him. In truth, she had given birth to a child she never baptized, and never buried.

At the hospital, a social worker helped her find an apartment in the Kreuzberg neighborhood, and made arrangements for Mares to study German, a language she was already familiar with from her time in Moscow. But she lived in a social housing complex, surrounded by Turkish families, and found it difficult to perfect a language she didn't have the opportunity to practice. Within a year she had been accepted into the university, where she gained employment as an assistant to Gaspar. In the evening she gave drama and staging classes, putting on plays with drug addicts who were made to take classes in return for social assistance from the government.

Nadine went to see one of Mares' productions, in which she played a modern Medea, in a new version Gaspar had written. In the play, Medea ended up killing her children for having terrorist blood in their veins. Evil must be rooted out, she said at the end, pulling a long, red silk handkerchief from her belly with bloodied hands. This brought the work to a close, and the curtain fell on the actors like a guillotine.

Mares and Nadine became friends. Nadine realized how much she'd missed having a close female friend, like Miranda when she was little. Nadine had trouble understanding Mares's German, with her marked Russian accent, but she came to speak Spanish fluently, even picking up Mares's Caribbean accent.

As they grew closer, Nadine left her student residence and went to live with her friend. Mares confided in her that she had been dating Gaspar for some time, their relationship was going well, and she spent more time at his apartment than her own. Nevertheless, she wasn't prepared to lose her independence and wanted to keep the new relationship a secret for now. She had the feeling the Kurd might appear at her house one night, and that this time he would finish her off.

On Tuesdays or Fridays, they would go out for walks along the Bergmannstrasse and the Maybachufer, delighting in haggling with the stallholders before they closed for the day, buying avocados and mangoes at bargain prices. Nadine had no memory of tasting tropical fruits before, and they reminded Mares of Cuba, despite being bought in a Turkish market.

They roamed the city carefree, until one day everything changed. Nadine had begun to feel concerned when she saw a photograph of her face front and center in the first of a series of critical articles published in the university newspaper, and then reprinted in the national press. With the support of the foundation where she worked part time, Nadine had started a campaign to bury the human remains of Nazi victims that had been preserved and stored for decades and were still being used in scientific experiments. This brought her both insults and support in equal measure. Some felt her campaign went against science, trying to erase the past; for others, it was about settling a debt with the victims and their families, bringing a chapter of the nation's history to a close.

The two women protected each other, including the time a group of skinheads recognized Nadine, making obscene gestures toward her. Mares called them neo-Nazi clowns, telling them all they were doing was inventing a false ideology simply to stave off boredom.

Then came the offensive telephone calls telling her to leave the past alone, that nothing good would come from continuing to remind people of the things the Nazis had done. Then anonymous letters containing death threats. One day as Nadine was leaving the apartment, a man stopped her, pinning her into a corner. Keeping her quiet by holding her throat with one hand, he ripped open the buttons of her jeans with the other, pushing his fingers between her legs.

"You think you're going to get your own way?" he said.

She opened her eyes and looked at him. She wanted him to know she would remember every detail of his face, so that whatever he did to her, if she survived, she could report him. But the only thing she managed to remember was the smell of yeast and garlic on her assail-ant's breath, his bloodshot green eyes, wide forehead, tattooed neck, and shaved head. She saw the beginning of a design on his arm, a kind of dragon, as he jabbed at her. Out of the blue she felt a surge of empathy for that woman she'd thought was so disgusting at Irma's trial.

"Go back to your own country, you piece of trash."

When the attacker carelessly released his grip for a moment, Nadine screamed. Loud enough for Mares to hear her. When she saw the skin-head assaulting her friend, Mares ran to them, barefoot. Startled, the man let go of Nadine and ran off down the stairs.

Nadine and Mares sat in the corridor. No one else had responded to her cry for help. The doors of the other ten apartments remained shut. From that day on, Nadine started to sleep at Anton's house in Dahlem Dorf, which was nearer to the university, and Mares decided to stay with Gaspar.

They both reported the attack to the university, giving a description of the man with the shaved head. A few days later, the foundation Nadine worked for announced a ceremony to honor the victims of racial hygiene programs, and to announce that all the human samples obtained during the Third Reich would be laid to rest.

· ◆ ·

Almost a decade after their first meeting, Nadine and Anton were planning their wedding. They had been living together for years, and Nadine was pregnant. It was about time, she thought: she was twenty-nine and he was thirty-one. The wedding, a simple affair, which only a handful of friends would attend, would be held on a day they'd chosen at random: the eighth day of the eighth month in the year eighty-eight.

When she heard the news, Mares told her friend the date they had chosen was highly auspicious and it meant she and Anton were making a pact that would last their entire lives.

"Nothing is forever," Nadine replied.

"It's not every day you marry on the eighth day of the eighth month of eighty-eight. It's a row of infinity symbols," Mares said, reminding Nadine of the gypsy woman who had read their palms in the square on a trip to Seville.

"You two are sisters," the woman had said. "It's more important to look the same on the inside than on the outside. You're united by loss."

Gypsies are wise, Mares repeated that day, as they walked past whitewashed houses in the sun, and from that day on they knew that even though they might marry, have children, and live far away from each other, they would never be parted.

"Eight, eight, eight, eight . . ." Mares repeated the wedding date, and after a lengthy pause went on, "Don't you think you should call your father?"

Nadine didn't have the energy to answer her. She felt ashamed, guilty, but tried to tell herself it was her parents who had abandoned her.

She had made an effort during the trial, but her father stuck by his wife, loyal to her, not the little girl they had rescued from a revolution.

"You're getting married, you're going to have a baby . . ." Mares went on.

Since moving to Berlin at eighteen, Nadine had lost contact with her father. Given that he hadn't spoken a word since then, it seemed pointless to write to him. In the beginning she would telephone her former landlady, Frau Adam, from time to time, to ask how the trial was progressing, until one day a woman answered the telephone and told her Frau Adam had died.

Nadine shook her head. It would have been easier for her to leave the past to the past, but she knew Mares wouldn't let the matter go. How could she convince her that it was impossible for her to make contact with the Taylors, that they had forgotten her the day the journalist had knocked on their door and announced her mother's real name? They no longer needed a rescued little girl. Parading her at the trial hadn't made the slightest impression on those deciding the verdict.

In truth, they had been in her thoughts recently, but Nadine didn't want to reveal this to Mares, and certainly not to Anton. He believed the Taylors were Nazis—even Jordan, an American by birth—and should have been unmasked years earlier. Now that she was pregnant, she found herself often thinking of her real mother too, her real father, and her German grandmother, the writer, whom she vowed one day to rescue from oblivion.

Mares didn't give up, standing with her arms crossed, waiting for an answer.

"They're not my real parents. My real parents died in Cuba."

The last time she heard about her adoptive father was in an article in the newspaper, which Anton showed her. Jordan Taylor, a retired electrician, American army veteran, had moved to Wesphalia to be near his wife, the imprisoned war criminal Irma Brauns.

Nadine was getting married almost exactly seven years after the woman who raised her—whom she had once called Mommy—was handed a life sentence for crimes against humanity.

25

Nadine was convinced you traveled to the future in an airplane, and to the past on a train. The times in her life when she'd been forced to think about the past, it was always with her eyes closed, almost against her will. Now, side by side with her seven-year-old daughter, Luna, and her old friend Mares, she was traveling west to Bochum-Linden, a city bordering the Netherlands, to settle a debt with her memory.

Since the birth of her daughter, Nadine had promised herself she would open her eyes and reconstruct her history, even if only from broken fragments, because at the end of the day "you are the sum of your mistakes." Her German literature professor, Theodor Galland, used to say this, quoting Ally Keller, the poet killed at Sachsenhausen, when he learned to his astonishment that Nadine was her granddaughter.

Nadine had struck up a friendship with Professor Galland, not through a love of literature, but because he had studied the few texts written by Ally Keller that he had been able to find, thanks to an almost archaeological persistence. Nadine had allowed him to borrow the letters written by the nun who had helped her escape from Cuba, in which she told much of Lilith's story. She had also lent him the only photo-

246

graph she had of her mother, and a copy of the poem Ally Keller had written for her daughter on her seventh birthday: *The Night Traveler*.

After the reunification of Germany, the East German archives were opened and Professor Galland gained access to documents that had been protected for decades in Humboldt University, where Ally Keller had published essays in the literary magazine edited by Bruno Bormann. They had found letters and annotated poems, donated to the university in memory of someone called the Holm Family after the war. They had even found fragments of Ally Keller's diary. Before he retired, Professor Galland hoped to gather enough material to prepare an anthology of Ally Keller's writing. He had been in touch with several universities across Germany in the hope of tracking down everything related to her.

Little by little, like pieces in a jigsaw puzzle, Professor Galland and Nadine put her family's past back together.

After the death of the scientist in charge of Aktion T4, the Third Reich's eugenics program, the scientist's family donated his archives to the research center where Nadine now worked full time. She was tasked with analyzing the documents, which brought to light further brain sample slides. These days it was more straightforward to gain permission for the remains to be laid to rest, but she was amazed to find a folder containing photographs of a naked little girl, measurements of her body and head, details about the nose, lips, eyes, and even a sample of her hair, under the name Lilith Keller. The girl, daughter of a German woman and a Black man, had been classified a *mischling*, and it was noted that despite her intelligence level being considerably above average, and her proportions being in line with those of an Aryan, the color of her skin and the texture of her hair confirmed she had inherited a genetic defect from her father's side. It was therefore recommended the little girl be sterilized by radiation, in order to stop the spread of racial impurity among Germans.

Staring at her mother's file, Nadine felt suffocated again, as during the trial in Düsseldorf. But on this occasion, she didn't want to forget. When she had closed that door before, it was because she wasn't ready to forgive. She photocopied the documents and handed them to Professor Galland so that he could complete her grandmother's testimony. She still had to investigate the story of her grandfather, but there was no mention of him in any of the letters or documents in the rescued archive. All she knew was that her grandfather had lived in Düsseldorf at the start of the 1930s, and that he had taken several trips. Nothing more. During the advent of the Nazi Party, several black musicians, later found to have been members of the resistance, had been killed in Düsseldorf, but none was ever found to be linked to Ally Keller. Nadine assumed that Franz Bouhler had died during the war, or of old age, which meant the only way she could reconstruct her past was to go to Cuba. The problem was this meant taking an airplane, which she didn't feel ready for. She would rather wait until her daughter was old enough to accompany her; together they could start to recover that part of their past. The only thing within her reach for the moment was to reunite with her adoptive parents and introduce them to their granddaughter.

Months earlier, Nadine had received a letter informing her that Irma Taylor, having had a leg amputated as a result of her diabetes, was to be granted amnesty and would be released in the coming days. The letter was from an organization dedicated to assisting war criminals who had served their sentences. In addition to notifying Nadine, since she was listed as Irma's daughter, they also passed the news to the witnesses who had testified against her in the trial. Jordan, who had visited his wife in prison every weekend, lived in a care home for the elderly in Bochum-Linden, where he hoped his wife would join him upon her release.

Nadine wrote to Jordan to tell him she wanted to visit them, to introduce her daughter, Luna. She never received a reply. So, while Anton was on a visit to New York for yet another legal battle with the auction houses, Nadine decided to go to Bochum-Linden.

"Are you sure you're ready to see them? Why now?" Mares asked her.

"A person can't spend their whole life forgetting, Mares," Nadine replied. "What good does that do?"

"And if they're the ones who aren't ready?"

"At least I'll know I tried."

Although certain she should take the trip, Nadine was also worried about how her adoptive parents would react when they met Luna. The little girl already felt she was different because the color of her skin was darker than her parents.

When she was very young, down in the florist's shop below her house, she had heard it said she was adopted, brought from a distant Caribbean island. The first-floor neighbor told the florist Nadine had gone to Cuba to adopt her, had snatched her away from the Communists. Luna marched up to her apartment, hands on hips, to confront her parents.

"Why didn't you tell me?" she demanded.

Hearing Luna dramatically relate the fantastical story of Nadine's escape from the island, on a boat in the middle of the ocean with the little girl in her arms, Nadine couldn't help but laugh. She decided then and there that her daughter was ready to understand the past in a way she herself never had been.

"I was the one who came from Cuba. I was the one who was adopted. And even if I *had* adopted you, I wouldn't love you any less. You're my daughter, and always will be."

Luna stood, not yet satisfied. "So, was I adopted or not?"

Nadine dug out photographs of her pregnancy, of the day Luna was born, Anton carrying her on his shoulders in the Tiergarten, the first train journey, summers by the lake. When Luna saw the photos, she felt she could remember every single moment.

"So why am I different?" she asked. "I'm darker than you two."

"Darker? We're all different, Luna," Anton interrupted. "Every single one of us. And no one is better than anyone else."

Nadine continued, "My father was Cuban; my mother was the

daughter of a white German woman and a Black German man. Even though my grandfather was Black, and they called him an African, he felt just as German as you and me, but in those days, people believed the German nationality had to be unique and pure," said Nadine.

"In those days?" Anton said wryly.

"You look just like your great-grandmother Ally, but combined with the beauty of your grandmother Lilith," Nadine reassured her, and Luna's face lit up.

From that day on, Luna was happy when she saw herself in the mirror. The little girl had Nadine's eyes, though hers were a gray that turned a pale green in the sun. She had inherited her great-grandmother Ally's fair hair, and her grandmother Lilith's dark skin.

Since Luna had taken her first steps and started to talk, they had called her "the little 'why' girl." She wanted to know the justification for everything. As she grew, so did her questions. She started to ask "when?" and "where?" to locate her reasoning in time and space. Nadine used to say the little girl wanted to flesh out ideas, make them tangible, so as to remember everything.

By "everything," Nadine meant every last detail. From a gesture, to how the furniture was arranged in the study, to the position of books on the shelves, to the order in which the crockery was set out in the dining room wood buffet. Luna even noticed if her mother changed the sequence of the colored cushions on the couch. She memorized all of her classmates' names and dates of birth, their addresses. She had a talent for languages. Luna imitated accents and could learn long and complicated poems with little effort. The only thing she struggled to memorize was mathematical formulas. She wasn't made for numbers and equations, only for words.

The train journey to Bochum-Linden was slow. What made Nadine most anxious was that she hadn't yet said a word to Anton about this trip. He believed it was important to grow up knowing the truth, and that the past should not be hidden. But he would have preferred it if Luna never visited Nadine's parents, not even at Christmas. It was one thing for the little girl to know who her adoptive grandparents were, and another to spend time with a war criminal.

· ◆ ·

Nadine, Mares, and Luna arrived in the city as night was falling and went to a little hotel not far from Bochum Weihnachtsmarkt. A few little bells still hung in the trees, left over from Christmas.

"We must bring Luna back next December," Mares said.

"We might never come back. Who knows?"

They had breakfast in the hotel and then headed to the care home for the elderly, a structure built opposite a park with tree-lined avenues, as though the little garden at the entrance to the building had been given a vast extension.

They found the name "Taylor" on the intercom and pushed the button for apartment 1C. No one answered. A moment later, they heard a buzz, and the door release was activated. They opened it and went through a reception area with a glass table in the center, a huge display of paper flowers on top of it. On the other side they saw a living room laid out with armchairs. They took the corridor to the left and looked for the third apartment in the maze. On the door below the number was written J. Taylor. They knocked on the door, but there was no answer.

"Maybe they've gone out," Nadine said, seeing Mares looking anxious. "They have no idea we're here, so I don't think it's that they don't want to let us in."

As they turned to go back toward the waiting room, they saw in the distance the silhouette of a man pushing a woman in a wheelchair.

"Is that Grandma in the wheelchair?" the little girl whispered. "Look, she has a leg missing."

"Don't point."

Nadine took her daughter's hand, as if the two strangers approaching might snatch her away.

"Relax," Mares said. "Everything's going to be fine."

The three of them stood aside to make way for the couple as they slowly headed their way. They could hear the man's labored breathing as he struggled to push the heavy wheelchair.

"We should have bought flowers," the man said, in English.

"Why bother buying flowers, they only die and end up in the trash," the old woman said, nervously stroking a rag doll. Her right hand was shaking.

Nadine recognized her father's voice. It was him. He had the same lilt, the same smooth tone. She didn't recognize her mother at all.

The man strained to open the apartment door. When he turned to close the door, he noticed the three visitors.

"What do you want?" he asked in perfect German.

"May we come in?" Nadine asked firmly.

Jordan pushed Irma in her wheelchair over to the dining room table to make room for them. Luna let go of her mother's hand and went in first. The three of them took a seat on the floral sofa, where they all sank down at once. Luna let out a giggle.

"Furniture just doesn't last these days," the man said. "Can I get you anything?"

The old woman kept stroking the rag doll. Luna couldn't take her eyes off it.

The man took some bags that were hanging on the wheelchair handles and set them down on the table.

Nadine cast her eyes all around the little room, illuminated only by the light from an interior courtyard. There were no pictures or ornaments. Only a table and four chairs upholstered in smoky gray, the floral sofa, and two dark-blue armchairs, their arms protected by white crocheted covers which were turning yellowish in the center. A pair of knitting needles and a bag of yarn lay on one of the armchairs. Opposite the sofa in the middle of the living room was a large trunk used as a coffee table. Several folded newspapers lay on it.

The man came over and picked up the newspapers.

"There's no news in them anymore, only gossip," he said, taking the newspapers through to the kitchen.

Nadine turned around and, in a corner, she spied a black-and-white photograph of the Taylors that had once hung in their Maspeth house. He was dressed in his military uniform, she in a white dress. Both looked impossibly young.

When Jordan came back, he spoke into the old woman's ear.

"Do you need the toilet?" he said, loudly enough for the three of them to hear him.

She said no with a little wave of her left hand, the one without the tremor.

She noticed Nadine staring at the photograph. "We were once young and happy too," Irma said. "We met just after the war. What a time that was. When I saw him walk into the hospital where I worked, I couldn't take my eyes off him. He was the most gentlemanly person I had ever seen in my life."

Irma continued talking with her eyes fixed on the floor, still clutching the rag doll. Jordan kissed her forehead.

"It was love at first sight," said Irma, "and we were soon married."

Jordan snuggled close to her, as if protecting her.

"What can we do for you? Do we need to fill out some papers?" Jordan asked meekly.

Nadine and Mares looked at each other, taken aback. Luna smiled. The old woman was making the rag doll dance.

Her father was still lost in his own thoughts, unable to see what was right in front of him.

"Mommy," she wanted to say to the woman. Afraid her voice might break, she couldn't get the word out.

It was hot and airless in the room, and Nadine felt sweat trickle down her back. She didn't know whether to confront her parents, reproach them for having abandoned her. In the end she couldn't decide who had abandoned whom, as she was the one who had left to study in

Berlin, never to return. She was grateful to them for getting her out of Cuba, sending her to school, teaching her German.

"Don't you recognize me?" Nadine said in English.

Nadine closed her eyes and saw her mother in a bedroom. She saw the yellowing leaves on the wallpaper, and the coverlet; she could smell the mothballs in the woolen overcoats. Was it the bedroom at the guest-house in Düsseldorf, or the one in the house in Maspeth? She heard her mother singing a lullaby in German, only now noticing her peculiar accent. What she hoped or wanted to recover simply didn't exist anymore.

"I'm Nadine," she finally said.

The man still didn't react.

Luna had begun a whispered dialogue with the rag doll, which looked as if it might start to unravel in Irma's calloused hands. Mares lifted the little girl to sit on her knees in an unconscious act of protection.

"Don't you remember your daughter?" Mares asked in amazement.

Mares held her friend's hand, trying to give her strength.

The old couple sat there, with blank expressions. They didn't want to hear. They were still caught up in the fog of the trial, the years spent in prison, the weight of shame.

"Irma, you should go to bed and get some rest," her father said, in the calm, friendly voice Nadine remembered from her childhood.

Hearing her mother's name brought back the smell of the house in Maspeth. Her parents didn't want to remember her. *Why should they?* she asked herself. She had only been part of their lives for a little over a decade. That was all. Everyone always wants to go back home, but perhaps the best thing to do was to leave, give up. There was nothing left to look for, Nadine concluded.

The man remained impassive. He pulled a chair out from under the table, and flopped down onto it, as if his knees refused to support him any longer.

"Maybe we should go," Nadine said, rising to her feet.

The three of them were walking toward the door, when they heard the old woman's voice behind them.

"Wait!" Irma said. "I have something for the little girl. What's your name?"

Luna said her name, looking at her mother to make sure she was doing the right thing, or if she should be quiet.

"Luna," the child repeated, pointing up at the sky in case the woman didn't know what her name meant in Spanish.

With a huge effort, the woman steered her wheelchair toward the trunk in the center of the room and opened it. It was full of rag dolls, all the same size, as if they were the same age, piled up like identical corpses. She picked one up and offered it to Luna.

"This is for you. It's been waiting a long time for someone to cuddle it."

The little girl ran over to the old woman and hugged her. Nadine's father sat with his back to them. Nadine asked herself how many rag dolls her mother must have made every day in prison.

"Thank you," the little one said. "What's her name?"

"You can call her whatever you like," the old woman replied, moving away, maneuvering her wheelchair toward the bedroom.

The man didn't get up to say goodbye. His eyes remained on the window, the blinds closed. But when his visitors reached the door, he suddenly called out:

"Nadine!"

She saw him walking toward her slowly, head down, trembling.

He couldn't bring himself to look his daughter in the eye. She heard him mumble something. The pounding of her heart drowned out her father's words.

"I'm so sorry," the old man repeated wearily.

Nadine's eyes brimmed with tears. She closed them. A second later she felt arms around her. She couldn't face opening her eyes. The old man's body was infinitely fragile.

Her father dropped his arms, stepped away, and turned his back on her.

When she opened her eyes again, Nadine saw him walking away toward the bedroom. She left the apartment in silence.

Mares and Luna were waiting anxiously outside.

Nadine took her daughter's hand. In the other, Luna was holding the old woman's gift. Luna showed her mother the doll.

Nadine took the doll and looked at it. The body was white silk; the eyes, two blue buttons; the braids, yellow wool; the lips, pink horsehair drawn into a smile; the dress, blue gabardine; over the dress, a white linen pinafore; and on the pinafore's hem, the doll's name embroidered in red, cursive lettering: Nadine.

26

When she got out of bed one morning, Luna Paulus declared she would have preferred to have been born in the new millennium.

"I've lost a decade in the last century," the little girl said, a book tucked under her arm.

She picked up a slice of toast and started to munch on it, standing behind her mother.

"Do you think you could sit quietly with us?" Nadine said, trying to focus on her newspaper. "Ten years is nothing. You're going to live through the whole century!" Turning to face her daughter, she asked, "Where's all this coming from, anyway? What are you worrying about?"

"You and daddy still treat me like a little girl."

"You are a little girl," her mother insisted.

"But I'm ten years old already!" Luna huffed.

Luna left the table and went back to her room. It was Saturday, and it had started to snow, so they would spend the day at home.

"She's begun keeping a diary, you know," Nadine told Anton without taking her eyes off the newspaper.

"She's been saying she looks like her great-grandmother," Anton replied. "She wants to understand where she comes from, where you come from. And . . . Nadine?"

"Yes?"

"I don't think you should read her diary."

"I only glanced at it," Nadine said.

Anton raised his eyes to look at her.

"If Luna finds out . . ."

"Anton, I know." She sighed.

"This all started when you took her to meet her Grandma Irma. She has even more questions now—she seems confused."

Luna had begun to fill notebooks with stories that began at the end, so that she didn't get lost in them, she said. Sometimes they were simply descriptions or conversations she had overheard between her friends at school. She trawled through magazines, cutting out words and pictures that made reference to Cuba or political terms like Communism or Nazism, pasting them down to make an endless collage, overlapping them on top of one another.

"One day it'll get so heavy we won't be able to pick it up off the floor," her mother told her, but Luna went on building that world beneath her feet.

Every evening when Nadine and Anton said goodnight, the little girl would stare at them for several seconds, holding their hands so they wouldn't leave the room.

Nadine thought Luna was scared of being left alone, or that she wanted them to read to her or sing songs for hours, until one day she realized what she was doing was imprinting them on her memory.

"Anton." She sighed. "Sometimes I think Luna's trying to make sure she doesn't end up like me."

"The two of you are the same, you can be sure of that, and she knows that too. That's how it is, our children come into the world to become a better version of us, don't you think?"

"She's realized I've spent my whole life forgetting, ever since I was born, and now she wants to remember everything."

Luna spoke Spanish with Mares; with Nadine and Anton she moved deftly between English and German, combining them and making up jokes that sometimes she was the only one to understand. She would wait for a reaction, growing frustrated when she was met with a long, awkward silence. Many nights Nadine and Luna would go on a "rescue mission," as Nadine called it, a mission during which she gradually introduced Luna to lost family members and the people who had surrounded them. Once she had opened the floodgates, Nadine began letting in people she had sometimes felt were merely figments of her own imagination. Even she was surprised to have set them free from wherever they had been hiding in her memory, never quite sure if they were real or a fantasy. But there were records that still existed of people like the Herzogs. And Franz's cousin Philipp, and the team of doctors who had tested Lilith's intelligence. And Martín's father who had served in Batista's cabinet, and Martín's best friend, Oscar, who had been killed in a plane crash. Their Katharinenstrasse apartment filled with faces that, over time, became familiar to them both. To Anton, they were like a tableau; the endless mimesis surprised and fascinated him.

Ally Keller wandered in and out of the stories, especially when they recited *The Night Traveler*. The little girl memorized the poem, and the two of them would delight in reciting it, inverting the meaning of the verses by giving them different inflections. Sometimes they read it with a musical lilt; or a summery, celebratory spirit; at others they made it wintery, leaving lengthy silences that gave the poem a tragic air. When they talked of Herr Professor, Nadine quoted famous lines from ancient poets; referring to Franz, she called him "the angel."

One night, when Luna was eight years old, she woke before dawn and went to her parents' bedroom. She stood in front of them and decided to wait for them to wake up. If Anton hadn't opened his eyes and seen her standing motionless in the dark, Luna would have stayed rooted to the spot for hours.

"Come and get into bed with us, Luna"

The little girl nestled between her parents and closed her eyes.

"Did you have a nightmare?"

Luna shook her head.

"What then? Too many ghosts? We'll have to tell mommy not to bring home any more books and papers from the library."

Luna opened her eyes and sat up in bed. Nadine woke with a start. The little girl took her parents' hands and very solemnly asked for their attention.

"I've decided I'm going to be a writer like my great-grandmother."

"Well, that's lovely, but it's time to sleep now," Nadine said, somewhat dismissively. "Tomorrow's a school day."

Anton was convinced his daughter already had her destiny all mapped out. He watched her filling notebooks and sheets of paper, which she kept neatly stored in the dresser drawer meant for her underwear. As far as she was concerned it was the ideal spot, the perfect hiding place for her texts to be safely hidden away. The following Christmas, her parents gave her a computer, to help with her writing, but Luna was used to writing by hand and kept the laptop for her schoolwork, which she always completed despite finding it tiresome.

Nadine gradually became convinced that Luna's obsession with writing served a sole purpose: not to forget. The only person Luna ever talked to about her writing was Mares, because it helped her decode her ideas when she went back to them. She had filled so many sheets of paper that no matter how hard she tried, she couldn't memorize all the words she'd written.

When the new millennium arrived, Luna reminded her mother and Mares they had a promise to keep: to go to Cuba. Nadine dodged the subject and Mares tried to put Luna off the idea. The truth was, neither Mares nor Nadine felt ready to go to the island. If Mares had agreed, Nadine might have faced her fears of flying on an airplane. But Mares said she wouldn't be welcome in Cuba. Ever since she had decided not to go back to the island after studying in Moscow, her mother had returned every one of her letters, and wouldn't answer her telephone calls. As far as her family was concerned, she was dead. Though they were somewhat better at remembering the dead, she noted with irony. At first, Mares had hated her family for turning their backs on her, though she knew that in her mother's view she was the one who had abandoned them. Over time, hatred turned to indifference, she explained to Luna.

For the first time in her life, Luna couldn't understand Mares. She felt her mother and Mares had conspired against her, making up the same past. They had both been given up, both had absent mothers they had run away from.

"In Cuba, they think I'm a *gusana*, a worm," Mares told her.

Luna didn't understand. What did it mean to be a worm?

"When someone goes to live abroad, or when someone leaves, they don't let you return," Mares explained, without elaborating, as if the subject wearied her. "To them, I'm a traitor. I'm sick and tired of Cuba."

Luna delighted in getting out of bed at night and slipping down the corridor to listen to the adults talking. *Adults can do whatever they like: go to bed late, eat whenever they feel like it, sit however they want*, she thought. She was always expected to have good table manners, she wasn't allowed to ask impertinent questions, raise her voice, or say bad words, or wrong words, as her father called them. No, no, no. Luna dreamed of being allowed to join in with those conversations in the dark, a steaming cup of cocoa in her hands as the others drank copious amounts of red wine and coffee. Her father would become impassioned, raising his voice to make his ideas heard, while her mother sat by him, as if seeking his protection, although Luna knew in fact it was to try to calm him down. Huddled together like that, Nadine and Anton almost seemed like one person. Luna was envious, not of her mother or her father, but simply wanting to be there, between the two of them, all three merged into one body. Her mother looked at her father as if she had just met him, captivated by his words. Then he would pause for breath, clear his throat, and stroke her arm. And Luna? Where did she fit in?

This was when the little girl realized: she was destined to live in the night. She and her grandmother Lilith were daughters of the moon. Daytime was for activities: school, music class, eating, bathing, getting dressed. At night she could write, read, watch television, eavesdrop on her parents' secrets, and rummage through closets, hidden drawers, and boxes of costume jewelry. At night she was herself. In the morning, she was someone else, the little girl everyone wanted her to be. Her great-grandmother Ally had known this and written a beautiful poem about it that seemed to speak directly to Luna across the years.

One day, without saying a word to her parents, Luna turned the house on its head. That was how Mares, overcome with laughter, described it when she saw it. The girl had taken all the books off the shelves and reshelved them with their spines facing inward. Luna's stockings never matched, and if she plaited her hair, one was always thicker than the other. She had gotten that quality from Anton's mother, Nadine thought.

When Luna's grandfather Joachim Paulus died of a heart attack in his sleep, her Grandma Ernestine decided to sell their apartment in Lucerne and return to Berlin to be near Luna. It didn't come as a surprise, because Luna's grandmother had spent her whole life doing what people least expected. She had worn a flowery suit to her husband's funeral, where he was eulogized as a hero who had restored German dignity through his tireless work in the restitution of Jewish property. He had been commemorated with a tree planted in his honor, naming him "Righteous Among the Nations" on a little hillside in Jerusalem. Standing at her side at the funeral, Luna had worn a blue blouse and a new green skirt. They were the only ones not wearing black.

After her grandfather's funeral, friends Luna had never heard of before filed through the house, men and women who spoke different languages and who remembered everything her grandfather had done for them. The house was filled with candles and flowers, platters of food, and a great deal of wine. There were hugs and kisses, together with tears and weeping. Luna was surprised to see photographs of her grandfather alongside heads of state on the front page of the newspapers. The old man she ate ice cream with in the middle of winter, without her grandmother knowing, whom she devoured chocolate bars with, who bounced her on his knee and told her stories of snow-topped mountains had never told her he was a hero, admired by so many. For Luna, he was simply Grandpa Joachim, whom she visited every Christmas.

They read in the newspaper that Irma Brauns had died, and Jordan Taylor too, just a few weeks after his wife. Nobody took flowers or lit candles for them. There was sadness in the Paulus family, but it was a different kind of sadness. At least in the Paulus house, they were proud of their dead. The news of Irma's death didn't appear on the front page, but the extensive article included a photograph of a young Irma wearing her Nazi uniform. She had choked to death, Luna overheard the adults say. A pulmonary obstruction. Luna felt her mother's pain. *Did she have time to look back over her life?* she wondered. After Irma's death, Jordan Taylor had spent the whole day beside her, in bed, as if he hoped she might wake up any moment, until the woman who usually helped Irma get up and wash arrived.

This caregiver had found Irma Brauns, whom the newspapers still delighted in calling "the Stomping Horse," cold and stiff. Perhaps she had asked for forgiveness, like those who know they are going to die. An absolution that only makes a difference to them, not those left living, or those who had died before.

After Irma Brauns's death, Jordan Taylor continued the daily routine he had followed every morning but did it without the woman he had dedicated his life to. After eating breakfast, the Taylors would cross the park opposite the care home garden, bordering the Christmas market, and stop at the flower stall. Then he would ask if she would like a bouquet. Irma would shake her head as she stroked the rag doll in her lap. "Why bother?" she would say. "Flowers only wither and die." After this they would return home. Her husband continued the ritual every day, pushing the empty wheelchair. To him, she was still there. Memory was a heavy burden.

One afternoon, Mr. Taylor had left apartment 1C on his own, without the wheelchair, and yet had made the same journey. As he stood at a traffic light, waiting for the signal to cross the street and enter the

Christmas market, Mr. Taylor had fallen into the road, or maybe he had let himself fall. The cars didn't have time to stop. When Nadine read about it in the newspaper, the shouts that had tormented her years before came flooding back, and she saw her father's body, his eyes still open, in the road. It was a scene she had already experienced.

Nadine was sad for several days. Much more so than when Grandpa Joachim had died, thought Luna. But Nadine wasn't grieving the loss of her adoptive parents; she had stopped thinking about them a long time before. She was sad because one night she had wished them dead, in Frau Adam's library, while the wife of another Nazi accomplice lamented the fact Nadine's mother had become a scapegoat for German remorse. That day she wished death, the worst kind of death, on her mother, her father, and Herr and Frau Adam. "Who was I to judge?" she said, weeping, to Anton, who did not know how to console her.

Although everyone in the house was suffering, each for their own loss, Luna was happy, as Grandma Ernestine was going to live with them for a time, while she sold the apartment in Lucerne and bought a house in the outskirts of Berlin, where it always seemed to feel like winter. To Luna, the cold nights were a joy. She had been named after a celestial body that orbited the earth and reflected sunlight, a fact she would point out whenever she was sent to bed early.

Ernestine bought a house on the shore of Lake Wannsee, near the home of the painter her husband had rescued, which had been converted into a museum.

"This way we'll never forget Grandpa," the old woman told Luna when she took her to see the house.

That summer Luna spent several weeks with her grandmother, decorating what was a classic German summer house—white, with a symmetrical garden—which her grandmother acknowledged was too big for just one woman. But memories take up a lot of space, she used to say, and she wasn't going to forget. Luna and Ernestine planted birch trees along the path that ran down to the lake, creating order out of disorder, as she told her parents when they came to collect her. The trees didn't follow a straight line, but were spread on either side of the courtyard, now a garden. They turned the back door into the main entrance, put the sofa in the dining room, and converted the library into a reception room.

Seeing the surprise on Anton's face, Ernestine hugged him.

"There's no better way to welcome someone than with books."

27

Nadine opened the door to Theodor Galland's office and saw Luna sitting on the couch, surrounded by yellowing sheets of paper. Luna got up, went to her mother, and helped her take off her jacket. A student, kneeling on the floor facing the couch, was sorting through envelopes with stamps of the Führer on them. Professor Galland, her old literature professor, was shielded behind his desk, surrounded by columns of books. When Nadine entered, the three turned to look at her. Nadine felt intimidated, wondering why they had summoned her to the university. She had had to leave work early, delaying the completion of a half-finished study, because they had told her it couldn't wait. There was a huge box on the desk, with a red gabardine coat on top. Inside were letters, documents. Nadine looked around at their excited faces.

"You should sit down," Professor Galland said with unusual formality. "I'm trying to put these letters in order."

Thinking this would be a short meeting, Nadine had perched on the edge of a table, as if ready to get up and leave. Now she took a deep breath, set her purse down on the floor, and sat down in a chair across from Galland. Clearly, this was going to take longer than expected. She didn't like surprises, as they all knew full well.

"We were wrong," the professor said. "I never imagined anything like this."

Luna picked up the documents scattered on the floor, one by one, placing them inside the box. Her expression was tense, and she was avoiding her mother's gaze.

"Do you mind telling me what's going on?"

"You're not going to like what you hear," the professor continued. "We found a letter from your grandmother."

"I thought you had already published everything of hers that survived," Nadine replied, uncomfortable, impatient. "I can see there's more than one letter there . . ."

"It's the last thing Ally Keller wrote. Your grandmother wanted to burn it, but Franz rescued it from the fire."

"Dear Franz . . ." Nadine said.

Professor Galland and Luna looked at one another, as if trying to decide which of them would deliver the news.

Nadine settled back in the chair. She tucked her graying hair behind her ears and fixed her gaze on a spot on the wall behind the professor. She noticed a clock there, just above a window that looked out onto a brick wall. The second hand quivered just before it ticked to the next minute mark, as if the shock made it bounce, as if it arrived in the future by inertia. *Why would someone have a clock behind them,* she wondered? Nadine reached the conclusion that it wasn't for the professor, but for his students and visitors like her, who interrupted his routine. She stared at the second hand, trying to stop it from moving. She couldn't face going back to the past again. How long would this go on?

They had already rescued her grandmother. The professor had published in a literary journal the poem that had accompanied her family halfway around the world. Saving that poem—which her mother had traveled with to Cuba, and which Nadine had then taken to the United States, and from there back to Germany, where her daughter had devotedly studied it, word by word, simile by simile, memorizing its lilt and rhythm—was the greatest tribute they could pay to great-grandmother Ally Keller. It was no accident that Luna had chosen to study German literature at university. Nadine saw the meeting between her daughter and Professor Galland as inevitable. She had set Luna's path in motion the day she'd decided as an undergraduate to take an elective literature course about German poets forgotten during the war. A course in which her grandmother was mentioned.

When the university archives were reopened after the reunification of Germany, Professor Galland decided to make copies of all available material to piece together the life of the woman who was embodied in that poem. He had traced as far back as Marcus, the Black musician who had disappeared and was probably killed before the war began. He had found archives belonging to Bruno Bormann, who Ally Keller called Herr Professor, as well as the writings of a young German man, Franz Bouhler, who had saved Lilith. With this material, the professor had published a fairly detailed study of Ally Keller's turbulent life and times and collected her haunting poetry in four slim volumes. The first was devoted to Marcus and music, the second to Bruno and literature, the third to Franz and love, and the fourth to Lilith and light. Nadine had now closed that painful chapter in her family's history. What more needed to be rescued?

These days, her daughter wrote through the night, holed up in the apartment her parents had bought in Mitte when Grandma Ernestine died. It pleased Nadine that her daughter, after finishing college, lived on the very same street where Ally Keller was thought to have written *The Night Traveler*. During the liberation, most of the buildings had been damaged or destroyed. She knew it wasn't the exact apartment, but Luna said she could feel her great-grandmother's presence, protecting her.

Luna kept her bedroom in darkness. She wrote by the window that looked out onto Anklamer Strasse, as if her great-grandmother had been reincarnated within her. She had already published her first collection of poetry, dedicated to Franz, the angel, and edited by Professor

Galland. Anton pointed out it was an achievement Ally Keller never accomplished while she was alive.

She should have listened to Mares, Nadine now told herself. Her friend believed that delving into the past could help heal certain wounds, but that some doors should be kept shut. Nadine couldn't understand her. *You can read what you want to, interpreting it whichever way you want*, she had thought. She was tired of living surrounded by ghosts. But now she knew her friend had been right.

The day in 1989 when they opened the borders and began demolishing the wall that divided the two Berlins, Nadine crossed to the other side with Mares, something that had previously been nearly impossible. For Mares it had been like going back to Cuba, where she wasn't wanted, where her mother considered her a traitor. They were so near and yet so far from the other side, she thought. All they had had to do was cross the road. A stream of people was coming and going from east to west, the only cardinal points that existed for Berliners. On the other side, time had stood still. There was fear, doubt. Young people were singing songs, some were stripping off their clothes as an act of liberation.

When they returned to the west, Anton was waiting for them in the doorway of their apartment block.

"How did you have the nerve?" he asked, shocked.

"I didn't want to miss this moment," Nadine replied.

"Four decades," Mares said somberly. "They've damaged our DNA The damage is physical. They destroyed more than a generation."

One afternoon, after the fall of the wall, Nadine decided to cross over on her own. She walked for hours along unfamiliar streets and avenues. The difference between the people on each side was striking. Some euphoric with victory. Others afraid, uncertain. They carried the weight of defeat, even though it brought freedom. *It's like being rescued from a cult*, Nadine thought. *You feel haunted, humiliated for the rest of your life.*

She wandered through the side streets of Mitte, previously closed to her behind the wall, losing herself in its courtyards. She saw an abandoned cemetery, a garden behind railings, a former school. Before long, she didn't know where she was. She had traveled back in time over years, decades. Disoriented, she ended up at a building with flaking paint and a rickety door. She approached it, running her finger over the bronze numerals. She wanted to know where she was, which street she was on, and if it still had the same number it had half a century before. She closed her eyes and saw her mother, age seven, desperately running, fleeing, chased by shadows.

Now, in Professor Galland's office, facing newly discovered texts by her grandmother, she wished she had Mares by her side. But her friend was no longer there. Mares and Gaspar had gone to Valparaíso, Chile, where they planned to live for a year or two while he taught at a Catholic university he had once been expelled from as a student. Nadine knew they would stay there forever. It's impossible to put down roots after surviving a dictatorship, she used to say. Mares had turned her back on the north to set up home in the south. She was tired of the grammatical nuances of a language she would never master. If she had been charmed by this city whose name, Valparaíso, held echoes of paradise, it was because it was surrounded by the sea. She was born in a place with water all around her and wanted to remain faithful to her name, she had once written in a letter to Nadine. They lived in a small apartment in the Concepción neighborhood, full of hills and steps that led down to the ocean. When Nadine came to visit, they would take a trip to the poet Neruda's house on Isla Negra, she said.

She imagined Mares on a beach in the Pacific.

Nadine had just turned fifty-five years old, and at that age, she felt there shouldn't be any surprises left to discover.

When her daughter's poetry book had been published and dedicated to Franz, it had generated a debate that neither Nadine nor the academic world was quite prepared for. Anton had spent his life ensuring the guilty didn't get away with what they had done, that they returned everything they had stolen, but his daughter painted a picture of the kinder side of Germany. In her poems, Luna was suggesting that not all

Germans were Nazis, they weren't all the same, and many young people had simply fulfilled something they were predestined for: to serve their country. Questioning the nature of that country might be valid now, but in those days, it was a matter of life and death. They didn't have a choice.

Franz had been one of these young people. His surname was associated with horror. One of his cousins had been part of the racial hygiene program designed to eliminate imperfection. The German race was perceived as damaged, and a Bouhler had set out to save it—albeit in a completely misguided way. But Franz had protected a *mischling*: Lilith. He had helped find her a new name, a new family, and a pass granting permission to disembark on a Caribbean island. Thanks to Franz, Ally Keller had been able to save her daughter. She hadn't survived herself, perhaps in part due to the pain of letting her daughter go.

This wasn't a new discourse, but Luna Paulus's book had revived the debate.

"Franz's daughter has donated a box of her father's papers," the professor explained. *Did he say "daughter?"* Nadine thought.

Luna's eyes were fixed on her mother. Nadine stood up and apprehensively brushed her fingers against the fabric of the red coat.

"It's Russian wool," she said.

"It seems it belonged to your grandmother."

Nadine carefully lifted the red gabardine coat out of the box, as if it were a living thing.

"There are several poems, probably the last ones she wrote, after she left Lilith at the port of Hamburg," Professor Galland said quietly. "As well as a letter your mother wrote to Franz from Sachsenhausen."

"So, Franz had a daughter." Nadine's voice was barely audible, but a faint smile passed across her face. "Our dear Franz—"

"Her name is Elizabeth Holm," the professor interrupted her. "While she was emptying her father's apartment, she came across the box, and in it an article I wrote on *The Night Traveler*. That's how she tracked me down at the university. The letter . . ."

"We should thank his daughter," Nadine said firmly. "To have kept all those old papers and an overcoat for all those years . . . When did Franz die?"

"Franz survived," the professor clarified. "His daughter put him into a care home for the elderly on the outskirts of Berlin when he got old and was suffering from senile dementia."

Luna went over to her mother, gently took her hand, and said, "Franz is still alive."

28

In her final weeks at the apartment, Ally Keller lived with her eyes closed. She stumbled around the rooms, trying to overcome the darkness she herself had created. At night she filled sheets of paper with a jumble of disconnected texts, the only way she could overcome time, her one true enemy.

Since they had watched Lilith climb the gangway on to the black, red, and white ocean liner, Herr Professor had been in bed with the flu, and the sound of his coughing penetrated the walls. Every morning and evening, Ally made him a tea with ridged cardamom pods and dry lavender flowers, sprinkled with a few drops of valerian. The scent of the infusion permeated the building. The thing that really soothed his cough, though, was a shot of Jägermeister that Franz had brought one night when he came to read them his latest grandiloquent poems. Ally had thought the drink was intended to make them sleepy, so they could bear to listen to him. The Jägermeister bottle was almost empty, and Herr Professor was still in bed, no longer proffering his customary speeches or literary quotes. It was as if he had said goodbye to the world and was now simply waiting for the end.

It had been more than a month since they'd had word from Franz. They had no idea where to find him or telephone him, and neither Herr Professor nor Ally dared to ask after him. They lived in constant fear that he had been arrested for having helped them get Lilith out of the country. Thanks to him, the little girl had been given a new identity and they had been able to send her to Cuba with the Herzogs, on a ship meant only for Jews. Ally's thoughts ran around and around in her mind; she felt at times they collided with those of Herr Professor, both of them blaming themselves for Franz's disappearance. In one night, they had lost both him and Lilith.

Ally grew accustomed to being awake both day and night. She only closed her eyes to think. All she did was write, because if she didn't, she would forget. As she didn't sleep, she didn't dream, and it was only in dreams—or rather nightmares—that she was able to conjure up her daughter. Without the memory of her, little by little the apartment became emptier by the day. Everything around her had lost its true dimension.

The morning Herr Professor appeared in her apartment, swamped by a dressing gown that now looked huge on him, Ally was standing by the window, the drapes drawn shut, resting her eyes.

In the gloom, Herr Professor saw sheets of paper piled up on the desk, the armchairs, in every corner of the room. The sheets were the path Ally had been leaving so she could find her way back to the starting point, which had become lost inside a maze.

"We're going to have to get rid of all this." In spite of his diminished appearance, Herr Professor's voice was firm, strong, and deliberate.

He meant Ally's handwritten manuscripts and copies of the magazines that had published her poems. Herr Professor had one of Ally's notebooks in his right hand. He was planning to edge toward the unlit fire and throw it in behind her back. They ought to have a bonfire, before it started to rain. It was too easy to leave tracks that would lead to Ally's ruin.

"There's nothing else I'm afraid of losing."

"I'm talking about your writing." Herr Professor slipped the notebook into his pocket without her seeing.

"What else can befall us?"

"I'm not talking about us, but Lilith, Franz . . . It's best we burn it all, get rid of anything that might compromise them."

Ally agreed with a nod. When she lowered her gaze, she noticed Herr Professor was barefoot.

"You can't walk around like that. You're unwell, it's dangerous . . ."

"A man can die but once," he said as he left the room.

Ally curled up in her armchair beside the fireplace. From there, the living room seemed enormous. It was June but there was still a chill in the air. Several rooms in the apartment had become off-limits to her, including Lilith's bedroom as well as her own. Ally's life now took place in the reception room, which was also the scene of goodbyes. She knew she was also about to leave, although she had no idea of her destination. She would stand in front of the only mirror in the apartment, searching for the vibrant blue that had once resided in her eyes. She had lost it. In the past, she had written about the death of colors, that tend to fade away, lose their radiance. Her hair, skin, lips, eye sockets had all taken on a coppery hue.

Ally felt unwell. Her limbs were heavy. Breathing was difficult. No air reached her lungs.

She lit the fire absentmindedly. She tossed on a log, then another on top to make a cross, and the fire rekindled. It was the last of the wood. The last thing she had, a burden she could turn into energy. As the flames grew, the crackling fire splintering the wood made her shudder. She collapsed back into her chair, her sacred reading nook where once she had always breathed peacefully, and she forgot what Herr Professor had said: she couldn't remember what she had to do. A few minutes later, her gaze fell on the papers strewn around, and remembered he had told her to throw them all in the fire. She felt relieved. She was edging closer to the end.

She grabbed a piece of paper, as if the poems were alive, and read a few lines that she barely recognized as her own. She read them aloud, unhurriedly, with the calm of someone no longer really there. She read them as if Lilith could hear. She didn't try to weave the words together, but rather scatter them. How many times would she have to say good-bye? How many deaths must she suffer? She read the words, or thought them. Was it written down, or were the words within her?

She heard footsteps on the stairs. The foundations shook. The time had come. She sensed the hunters, poised to shoot. Who were they looking for? They were in a hurry. Some were running. There could be two, three, four of them. The sound of the footsteps swelled, pounding down the corridor, coming and going. She felt them getting closer, almost on top of her. Only the living can be hunted. She had already died.

There was a knock on the door. A sharp rapping that reverberated through the apartment and made her react. The poems, her writings, the loose sheets of paper, she had to burn them. Hadn't she heard Herr Professor? She wouldn't be doing it for herself—for her there would be no salvation—she would do it for the others. Faltering, she let the first sheet fall into the fire, watching how it was consumed within seconds. Then another, and another and another. The fire lit up the living room. She had to keep going. She should throw them all on at once. She looked for her red gabardine, lying on a chair. Folding it out on the floorboards, she started to pile the sheets of paper onto it. Something that had once seemed easy was now a terrible burden.

Suddenly, the door was kicked open. Just as she was picking up the red coat, a hand reached out to stop her. She spun around and saw a soldier who looked at her kindly.

"Fräulein Keller, let me help you with that," the man said, with the hint of a smile, holding the coat that harbored her words.

There were three more soldiers behind him. She felt they carried the weight of the entire German army, that they had brought the impatience of the whole city with them into her home. The friendly soldier didn't take his eyes off her, as if she might run away or vanish into thin

air. He was studying her, and then the room. His eyes took in every corner, the drawn drapes, the unlit lamps. Ally lived in darkness.

"I'm sorry, Fräulein Keller, but you'll have to come with us." His
voice was like a caress.

The other soldiers retrieved the papers Ally had wrapped in the
gabardine coat, and placed them, along with the other sheets that still
lay around the room, into a box one of them was holding. Ally's coat was
put back on the armchair. It had been saved from the fire. She went over
and quickly brushed her fingers against it, one last time. They could take
her now. The red gabardine was no longer hers. She would go down the
stairs, cross streets full of soldiers. She knew they were pursuing her and
her writing. She went over every line of the verses in her head, realizing
she had never once mentioned her daughter's name in any of them. Nor
the Herzogs. How would they ever know that Lilith was light? She did
mention Franz, but not by name. She talked of the angel, as Lilith had
called him. She had to protect him.

The fire in the fireplace burned itself out and the room grew dark.
She could almost have escaped then, opened the window and thrown
herself out into oblivion. The wind would carry her wherever it pleased.
But the friendly soldier had her in his grip.

She heard a crash outside, followed by a groan. There was laughter,
too. Someone was happy. Then more groaning. A heavy body thudded to
the floor. The soldiers looked at one another, as if awaiting an order. At
that moment she knew the person in charge, the one who was behind this,
was still outside. One of the soldiers went out to see what had happened.
Seconds later, he returned. He told the others that it was time to go. All of
them, her included. The weight of her legs dragged her down. She walked
between the soldiers.

Out in the corridor, the lightbulb blinded her. A soldier was struggling to lift an inert body from the top of the stairs. Ally saw the head
hanging down over the step, as if it had detached from the body. The
head hit the step first, then the body toppled after it and rolled into a

ball. The image appeared distorted, fragmented, broken up in between the soldiers' polished boots. When they saw her, they straightened up, and the light filtered past them. Ally lowered her gaze toward something she didn't want to see. The body was covered with a wine-red dressing gown, with dark stains on one shoulder. The blood had turned black on the red silk. Ally let out a cry, and it frightened her. She hadn't heard herself. She didn't even know she was still capable of making a sound. She went down on her knees.

"Bruno, can you hear me? Wake up . . ." Ally whispered, into his ear so that no one else heard. "It doesn't matter what they take. They won't find Lilith's name on a single page, or the Herzogs. Nothing."

Herr Professor didn't react. Every attempt to draw oxygen into his lungs made him wince with pain.

"Bruno," her voice cracked. "Don't leave me all alone . . ."

Ally felt tears running down her cheeks. She held the professor's head and swept the white hair off his forehead. She gently dabbed at a thin line of blood that escaped from between his lips, threatening to become a river. Herr Professor opened his eyes, and she helped him come to.

"We must go downstairs," the kind soldier said.

Ally didn't see him. She wanted to forget every face. Forget. She was prepared to go down, to take the path to sacrifice.

Ally kissed Herr Professor's forehead, and a fleeting smile played on his lips. She looked at the nearest officer and lashed out.

"Why are you arresting him? He's an old man."

"Do they need a reason?" Herr Professor mumbled, beginning to recover.

Ally helped him sit up, and he gripped the iron banister with his right hand, grimacing in pain. His left arm hung limp by his side. Ally held Herr Professor around the waist, and they attempted to stand, together, as if they were one body. With great difficulty, they started down the stairs. Ally counted each step one by one. She noticed every vein in the marble, desperately committing it all to memory. A soldier opened the door at the bottom. The sun was shining. Ally had thought it was the middle of the night; she had lost all notion of time. Could it be midday? She had always traveled by night with Lilith.

The breeze brushed over them. There was a car waiting. When they crossed through the main doorway, Ally noticed an officer to her right. Each time a soldier passed in front of him, they gave a victory salute. They had triumphed over a woman and an old man. This is the way wars begin. First, they crush the smallest, the most insignificant. What was so frightening about them? Ideas.

"We have the documents you wanted, sir," the kind soldier reported to the officer.

There it was. *Her poems had already become mere "documents,"* thought Ally.

The professor climbed into the car first. She followed. He hung his head between his knees; Ally didn't know whether from pain or shame. The soldiers continued to salute the officer, with their heroic gesture. They had saved the papers from the fire, as he had ordered. *Perhaps the old man had simply fallen, and now he had recovered,* Ally thought. *They would take them to the station now, to be interrogated, and from there they would take them to Oranienburg,* she told herself.

Her eyes misty, she turned to look at the entrance to her home one last time. It was her gesture of farewell. She saw the enormous door knocker, the bronze number 32 that had turned green over time. She saw the wooden door planks, now so far away, and the sidewalk cobblestones. Her eyes lingered on the officer's shiny, heavy boots, the impeccable uniform, with its Germanic runes and silver skulls, the revolver in its black leather holster, the belt, the shiny jacket buttons, the black swastika in a white circle drawn on the blood-red armband. *The beauty of power,* she thought. *Perfect symmetry.* She got as high as the officer's wide, straight neck. He had been keeping watch at the entrance of the building. He hadn't dared to enter her apartment. She recognized his pursed lips. She saw his nostrils opening and closing, and she came to a halt at his eyes. Those blue eyes that once used to make her feel sleepy. *Why did she have to see his eyes?* she asked herself.

Ally lowered her gaze. There was nothing more to remember. Wasn't it easier to forget? She was overwhelmed, light-headed. A sudden sharp pain in her belly made her shudder. In the darkness, she felt for Herr Professor's hand. She summoned every last shred of strength, and as the car pulled away turned again to look at the officer. A cloud passed slowly above him. In shadow, Ally recognized him.

It was Franz.

29

Ally Keller's naked body lay on the white-tiled table. The table was a rectangular slab in the center of the room, almost an extension of the floor, walls, and ceiling. Every surface was tiled. On either side of the doorway were two glass-fronted metal cabinets, painted a shade of pale green. At the far end of the room was another door, also flanked by similar cabinets containing instruments laid out in size order, and glass jars with labels that identified what was inside them. A long, narrow table ran along one of the side walls, below three equidistant windows. There was a third table in the room, parallel to the one Ally's body lay on. In the center of each was a circular gold-colored drain pierced by dozens of tiny holes. The room was perfectly symmetrical. Above each table, three lamps hung from a dark tube. The light was intense, leaving no possibility of shadows. Nothing could survive the white of the tiles.

A doctor and nurse entered the room. Ally knew who they must be, she didn't have to open her eyes to recognize them. Under the weight of her eyelids, in the darkness, her perception was heightened. The doctor, whose spotless military uniform could be glimpsed beneath his white coat, moved toward the table where Ally lay, ignoring the body of the old man stretched out on the other one. Ally's body was as cold as the windows in midwinter, cold as the long silver instrument he began to insert between her legs, with a surgeon's precision. When the instrument reached its deepest point inside her, Ally opened her eyes. The blue had disappeared from her irises. The doctor looked around for the nurse, who came to stand at the head of the table, ready to restrain the patient should that become necessary, but Ally remained inert, in a torpor. Perfection was sharp, cutting. Never before had whiteness been so painful.

Removing the instrument from Ally's body, the doctor dropped a bloody lump onto the table, a piece of flesh still attached to the woman's body by a thread. The dark mass spread across the white tile. The nurse and doctor observed it, watching to see if there was any reaction, any pulse. How long could it survive now that it was no longer inside, being fed? They were trying to detect the merest beat, the slightest movement, some sign of life, Ally thought, knowing she was completely bloodless. She had been on the table for twenty-four hours. They had cleaned and emptied her body, there couldn't be a single drop of blood left inside her, and yet she was still alive. Why her?

All she wanted was to put out the light. She no longer cared that they took the only thing left inside her, but she couldn't bear the brightness. It was like burning on a bonfire. She had been close to the end so many times by now that she was too exhausted to go back over her life yet again. She had heard it said that being close to death, one goes back, to the start, to see what you were, or could have been, settle your debts, and start to bid farewell to the world. She had been saying goodbye for months. At the very end, it made sense she should let go, alone.

When she had arrived at Grolmanstrasse police station, Ally knew Franz had betrayed them. She had seen him at the door to their apartment block, and yet for a moment she thought of protecting him. In that instant, her chest had tightened, her hands grew clammy, and she was overcome with doubt. She wanted to make excuses for him. He was a German soldier, he had to protect his future. She was convinced fear makes us wretched. Delirium bored into her, leaving her breathless.

When the interrogation began, a woman with slicked-back hair and red lips tried to win her trust in the windowless, pictureless room they took her to. The only furniture consisted of a table and two chairs. Fortunately, it was dark. The woman wanted to know how she had been able to get the little girl into Cuba, why she had been allowed to disembark there. It was thought that all the passengers had been sent back again.

It would have been better if she'd had Herr Professor by her side. He always had an answer for everything. He could calm the most deranged, even control their thoughts. But they had left her on her own, and she didn't know what the woman wanted. She was prepared to give her what she was looking for. She had nothing left to lose.

When they took her from the police station and made her climb up into the back of a covered truck, she knew she would never see Franz again. At the far end of the truck, she saw Herr Professor, still in his silk robe, and she pushed her way through people to get to him. They had split up the families. Thankfully, they hadn't been able to tear her daughter from her. They were too late. They eventually drove out of the city, and someone said they were being taken to Sachsenhausen. Ally let out a sigh, relieved. *No one comes back from Sachsenhausen*, she said to herself, remembering Paul, the Herzogs' son. She had reached the end. Yet another ending.

When they arrived at the camp, they split up the men and women. They took away all their clothes. They gave her a blouse and skirt made of rough, uncomfortable fabric. They were made to stand outside in the sun. Her blouse had an inverted red triangle, and they separated her from the women with purple triangles, and from those with the yellow star. She could make out the men on the other side of the camp. Herr Professor was wearing a pink triangle.

She knew the group she was allocated to were the privileged ones. As such, in spite of the fact they all had the same fate, some deaths would be better than others. She was with Germans, all of them racially pure, she heard someone say. They had access to paper and pencils, and they were allowed to send one letter each month. They fed them well, in a place where soup, a raw potato, moldy bread, an onion, and watery coffee could be considered a luxury. Once a week she was permitted to wash before going to the station house, as some of them called the place that others named the butcher's shop. In reality, it was the infirmary. Those Germans who could prove they had no genetic flaws or mental imbalance, those who were racially pure, were made to give blood. The soldiers on the front needed it, the nurse told the women, and they agreed, and why wouldn't they, in exchange for a cold shower and a pencil and paper?

Let them drain all her blood: they would be doing her a favor, thought Ally. Every time she left the infirmary, pale and breathless, she would look toward barrack 38, thinking of those who weren't fortunate enough to be bled dry in exchange for a shower or a raw potato. No attention was paid to the barrack with the pink triangle, for the effeminate prisoners. Their belongings were never checked for smuggled knives, rusty and with barely any blade that they might cut their veins with. The others marked with the pink triangle would be ordered to clean up the blood. Life fights on, even outside the body. Every cell strives to endure, not stopping until it finds a whisper of breath. Such is the desperate act of survival.

In return for onions and chunks of bread, Ally tried to find out what was happening in the barracks where they kept the men with the pink triangles, hoping to find out if Herr Professor was well, if he was still alive, if he had recovered from the blow to the head, but the answers she received were vague. Two or three corpses were carried out each day.

After two months there, Ally began to write her farewell. It would be a long letter, and it would be written to Franz. She wondered if she should note the date, or where she was being held. *He would already know that*, she told herself. She wanted to reproach him, but what would she gain by that? She wasn't trying to be rescued. Several times she questioned whether she should tell him, but in the end, she decided she should. Everyone was asleep in the barracks. The silence was a wonderful luxury. When the lights were switched off, the crying began. There was always someone sobbing, or quietly moaning, and the litany accompanied that of hunger, the symphony of anguish, the empty stomach. Ally didn't need light. She grabbed the pencil and etched the first stroke, then a second, and kept writing, uncontrollably. The first thing she wrote was what she herself didn't even dare say out loud. There was still someone to save, though there were still five months to go, which to her seemed like an eternity: she was pregnant.

The first letter was the shortest. The shared secret tasted of vengeance. There are many ways to settle a score. Hers was to make him feel guilty for everything he had done to Herr Professor, the Herzogs, and Lilith, who regarded him as an angel. He denounced them for what Ally had published. He sent them to Sachsenhausen. He got rid of her daughter and the Herzogs for a clean and pure Germany. She wished him dead every minute, every hour. But there was a child on the way. Now Franz had to decide whether or not to save his own child. It was her last and only hope.

The second letter would take her longer. The final act of vengeance is more difficult to sketch out. Her words grew like the cells dividing in her belly, the secret she felt as a constant fear. She had heard pregnant women were disposed of. If they found out in the infirmary, would they refuse to extract her precious blood? Everyone knew the doctor's assistant, whom they called "the butcher" and hated even more than the doctor, as she was the one who stuck cold spatulas between their legs to check whether they were pregnant, and it was the nurse who punctured their arms with a thick needle, searching blindly for a strong vein.

The butcher presented the greatest threat, Ally was sure. She slept in barrack 38 and wore a yellow star, but she was free to wander through the camp and go where nobody else could. She spent the day in the infirmary, playing with fetuses stored in thick yellow liquid inside glass jars, labeled with their gestation period.

Some said she had been a bloodthirsty midwife, others that she was once a prestigious doctor, one of those who dedicated their lives to bringing children into the world. Since arriving at the camp, the only way she had been able to save herself had been to participate in the experiments carried out in the infirmary. She was in charge of the pregnant women, whom she could recognize at a distance. She went from barrack to barrack, checking bellies to detect any that were swelling, despite the lack of food. It was said she told the women the only way to survive was to get rid of their unborn babies. The camp commander didn't want children, pregnant women, old people, or the sick. And who would want to bring a child into a world like this? Who was more cruel—the butcher, or the mother giving birth to live bait for the enemy?

So, the butcher would take the pregnant woman from the barracks in the middle of the night, sit her against a brick wall, on the dirt and the stones, spread her legs, and without pity or hesitation, introduce her hand then her arm, and remove whatever was in the woman's belly. If anyone in the camp succeeded in hiding her pregnancy, the butcher would be there at the birth, make the mother say goodbye to her newborn, and then proceed to drown it in front of her, to teach them all a lesson.

"Is this what you want?" she would shout, so that everyone in the barracks would hear. "Isn't it better to tell me in time so you don't have to live with that guilt?"

Then, not even stopping to wash her hands, she would climb into her bunk and fall asleep within seconds.

Fortunately, the butcher didn't pass by Ally's hut, and as time went on, with less blood in her body every day and the baby consuming her, she lost weight, her uniform hanging off her. Her belly grew, devouring her, but she lost muscle mass and could therefore hide it under her clothes.

She hoped, as she wrote of her agony, that Franz would arrive one day soon to save the baby.

A few days before Christmas, during the final blood withdrawal of the year, the doctor spoke to her when they were on their own.

"I know you're pregnant," he said to her quietly. "Your baby is going to be safe."

All Ally could muster was a smile. Her baby was going to be born. Another child she would have to abandon. She was convinced Franz had received her letter, that had been more like a plea. He wouldn't have to change the baby's name or hide the color of its skin or prove to a commission that its measurements were correct and its intelligence superior. The baby would not violate any of the new laws and could therefore exist.

"When will the baby be born?" the doctor asked.

Franz was determined to save the child and had been in touch with the doctor, Ally told herself. She touched her belly, feeling the size of her baby, who seemed enormous. It was her way of telling the doctor there were only days left before it came into the world. The doctor nodded, and she knew he was on her side. They had to keep the butcher away from her. Ally would tell him when her water broke, or if she started having strong contractions. When she left the infirmary, her blood depleted, she felt the baby's strong kicks. It was alive.

As the new year began, Ally finished the long letter she considered her farewell. She had ceased to exist months ago. A new decade was starting that was meaningless to her but not to the baby about to be born. She stayed in bed during the day under the doctor's special dispensation and at night she counted the heartbeats of the baby as it wriggled constantly. She stayed like this for two days, without eating, lying in her own urine and excrement. Nobody cared about her.

Ally closed her eyes, and let her child take over. At that very last moment, she realized she had to give in. No pain or duress could make her cry out, contract, or push. The baby had all the power in the world, and she prayed harder than she ever had before, pleading with God to save her child, to let it live, so that one day, when the world once more became the world, when no one had to travel at night or live in darkness, or prove their intelligence or their perfection, Lilith and this baby would meet. Was that too much to ask?

· ✦ ·

She awoke. She was still alive on the white-tiled table, and they were hosing her down with cold water. The water ran down the drain under her back. Her belly was inflamed, but the baby wasn't moving. There is nothing more comforting than the weight of something living. She wanted to shout out for it to move, nudge it roughly to wake it up, to show everyone it was still alive. She saw the doctor, the nurse, and an officer. A woman was cleaning the blood off the floor. Whose blood was it? They had tossed a body on the table next to her. She felt the stream of water once more. They called him "the old man," but she couldn't see him. A heart attack. He had come from the barracks with the pink triangles. They would open him up and examine his insides, looking for the error. Perhaps they hoped to discover his organs were as pink as the triangle. Ally knew it might be Herr Professor. Nothing in life happens by chance, though perhaps she was just hallucinating all of it. Even if she opened her eyes, she wouldn't be able to see him. Perhaps he had felt her presence before they cut him open and had let himself die.

She saw a movement against the light. The doctor had his back to her. In one corner was a woman who wasn't wearing a white coat. It was the butcher. Had she come for her? It's harder to survive without words.

"Relax, relax," said the doctor, in the most comforting voice she had heard in her life.

The doctor sponged her forehead with a warm, wet towel. It was the only thing she felt. After that Ally lost contact with her body, with the newborn baby, with the cold tiles. As if she had escaped from the room, she looked down on the camp's seventeen lookout towers, with their guards. She saw the village beyond the camp, its snowy streets and terraced houses, where everyone would be celebrating the goodness the new year would bring. Just a few meters from the camp, families lived peaceful lives. Perhaps they were the guards in the lookout towers, the women who ran the kitchens. Did the doctor and nurse live around the corner? Did they tell their neighbors what they did for a living?

When she returned to the icy table, they had already cleared away the corpse next to her. She was the only one there, apart from the doctor and nurse. The butcher had left. Was her child safe? There were no bloodstained sheets, no bowls of hot water, and her baby was not at her breast. Her breasts were empty, as dry as her belly. There was nothing more for them to take. The nurse put the placenta into one of the jars of formaldehyde and attached a label.

The doctor came alongside her, trying to detect her dying breath. Ally felt two cold fingers against her neck.

"It's a girl," the doctor whispered, watching for a reaction.

Ally felt his warm breath and wanted to smile gratefully, but her lips were frozen.

"Is she still alive?" asked the nurse.

"I don't think so . . ." the doctor replied.

Once again, he placed two fingers on her neck to check her pulse: the last one. He turned away and left the room. Ally heard the door slam. The nurse had switched off the lights before leaving.

It was dark. Once again, Ally was ready to travel at night.

30

When she left Professor Galland's office, Nadine felt she was on the edge of a precipice, flattened by the contents of a letter that should never have seen the light of day. She wasn't ready to forgive and walked for hours. Anton called her cell phone again and again in desperation, without getting an answer. He chided Luna for not going with her mother, who had said she wanted to be alone. Luna telephoned halfway across the world to speak to Mares, who promised she would get on a plane to be with her friend if she needed her.

As she roamed the streets, Nadine tried to understand why she was overwhelmed by a feeling of guilt. She should have looked for those she never knew: Franz, her mother, her grandmother, Herr Professor, even if only to visit their graves. She had refused even to go near Sachsenhausen, now turned into a dark museum where perhaps the remains of her grandmother and Herr Professor were spread on the earth. She had trusted that her daughter would take charge of rescuing them, as she had done with Ally. Now she was the one who needed to bring them all back.

Nadine sat on a bench in the Tiergarten, with the letter her grand-mother had written lying open on her lap. It had taken seventy-four years to reach her. Nadine felt she was passing through, like a tourist walking in the shadow of something that should be long gone, but still endured. A swastika on a forgotten wall in the Bismarckstrasse, the eagle with the hooked cross between its talons, the red marble at Mohrenstrasse station that came from the Führer's New Reich Chan-cellery, Albert Speer's lamps along Strasse des 17 which nobody had the desire to tear down, the inerasable footsteps of the Führer's dream city.

She put her phone aside and unfolded the two withered sheets. *Before her was one of the keys to her past*, she thought. The essence of Ally, her grandmother. She tried to decipher the order of the letters. One, penned in hasty handwriting, loose sentences, full of questions; the other, in small, almost illegible handwriting, as if she were taking advantage of every millimeter on the blank sheet. In both letters, sev-eral paragraphs had faded away, as if the sheets of paper had survived a shipwreck.

On one, there was no date or addressee.

> *You took my Lilith from me. What was my daughter's sin? Did losing her make me more pure in your eyes?*
>
> *Yes, we were a disgrace to you, but it was too late. I still am. There were my published poems. You can't get rid of them. The past, Franz, always condemns us.*
>
> *In the end, my daughter traveled by night: she is safe. Away from this hell, from you, from everyone.*
>
> *Now I just want you to know that you will never be able to get rid of me. You are tainted too. I am pregnant. Your child will be born in a cell.*

The other letter was dated.

Sachsenhausen–Oranienburg, January 1, 1940

Franz,

> *We have little time left.*
>
> *Your son is about to be born.*
>
> *Every time he moves, every time he gives me one of his kicks that shake me, that bend me with pain, he makes me happy. He is alive, eager to come into the world.*
>
> *The days are long, the nights are too short.*
>
> *In the evenings, I talk to our son, I tell him about Lilith, his sister. I know that one day he will find her, when the war is over, when we tire of being beasts.*
>
> *Franz, I do not come to blame you, it would be pointless. I only ask you, in the name of the love we once had for each other, to think now of our son. You have the chance to save him. Saving him will save you too. It is impossible to live in darkness for so long. I know that someday it will dawn again.*

She was reading fragments of the letter aloud when she received a phone call. It wasn't Anton or Luna, and she decided to answer. Night had already fallen.

"If I could be by your side now, I would," Mares said. "You should come to Valparaíso."

Nadine was silent for a moment, then said, "Remember the time we visited the Pergamon Altar?"

"Nadine, dear, listen to me. Anton and Luna are worried. I think it's time you went home."

Nadine wanted Mares to remember the visit to the Pergamon Museum, where they had seen an old man weeping inconsolably in front of the magnificent ancient Greek altar. Nadine had assumed he was on the losing side, yearning for a Germany that never existed, a thousand-year Reich that had crumbled in a decade. Mares, on the other hand, saw him as a victim of the Nazis, for whom the symbolism of the altar conjured painful scenes that prompted tears of loss. They had just walked through a U-Bahn station and seen the model of what Berlin could have been. It was now possible to exhibit the legacy of Albert Speer, the great architect, the Führer's best friend, the man who had captivated everyone with the imposing size and spare symmetry of the buildings he created, designed to stick in the memory, and which would survive his own ruin.

Mares listened to her friend, trying to make sense of her rambling conversation. To Nadine, Franz and Albert Speer were similar types, both were experts in make-believe. If he had wanted to, he could have known what was happening in Germany, the architect had admitted during his trial after the war. In the end, you only see what you want to see, Nadine insisted. It was easy for Speer to convince others he was repentant. The architect, who had been the Reich Minister of Armaments and War Production, had listened to the witnesses against him with kindness and sympathy. This set them apart from the Nazis who denied the horror. There was one particular gesture of his that blinded his accusers. Speer had once visited an underground weapons factory and taken pity on the workers' conditions, ordering the building of a barracks for them to live in, and insisting that they be properly fed. In truth, he was saving his cannons. For his part, Franz had taken great pains to save Ally Keller's final poems. In the end, a gesture of kindness can prevail. Ally had told him that in the last letter. By saving their son, he would be saved too.

The day of the downfall, after saying goodbye to someone he thought of as a friend, Albert Speer had not carried out the Führer's order to burn Berlin as Nero had burned Rome. He managed to seduce the Führer and now he once more displayed his talents and captivated the tribunal: he was the only one who showed remorse in court. In the end what he did or did not know was irrelevant. He was locked up in a cell with a yard in Spandau, a former Prussian fortress. In there he brought his Germania to life, secretly writing his memoirs on toilet paper, smuggled out by a compassionate guard.

The great architect was condemned to twenty years of tedium, a sentence he accepted until midnight of his last day in prison. The man who had been in charge of the armaments factories of the third and final Reich, died in glory, a millionaire, in a magnificent Art Deco hotel in London, as he was preparing to give a television interview. A blood vessel in his brain exploded.

In Lucerne one Christmas, at the home of a French friend of her in-laws, Nadine had heard another guest say that to understand is to forgive.

"I find it very hard to understand," Nadine replied.

Mares voice on the phone brought her back to the present. "You and Anton should come visit me. Bring Luna. It does you good to leave the city once in a while."

Before she said goodbye, Mares made Nadine promise she would travel to the end of the world, as she called the Chilean city where she now lived.

Arriving home, after reading the long letter a second time, she saw Anton at the window. When she got upstairs, he hugged her. Anton could feel her shivering.

The following morning, the first call Nadine made was to Elizabeth Holm.

Ever since Elizabeth had donated Ally Keller's texts to the university, she had been waiting for a call from a relative she thought would probably not be willing to accept her. It was the only way she was able to fulfill her mother's final wish. The letter had been a recent revelation for her too. Her father had never told her anything about her mother, nor that she had a half-sister whom they had sent to Cuba. She had grown up a child of the war, alone, with no past and no descendants.

Nadine sensed Elizabeth had been waiting beside the telephone for days. Her voice was soft, and she gave every word the same intonation. She didn't drop a syllable or add any. They met in the afternoon at Elizabeth's apartment.

"My father was—*is*—a good man," Elizabeth Holm said, her eyes fixed on the window. She held a steaming cup of coffee, but she still hadn't taken a sip.

Nadine and Luna Paulus, two strangers, had bombarded her with questions from the moment she had opened the door, as if she had any answers.

Nadine ran her eyes around the room looking for some kind of phsyical object that would connect them, while Luna stared at Elizabeth. The person sitting in front of them was her mother's closest relative, her half-sister. Nadine hoped to find a piece of Lilith in Elizabeth. Lilith lived somewhere in this stranger, in her gestures, her tone of voice, her drooping shoulders, her hands clinging to the cup as if it were a shield. Lilith and Elizabeth shared the same mother, they must have something in common. But only one was the traitor's child.

Luna tried to recognize her great-grandmother in the woman's profile, the lost blue of her eyes, the weight of her eyelids. She couldn't see any likeness. Of course, Ally Keller had died at twenty-five, much closer to the age Luna herself was now.

Seeing her by the window, Nadine felt that in her own way, Elizabeth was also saying goodbye. It's impossible to bear such a heavy load as one's journey nears its end. Elizabeth raised the cup of coffee time and again, savoring the aroma, but without taking a sip. She brought it to her lips, then paused nervously. She'd never gone back to Sachsenhausen, she said. She never could. On her birth certificate, issued belatedly, it had been recorded that she was born in Oranienburg and not the concentration camp where her mother had actually brought her into the world. Yes, Ally Keller was registered as her mother, but her father had told her that Ally had died during childbirth. A young love affair cut short by the war, that was all he had said. He was only twenty-one years old, and had been called to the front line, as everyone was in those days. Nobody could refuse. Elizabeth had grown up with her paternal grandmother, in the same apartment where she still lived. She hadn't known the grandfather who had died in the Great War, leaving her grandmother pregnant with Franz.

The only thing Elizabeth remembered from her childhood was, one night, plunging into a river with her grandmother, tied together with a rope around their waists, the pockets of their overcoats filled with stones. Fleeing the bombing in Demmin, to the north of Berlin, they had gone to stay with one of her grandmother's sisters.

"What was a five-year-old girl doing in the dark, icy waters of the River Tollense?" she said she asked herself for years.

One day her grandmother helped her decode the nightmare that had been tormenting her. Her grandmother's sister had not survived. The waters swept her away, along with hundreds of other villagers who chose to take their own life rather than live as the defeated. She and her grandmother were saved by soldiers of the Red Army, or so she was told.

The German army had abandoned the village and blown up the bridges over the river. Where could they run? The Red Army was closing in, determined to destroy everything they found. Almost all the families of the village had disappeared beneath the waters of the three rivers surrounding the village. Yes, she and her grandmother had been saved, but the horror never left her. They had wandered around for days, sheltering among the debris, eating scraps, before returning to a Berlin they no longer recognized. This is what her grandmother had told her, but all that existed for Elizabeth was the moment in the water, the sky above them, and a rope around her waist so she couldn't move. And the stones, those stones dragging her down to the bottom of the river. Her grandmother had intended for them both to die that night, but for some reason they had not.

Her days in Berlin were marked by the constant sound of sirens. Elizabeth couldn't understand why, if the Reds had already taken the city, bombs continued to fall, perforating streets and shelters. One day you had neighbors, the next you didn't. One day there was a row of terraced houses, and when the sun came up, the block was reduced to a huge lump of cement and bricks. She could still hear the sound of the sirens, Elizabeth said.

The war had continued after the liberation, for her at least. As a little girl she had decided never to marry or have children. The men were taken to the front, and you ended up losing your children too. She remembered the way her grandmother had scoured the streets of liberated Berlin, looking for food. She would return home dirty, bleeding, with a chunk of bread or a couple of potatoes. On the best days she might bring a chocolate bar handed out by an American soldier.

Nadine knew Elizabeth was just another victim. Sometimes people let themselves die. Her mother had been able to choose. Perhaps her grandmother too? She imagined the little girl among the rubble. What would the city have looked like out of that window seventy years earlier?

Three years after the liberation, Franz came home. Elizabeth smiled when she said her father's name.

"You see? That's why one shouldn't leave," she added.

If she and her grandmother had left, where would Franz have come home to? The only token the little girl had of her father was a photograph of him in uniform.

"He was handsome," she said. "But the man who returned was hunched, dragging one leg, and without a drop of life in his face. He had sunken eyes, and his skin had darkened and taken on a greenish tinge."

Elizabeth still remembered her father's smell, like that of a dead animal. From that day on, Franz was always an old man to her.

After he returned, Elizabeth had a name, documents, a passport. Her father decided to take his mother's surname, and everyone in the house became a Holm. They wanted to erase the name Bouhler, as if in doing so they could amend the past.

Elizabeth had gone to study in Moscow. She was just another foreigner there, and they looked down on her. She became a teacher, and when she came home she found out that her grandmother had died. She had been buried without a tombstone, and a wall now divided the city. Her father worked in a library, classifying books. He once told her he had dreamed of becoming a writer, but the war made decisions for people, took away their free will, turned them all into shadows.

Elizabeth's first job had been in a school, where she was greeted with distrust. She taught Russian to children who had no interest in the language, and who treated her like a spy or an informer. Everyone was frightened of one another. Your neighbor had become your enemy, listening to your every thought.

One day the Stasi took her father, and she didn't see him again for more than a year. They had loaded him into a van as he left work, taken him away without even asking his name. A woman who said she worked with him called Elizabeth that night, telling her he wouldn't be coming home. Elizabeth didn't ask questions. They both knew the phone might be bugged.

"They took him in a van," she said.

Everyone knew what that meant. When a man in plain clothes asked you to get into a van with no windows, you knew your fate. There would be no accusations or trials. You would just disappear, and that would be that. Then one day they would let you go, and you would have to start again from scratch. What could she do? Nothing. What could anyone do against the Secret Police? She was fortunate that she didn't lose her job at the school; she could continue to teach.

The afternoon her father returned—how many times is one allowed to return?—neither of them dared talk about why he had been taken, or what had been done to him. The past never goes away, however strong might be the desire to forget. Elizabeth eventually pieced together that her father had been denounced by a jealous library administrator who wanted to give Franz's job to a nephew of his. He accused him of being a Nazi officer who had never stood trial. *What about those years he had spent in Soviet prisoner of war camps?* Elizabeth asked rhetorically. According to her father, he had been better treated there, because he had been an officer and had turned himself in and collaborated with the Allies, than by his fellow East Germans, who had tortured him in the basement of a building that didn't appear on the map of Berlin, where they locked away the politically disaffected.

Being a Nazi wasn't the thing that most concerned the Stasi, but rather certain telephone calls he had received from a military colleague who had survived the war and was writing a memoir in West Berlin. Her father had told them he had no recollection of the man, that time and hunger had wiped his brain clean. Even so, the Secret Police had subjected him to extreme cold and heat, locking him in a solitary cell for weeks, with no windows and a lightbulb permanently lit. Her father began to wish he had never been brought into the world. He had been born into an era nobody should have had to endure.

Franz was never able to go back to the library, and one day he gave up looking for work. There was only so much an old man like him could do, so he stayed at home reading, or wandered the city. He eventually gave up going for walks when he noticed he sometimes struggled to work out where he was and would have difficulty finding the way home.

One night, when her father had been in bed for several days with a flu that left him feverish, Elizabeth heard the name Lilith for the first time. She had thought she must have been an old flame. When she asked her father who the woman in his nightmares was, Franz blushed, then fell into his habitual silence. By then he was confusing past and present. Sometimes he woke up believing he was in the Soviet prisoner of war camp, at others, that he was in a Stasi cell. He would fall to his knees and pray—he, who had never before believed in God.

Soon he began calling Elizabeth "mother." Elizabeth bore a striking resemblance to his mother, Franz would say when he woke in a more lucid state. Elizabeth accepted her father's mental deterioration as she had accepted everything else life had thrown at her, until one night, much to the neighbors' alarm, he ran out into the street naked, shouting her mother's name: Ally.

He underwent a multitude of tests and Elizabeth held on to the hope that some magic pills might bring her father back, rescue the calm, gentle man he had once been. They visited numerous doctors and hospitals, where he was given brain scans and subjected to group therapy that made him increasingly ill-tempered, until he was eventually diagnosed with senile dementia. He deteriorated rapidly. Two months later he was lying in bed, refusing to get up, shower, or eat. It broke Elizabeth's heart to listen to his incessant whimpers, so in the end she made the difficult decision to send him to a care home for the elderly, Senioren-Domizil. She always hoped he would recover, that this was merely a passing illness, but he never spoke or walked again. He had given up.

It was then that Elizabeth decided to clear out his bedroom. She donated his clothing and shoes to charity and disposed of everything her father had accumulated over the years: newspaper clippings, magazines, theater programs, instruction manuals, receipts. In a corner at the very top of the closet, she discovered a heavy and battered box. She could sense that whatever was inside was different from the rest.

She lifted it and placed it on the dining room table, where it remained unopened for several days. Elizabeth ate breakfast, lunch, and dinner looking at the box, as if it were a guest at the table. Finally, she looked inside. The first thing she saw was a recently published literary magazine. Her mother's name was written on it, and so Elizabeth read *The Night Traveler*. She guessed the red gabardine coat must have belonged to her, along with all the other papers in the box. It was the first time she had ever felt close to the woman who had brought her into the world. Then, at the bottom, she found the letter and discovered she had a half-sister named Lilith.

She could have thrown all the yellowing papers into the trash, along with the red gabardine coat. She could have chosen to forget. But then she came across the name of the professor who had rescued and studied her mother's texts and decided to telephone him. Her half-sister, though older than Elizabeth, might be alive. Perhaps her father had looked for her before, to carry out Ally's wish, only to find ashes, or closed doors. In any case, what did she have to lose? Had she done the right thing? She couldn't yet be sure. She wanted to believe she had, she said, as if waiting for confirmation from one of them. Nadine said nothing. Luna looked around at the house, frozen in time as if the wall between the two Germanies were still standing.

"And what about Lilith?" Elizabeth asked, her voice unsteady.

Luna snapped out of her daydream, waiting for her mother to answer. Nadine wavered.

"My mother died in Cuba," she said. She didn't want to tell her that it was likely she had taken her own life. "The war never ended for her. But she was able to save me . . . She sent me on an airplane, alone, when I was very young, and I was adopted by a family in New York."

Hearing herself speak, Nadine realized the war hadn't ended for her either. She had lived through one war after another. War was getting on an airplane, a courthouse waiting room, a rag doll with her name on it.

Elizabeth's face fell. The reason she had taken the box to the university and welcomed Nadine and Luna into her home was that she hoped to fulfill the final wish of the mother she never knew: that her two daughters would one day meet.

"We'd like to visit Franz," Luna said.

Nadine thought that if Franz had taken refuge in oblivion and lay in a bed in a care home for the elderly, what sense was there in confronting him? She couldn't understand what else her daughter wanted to know, why she continued to interrogate Elizabeth as if hoping for a miracle. Franz wasn't going to wake from his unresponsive state, and he was the only one who had known her mother and grandmother.

"You must understand, there's not much to see," Elizabeth said, at last putting her cup of coffee down on a table covered with a fraying lace tablecloth. "My father can't leave his bed, he doesn't move. He can barely say a word. He's ninety-five years old."

Nadine knew Luna had been storing up every word, every gesture, and that later, in her apartment, she would write until dawn, filling notebooks with her impressions, to preserve every moment. She was the one who needed to meet Franz.

"I've written about him, or rather the memory my great grandmother had of him," Luna said. "Now, with this letter . . ."

Elizabeth glanced at Nadine. She wanted to know what she thought. Nadine nodded her assent.

"You have the right to meet him," Elizabeth said. "It would be best to visit in the afternoon . . . Perhaps Friday?"

Nadine stood up. Luna was already by the door, her eyes still on the unsipped cup of coffee. Elizabeth remained in her armchair by the window, but realizing the visit was coming to an end, she rose to her feet.

"I can't drink coffee at this hour, I'd never sleep," she said to Luna.

Nadine and Luna waited for Elizabeth to open the door. Luna was the first to leave. Once they were out in the corridor, Nadine went back to Elizabeth and hugged her. The old woman stood still, eventually lifting her arm to stroke Nadine's back. Luna watched from a distance.

They crossed Gustav-Adolf-Strasse without knowing in which direction they were going. They walked for a long while, until they arrived at Jüdischer Friedhof, with over a hundred thousand graves. Luna sensed the reunification had not made a great deal of difference to life in this neighborhood. The women still dressed as they did in the Soviet era. The streets were dirty, graffiti covering every passageway. The smell of the city was different over here, sweet yet rancid.

"If you like, I'll come home with you and stay over," Luna told her mother.

"There's no need. You'll have a lot to write tonight . . ."

They embraced, and Nadine watched Luna walk away until she disappeared around a corner.

31

Four Days Later
Pankow, May 2014

At Eberswalder Strasse station on Friday, Nadine took the yellow tram toward Warschauer Strasse. Taking the Strassenbahn was always a journey into the past. She was just one of the crowd. She felt disoriented and so busied herself with naming the stops one by one. Luna was making her own way there, and they would meet at the seventh station, on the corner of Landsberger Allee and Danziger Strasse. Nadine arrived early. She had thought the journey would take longer. She decided to sit and have a coffee, but when she got off the tram there was no café or little restaurant among the identical austere buildings, their windows so small it was as if they were meant to keep the sunlight out. Or the people in.

She decided to wait for her daughter in the fresh air. She had already sent her a message, and Luna had replied to say she was on her way. Nadine was in a hurry. She wanted to get the meeting over with, consign it to the past, put it somewhere it wouldn't be able to upset her. *It was probably too late to go back home*, she thought. She would have liked to lock herself in her room, then go on a trip with Anton far away from

Berlin. She asked herself once again why she was going through with a meeting that had kept her awake the last few nights.

Closing her eyes, she waited for a sign. She began to count to relax and heard Anton's voice. He had told Nadine they were making a mistake. "But Luna needs to see Franz in person," she replied. It was Luna who was going to confront Franz; it was Luna who had inherited the story, and who seemed determined not to let it fall into obscurity. Luna was convinced she had to face him, to find out how Franz had gone from Ally's guardian angel to her betrayer, to the keeper of her memory. That's how she had explained it to her parents. If Anton had asked her not to go, and also managed to convince their daughter, Nadine would not be sitting trembling on a frozen bench outside a tram station in the middle of nowhere. But saying no to Luna was like attempting to stop the tides. Her daughter needed to give her ghosts a face.

Without realizing it when she put it on, she was wearing a dark gray dress, as if in mourning for someone she had once known. She had spent years feeling guilty about her silence, for always taking the path of least resistance. She had lived her whole life by the adage: "If you can't remember it, it didn't happen." She had spent her entire youth turning her back on her past, until her daughter was born.

Nadine's shoulders felt heavy. Why did her daughter have to become a character in a story she didn't belong to? She could have kept Luna well away from the old poem and her grandmother and mother's obsession with darkness.

As she waited, sounds intensified, colors merged, shapes changed density. People poured out of Strassenbahn M10, but not her daughter. Everyone was heading somewhere, with purpose. Everyone had a destination. Cars gave way, bicycles came from the opposite direction. She heard a policeman's whistle. Children were running, avoiding the motorists. She saw herself surrounded by fragments. *What was she doing there?* she wondered time and again, until she saw her daughter step off the last yellow carriage of the Strassenbahn.

Nadine swallowed hard, desperately trying to locate a single drop

of saliva. Among the darkly dressed passengers, Luna was like an apparition. She was wearing her great-grandmother's red gabardine coat.
Nadine's heart overflowed as her daughter approached with an unusual
calmness about her. Her steps were deliberate, unhurried.

Luna embraced her mother and Nadine thought, not for the first
time, that her daughter represented everything Nadine had ever wanted
to be and to do, but never had out of fear. Or only with the lethargy of a
victim. She had been defeated. Her daughter had not.

A gust of wind brought her a feeling of surprising steadiness. She
sensed the oily smell of the trams, the screeching of the electric cables.
She held out her hand to her daughter, and together they left the station
behind. She finally dared acknowledge the obvious. Her daughter had
cut her hair to her jawline and had lightened it. With her hair short, the
waves were less pronounced.

"Every time I see you, I sense more of Ally in you."

Her daughter smiled, leaning her head against her mother's shoulder
for a few seconds. It was a gesture of approval, don't be afraid, everything
will be all right. Luna had spent hours writing last night, remembering
and reconstructing faces that were missing pieces. Without having been
aware of it, Nadine had been tracing a direct line to Franz since the day
she had come to Germany, a line that Ally Keller had begun, and that
Lilith continued. It was up to her and her daughter to finish it.

The journey to the six-story building that had been converted into
a care home for the elderly felt somehow familiar to Nadine, as had the
meeting with Elizabeth Holm. Nadine's aunt had always been there but
had remained invisible for them until they had finally decided to see her.
They had been to this residential home before, in this life or another,
Nadine wanted to tell her daughter. She felt like Ally Keller, hand in
hand with Lilith, though this time around she wasn't sure who was who.
Everything around her seemed small. Her daughter was leading her
now, and she let herself be guided along paths others had followed.

Nadine looked up and saw there were black clouds obscuring the
sun. She looked at her daughter and wanted to tell her they were safe

now that night had fallen. They turned a corner and saw a pleasant garden—immaculate, symmetrical—in the middle of the barren urban landscape of Soviet-era buildings. The Altenheim was a rectangle, with rows of small windows and a door in the center. Nadine thought it looked like an ocean liner, lost at sea, where troubled souls went to end their days. Franz was one of them. The faded yellow walls stood out against the green lawn.

The garden was completely still. Nadine wished for another gust of wind or, even better, a tornado. The knotty branches and dry leaves made spring feel like autumn there, as if the disorder reigning in the old people's minds also defined the seasons. Elizabeth was waiting for them at the foot of the six semicircular steps at the entrance, a nervous smile on her face. She seemed to be part of the place's geometry. In the afternoon shade, and from a distance, she looked younger. Her wrinkles had disappeared, and her hair was tied back, strands twisted inward, making her head appear bigger, her face more full. She was wearing a cream-colored skirt and a greenish silk blouse with a puffed-up bow. Her shoes were black and bulky.

When Nadine and Luna approached, Elizabeth curiously fixed her gaze on her mother's old red gabardine coat and held out her hand, per-haps forestalling another awkward hug. "It looks good on you, Luna," she said.

As they went into the building, Elizabeth said, "Most of them are in their nineties like Dad, but some are over a hundred years old."

Nadine shuddered. The old people in wheelchairs barely moved. They were like salt statues, swaying with the ebb and flow of the tide. Even the receptionist had her eyes riveted in a book. Occasionally one of them made a slight movement—a gesture, a sigh, someone turning to look at them only to immediately return to their original position—just enough to confirm they were still alive. All the people in the home had survived the war, had been a part of it. They all knew what it was to be defeated. Luna sensed these walls were built on silence.

"My father is on the sixth floor," Elizabeth said. They took the right-hand corridor, going past a bright, open room that led to the elevators. "Many of them recuperate their memory here, but not Dad. For him, returning to the past just doesn't stimulate him. Quite the opposite. Since arriving, he's refused to take a step or say a single word."

Elizabeth paused so that Nadine and Luna could take in the way the room was decorated.

"It was done recently," she explained. "The doctors think that surrounding the patients with things they're familiar with helps them recover lost abilities."

On the shelves there was a nickel-plated hairdryer, its cord taped up, covering the cracks, together with magazines from the '60s, '70s and '80s. There were cans of cabbage and stuffed peppers, the kind that were sold three decades earlier, as well as boxes of Spee and FEWA brand detergent. Books in Russian, a battered old record player, several different-size radio sets, Zenit cameras, and a military cap with the red hammer and sickle symbol. Yellowing photographs of the May 1st marches, with everyone wearing red neckerchiefs, and rolls of Orwo 400 ASA film. On the main wall hung a small painting of the Honecker and Brezhnev kiss, and around it images of Red Square and the Baltic Sea. There was even a watercolor painting of the Berlin Wall, without the barbed wire, covered in flowers. On the table in the middle was an orange telephone, and small red paper flags were dotted around the room.

"Yesterday was May first," Elizabeth said, picking up one of the flags. "Labor Day. There was a little party."

Elizabeth told them that whenever the old people walked through the room before returning to their bedrooms, the tension in their faces eased a little. Before, they were often agitated, their breathing ragged, as if lost in the woods. But now, thanks to evoking the past, they began to recognize their children and grandchildren for a few minutes and could even hold a conversation with some thread of logic, even if it was repetitive. Memory was there, it simply had to be reactivated.

"Those who improve can at least sleep soundly, without feeling so lost, like Dad."

It occurred to Luna that some might have to go even farther back to recuperate their memory, one or two decades farther, but there are certain pasts that nobody wants to recover. *It was best that those memories remained repressed*, she thought. As they stood next to each other in the elevator, she wanted to ask Elizabeth if they had tried showing Franz a photograph of himself in his Nazi uniform. The inside of the elevator was paneled in dark-striped Formica, and there was a huge brown telephone with hand-painted numbers beside the buttons.

"We're back in East Germany," Nadine said.

"That's the idea," Elizabeth replied.

Elizabeth told them that the staff called the sixth floor the "last stop," since this was where the residents with the most acute dementia had their rooms. The elevator came to a halt, and the door began to open shakily. Elizabeth had to push it with her hand.

The sixth floor was shrouded in darkness, making the walls appear gray. There was a neon light at the end of the corridor: a long, bare tube. All the windows and doors were closed. The musty smell of damp was overwhelming. Nadine could hear a subdued moan coming from somewhere on the floor, repeating like an excruciating echo.

Luna imagined all the possible ways the meeting might go. Would the old man be sleeping, or have his eyes closed throughout, or keep his gaze fixed on the window, not looking at them? Luna was convinced she would recognize him. She would try to identify the face her grandmother described in fragments of poems. She would wipe away the decades that had befallen him, and the real Franz would resurface. She would have liked to read him one of the poems, but there was no point. Elizabeth had explained that Franz had stopped acknowledging the outside world. It was like his brain was battling a whirlwind that occupied it completely.

They reached the end of the corridor. Elizabeth asked them to wait, she would go in first and try to make Franz comfortable, air the room a little. Standing in the doorway, Nadine and Luna were hit by the smell of urine and stale sheets. All they could see of the room's interior was a window, its drapes closed. The bed must be to the left. Elizabeth tried to open the window, but it was jammed. She looked around at Luna, a pained expression on her face, trying to convey that she was doing her best, that she didn't want them to feel disgusted when they saw her father.

"I'm going to find a nurse to change his catheter and bring clean bed sheets," Elizabeth said, hurrying out with her head down.

Nadine and Luna watched her leave. She didn't have to get her bearings to find the nurses' station. She knew the sixth floor from memory. As she moved farther away down the corridor, she was swallowed up by darkness.

Nadine and Luna held hands, not moving. Luna could feel her mother's heartbeats, and wanted to break away, follow her own rhythm. Nadine let go. Luna stepped inside the room, her eyes fixed on the window. She came to a halt in the middle of the room, and before looking at the bed, turned and observed her mother. Nadine inched closer to the door, finally entering the room and standing a few feet behind her. Luna closed her eyes for a second or two, and when she opened them, she turned and looked at Franz.

The first thing Luna saw was the old man's face, sunk into the pillow as if his head were all that was left of him, his body swallowed by the sheets and mattress. He had lost his hair. He had no eyebrows or eyelashes. His shiny skull was covered in liver spots. His nose was long, his lips thin; his eye sockets were dark patches. Lying in his yellowing bed sheets, Franz was no more than a dull patch. Luna wanted to see her great-grandmother's lover, the grandiloquent poet. She wanted to hear the commanding voice of the officer standing at the entrance to building number 32. She wanted to see him arm in arm with Ally Keller, wandering in the rain along Unter den Linden.

Suddenly, the room felt tiny, and the air became dense. Franz slowly opened his eyes. As he lifted his wizened eyelids, his breathing became agitated. The merest movement consumed what little energy he had in him, provided by the intravenous drip attached to his arm. The needle seemed to directly enter his bone, unable to supply it with the vital liquid. In the darkness of the bedroom, all the light streaming from the corridor fell on Luna, intensifying the red of her gabardine and the golden tones of her hair.

For a moment, Luna felt daunted by Franz's empty eyes. *That's enough*, she thought. Perhaps she should have listened to her parents—this meeting should never have taken place. The Franz she had before her now was not the Franz of the poems. This one had drowned in his own urine and excrement and ceased to exist. Luna wanted to tear her eyes away but couldn't. She sensed a connection with Franz; he was holding her gaze.

Franz's breathing was becoming increasingly agitated. Every gasp of air that reached his lungs made his whole body shudder. Luna tried to read his eyes. His irises were blurred with blood vessels, woven into an endless map. Franz opened his eyes as wide as he could, and Luna closed hers. She felt exhausted, drained of her energy, on the brink of walking out and leaving the decrepit old man in peace.

"Ally." Luna heard her great-grandmother's name.

The voice was weak, but it wasn't the voice of an old man. She opened her eyes and saw Franz's face for the first time, under the shadows and wrinkles.

"Ally." The voice emerged from the bed sheets. "Forgive me."

Luna looked at Franz, then at her mother, then back at Franz, as if he wouldn't let her go. Nadine had covered her face with her hands and started to cry.

"Forgive me," the old man said, louder this time.

Luna didn't know whether to go to him, call the nurse or Elizabeth, or run to her mother's arms and flee. Was she dreaming? In front of them was the man who had betrayed their family. Luna suddenly felt nauseous. Who was she to grant him forgiveness? Who was she to withhold it? She stood rooted to the spot, until Franz began to howl, a loud, unending cry of pure anguish.

Nadine took Luna by the hand, and they hurried out of the room and into the empty corridor. They headed for the stairs, not wanting to wait for the ancient elevator. Before they started down, they saw Elizabeth running, a nurse beside her. Franz's shouts were like a siren that couldn't be silenced.

Outside, in the peaceful garden, the sound of his wailing continued to echo in their heads.

32

One Year Later
Havana, May 2015

Luna Paulus hadn't written a word since the day she visited Franz in the care home for the elderly. She spent sleepless nights alone, organizing her great-grandmother's letters and poems. There was nothing left to decipher. It seemed Franz had lived to the age of ninety-five so that he could see Ally Keller one last time and ask for her forgiveness. The morning following their visit, he was found dead of a heart attack.

Elizabeth told Nadine he had died peacefully, with a smile on his face, and that he hadn't suffered. This is always a comfort in the face of death. But by the time they found him he had already gasped his last breath. It was impossible to know how much he had suffered. There was no wake, no death notices, no procession of friends filing past him. He was buried at Friedrichsfelde cemetery, alongside his parents. On the tombstone they engraved his real last name, Bouhler, and the dates of his birth and death. Luna thought they should have followed tradition and written everything the deceased had been in his life: soldier, Nazi, prisoner, poet, student, librarian, survivor. Elizabeth instead chose the laconic phrase: "Here lies a good father." There were no angels or crosses on the tombstone. No one left flowers or stones.

312

Nadine telephoned Mares to tell her the news.

"Now he can say sorry face to face to Ally Keller and Bruno Bormann, and God knows how many others, floating about up there in heaven," Mares concluded.

But Nadine knew Mares didn't believe in heaven or paradise, and much less so in hell. God was a difficult presence to understand, especially given how she had suffered at the hands of Communism and her husband. However hard she tried, she simply couldn't have faith. For her it was too abstract a concept. Faith was something you were born with.

Aunt Elizabeth left the way she came in, without preamble or farewell. Nadine met up with her a couple of times. They had dinner in a dull restaurant in Weissensee, and during an awkward silence, feeling guilty that she hadn't invited Elizabeth to have dinner with them at home, Nadine blurted out that she must come to Luna's wedding when the time came. Anton had never seen Elizabeth in a good light. He said that, deep down, there would always be something of the Nazi in her, her father, and her grandmother. In any case, Nadine's offer had only been a polite gesture, as she was certain Luna would never marry. Since she was a little girl, Luna had been adamant there was no way she would walk down the aisle of a church in a white dress, much less stand at an altar and promise to tie herself exclusively to one person for the rest of her life.

After that dinner, Elizabeth must have felt she had been accepted into the family, because she admitted to Nadine that she had been battling an illness for years, and that the time had come to give up the fight. Elizabeth had kept going thanks to chemotherapy and radiation treatments because she couldn't bear to leave her father alone in the care home. But now that he was gone and finally at rest alongside his parents after so much suffering, it was time for her to throw in the towel. Nadine offered to visit her, but Elizabeth declined. She couldn't cope with pity at this stage. She would be admitted to the hospital, and when she died, someone would call Nadine. She promised.

It was Elizabeth's lawyer who telephoned. The woman she had

never called aunt had died, leaving her entire estate—a modest bank account and a gloomy apartment—to her grandniece, Luna Paulus.

Eight months after first meeting Elizabeth, Luna and her mother returned to her apartment. The first time they were there, it had seemed small and dark, but now it appeared huge. They opened the windows to let the air in.

"I'm not ready to open drawers," Luna said. "I think it's best we leave it as it is for a while."

Seeing her daughter looking so lost and unable to take her usual comfort in writing, Nadine summoned all her strength and told Anton she was finally going to fulfill the promise she had made Luna when she was ten years old. They would board an airplane together and go to Havana.

"It will only be a weekend. I can't take any more time off work."

Three days would be enough time to visit her parents' graves, lay flowers, and see the house where she was born, she told Luna. She just wanted to breathe the air of the island, feel the tropical sun on her face. She would go to the port too, to see the bay where the ocean liner that brought her mother to Cuba had been anchored for a week.

"I have nothing else to do in Havana," she said to Anton. "It won't be a tourist trip, more like a . . ."

She left the sentence unfinished. She wasn't returning for her daughter. She was facing her own fear, or rather leaving it behind. That was the real reason.

Luna asked her mother if she was really ready to take such a long flight, and Nadine reminded her that distance was an illusion, and that she had already triumphed over time. There was nothing more to go looking for in the past, Nadine assured her. This was about Nadine honoring the memory of her mother.

The meeting with Franz had given Nadine a strange sense of peace. She was tired of looking for people to blame. In the end, everyone was guilty, if you did enough digging.

The day they flew to Cuba, Anton went with them to the airport.

Nadine was in good spirits. It was the first time she had ever been back to the country where she was born since the day she had traveled alone in a huge airplane to start a new life with complete strangers. Now she was returning, hand in hand with her daughter.

"You're my lucky charm," she told Luna as they sat on the airplane, about to take off. "I was a little girl who never liked adults," Nadine said. "Adults always seemed like sad, solitary creatures to me. I'd never have believed I'd get back on an airplane, much less with my daughter. Thank you for coming with me."

The flight was shorter than some of the train journeys they had taken. She realized that time feels different depending on one's age. When she traveled at the age of three, it had seemed like an eternity, as if she had lost decades of her life. This time, crossing the Atlantic went by in a heartbeat. She closed her eyes not long after takeoff, and when she opened them, Havana was a dot on a long, narrow island stretching out beneath their feet.

They were the first ones down the airplane steps. "If it's this hot in May, what must it be like in midsummer?" Luna said to her mother. Nadine couldn't answer, overwhelmed by the smell of gasoline that assailed them as they boarded the terminal bus.

They joined a long line to pass through immigration. A small, dark-haired man with big eyes questioned them.

"You're Cuban?"

"I don't think so," Nadine replied, immediately annoyed at her answer. You either are or you aren't. She was not Cuban. "I was born in Cuba, but I grew up in the United States. We live in Berlin now."

"In the 'Rada' or the 'Rafa'?" the man asked, using the Spanish acronyms for the former two Germanies. He was looking at her with a puzzled expression.

Nadine didn't understand the question. She thought it was because her Spanish had become too European, that she needed to get used to the way they spoke on the island.

The officer looked at her passport, then at her, back and forth, as if doubting her. A white woman with pale eyes, blond hair, and a dark-skinned daughter, both with the same foreign last name. And it was the mother who, according to her passport, had been born in Havana.

"Mum, he's talking about West Germany and East Germany," Luna whispered.

"Oh, there's been only one Germany for almost twenty-five years now."

"But you haven't answered my question."

"My daughter was born in West Germany. My mother . . . Well, my mother was born when there was only one Germany, before the war."

"But if you were born in Havana, as far as we're concerned, you're Cuban, and always will be. What year did you leave Cuba?"

"Many years ago, I doubt you were even born."

"Answer the question." The man seemed put out.

"In 1962. I was three years old."

"You went to Germany?"

"I traveled to Miami."

"Ah, with the *gusanos*."

Luna's eyes widened. She remembered what Mares had said. Mares was a *gusano*, a worm, and now so too was her mother. Did that mean she would become one too?

"My mother was German. I went to New York from Miami, and then we went to live in Germany. Yes, Federal Germany, your 'Rafa'."

Saying "we" felt strange to Nadine. The man thumbed through page after page of her passport as if he wanted to tear it to pieces to discover some error. The dim light in the terminal, the humidity, and her desperate thirst started to make Nadine feel uncomfortable. The man's questions didn't intimidate her. She had no reason to feel nervous, she told herself.

"We can get a drink of water soon," she said to Luna so the official would hear.

"I'm fine, Mom."

Nadine knew that was true. She was the one whose legs had begun to tremble. But what was the worst that could happen? Even if they took her to a cell and interrogated her for hours, in the end they would have to let her go back to Berlin, in the same airplane they had arrived in. Another nine hours shut up among the clouds.

Without saying a word, the immigration official took both passports and left the cabin. They waited for a minute, then two, three. To Nadine it felt like hours.

The man returned, but this time he stood behind them.

"Come with me."

They walked down a corridor with better air-conditioning, and at the end saw a tall, slim man with a sun-beaten face waiting for them in a doorway.

He indicated for them to take a seat and gave them each a bottle of water. They drank. The thin man was all smiles.

"How was your journey?" he asked in English.

"Fast," Nadine replied, defiantly.

"I'm glad to hear it. Here are your passports. Welcome to Havana."

Nadine and Luna were unsure whether they should leave the room or wait for someone to accompany them to cross the line between here and there, past and present. Nadine wanted to know when she could start to feel confident.

The man stood up, asked them to follow him, and in the baggage claim area pointed them in the direction of a woman dressed in military uniform, with a very short skirt and fishnet stockings, who was waiting with their small suitcases.

As they headed for the exit, toward the light, they saw a crowd gathered on the other side of the glass door. When at last they emerged, Nadine spotted their names on a handwritten card someone was holding in their hands: *Señora y Señorita Paulus*. Underneath was printed *Hotel Nacional*.

The man with the card led them to a minivan, where they joined other tourists. Most of them were German, and they seemed restless, perhaps because they had been kept waiting. Nadine didn't know what she was doing with this group of German tourists, back on this island where she had been born.

She closed her eyes and wished that when she opened them, she would find herself back in Berlin. With her eyes squeezed tightly shut, she tried to tell herself she had never left Germany, that she was just having one of her many nightmares in which she was transported back to the big house in Vedado where she was born, or the streets of Maspeth, the courtroom in Düsseldorf, or the Christmas market in Bochum-Linden. Nadine knew Luna was taking in every single detail of the journey, from the light to the smells. She saw her face flush, her eyes open wide, gripped by every gesture, every phrase.

· ✦ ·

Havana was like a city in miniature, a city that time forgot. The Hotel Nacional was on a hill by the coast. Their room had a sea view.

The cemetery was a palace where everything was white and shiny. The Bernal family vault was still intact, as if someone had been taking care of it. But then marble is everlasting, surely no one had been anywhere near it for decades, much less knelt down to light a candle. They had left white lilies on the tombstone. Lilies are planted in spring: the lilies had given off a heady aroma, which meant they were nearly dead. They had also visited Guanabacoa cemetery, to pay their respects to Alfred and Beatrice Herzog, the Jewish couple who had saved Lilith. They left some shiny black stones on their graves.

They went down to the port too and crossed the bay. In the Morro fortress, at the foot of a huge stone wall corroded by time and salt water, they looked back at Havana. That would have been how the people who had journeyed with her German mother would have seen it, the ones who weren't allowed to disembark from the *St. Louis*. All of a sudden Havana seemed far away, unreachable. Nadine felt like one of the nine hundred and thirty-seven passengers, as if she hadn't been born in Havana. Why had she come back? It's impossible to return to a place you have no memory of having ever been.

It was time to see the house where she was born, and where she had always presumed her mother had taken her own life. When they got to the house in Vedado, Nadine and Luna got out of the car and took a few photographs of it. It was so much smaller than Nadine had imagined, practically a doll's house. An elderly woman emerged from the house next door and watched them as Nadine and Luna opened the iron gate to the garden and approached the front. They knocked, insistently, and when no one came to open it, they began to walk away. That's when the elderly neighbor made her way with surprising speed along the sidewalk to intercept them.

The old woman, tears streaking her face, took hold of Luna's hands. "You must be Nadine," she said in Spanish.

Before Luna could correct her, Nadine asked, "Did you know my mother?"

"How foolish of me. Of course, dear, you're too young to be Nadine, but I must say, the young lady reminds me so much of señora Bernal."

The old woman hugged Nadine. Several seconds later, when they were still locked in an embrace, Nadine gestured to her daughter as if unsure of what she should do. Luna shrugged, equally baffled.

"Let's go to my house," the old woman said. "My name is María. I lived next door to your mother for many years."

The two followed her without asking any questions. María ushered them into a house that appeared to be quite similar to Lilith's, invited them to sit down, and excused herself. The walls were covered with several layers of undefined colors of paint. Depending on the light, they could look yellow or pink. There was dark wood and wicker furniture. A family photo of a young lady standing next to a man in a suit and holding a child hung in the middle of the wall facing the street. In the yellowish image, Nadine could see that the young lady was the old woman they had just met. A small altar with a virgin and a candlestick stood in a corner of the room.

María returned with a silver tray carrying two glasses of water. She put the tray on the coffee table, handed them each a glass, and pulled a white candle and a box of matches from her pocket.

She lit the candle in front of the virgin and crossed herself. It seemed as if she was praying to her. They couldn't hear what María was saying to the virgin.

"I used to pray the rosary for your mother every afternoon," she said as she sat next to Nadine. "You have no idea how much I asked my Caridad del Cobre Virgin to perform a miracle so that Lilith could be reunited with her daughter. The day we put your mother in the care home I promised her that one day you would come to meet her. No one forgets their real mother."

Nadine couldn't believe what she was hearing. "As a child, I was told my mother had committed suicide shortly after I was sent away," she said with a lump in her throat. "If I had known she lived to be an old woman, I would have rushed over to meet her. I never imagined—"

"Why on earth would you have thought that?" said María with a look of shock. "God has blessed us. God always hears our prayers . . . Nadine, your mother is alive."

Nadine covered her face with both hands and burst into tears.

"Are you sure?" asked Luna. "Do you know who we're talking about?"

"Señora Lilith Bernal. Who else? You have no idea how much Lilith has suffered. First, she lost her husband, then you. That's what a revolution does, it annihilates families. Look at me, a widow with my son in prison. I haven't abandoned this damn country because I can't leave my son in jail. And do you know why he's in jail? Just for thinking differently."

"Can we go see her right now? Would you take us? We have a car waiting for us outside."

"Listen, *mija*, I don't want you to get your hopes up. Lilith is old and gets confused sometimes. She's not crazy, but she lives in her own reality. She can't walk but thank God the nuns take good care of her in Santovenia."

"Is she sick?" asked Nadine.

"Not sick, what we are is old. And there's no cure for that. She suffered a lot from a very young age. I used to go to see her every Sunday after Mass; now I go once a month. You don't know how hard it is to get there by bus. But tomorrow is Saturday. We can go visit her early."

"And who lives in my grandmother's house?" asked Luna.

"Some communists. You know, the first chance they get, they take our houses and keep them. They're traveling now to I don't know where. He's a soldier, I think, or a diplomat, who knows."

María got up from the couch and left the room without explanation. She returned with a crumpled plastic bag. Inside was an envelope.

"The day your mother almost burned down her house, she had this letter in her hand," she said and handed the bag to Nadine. "You were about to turn eight years old."

Nadine took the bag. She didn't dare open it. Her heartbeat was so loud, she could barely hear María.

"We're going to see my grandmother tomorrow," Luna said. "I think we'd better go back to the hotel now so you can rest."

"Lilith is going to be so happy," María said. "And thank God you both speak Spanish."

They said goodbye with another long hug. On the way back to the hotel, Nadine didn't dare read the letter. Once they were back in their room, she took a shower and waited for Luna to fall asleep so that she could read her mother's words on her own.

At the foot of the window, with a view of the sea, Nadine read the letter aloud.

33

Starting the first of January 1967, when her daughter would have been turning eight years old, Lilith began celebrating Nadine's birthday alone. There was no cake, no blazing white candles, one for each year of her daughter's life. Every year, Lilith held only one candle in her hand and, with her eyes fixed on it, she sat in the middle of the dimly lit dining room. *How can I celebrate my daughter's birthday with one candle?*

On the table lay a small pink envelope with no inscription containing a letter that she had written twenty-one years ago. At the sight of it, she smiled but was immediately struck by sorrow. She didn't have the indigo-blue box with her.

She had spent the whole night wondering how she had been able to get used to a life without her daughter. Since that day, almost three decades ago, she had lived in darkness. At night, she wandered the city, its sidewalks shattered by the powerful roots of ceiba and flame trees. During the day she wrote unaddressed letters.

She had lived on an island with a new identity and a new family. She had learned a new language. She had wiped away the past like someone cleaning a foggy mirror. Since she had abandoned her daughter, none of that meant anything to her.

Not long after sending Nadine to New York, the nuns of the St. Catherine of Siena convent had been expelled from the country. Nadine went to the convent's registry office, inquired, and was told that there were no records of the departure of a three-year-old girl named Nadine, nor of anything called Operation Pedro Pan. They looked at her as if she was hallucinating.

Eventually she became the caretaker of the Bernal family mausoleum at Colón cemetery, which she visited every Friday. She would buy flowers and argue with the seller in German, claiming that they were wilted, that she wanted her flowers to have roots.

Lilith was once again a foreigner in Cuba. She spoke to herself in German and the neighbors thought she had gone mad. María, who lived next door, began to visit her in the afternoons and did her shopping in the bodega. If Lilith ate, it was thanks to María who, with religious devotion, brought her a plate of hot food every evening and prayed the holy rosary in a subdued voice so that the neighbors wouldn't hear her. When she finished, María would hide the rosary in her blouse. When she asked her how she felt, Lilith would answer in German.

Lilith would write letters and take them to the post office. At first, the post office clerk would explain to her that since the letter had no address, he couldn't accept it. She would still leave the letter on the counter every week until the clerk finally began to accept them and even stamp them in front of her just to see her smile and get her to leave as soon as possible.

One day she went to the post office and saw that it had been closed. "Nobody cares about letters on this island," an old woman told her. "Since the communists came into power, they don't want us to know about the world. It's been years since I've received a letter from my daughter in Miami."

Lilith turned around, locked herself away in the Vedado house, and for years continued writing letters. The rooms were slowly flooded by ink-stained sheets of paper with illegible phrases. The doors began to come off their hinges, and dust and cobwebs took over the corners as if no one had lived under that roof for years.

María felt compassion for her neighbor. She herself had a son imprisoned by the communists who wouldn't even let her visit him. When Lilith was about fifty years old, María decided to go to Calzada del Cerro and begin the process of getting Lilith, who had no family, accepted into the Santovenia care home.

"If she has mental problems, she should go to a mental institution," one of the care home directors told María.

"She's not crazy," said María. "She lost her parents, her husband, and her daughter. She is sad and cannot take care of herself."

A year later, during the Christmas holidays, which had been banned by the government for a decade, she was informed by the care home that a bed had been vacated and that she could initiate her neighbor's registration.

María filled out all the forms but decided that she would wait until the New Year and take Lilith to the care facility in early January.

At noon on January 1, 1988, María saw a column of smoke coming from Lilith's house. By the time she reached it, other neighbors had already broken down the door and doused the fire with buckets of water.

"Who would think of lighting a candle in this house?" said a man who emerged from the house soaking wet, holding an empty bucket in his hand, and dragging scorched papers.

Lilith remained on her feet down the hall with an envelope in her hand. María led her into the living room and they sat down together.

"Wait for me here," María said. "I've found you a home where they'll take care of you, and you'll be able to write all the letters you want to your daughter without being bothered. That said, they won't let you light a candle there."

Lilith smiled. When her neighbor left, she closed her eyes and pretended to savor the cake she was never able to bake and the eight candles she hadn't been able to get or blow out. What would be her wish this time? Why make it if her wishes had never come true? Abandonment had always had a day and a time.

María returned and the two of them sat in silence in the living room.

"They'll come to get you soon," she said. "Even though it's a little far away for me, I promise I'll come visit you on weekends."

Two hours later a car pulled into the driveway and honked the horn.

"It's them," María said and got up. "You'll see how well you are going to be in there."

María walked out first and Lilith followed her.

Standing at the threshold of her home that night, with the old pink envelope without an inscription in her hand, Lilith recited by heart the poem her mother had given her on her eighth birthday. Before getting into the car flanked by two men, one in olive green and the other in white, Lilith turned and looked for María, who ran toward her. The neighbor took the envelope Lilith held out to her and hugged her.

"We have to go," said the man in white. "You can visit her on Sundays," he said to María. "Just give her some time to adjust first."

The car began to move and, with the windows down, Lilith felt like the wind would set her free. Yet, as if it had never been erased from her memory, the air was still heavy with gunpowder, ash, leather, and metal. Nothing had changed for her. The city was still covered in broken glass. *One dreams of freedom as one dreams of God*, she said to herself in German. Whose voice was this? She couldn't even recognize her own voice.

Once again, dreams and God had ceased to make sense to her. She liked to think that, along the way, she was leaving a trail behind her that would lead to wherever they were taking her. So that someday, when her daughter returned—because she was convinced that she would return—she could find her. Full of hope and with a smile, she shed a tear: the last one.

At that moment, she spoke aloud the contents of the letter she'd handed to María, the letter she'd written to her Nadine, in German, her mother tongue, and let the wind carry the words as far away as possible, like when one throws a glass bottle with a message into the sea:

Havana, January 1, 1967

My dear Nadine,

Your father and I dreamed of you before we had you. The night we got married, Martín caressed my belly and predicted that you would be a girl.

So before you grew inside me, I already called you Nadine, my Nadine. I imagined you with your big, curious eyes wanting to recognize everything within your reach. The first time I felt your heartbeat, when you gave your first kick, when you moved as if you wanted to come out and cling to me, I ran to tell your father. You brought us so much happiness.

On the New Year's Day when you were born, we didn't need champagne or music. You were our celebration. Even though the city was in turmoil and the world was upside down, you brought us peace, my Nadine. From the moment I held you in my arms, I clung to you. That day I loved your father even more when I saw him with you, as if the two of you had known each other all your lives. You and he were one and you latched on to his finger. It was in that instant he made a promise: one day you would fly together, the two of you alone.

I prayed that night would last forever, and we watched you sleep, we counted your sighs, and every time I nursed you, I was the happiest woman in the world.

I want you to have only that happy memory of us, because yes, Nadine, your father and I were very happy by your side.

And now I must ask for your forgiveness. Today, on the day you turn eight years old, the same age when I blew out my eight candles in Berlin and made a wish that never came true: never to be separated from my mother, that together we would flee from hell. At that age, my mother sent me with two strangers to an island on the other side of the ocean and I never understood how she could've done that to her only daughter. I cursed, I wanted to forget her, I promised I would never speak German again. I wanted to erase my eight years with her.

You had to be born so that I could understand my mother. The night I started labor contractions, before I even heard your first cry, I forgave my mother, because I knew that I was alive and, if I had the chance to become a mother, it was thanks to her. I learned that sometimes the only way to save what you love the most is by abandoning it.

My dear Nadine, you have no idea how much guilt I felt for not having understood my mother. I know that when the day comes for me to say goodbye to this life, I will return to her arms. And I pray to God that when I run out of breath, He will allow me to take refuge in my mother so that I can tell her how much I have loved her.

My dear Nadine, I had to abandon you too, and I know understanding this is difficult at your age. If I am able to bear the pain of not having you with me every day, it's because I know you're alive and happy, even if I'm not the one who wakes you up every morning with a kiss.

Someday you will grow up, maybe you will curse me, but I hope that when you become a mother, you will understand me. A mother never forgets her daughter, even if she can never hold her in her arms again.

Here, on this island that now must seem far away, I'll be

waiting for you. I will hold my breath, my last, until the day you arrive. Today, that is my only wish.

Forgive me, my Nadine.

I love you with all my heart.
Your mother,
Lilith

34

Twenty-Seven Years Later
Havana, May 2015

Early in the morning on Saturday, Nadine and Luna, along with María, traveled by car to the Santovenia care home. The Calzada del Cerro was a cauldron. The sun hit the pavement and made it spew smoke as if it were about to melt. Cars cut them off in the middle of the road, ignoring the traffic signs; pedestrians darted in front of them on the brink of getting run over. The driver shouted at anyone who got in his way. The three passengers, however, were silent. To Nadine, this part of the city appeared to be in a state of war. There were armed police officers on every corner and long lines at shop entrances. The deafening thunder of trucks and crowded buses shook her. The driver slammed on the brakes every time he spotted a massive pothole in the middle of the road, and, in the absence of seatbelts, they had to cling to the car's roof and door handles.

Suddenly, they turned a corner and entered a quiet tree-lined street. The car stopped in front of a palatial building, now seemingly neglected, that took up the entire block.

"This villa belonged to the Counts of Santovenia," said María. "Nadine, Havana used to be a very elegant city."

Luna and María got out first. Nadine closed her eyes, inhaled deeply, and caught her breath. She had stayed up all night, repeatedly reading the letter from her mother that she now kept in her purse.

María had called the care home to let them know that she would be arriving with Mrs. Bernal's daughter and granddaughter first thing Saturday morning. She was told they would be waiting for them with Lilith bathed and dressed for the visit.

They crossed the enormous barred gate and were welcomed by a nun in a pink habit.

"God's miracle," said the nun. "The Virgin's miracle."

The corridor of white-and-gray marble slabs was dotted with empty armchairs leaning against the walls. They were taken to an inner court-yard where a small fountain quietly burbled.

"She doesn't speak much, but I know she'll understand you," ex-plained the nun. "She likes to be in the shade."

Nadine caught sight of her mother on the other side of the court-yard. During those early morning hours, there was no one else in the gardens. From afar, her mother seemed small to her, as small as if she were an eight-year-old child. Nadine thought she'd be nervous, that her legs would buckle, but in that instant, she was filled with energy. She hurried forward and was the first to reach her mother.

In the shade, her nostrils were filled with the scent of violets. Lilith's hair was short and white. Her skin was smooth, wrinkle-free, but her arms were covered with dark spots. She clasped her hands on her legs; her gaze was lost. As Nadine drew near, Lilith turned to look at her. Her eyes swept over Nadine's face. When Nadine took her hands, her mother smiled. Suddenly, she felt Lilith's hands trembling. She believed her mother had recognized her.

"Her hands are shaking," Nadine said and turned to Luna.

Luna began to cry.

"We have nothing to cry about," Nadine said, though her own eyes were moist.

Luna bent down and gave her grandmother a kiss. Nadine tried to hug her, carefully. Lilith felt small, fragile. The scent of violets sur-rounded her.

With trembling hands, Lilith began to caress her daughter's face from her forehead down to her cheek. She repeated the motion again and again, as if she were a blind person whose fingertips would tell her what Nadine looked like. *Her hands are as soft and warm as a newborn's,* Nadine thought to herself.

Like a murmur, they heard Nadine speaking in German to her mother. Nadine told her about her life in New York, about her studies in Berlin, about the day she met Anton and fell madly in love with him. About Luna, who inherited her great-grandmother Ally's talent. All the stories she told her were happy ones.

"We have another poet in the family," she said.

"Like my mother," Lilith whispered in German. "I knew that some-day we would meet, even if I was already very old."

"If only I had known it before!" said Nadine.

"My dear daughter, I always had hopes. There are so many questions without answers. You don't know how hard it was for me to understand my mother, that she sent me alone to Cuba. Can you imagine?"

"It's the war, Mom. We are all victims of war."

"The war . . . We lost everything, but I have you and my grand-daughter. I can die in peace now. I did the best I could, my little Nadine. My intention was never to abandon you."

For the next few hours, they would chat for a few minutes, then sit in silence, relishing simply being in each other's presence.

"Come with us to Berlin," Nadine said.

"No, my little one. I can't even move anymore. Besides, your father is buried here. It's my turn to stay by his side."

Lilith held her daughter's hand and squeezed it as if she wanted to be sure she wasn't dreaming.

Suddenly, Lilith started nodding off, as if falling asleep.

"It's time for her to rest," said the nun, who had been standing nearby. "It's been a lot for one day."

They had only spent four hours in the care home, but for Nadine it had felt like a blissful year.

Nadine wanted to return, but the next day they would fly back to Berlin. She had to find a way to get back to Havana as soon as possible. She dreamed of being able to take her mother to Berlin, but she was afraid that, in her fragile state, she would not survive the crossing of the Atlantic.

When they arrived back at the hotel, Luna hugged her mother.

"Are you going to let me read the letter?"

"Like Ally's poem," she said, handing the pink envelope to Luna, "this letter belongs to you." She paused. "You go back to Berlin. I'm going to stay with my mother for a little while."

35

The night Lilith died, Luna said goodbye to her parents, put on the red gabardine coat, left the apartment, and went out to walk the streets of Berlin until dawn. The city looked different to her now, as if it were an extension of the places she had left behind in Cuba. In Havana and Berlin, she felt the past beneath her feet.

The night Lilith died, it occurred to Luna that by "rescuing" her, Franz, and Elizabeth, she'd given all three of them the chance, for better or for worse, to bid farewell to the people they loved the most. Perhaps they'd left the world knowing that their lives weren't as hopeless as they'd believed. "You can't leave life carrying a heavy load," she had heard her grandmother Ernestine say on more than one occasion. "To get to the other side, you must travel as lightly as possible."

The news came in a brief phone call from María. Luna and her parents had been organizing a trip to Cuba for December. The three of them were planning to spend Christmas with Lilith.

The month Nadine had spent in Havana had filled Anton and Luna with anxiety. She only managed to talk to them once a week. Anton had to go to the Cuban embassy in Berlin to extend Nadine's stay. They treated him as if he had committed a crime. In Havana, they made Nadine go to the reception desk at the Hotel Nacional every night, and there they'd begrudgingly extended her stay one day at a time until the night she received a document from a Cuban government official stating there was no possibility of extending her visit any further.

Nadine felt that as the days went by, Lilith was fading away. They spent the afternoons together in the central garden of Santovenia as if they had never been apart. Lilith talked about her father, the musician, as if she had known him. She said that she and her mother had lived with him in Berlin. At first, Lilith seemed more lucid than she'd imagined she could be, but in time, Nadine realized that her mind wandered and allowed her to rewrite her own history.

"This has always been our home," Lilith once told Nadine. "I was very happy here with my parents."

The day she had to leave for Berlin, María advised Nadine to just say goodbye to her mother as if she was coming back the next day.

"It is very difficult for Mrs. Bernal to understand time," María told her. "For her, every day belongs to the past."

Since returning from Cuba, Nadine called María every Sunday after her visit to see Lilith in Santovenia. She now paid for María's trips to the Cerro and sent medicine to her and her mother, attempting to overcome every barrier to get a package to Cuba. Sometimes it was via Madrid, sometimes via Miami. Nadine made a donation to the Santovenia care home through a Catholic organization in Galicia. Once a month, she would call the care home and one of the nurses would put the receiver to Lilith's ear. Nadine would speak to her mother in German, telling her that soon the city would be covered in snow, that her granddaughter had become a writer like Ally. What she had refused to tell her about was the existence of a sister, Elizabeth, who had only recently died. Why make her suffer with stories that even Nadine and Luna still couldn't fully understand.

Luna suspected that this Christmas would be her grandmother's last, and when the phone rang, she sensed the bad news as soon as she heard María's voice. Her mother nervously snatched the phone from her when she mentioned her name.

Nadine listened attentively to María, and Luna saw her lips purse. Her mother's eyes filled with tears. Anton walked over to his daughter and hugged her, then went to Nadine. When she finished, Nadine fell into her husband's arms and broke down. Luna was startled by her wailing. It was the first time she had ever seen Nadine mourn her mother's death, Luna realized. As a teenager, the news that Lilith had died in Cuba had never felt real to her mom. Now Lilith was a real human being.

Nadine told Luna about María's call in a whisper. Lilith had probably died around midnight. They found her at dawn. María assured her that ever since Lilith was reunited with her daughter and granddaughter, her eyes had been filled with light.

"Lilith was still alive only because she had never stopped dreaming of that reunion," she told Nadine.

The care home already had all the information regarding the Bernal family mausoleum in the Colón cemetery. It would be a simple burial; there would be flowers, prayers. Nadine promised she would come to Cuba as soon as she could. Nadine told María that she wanted to give her a hug, that doing so would be like hugging her mother for the last time. Nadine was now the new guardian of the Bernal family mausoleum.

After Luna had said goodbye to her parents and left their apartment, she wandered aimlessly through the city and ended up on one of the streets that led to the Tiergarten. She sat down on a bench, closed her eyes, and let her mind wander freely.

As the sun rose, the Tiergarten was a bench, a streetlamp, a tree, and a little girl running, always returning to her mother's arms. She saw Ally and Lilith in the sunlight. They no longer had to hide.

In her mind, Luna boarded the number four on Tiergartenstrasse, passing open windows and doors, stores filled with antiques for sale. South of the Brandenburg Gate, rows of terraced houses faced the park. She went into the Herzogs' lighting store. Nowadays there was one on every corner of the city, a city bathed in light. The bell tinkled as she walked in; she was dazzled by a ceiling lit by hundreds of multicolored bulbs. She heard Beatrice and Albert welcome her: *Shalom.* Behind the counter, Paul, their handsome son, was helping a customer.

Luna left the shop and continued on her way, as clouds of fine drizzle gathered above her on Unter den Linden. She drew her red gabardine coat tightly around her and stood looking at the blossoming lime trees.

She must hurry, they were waiting for her. She closed her eyes more tightly, and in an instant she arrived at Anklamer Strasse, at the building bearing the number 32 in greenish bronze. The heavy wooden front door was freshly painted, the paving stones of the sidewalk were immaculate. Luna opened the door easily and went inside. To the left, at apartment 1B, she stroked the mezuzah hanging at an angle on the top of the doorframe and climbed the stairs.

Luna followed the map she herself had drawn. On the third floor she walked to the end of the corridor, which lit up as she advanced. She opened the door to an apartment and was struck by the smell of leather and parchment. Herr Professor, sitting in a velvet armchair, was reading aloud. Luna moved closer so she could hear him. "What is past is prologue." Reclining on the sofa, bare-chested and gleaming like a Greek sculpture, Franz was trying to sleep, lulled by his maestro's voice.

Luna left the apartment and opened the adjoining door. As she went in, she saw Ally Keller and her husband, Marcus, standing by the window. She heard Lilith's voice calling to them. They didn't react. The little girl repeated "Mommy," louder this time. Then after a pause, she said "Daddy." Marcus ran to her, twirling her in the air. Ally turned around. She smiled. The candles along the dining room table were lit. Sitting at one end of the table were Lilith and Martín, with a baby in their arms. Over to one side, Nadine and Anton stood chatting. Luna tried to make out what they were saying, but everything was spinning around her. The walls began to fade away. Luna looked up. The ceiling had disappeared. She burst into tears, as she had once cried for her grandmother, for her great-grandmother, as one only weeps for the dead, with despair. She looked for a mirror, needing to know who she was.

She realized it was night again: maybe it had never ended. From her apartment window she saw a couple crossing Anklamer Strasse. When they reached the corner, the strangers turned and looked up at her. Luna saw herself, sitting in the nook by the window in her own apartment.

She spent the next several hours of the night organizing her great-grandmother's forgotten letters and poems. There was nothing left to decipher. The yellowing letters sent from Sachsenhausen and the pink envelope with no inscription now lay on the wooden floor. Sheets of blank paper covered the table. Emptiness had always intrigued her. She had to begin but didn't know where.

Luna's eyes filled with tears that weren't hers. One of her many lives had begun. She started to write on the blank page. Someone else was making the marks, all she was doing was moving her hand. She tried to decipher what she had written before, the random words, but couldn't. She read it aloud. All she heard was silence. In the midst of the stillness, words were forming, coming to her one by one. She lost all sense of time; she didn't know the day of the week. Not even the year.

She read what she had written. Calm, protected by the shadows, she could now make out the voice guiding her. Suddenly, she heard it: *By night, we're all the same color . . .*

Day dawned, bright and clear.

Author's Note

Eugenics

Germany's laws of "racial hygiene" came into effect in 1933, and Adolf Hitler's government subsequently approved the policy of forced sterilization. About 20 percent of the population was considered to have genetic or racial defects. First, the Nazis began by sterilizing the mentally ill. Next were the *mischlings*: those with one Aryan parent and one of another race, principally Black or Jewish. In 1935, the government unanimously passed the Reich Citizenship Law and the Law for the Protection of German Blood and German Honor, which classified citizens according to their racial heritage.

Eugenics is the quest for a superior race through the enhancement of hereditary traits. Eugenics policy in Germany was inspired by research being carried out in the United States and worldwide from the end of the nineteenth century. Nazis created the Aktion T4 program to kill or sterilize over 275,000 people. Females were sterilized using X-rays and males by vasectomy, often without anesthesia. Many Afro-German children, labeled "Rhineland bastards," were removed from school or gathered up in the streets and taken to medical facilities to be sterilized. Racial mixing, especially with colonial Africans, was deemed a racial offense.

German laws of eugenics were specifically based on the research of doctors from Pasadena, California. In the first half of the twentieth century, the method these doctors had developed gave rise to the involuntary sterilization of some 70,000 people in the United States. Sterilization continued to be practiced in certain states, including Virginia and California, until 1979.

MS St. Louis

On the evening of May 13, 1939, the transatlantic ocean liner *St. Louis* of the Hamburg-America Line (HAPAG) set sail from the port of Hamburg bound for Havana, Cuba. Some nine hundred passengers were onboard, the majority German Jewish refugees. Some were children traveling without their parents.

The refugees all had permits to disembark in Havana issued by Manuel Benítez, the general director of the Cuban Department of Immigration, with the support of the army commander Fulgencio Batista. The permits had been obtained through the HAPAG company. However, a week before the liner sailed from Hamburg, the president of Cuba, Federico Laredo Brú, issued Decree 937 (named after the number of passengers aboard the *St. Louis*), invalidating the landing permits signed by Benítez.

The ship arrived at the port of Havana on Saturday, May 27. The Cuban authorities would not allow it to dock in the area assigned to the HAPAG company, and so it was forced to anchor in the middle of Havana Bay. Only four Cubans and two non-Jewish Spaniards were allowed to disembark, together with twenty-two refugees who had obtained permits from the Cuban State Department prior to the ones issued by Benítez.

The *St. Louis* sailed for Miami on June 2. As it approached the U.S. coast, Franklin Roosevelt's government denied it entry into the United States. The Mackenzie King government in Canada also refused the ship entry.

The *St. Louis* was therefore forced to return to Hamburg. A few days before it arrived, the Joint Distribution Committee (JDC) negotiated an agreement for several of its member countries to take in the refugees. Great Britain accepted 287; France 224; Belgium 214; and the Netherlands 181. In September 1939, Germany declared war and the countries of continental Europe that had accepted the passengers of the *St. Louis* were soon occupied by Hitler's forces.

Only the 287 passengers taken in by Great Britain remained safe. Most of the other passengers from the *St. Louis* suffered the horrors of German occupation or were killed in Nazi concentration camps.

Operation Pedro Pan

Between December 1960 and October 1962, some 14,048 children left Cuba without their parents, on commercial airplanes, as part of an operation coordinated by the Catholic Church and supported by the United States government. The U.S. Department of State authorized Brian O. Walsh, a young Catholic priest in Miami, to bring the Cuban children into the country without visas. Many of the parents who sent their children to the United States faced political persecution under Fidel Castro's regime, which was established by force on January 1, 1959. Others were involved in clandestine activities and feared they would lose their parental rights, or that their children would fall victim to political indoctrination at school. The Communist government closed Catholic schools, seized all property belonging to the church, and took control of private companies.

Operation Pedro Pan takes its name from the classic J. M. Barrie novel about a boy who never grows up and who lives on the mythical island of Neverland. The program constituted the largest politically driven mass exodus of children in the Western Hemisphere in modern history.

In October 1962, as a result of the Cuban Missile Crisis involving the United States, Cuba, and the Soviet Union, all air traffic between Havana and Miami ceased, leaving many child refugees in limbo, awaiting the arrival of their parents. Many of these children were sent to different cities across the United States. Some remained under the care of the Catholic Church; others were taken in by families, placed in homes for juvenile delinquents, or sent to orphanages. A large number of them forgot how to speak Spanish, and some never saw their parents again.

Acknowledgments

The Night Travelers took me four years to complete, but what first began with *The German Girl* and then *The Daughter's Tale*, three independent novels united by the MS *St. Louis*, involved several decades of research. Certain chapters of *The German Girl* date back to 1997.

I first heard about the MS *St. Louis* through Tomasita, my maternal grandmother, the daughter of Galicians who came to Cuba at the start of the twentieth century. My grandmother was pregnant with my mother when the ship dropped anchor in the port of Havana. Since I was a child, I had heard that Cuba would pay for a hundred years to come for what it did to the Jewish refugees from Germany.

To my grandmother, my deepest gratitude.

During one of our many Manhattan brunches, Johanna Castillo, then an editor for Atria Books at Simon & Schuster, asked me why I'd never written a novel. She had read my first book to be published in the United States, *In Search of Emma*, a sort of memoir, and told me she saw my potential to write fiction. My response was that every writer has a novel tucked away in a drawer somewhere. That day, *The German Girl* first started to take shape. At a subsequent brunch, I showed her everything I'd put together about the MS *St. Louis*, including documents and original photographs. Within days I signed a contract to publish the novel.

To Johanna, my friend, editor, and now literary agent, for believing in me. It is thanks to her that my three novels exist.

If in the second act of *The Night Travelers* I brought Batista's Cuba to life, committing myself to studying his books, his contributions, and his mistakes, it was thanks to my maternal grandfather, Hilario Peña y Moya. My grandfather was a passionate Batista supporter, even during the 1959 revolution. He never tried to hide his ideas from family or friends, or even from strangers. Ideas that might have landed him in prison at the time. As a child, I remember that when Batista died in exile, my grandfather's friends filed through the house to offer their condolences.

To the entire team at Atria Books, and Simon & Schuster, my publishing house, for all they do to ensure my books reach new readers every day.

To Daniella Wexler, my faithful editor, and her assistant, Jade Hui, at Atria Books, all my gratitude. Thank you for making me sound better in English.

To Peter Borland, my wonderful new editor, thanks for your vision. I know that with you, my books will soar. Here's to a long journey together.

To Libby McGuire, for her belief and her passion for my books.

To Wendy Sheanin, for her passion for books and for helping my novels find many more readers.

To Gena Lanzi, Katelyn Phillips, Tamara Arellano, Sean deLone, and the whole team at Simon & Schuster, my heartfelt thanks.

To Annie Philbrick, for her passion for books, for reading me, for her friendship. A friendship that grew out of an eventful trip to Cuba, where on the first day we arrived in Havana, we happened to sit across from each other in a restaurant on the river. Since then, Annie has become the "madrina" (godmother) of my novels.

To the editorial team at Simon & Schuster Canada, in particular the publicist Rita Silva, for their support.

To the editorial team at Simon & Schuster Australia, and particularly Dan Rufino, Anna O'Grady, and Anthea Bariamis. Thank you for your editorial input and for the opportunity to travel and meet my readers in your beautiful country.

To the Australian author Thomas Keneally, for supporting *The German Girl* and welcoming me into his home in Sydney.

To Berta Noy, my Spanish editor, who always believed in me and acquired the rights to *The German Girl* in Spain and Latin America. Thank you to the entire team at Ediciones B, Penguin Random House, especially my editor, Aranzasu Sumalla, in Barcelona; Gabriel Iriarte, Margarita Restrepo, and Estefanía Trujillo in Colombia; and David García Escamillo in Mexico.

To Louise Bäckelin, my editor at Förleg in Sweden; to my editors at Boekerij, The Netherlands; Gyldendal Norsk, Norway; Simon & Schuster, UK; Czarna Owca, Poland; Dioptra, Greece; 2020 Editora, Portugal; Politikens Forlag, Denmark; Matar, Israel; Alexandra, Hungary; Topseller, Portugal; Bastei Lübbe, Germany; Presses de la Cité, France; Chi Min Publishing Company, Taiwan; Casa Editrice Nord, Italy; Jangada, Brasil; Epsilon, Turkey.

To Nick Caistor, my English translator. Besides being a brilliant translator, Nick is an excellent editor.

To Alexandra Machinist, who, as my literary agent, negotiated the publication of *The Daughter's Tale* and *The Night Travelers* with Atria Books.

To Esther María Hernández, for refining the Spanish of everything I write. Thanks to her I sound better in my mother tongue, which at times suffers from my having spent decades in the United States.

To María Antonia Cabrera Arús, for her precise copyediting in Spanish and her critical eye.

To Cecilia Molinari, an excellent editor, copyeditor, and translator, and a dear friend. Thank you also for having contributed, with Faye Williams, to the English translation of *The Night Travelers*.

To Néstor Díaz de Villegas, author, essayist, painter, poet, for getting me closer to Batista, and for his insightful comments. For our conversations on books and authors.

To Zoé Valdés, author and ardent Batista supporter. Thank you for your constant support.

To the writer Joaquín Badajoz, for giving me a final reading of the manuscript in Spanish before sending it to my publishers in Barcelona. It was a luxury to have his recommendations.

To the writer Wendy Guerra, a sharp and passionate reader of my manuscript, for her beautiful words.

To Andrés Reynaldo, knowledgeable author and reader. I will never forget his comments on everything I've written.

To Mirta Ojito, for patiently reading my drafts and listening to my ideas, and for her advice, friendship, and passion for reading.

To María Morales, who always has something to add to my characters and their stories.

To Carole Joseph, who always listens patiently to my literary projects even when they are nothing more than an idea.

To Laura Bryant, for tirelessly promoting everything I write. Thanks to you we received the first offer to bring *The German Girl* to the big screen.

To Clemente Lequio, for believing in my books.

To the team at Hollywood Gang Productions: Gianni Nunnari, Andre Lemmers, and Jacqueline Aphimova.

To Katrina Escudero, my film and TV agent.

To Verónica Cervera, an excellent reader and friend who is always prepared to read my manuscripts.

To Herman Vega, for his friendship, and for the cover designs that help me write.

To Yvonne Conde, a writer and one of the girls of Operation Pedro Pan, for answering all my questions about the exodus of Cuban children, and for her observations when she read the manuscript.

To Ania Puig Chan, who helped me re-create certain Berlin streets, as well as the care home for the elderly.

To María del Carmen Ares Marrero, who inspired one of the characters, Mares.

ACKNOWLEDGMENTS

To Ana María Gordon, Eva Wiener, Judith Steel, and Sonja Mier, the real girls of the MS *St. Louis*, for being an inspiration in everything I write. Thank you for keeping the memory alive.

To my family, who are the first to support me with each of my books.

To my mother, for being the first reader and for passing on her love of reading and cinema.

To Emma, Anna, and Lucas, who always help me find names for my characters. Thank you for your patience while I was shut away writing.

To Gonzalo, for his support and love over more than three decades.

Bibliography

Agote-Freyre, Frank. *Fulgencio Batista. From Revolutionary to Strongman*. Rutgers University Press, 2006.

Aitken, Robbie, and Eve Rosenhaft. *Black Germany: The Making and Unmaking of a Diaspora Community, 1884–1960*. Cambridge University Press, 2013.

Aligheieri, Dante. *La divina comedia*. FV Éditions, 2015.

Baker, Jean H. *Margaret Sanger: A Life of Passion*. Hill and Wang, 2011.

Barberan, Rafael. *El vampiro de Düsseldorf*. Sonolibro Editorial, 2019.

Barrie, J. M. *Peter Pan*. Signet Classics, Penguin Group (USA), 1987.

Batista, Fulgencio. *Piedras y leyes*. Ediciones Botas-México, 1961.

Batista, Fulgencio. *Respuesta . . .* México, D.F., 1960.

Batista, Fulgencio. *The Growth and Decline of the Cuban Republic*. The Devin-Adair Company, 1964.

Beck, Gad. *An Underground Life: Memoirs of a Gay Jew in Nazi Berlin*. University of Wisconsin Press, 1999.

Bejarano, Margalit. *La comunidad hebrea de Cuba*. Instituto Abraham Harman de Judaísmo Contemporáneo, Universidad Hebrea de Jerusalem, 1996.

Bejarano, Margalit. *La historia del buque San Luis: La perspectiva cubana*. Instituto Abraham Harman de Judaísmo Contemporáneo, Universidad Hebrea de Jerusalem, 1999.

Bilé, Serge. *Negros en los campos nazis*. Ediciones Wanáfrica S.L., 2005.

Black, Edwin. *War Against the Weak: Eugenics and America's Campaign to Create a Master Race*. Dialog Press, 2012.

Blakemore, Erin. "German Scientists Will Study Brain Samples of Nazi Victims." *Smithonian Magazine*, May 5, 2017.

Brozan, Nadine. "Out of Death, a Zest for Life." *The New York Times*, November 15, 1982.

Campt, Tina M. *Other Germans: Black Germans and the Politics of Race, Gender, and Memory in the Third Reich*. The University of Michigan Press, 2005.

Carr, Firpo W. *Germany's Black Holocaust: 1890–1945. The Untold Truth: Details Never Revealed Before*. 2012.

Castro, Fidel. "*Discurso pronunciado por el comandante en jefe Fidel Castro Ruz en la reunión celebrada por los directores de las escuelas de instrucción revolucionaria, efectuada en el local de las ORI, el 20 de diciembre de 1961.*" *Fidel, soldado de las ideas*. www.fidelcastro.cu

Castro, Fidel. *La historia me absolverá*. Ediciones Luxemburg, 2005.

Chao, Raúl Eduardo. *Raíces cubanas: Eventos, aciertos y desaciertos históricos que por 450 años forjaron el carácter de lo que llegó a ser la república de Cuba*. Dupont Circle Editions, 2015.

Chester, Edmund A. *A Sergeant Named Batista*. Grapevine Publications LLC, 2018.

Cohen, Adam. *Imbeciles: The Supreme Court, American Eugenics, and the Sterilization of Carrie Buck*. Penguin Books, 2016.

Conde, Yvonne M. *Operation Pedro Pan: The Untold Exodus of 14,048 Cuban Children*, Routledge, New York, 1999.

De la Cova, Antonio Rafael. *La guerra aérea en Cuba en 1959: Memorias del teniente Carlos Lazo Cuba. El juicio por genocidio a los aviadores militares*. Ediciones Universal, 2017.

Díaz de Villegas, Néstor. *Cubano, demasiado cubano*. Bokeh, 2015.

Díaz González, Christina. *The Red Umbrella*, Alfred A. Knopf, 2010.

Domínguez, Nuño. "*Alemania reabre el caso de los asesinados por la ciencia nazi.*" *El País*, 22 de mayo de 2017.

Dubois, Jules, *Fidel Castro: Rebel—Liberator or Dictator?* The New Bobbs-Merrill Company, 1959.

Evans, Suzanne E. *Hitler's Forgotten Victims: The Holocaust and the Disabled.* The History Press, 2010.

Fernández, Arnaldo M. "*Historia y estilo: doble juicio revolucionario.*" *Cubaencuentro,* February 13, 2019.

Fornés-Bonavía Dolz, Leopoldo. *Cuba cronología: Cinco siglos de historia, política y cultura.* Editorial Verbum, 2003.

Gay, Peter. *Weimar Culture: The Outsider as Insider.* W.W. Norton & Company, 2001.

Gbadamosi, Nosmot. "Human Exhibits and Sterilization: The Fate of Afro Germans Under Nazis." CNN, July 26, 2017.

Goeschel, Christian. *Suicide in Nazi Germany.* Oxford University Press, 2009.

Gómez Cortés, Olga Rosa. *Operación Peter Pan: cerrando el círculo en Cuba. Basado en el documental de Estela Bravo.* Casa de las Américas, 2013.

Gosney, E. S., and Paul Popenoe. *Sterilization for Human Betterment: A Summary of Results of 6,000 Operations in California, 1909–1929.* The Macmillan Company, 1929.

Grant, Madison. *The Passing of the Great Race.* Ostara Publications, 2016.

Hitler, Adolf. *Mein Kampf.* Mariner Books, 1998.

Koehn, Ilse. *Mischling, Second Degree: My Childhood in Nazi Germany.* Puffin Books, Penguin Books, 1977.

Kühl, Stefan. *The Nazi Connection: Eugenics, American Racism, and German National Socialism.* Oxford University Press, 1994.

Lang-Stanton, Peter, and Steven Jackson. "*Eugenesia en Estados Unidos: 'Hitler aprendió de lo que los estadounidenses habían hecho.'*" BBC News Mundo, April 16, 2017.

Lelyveld, Joseph. *Omaha Blues.* Picador, 2006.

León, Gustavo. *De regreso a las armas: La violencia política en Cuba: 1944–1952. Trilogía de la República. Tomo II.* 2018.

Lowinger, Rosa, and Ofelia Fox. *Tropicana Nights. The Life and Times of the Legendary Cuban Nightclub.* In Situ Press, 2005.

Luckert, Steven, and Susan Bachrach. *State of Deception: The Power of Nazi Propaganda.* United States Holocaust Memorial Museum, 2009.

Ludwig, Emil. *Biografía de una isla (Cuba).* Editorial Centauro, 1948.

Lusane, Clarence. *Hitler's Black Victims: The Historical Experiences of Afro-Germans,*

European Blacks, Africans, and African Americans in the Nazi Era. Routledge, 2003.

Machover, Jacobo. *Los últimos días de Batista. Contra-historia de la revolución castrista.* Editorial Verbum, 2018.

Martin, Douglas. "A Nazi Past, a Queens Home Life, an Overlooked Death." *The New York Times*, December 2, 2005.

Massaquoi, Hans J. *Destined to Witness: Growing Up Black in Nazi Germany.* William Morrow and Company, 1999.

Meyer, Beate, Herman Simon, and Chana Schütz, eds. *Jews in Nazi Berlin: From Kristallnacht to Liberation.* The University of Chicago Press, 2009.

Noack, Rick. "A German Nursing Home Tries a Novel Form of Dementia Therapy: Re-creating a Vanished Era for Its Patients." *The Washington Post*, December 26, 2017.

Ogilvie, Sarah A., and Scott Miller. *Refugee Denied. The* St. Louis *Passengers and the Holocaust.* United States Holocaust Memorial Museum, 2006.

Ojito, Mirta. "Cubans Face Past as Stranded Youths in U.S." *The New York Times*, June 12, 1998.

Ortega, Antonio. "A La Habana ha llegado un barco." *Bohemia.* Number 24. June 11, 1939.

Osterath, Brigitte. "German Research Organization to Identify Nazi Victims that Ended Up as Brain Slides." DW, May 2, 2017.

Peña Lara, Hilario (ex-captain of the Rebel Army). Private Archive.

Plant, Richard. *The Pink Triangle: The Nazi War Against Homosexuals.* Henry Holt and Company, 1986.

Prieto Blanco "Pogolotty," Alejandro. *Batista: "El ídolo del Pueblo."* Punto Rojo Libros, 2017.

Procter, Robert N. *Racial Hygiene: Medicine Under the Nazis.* Harvard University Press, 1988.

Riefenstahl, Leni. *A Memoir.* Saint Martin's Press, 1993.

Riefenstahl, Leni. *Behind the Scenes of the National Party Convention Film.* International Historics Films, Inc., 2014.

Ross, Alex. "How American Racism Influenced Hitler." *The New Yorker*, April 23, 2018.

Sarhaddi Nelson, Soraya. "Nursing Home Recreates Communist East Germany for Dementia Patients." *NPR*, January 22, 2018.

Sartre, Jean-Paul. *Sartre on Cuba: A First-Hand Account of the Revolution in Cuba and the Young Men Who Are Leading it—Who They Are and Where They Are Going.* Ballantine Books, 1961.

Schoonover, Thomas D. *Hitler's Man in Havana: Heinz Lüning and Nazi Espionage in Latin America.* The University Press of Kentucky, 2008.

Seaton Wagner, Margaret. "A Mass Murderer; The Monster of Dusseldorf. The Life and Trial of Peter Kurten." *The New York Times*, July 9, 1933.

Speer, Albert. *Inside the Third Reich: Memoirs.* The Macmillan Company, 1970.

Spotts, Frederic. *Hitler and the Power of Aesthetics.* Harry N. Abrams, 2018.

Taborda, Gabriel E. *Palabras esperadas: Memorias de Francisco H. Tabernilla Palmero.* Ediciones Universal, 2009.

Taveras, Juan M. *El negro y el judío: El odio racial.* 2017.

Thomas, Gordon, and Max Morgan-Witts. *Voyage of the Damned. A Shocking True Story of Hope, Betrayal, and Nazi Terror.* Amereon House, 1974.

Torres, María de los Angeles. *The Lost Apple. Operation Pedro Pan, Cuban Children in the U.S., and the Promise of a Better Future.* Beacon Press, 2003.

Triay, Victor Andres. *Fleeing Castro: Operation Pedro Pan and the Cuban Children's Program.* University Press of Florida, 1998.

Truitt, Dr. W. J., and T. W. Shannon. *Eugenics: Nature's Secrets Revealed. Scientific Knowledge of The Laws of Sex Life And Heredity, or Eugenics: Vital Information for The Married and Marriageable of All Ages; a Word at The Right Time to the Boy, Girl, Young Man, Young Woman, Husband, Wife, Father and Mother; also, Timely Help, Counsel and Instruction for Every Member of Every Home, Together with Important Hints on Social Purity, Heredity, Physical Manhood and Womanhood by Noted Specialists.* The S. A. Mullikin Company, 1915.

United States Government Printing Office Washington. Committee on the Judiciary. *Hearings Before the Subcommittee to Investigate the Administration of the Internal Security Act and Other Internal Security Laws of the Committee on the Judiciary United States Senate Eighty-Sixth Congress. Second Session Part 9.* August 27, 30, 1960.

United States Holocaust Memorial Museum. *Deadly Medicine: Creating the Master Race*. United States Holocaust Memorial Museum, 2008.

United States Holocaust Memorial Museum. *Voyage of the Saint Louis* (catalog).

Valdés, Zoé. *Pájaro lindo de la madrugá*. Algaida, 2020.

Whitman, James Q. *Hitler's American Model: The United States and the Making of Nazi Race Law*. Princeton University Press, 2017.

Wipplinger, Jonathan O. *The Jazz Republic: Music, Race, and American Culture in Weimar Germany*. University of Michigan Press, 2017.